The Garden of Earthly Delights

THE GARDEN OF EARTHLY DELIGHTS

Nicholas Salaman

HarperCollins*Publishers*

HarperCollins*Publishers*
77–85 Fulham Palace Road,
Hammersmith, London w6 8jB

Published by HarperCollins*Publishers* 1993

1 3 5 7 9 8 6 4 2

Copyright © Nicholas Salaman 1993

The Author asserts the moral right to
be identified as the author of this work

A catalogue record for this book is
available from the British Library

ISBN 0 246 13771 1

Set in Linotron Ehrhardt by
Rowland Phototypesetting Ltd
Bury St Edmunds, Suffolk

Printed in Great Britain by
HarperCollinsManufacturing Glasgow

The poetry of history lies in the quasi-miraculous fact that once on this earth, once, on this familiar spot of ground, walked other men and women, as actual as we are today, thinking their own thoughts, swayed by their own passions, but now all gone, one generation after another, gone as utterly as we ourselves shall shortly be gone like a ghost at cockcrow.

G. M. TREVELYAN

Acknowledgements

When Hitler visited the North German town of Munster in 1934, he expressed a wish to see the Cathedral; but Bishop von Galen, with great bravery, refused to let him in. Indeed, it is likely that the Führer would have had him arrested on the spot, had it not been for the fact that the crowd – which had originally welcomed their Leader and his bodyguard with great acclaim – started to turn ugly.

The reason for the Bishop's resolute stance was partly a matter of history.

Four centuries previously, Munster had already had its Thousand-Year Reich and its totalitarian state, and the baleful shadow of that terrible time still oppressed successive generations of its citizens.

This book concerns the Religion of Love as illustrated in *The Garden of Earthly Delights* – painted by Hieronymus Bosch in a town not eighty miles from Munster. At the same time, its story involves the creed of hate which took form in that unhappy city.

I have named the city Rensburg in the book. Of course it is loosely modelled on Munster; as are some of the characters based on real-life Munster originals. I could, I suppose, have given them all their proper names and written a closely modelled history. But a historical novel is never that close. Nor should it be judged on its pinpoint accuracy. Certainly there must be no glaring historical howlers for the average non-specialist reader, for example steam engines in the sixteenth century; and I have tried to do a little better than that.

On the whole, though, the drama, the idea, the style, must take their course, and be judged on that alone (as if it were not enough). I have eschewed 'prithees' and 'forsooths' since those in their day sounded no more dated than 'there you go' does to us. I have simply arrived at a contemporary idiom without too much 'argot'. In language, too, research is in the end a monster which devours writer and reader alike.

I have, however, given Bosch his real name. There seemed no getting away from the fact that he painted the triptych of *The Garden of Earthly Delights*, sometimes called *The Millennium*. But as so little is known about him, I thought I could take a few liberties without too many art historians getting hot under the collar. I have also, with a little licence, used Bois le Duc (so called under the Burgundians) or (if you prefer the Dutch version) 'sHertogenbosch, after which Bosch took his name.

I have taken History and tried to form an idea around it – the opposite of some historians who take an Idea and try to extrude History.

On the art-historical side, I have followed Wilhelm Fränger's interpretation of Bosch's remarkable picture. That is, I have taken the picture to be a complex and exhaustive visual 'bible' of the Adamite sect to whom love was the height and the breadth of life and the passport to union – through the beloved – with the Eternal Spirit itself.

I am well aware that there are other interpretations of this inscrutable (or only partly scrutable) painting, but since this is a novel and therefore my game I have gone along with Fränger.

It may well be that the picture is yet another late medieval moralization on the Sin of Lust, but I do not find this notion interesting.

Shakespeare no doubt would not have found Richard III such fun if he had really been (as some believe) misrepresented by the Lancastrians – and was in fact a straight-backed man and a model uncle.

There is something in this picture – and indeed in Richard III – which leads me to doubt the dull interpretations.

Finally, I am indebted more than I can say to Norman Cohn's excellent book *The Pursuit of the Millennium*. This indeed is history – concerning the millennial obsessions that have sprung up in Western Europe from the earliest days of Christianity, based on ancient Jewish traditions of the End of Things, appealing especially to the poor and dispossessed. These continued as a strand throughout the Middle Ages and beyond, every now and then throwing up knots of religio-fanatical communism that caused both practitioners and persecutors alike endless trouble. It is a lucid and riveting account; and I have drawn considerably on his narrative of 'The Messianic Reign' in Munster.

I cannot thank him or his publishers Secker & Warburg enough for this kindness in allowing me to do so, and I respectfully acknowledge his influence on the book – along with that of Bishop von Galen, poor (traduced, I fear) Hieronymus Bosch and the late Wilhelm Fränger (and his publishers Faber & Faber), who first fired me with interest in his view of Bosch's *Garden*.

It may all seem a long way away, the early sixteenth century; a small German city state. But in an age when sex has been promoted to the forefront of our culture, and religion has been pushed to the back, it may be that the Religion of Love counterpointed by the Power of Darkness still has something of interest for us today.

Part One

My mother groaned, my father wept,
Into this dangerous world I leapt,
Helpless, naked, piping loud
Like a fiend hid in a cloud.

Songs of Experience
WILLIAM BLAKE

Prologue

Darkness and the smell of straw and blood.

Outside, in the wan light of dawn, mist rose on the river marshes like the exhalation of a fever.

Spring had been late this year, and indeed there had been many in the town who doubted whether it would ever come at all – for it had been widely rumoured, and generally prophesied, that this year of 1500 would be the one appointed for the end of the world.

Well, it had not come yet. And, though there were some who occupied themselves in prayer and ceaseless contemplation of the Last Things, others had to carry on with life as best they could.

One such, in a slatternly midwife's hovel on the edge of the town, was the small boy who had just been born.

'Is he all right?' a girl's voice whispered exhaustedly. 'Why doesn't he cry?'

'He'll cry, he'll cry,' muttered the old trollop who handled such matters as unwanted or secret births in the town. 'Poor little bugger, he'll have plenty to cry about.'

There was the sound of a slap and a wail of tiny indignation. A shape appeared in the rectangle of doorway, framed against the grisaille of the dawn.

'Is it over? Is it all right? Can I come in?' a man's voice whispered anxiously.

'You stay out there. I've got to clean her up first,' grumbled the crone.

'But is she all right?'

'It's a boy,' the girl answered.

'I don't care about that. About you . . .'

'I'm . . . fine . . .'

'She's very weak,' said the old woman. 'Little bugger took his time, didn't he?'

'I'm sorry, darling,' the man said. 'Is there anything I can do?'

'Haven't you done enough?' said the midwife.

'Silence, woman.'

'Just . . . stay near . . .' said the girl.

'I will, my darling.'

'Darling, darling,' grumbled the crone to herself. 'Should've thought about what he was doing, shouldn't he? Giving a nice girl a babby.

3

That's not very nice. And what's to become of the little bastard, I should like to know?'

'Do what you like with him,' said the man's voice coldly from outside. 'Float him down the river if you like. Make a little Moses of him.'

'No,' cried the girl's voice. 'Our baby . . . you wouldn't . . .'

'He came between us, didn't he?' The man's voice was hard. 'He is the reason we have to part. He was the snake in our grass.'

'It's not his fault, poor little thing.'

'Everything was all right before.'

'All right?'

'It was Paradise. We were Paradise.'

'You were married.'

There was a pause.

'I am married,' he said heavily.

'So it was not all right,' she told him.

'I love you,' he said.

'I know.'

'Stop your blathering and get your knees up,' ordered the old woman. 'Let's get some of this muck off you. Love? I wish I had sixpence for every time I've heard that word used as an excuse for trouble. It's a filthy word if you ask me. Just a passport to spread-your-legs . . .'

'Be quiet, you old witch,' said the man.

The old woman cackled. She had asked for payment beforehand.

'Touchy, are we?'

There was another pause punctuated by the baby's mewing.

'So what am I to do with the babby?' the midwife asked again.

'Arrangements have been made,' said the man. 'Just get it ready and I will take care of it.'

'Him . . .' corrected the girl. 'Poor little boy . . .'

She started to weep, and the man made as if to come forward.

'You keep out,' said the old woman fiercely, moved in spite of herself. 'You've done enough mischief for one twelvemonth.'

Chapter 1

To be brought up by stern and unloving parents is bad; but to be raised by a sullen couple to whom you are not related even by the unreliable ties of blood is immeasurably worse.

Julius often wondered as a very young boy what he had done to make his parents dislike him so much. And he was only six or seven when he discovered that they were not his parents at all.

'What is the point, Dirk?' his 'mother' had grumbled to her husband one day after the boy had committed some trifling misdemeanour. 'He's not ours. Why should he even think that he is? He's a bastard.'

'He's a bastard,' agreed her husband, a butcher.

'You're a bastard, boy,' she continued nastily to Julius.

She had been saving the news up for some time.

'What is a bastard, please?' Julius had asked with trembling lip.

'A bastard is a booby, a bloody nuisance to everybody,' his 'father' had said.

Julius wondered whether being a bastard was a beatable offence. There were many such offences in the butcher's house in Magpie Lane. Not liking the smell of meat was one of them. It wasn't his fault if that warm, sweet, slightly sweaty smell made him walk around with held breath and pinched mouth and nose. If he didn't, and caught a great whiff of one of the veal collops his father would bring in for his dinner, he would sometimes be sick on the spot. And that would ensure an even bigger beating anyway, so you might as well pinch your nostrils and have done with it. Oh, how he had suffered from that meat. It was all right when it was cooked but somehow raw – with all those tubes and sinewy bits and blaps – it made you go pale just to think about it. And of course it would have to be his father's business.

'That's your bread and butter, boy,' his father would say. 'That's the roof over your head. Too good for it are you? Smell it, that's life.'

Not that the sullen couple were exactly cruel or even – by their neighbours' standards – especially violent. They were simply chilly. They didn't believe in love or affection. Even to each other, they preserved a cool indifference in their demeanour. If they ever made the beast with two backs – and there were no other children in the house, so perhaps they did not – you felt it would have been with the same expression they used when cutting the fat off a kidney.

5

'A bastard,' said his wife, 'is an unwanted child brought into the world by a mother who isn't married.'

Julius had no idea at that time how children were brought into the world at all, but he knew about unwanted.

'Don't you want me, then?' he asked, and added, 'Mother?'

'Mother? Mother? Hark at the child. Can't you get into your thick head what we're trying to tell you? I'm married, aren't I? Didn't I just say a bastard mother is unmarried?'

'You mean . . . you're not my mother?'

Her husband clapped his meaty hands ironically.

'Clever dick. Got it in one.'

'But . . .' and his lip trembled again, not at the news that these people weren't his parents, but at an intimation of the terrible loneliness of the world. '. . . where are my parents? Who am I, then?'

It was a cry that would recur constantly later.

'Where are my parents? Who am I?'

'Ah,' said the butcher, knowingly although he did not know, 'that would be telling, wouldn't it?'

From that moment his will added weight to a tendency his surroundings had already encouraged. If his parents didn't need him, he did not need parents. He had to stand alone. It was a loveless upbringing for a child of love and it was not surprising that he knew nothing of the meaning of the word.

Things were little better at school. The other children all seemed to have good, solid parents behind them – bastards usually went to the poorhouse – and he did not enlighten his fellows as to the true nature of his relationship with the butcher couple. He instinctively felt it might have been revealing a chink in essential armour; but the knowledge worked upon him inwardly. He himself felt the stigma of being different; and of course that communicated itself to the boys. Solitude was his game.

There was one boy in particular – an uncomfortable, restless sort of fellow, a year older than he – called Paul Uitwaarden, who delighted in tormenting him, trying to break down the barriers of his self-sufficiency.

Uitwaarden had the gift of mimicry and the ability to read his fellows.

'Bathtard, bathtard,' he lisped, apeing a childish peculiarity Julius had.

How had he discovered? wondered Julius. Doubtless the butchers had been blabbing.

'Bastard,' cried the other boys. 'Poor little babby left on the thtepth . . .'

Julius, however, was not a coward, and one day fought Uitwaarden and punched him in the mouth, making him lisp perforce through swollen lips.

6

'I'll pay you for that, thee if I don't,' said Uitwaarden, wiping skin and blood from his teeth.

When Julius returned home, with a bloody nose and torn clothes, he was berated for quarrelsomeness.

It was, as it happened, however, a good school of its kind. And he studied there diligently – another reason for the suspicion of his contemporaries who were mostly indifferent to knowledge and the dawning wonders of the New Learning, and couldn't wait to join their elders in the family trade.

The dominus, a strict old buzzard by the name of Pieter Preger, with a shrewd cane, was not so hardened by the obduracy of the boys that he could not perceive in Julius a certain thirst for learning – a thirst encouraged by the butchery and boredom of his home life. And, though he beat Julius as frequently as any of the lads, he did not lay it on so hard; and when he gave him extra lines to copy after school, he made sure that they were of a quality guaranteed to quicken the interest as well as a length necessary to allay persecution or any hint of favouritism.

By the time he was twelve, then, Julius had a reasonable mastery of Latin, a little Greek, some French, some Euclid and a decent hold on Grammar and Logic. He had also discovered a talent for drawing which, merely as a habit of childish doodling, developed as a result of visiting the various churches of the town and trying to copy some of the paintings with which they were adorned – van der Weyden, van Eyck, Geertgen tot Sint Jans, and the local artist, Hieronymus Bosch (whose pictures, teeming with nightmarish creatures and brutish humanity, particularly fascinated him) were all represented. And, of course, the new printing had unleashed a steady stream of books illustrated with woodcuts – some by Italians, others by the German, Dürer – against which he would pit his skills or lament his shortcomings.

There was no teaching of art in the school. One day, however, Old Preger sent for him.

'Martens,' he said (that was the butcher's name), 'many of the boys are now becoming apprentices. Are you going to follow your father into butchery?'

Julius could scarcely suppress a shudder.

'I thought perhaps you would not. I have been looking at some of your drawings, and I believe we might be able to place you with one of our town's most illustrious painters. He has asked me for a suitable lad to help around his studio. Would you be interested?'

'Indeed I would, sir.'

Julius could hardly contain his excitement. And then he thought of the butcher and his wife. They would never let him do something that smacked so much of doing nothing. He had heard them talking about

7

painters. Besides, they would surely expect him to help out in the shop, or – worse still – in the abattoir.

To his surprise, however, the butchers went along with the apprenticeship – especially when they heard it was going to be to Mr Bosch, whose name was not without honour in his own country (had he not designed the stained-glass windows in St John's Church?), and who was married to the only daughter of a well-to-do local nobleman.

'He's a right one, and no mistake!' said the butcher's wife. 'Have you seen that *Judgement* in St John's? Goblins and ghouls and dreadful goings-on. You wouldn't think he knew about that sort of thing at all, him looking so respectable. Puts you right off the end of the world.'

'Never mind that, wife,' said the butcher. 'He's going to take young Julius off our hands and that's a mercy. Wouldn't have been any use in the knacker's yard, would you, Lily?'

He had thought it was the funniest thing in the world when he hit on the nickname for Julius.

'No,' said Julius, too pleased to be going to the painter to be vexed at the reiterated insult. 'No, I would be quite useless.'

'There you are, you see,' said the butcher to his wife. 'Consider the lilies of the field. They toil not neither do they spin. Painting's the best thing for a lily.'

'Painting's too good for a lily,' said his wife.

But no attempt was made to stop him, and in due course he presented himself at the famous painter's half-timbered house, the Red Cross in the Cloth Market, the smartest street in town.

Chapter 2

The next three years brought a transformation in Julius's life. Not that Bosch himself was an easy master; by no means. He could be abrupt, cantankerous, strangely abstracted, impatient, vague, overbearing, uncompanionable, mean – but he could be forgiven, for he had much to teach.

Of painters and paintings, his knowledge was prodigious. He had travelled a little – to Louvain and Antwerp to help the great du Hameel with his work on the cathedral spire. But his main peregrination seemed to have been in the realm of the mind. It was as if he had access to some secret store out of which he plucked more wisdom than you would have thought one man could carry.

His clothes were homespun – garments that went with the tonsured hair and proclaimed him a member of the Brotherhood of Our Lady of which he was a 'notable'. His house, however, was full of beautiful things that he had picked up in some manner not fully clear to Julius.

His wife, Aleid, who was some five years his senior and no longer in the first flush of youth – being now in her late fifties – was still one of the beauties of the house. She had a grave, pale elegance like an old statue; and, though she did not say much, when she did speak her quiet voice seemed cut in marble. There was a kind of cool resignation written on her features. She was the one person to whom Bosch seemed to pay attention.

It was clear she did not much like Julius.

They had no children, nor could Julius imagine them having any. Children would have interrupted Bosch's thoughts, cracked the marble.

A pattern of days was now established that varied little as the months went by.

Every morning, Julius would leave the butcher's house where he was now treated almost with the respect due to a lodger, and arrive at Bosch's private studio at seven. Bosch had a second studio – what he called his workshop – in another street where three or four artists worked on his larger commissions, on designs for stained-glass and his architectural enterprises, but his private studio was where he originated his most important compositions. Here Julius would light the studio fire, mix the pigments for the day, and run whatever preparatory errands his master ordained. Sometimes he was allowed to fill in a little background. Mostly he was made to watch.

There was one deference Bosch seemed to feel, greater even than his consideration for Aleid his wife, and Julius learned about it.

One day he accompanied his master to help with the decorations for the annual Swan Banquet of the Brotherhood of Our Lady. (The swan was the emblem of the Brotherhood and one or two roast swans invariably appeared on the menu of the feast.) The occasion was one of great note in the town, and of course Julius had heard much about it before. It was a considerable treat to be allowed to come as close to its solemnizing as this.

As Julius placed the carefully painted, almost magically lifelike swan effigy that his master had created for the occasion on a wall-bracket overhanging the end of the table, a tall man with black hair, strong features and an expression of the greatest authority entered the room.

Julius was astonished to see his master – who normally bowed the knee to no man – humble himself in the stranger's presence.

'Grand Master,' he murmured. 'We did not expect you.'

'I have come for the Feast,' said the man in a strong voice with a trace of foreign accent to it. 'And to see how our Garden grows.'

'It is coming along,' said Bosch, though Julius did not know what he was referring to.

There was no garden picture that he knew of in the studio.

'And this is your apprentice?' asked the man, fixing Julius in the great beam of his gaze.

'Yes,' said Bosch. 'Name of Julius.'

'A good name for a soldier. A name for the times. You must wield your brush like a sword, not your sword like a brush, young man.'

'Yes, sir,' said Julius.

'You have had trouble, my lad, and you will have more. But what is the use of a strong horse if he cannot carry a burden?'

'Not much, I suppose,' said Julius.

'You suppose right. Do your work well. Learn from your master. We will need you in due course. You will know me again, hmm?'

'That I will,' said Julius.

It was not a face you could easily forget.

'And now abideth Faith, Hope and Love; these three,' said the man. 'And the greatest of these is Love.'

With that he walked out.

'Who was that?' asked Julius as he returned home with his master.

'Who was who?'

'The man who came in and you called Grand Master.'

'Oh, him,' said Bosch. 'He's a free spirit.'

'What is his name?'

'Nameless Wildness, I shouldn't wonder.'

'Oh.'

There was a pause. He could never tell when his master was making a joke.

'He didn't seem very wild,' said Julius.

'What on earth has that got to do with it?'

There was another pause.

'Oh, very well, then,' said Bosch suddenly. 'His name is d'Almagaes, he is a Jew received some years ago into the Church and baptized in front of Duke Philip the Fair. He is enormously wise and limitlessly rich and the Grand Master of our Order.'

They trudged on in silence.

'Your father was a man of my acquaintance,' said Bosch at last.

Try as he would, Julius could get no more out of him than that. He had the absurd notion that the mysterious Jew might after all be his parent. Not that it would cut any ice with him. He did not need parents – especially not the sort that could desert him.

Why had he talked of Love? And what was that, anyhow?

Chapter 3

Three events stood out in his mind when, in later years, he tried to recall his apprenticeship; though in a sense they were all bound up with the first of them.

He understood early on from Bosch that his assistance was only required on the 'nuts and bolts' of the work. As well as background, he was sometimes invited to help with a little varnishing in the outer studio when certain pictures emerged from the inner sanctum. These were what Bosch called his bread-and-dripping paintings (although Julius considered them wonderful enough); works like an *Adoration* or a *Crowning with Thorns* which were destined for the Cathedral or one of the local churches.

There were, however, other works undertaken in Bosch's inner room which he laboured upon and finished privately. The models came and went by another door, and so did those for whom the paintings were effected.

Whenever Julius made reference to these matters – which he sometimes did in the early days, for he was naturally curious – his master would silence him brusquely, telling him to mind his own business.

However, on one occasion, when Bosch had left the studio to attend some Brotherhood function, Julius found that the inner studio door was unlocked, and (greatly daring, for he knew the old man's capacity for wrath) he ventured in.

To his disappointment, the room seemed conventional enough save for a tame owl that sat motionless and unblinking in a cage that hung upon the wall. Julius had been expecting more mysteries than that – the trappings of alchemy, or, more pruriently, some of the fleshy Italianate nudes which had started to be so talked about. He had reached an age when images of women's bodies had started to occupy his mind.

There were merely two paintings in evidence, both draped with cloths and standing on easels. He advanced upon the first and gingerly uncovered it, hoping for pink bodies, but there were none. Instead a scene was disclosed which, like so many of his master's creations, was to haunt him for the rest of his life. It was the front of a triptych that had sustained, it seemed, some minor damage which Bosch was in the process of repairing or correcting.

A traveller or beggar, shabbily dressed with a hole at the knee, and wearing an expression of weary resignation tinged with fleeting annoyance (for he was fending off a snarling dog), was limping through a cheerless landscape towards a rickety little bridge. Bones and rubbish littered the foreground and behind him, to the left, a violent robbery was in progress. To the right, a couple danced with lascivious joylessness to the music of a feckless bagpiper, while in the background a crowd gathered beneath a gallows whose ominous dimensions crowned a low hill . . .

It could have been a scene of the utmost dreariness, but under Bosch's touch it evoked a strange sense of recognition in the viewer. Yes, thought Julius, young as I am, I seem to have travelled some of that road, alone. I am on it. I will be there. Danger, sin and death seemed to oppress the traveller from every side. And yet there was more than that – a feeling, too, that there was hope if only one knew where to look for it.

Julius tried to open the triptych, eager to find out if the answer lay hidden, but it was held fast by a locked catchment.

He turned at length to the other picture under its shroud. This held an image as extraordinary as the other had been familiar.

In the darkness of what seemed like eternal night – or the land of the shadow of death – shone a great light, emerging in a tremendous cone of lucent perspective from a source into which two blest figures were disappearing, while another, ushered by an angel, was already entering upon its glorious circumference.

In the foreground, two more hopefuls, attended by angels, were making their way in supplication towards the source of eternity, while strange writhing things flung their toils in a desperate attempt to divert these latest candidates.

The composition was so simple and yet so strong, so extraordinary and yet so curiously natural, that Julius could do no more than gaze at it in fascination for several minutes.

He had the oddest feeling of recognition, that (yes) this was what it was like – the corridor of light down which you must pass, the waiting guide clothed in brightness, the traumas of the dark brushed aside . . . But how did the old man know? Julius had never heard of the image painted or even described in this way before. Only later, when he fell into conversation with a plague victim who had been left for dead, did he hear of something that almost exactly mirrored Bosch's painting.

Now he stood and marvelled, and at last, fearful of his master's return, he replaced the cloths and went back to his workroom where he remained, vacantly stirring pigment, while his mind followed the desolate path of the pilgrim and at length soared again, sucked up into that tunnel of light, to knock at the secrets of the blest . . .

'What, boy? Not finished yet?'

It was his master back again.

'Oh? Sorry . . . Sorry, Master.'

'Your young men shall see visions,' quoted the old painter – he had become marginally more communicative of late. 'Let us hope you will one day have the skill to put them down on canvas. But not if you mix good paint like that. That pigment is like sow's vomit.'

'Sorry, sir,' said Julius, again.

His eyes, his very heart dazzled, as though he had glimpsed God.

Chapter 4

Bosch suggested to Julius one day that he prepare to become a novice of the Brotherhood of Our Lady, and he embarked upon a twofold course of instruction. The first came from a priest involved in the Brotherhood – as many were in the days when its secrets were still unknown to the authorities. He simply prepared Julius for Confirmation, which in due course he received. The second part of his course was administered by the dark-haired man whom he had met on the eve of the Swan Supper – the Jew, no less, d'Almagaes himself, who now appeared at irregular intervals and provided instruction that was not at all what Julius had been expecting.

He had anticipated a little background information on the Brother-hood's history and establishment, some practical preparation for those areas that they seemed mainly to be involved in – prayer meetings, funeral pomps, almsgiving and food distribution to the poor – better still, he had hoped to receive lessons in playing a musical instrument, for the Brotherhood supplied an orchestra for the Cathedral. But it seemed that beside – or perhaps behind – this formal religious aspect was another altogether more, how should he call it, more philosophical, more humanistic, and (though it was not said) more heretical. The name Erasmus was raised, classical mythology was discussed; the place of art, the nature of man, the meaning of evil, the doctrine of reincarnation – all these courtly ideas were subjects which the Jew with his finely modulated voice and his glittering eyes touched on with animation and scholarship.

This intermittent course of instruction lasted a year. And, almost throughout that time, Julius still fostered the notion that the Jew was actually his father. There was no particular reason for it. They were both fresh-complexioned. There was some passing resemblance in feature. It was simply a feeling that he had. He never mentioned it to d'Almagaes, for he felt that it would have been an admission of need on his part. He did not, would not, need him, and he tried to maintain a resolute indifference to the man's considerable charm.

'Ssso,' said the Jew one day, in his curiously sibilant voice, 'you are ready now, Julius. I think it is time we admitted you as a novitiate.'

Julius was suddenly filled with alarm. There was a curious tone of completion, of finality in the man's voice.

'Does that mean . . . no more lessons?' he asked.

If he didn't need the man's company, he needed the wisdom. It was a path of gold.

'No more for the moment,' said the man. 'I am called away. Your master Hieronymus will take my place.'

'But there is much more for me to learn.'

'You have enough for the moment. You are young. You must learn to paint as well. That is most important to us. You know how, in the Dark Ages, it was the illuminators and scribes who kept religion alive. Today it is our painters who convey the mysteries. Words are too crass. This printing turns everything to fodder. Paint, and learn to live and to love.'

'But, Father . . .'

There, he had said it; a bait to get the man to continue his teaching.

The Jew looked long and hard at him.

'You have one father,' he said at length sternly. 'Only the One. Do not call me father or think of me as such.'

Julius's eyes filled with tears – ridiculous, that was not what he wanted at all – and the Jew seemed to relent, putting a hand on his shoulder.

'You will come at length,' he told him, 'to joys unimaginable. But the road is not easy. Remember the pilgrim. You must have patience. You will not see me again for a long time but, when you do, you will know you are near the end.'

Chapter 5

The third of the events to leave a lasting impression, flickering like a candle down the shadowy corridors of his recollection, was centred around the Brotherhood's involvement with theatricals. Indeed, they had a theatrical company that specialized in strong, dramatic performances of various kinds. Mystery plays for the various churches, pageants for the guilds, burlesques and comedies, masques of the Nine Worthies, *Patient Griselda and the Trials of Virtue*, devil dances, ballets of skeletons and ghosts, farces, diableries . . . The thirst of the town for such entertainments was unslakeable.

Apart from the fun of taking part in these productions, there was the business of designing and preparing the props and costumes, which often fell to his master's dispensation as 'Insignis Pictor' of the town.

Iron helmets, false leather noses like elongated cod-pieces, painted finery, masks of cloth and hide, embroidered cloaks, gonfalons of silk and cloth of gold, armour made of wood and leather, coloured lanterns and reflective oil torches . . . all these passed through the Bosch studio. And, to Julius's surprise, the old man took a keen interest in such frivolities, often taking time off from more important work to sketch the helmets and the noses, the comical beards and wigs, making crazy little nightmarish creatures out of them, and wearing the most serious expression imaginable while he did so.

It made Julius laugh to see him frowning over his drawing of a moth whose wings were giant stage ears, or a helmet fitted with tiny menacing arms and legs and a face that pouted and sneered with vainglorious aggression.

But when he did so, the old man would round on him.

'Don't laugh, boy. Out of the trivial, nightmares are made. Great things may be achieved with small effects.'

'I'm sorry, Master.'

'Have you learned your next part? What are you?'

'The boy David.'

'Look what he did with a piece of leather and a stone.'

The sinister creations would appear in the next Danse Macabre or Hell scene for a triptych, and Julius would feel chastized.

It was at a rehearsal for one of these Devil Dances that Julius sensed someone tugging softly at his sleeve.

'Yes?'

He half-turned, still looking at the stage. He was on soon.

'Can you get me into this, Julius?' said a voice, insinuating, coercing.

It was his erstwhile persecutor Uitwaarden. Julius had learnt some years since that Uitwaarden himself was a bastard. It seemed to him a particularly pernicious thing to tease another for what you felt was your own shortcoming (though, of course, he learned later that this is one of the prime reasons for teasing). So he did not look too kindly on Uitwaarden's request.

However, he went through the motions of re-union.

'What are you doing now?' he asked.

Uitwaarden looked slightly sheepish.

'I'm an apprentice,' he said.

'What in?'

'Pastry. All I could get. No connections, that's my trouble. I'm a bastard, you see.'

'Yes, I know.'

'Oh. You knew, did you?'

'Yes.'

'You're a bastard too, I seem to remember.'

'That's right.'

'But with connections, I suppose.'

'I'm an apprentice too.'

'Yes, but to a painter . . . *the* painter . . . mad old Bosch. I heard about that. I dare say your dad was some randy old noble, getting you a job like that. Mine was a village mayor, worse luck. A pastry cook! I ask you.'

'Nothing wrong with pastry. I like pastry,' said Julius, feeling that tarts and pies needed sticking up for, and wondering once again if his father really could be the rich Jew.

'Pastry's not a place for heroes,' replied Uitwaarden.

Julius couldn't help seeing what he meant. He rather wished, however, that he would go away. There was something derogatory, oppressive about the boy.

'You will get me into the next play,' he said.

It may have been a question but it sounded like a statement.

'I'll try,' said Julius doubtfully.

'I would go for this one but it's only a pageant.'

The next play, as it happened, was the Mystery concerning the boy David and King Saul, which Julius had discussed with his master. He had already been cast. But, because he was a kind lad and Uitwaarden seemed to have set his heart upon it, he prevailed upon the producer to give him an audition, and a brilliant job Uitwaarden made of it.

The trouble was, he was too brilliant. He had even re-written some of the speeches and done it superbly – but it was not the producer's idea of David.

'David is a lowly shepherd boy. He does not think of himself as a hero. You would do very well as Saul but you are not yet big enough. Come back in a year or three, boy, and Saul is yours.'

But this was no sop to Uitwaarden, who ground his teeth and looked daggers at Julius.

'Friends in high places again, eh? I was better than you, anyone could see that. You take "lowly" to new depths, Martens. That's the second time you've done me down. Remember what I said before?'

'No.'

'I said I'd pay you back. Now you've got it coming to you twice over, you bastard.'

'Bastard yourself.'

'A bastard's a real bastard if he doesn't know who his father is.'

'Don't take it like that,' Julius said. 'It's only acting.'

Uitwaarden's face went white with rage.

'Only acting?' he hissed.

He gestured around him, throwing his arms wide to indicate the hall, the town, the world.

'What else do you call this?'

Chapter 6

Never easy, sometimes mocking and even bullying, wry, cantankerous, his conversation full of snatches of reference to obscure painters and poets, Julius's master now began to talk to him of other things besides form, light and colour as they went about their business in the studio.

Julius had asked him about the Beghards and Beguines who occasionally appeared in the town – strange, sometimes troublesome itinerant beggars who believed in odd fantasies of Doomsday. He had heard that they belonged to a Brotherhood of the Free Spirit.

'It is said . . .' Bosch's voice had become somewhat frailer recently, and indeed his wife had given precise instructions to Julius in her chilly voice that he should not be tired '. . . it is said that the origins of their beliefs – at least of those who know what it is they believe in, for there are many rascals on the road – stem from the teachings of the Jews and Early Christians. There existed a tradition which dealt with the final state of the world. A Millennium was foretold – not necessarily limited to a thousand years but often so – in which, after certain tribulations and a final battle with the hosts of Antichrist, humanity would inherit the Earth – and enjoy it in lasting happiness and goodness.'

'Do you believe that, sir?'

'I believe that such doctrines existed and continue to exist. Look at the Picards and the Taborites . . . the Drummer of Niklashausen and Thomas Muntzer with his Peasants' War . . . Look at the *Book of Ezra*. Consult the *Book of Revelations*. But I do not believe that this happy state will be achieved by the generality of men. Perfection must be deserved. Those who wait for it as geese wait for corn or children for sweetmeats will be bitterly disappointed.'

'I shall not wait for it like that, Master.'

'That's as may be. I dare say you'd wait and guzzle if you could. I have asked the Brethren if they will admit you fully. We shall see. I doubt if you're up to scratch, personally. Presently you shall go to Florence and learn to draw the human figure in a manner that I have never attempted. You shall talk to the heirs of Pico della Mirandola and Ficino, the neo-Pythagoreans and Platonists who praise our great Original, Adam. They regard him, let me see . . .'

Here his master fumbled at a book he kept in his studio, leafed

20

through it, found what he wanted and turned to Julius portentously, lowering his voice still further.

'Adam,' his master read, 'is a Protean expression of the universal process of transformation, and I place his nature between animal and divine.'

'I don't quite understand, sir.'

'Listen, boy. "I place his nature between animal and divine, for if he gives way to the urgings of sensuality, he will grow savage and become a beast. If he follows reason, a divine being will arise out of him. But if he develops his intellectual powers, he will be an angel and a Son of God. And when at last, discontented with the destiny of created beings, he withdraws to the centre of all being, then he will become one with God, one spirit, and raised up to the solitary heights where the Father reigns over all things, he too will erect his throne over all that is. Hence Asklepios of Athens had good cause to say that this ability to transform oneself into all kinds of different beings is represented in the mysteries by the symbol of Proteus. And hence the Pythagoreans, too, as well as the Jews, celebrate a festival of the Metamorphoses." Do you understand now?'

Julius did not understand, not in the least, but he didn't like to irritate his master.

'I ... think so ...'

'I myself have been an owl. You have seen the owls in my paintings?'

His eyes glowed fiercely. He's making fun of me, thought Julius.

'Yes.'

'The owl, of course, is symbolic. But it is also myself. The watcher. It is a little joke I have with the Grand Master.'

'Ah.'

Was the old man mad or was he truly a magician as well? Certainly he mingled with alchemists and mountebanks.

'Next week, if I am free from this cold ...' Bosch continued, and then stopped, leaning against the wall and coughing.

Julius came forward to help him but Bosch waved him away.

'Next week, when I am free from this cold,' he went on, 'I shall take you to the Cathedral Church of St John to see my altar-piece of *The Last Judgement*. It is fitting, since we were talking of Doomsday.'

'I have seen it, sir.'

'You have seen it but you have not seen it. I shall read it to you so that you may get it into your noddle – if it's capable of holding anything more profound than a saveloy.'

'I shall enjoy that, sir. Sir?'

'Yes, boy?'

'Do you really mean that about Florence? Shall I go there?'

'In good time, boy, in good time.'

'Hieronymus.'

It was his wife calling from the studio door. She did not come in. She never came in.

'Yes, my dear?'

'It is time to come home. Remember what the doctor said? It is cold in the studio. The boy is keeping you.'

She fixed Julius with her cool, stone-coloured eyes.

'Not a bit of it,' said Bosch. 'It is I who am keeping him. So much to learn, so little time, eh boy? *Arse longa, vita brevis?* And how damn *brevis* it is!'

'Yes, sir.'

'Pish,' said his wife.

Julius suddenly realized what it was that made Bosch so abstracted, odd, withdrawn, wry, unpredictable. He was unhappy and terribly lonely.

Why on earth could that be? thought Julius, the realization coming as a shock to him. He's an Insignis Pictor, isn't he, with the world beating a path to his door?

But the unhappiness of the successful old is not accessible to the unsuccessful young.

Chapter 7

The old man had recovered sufficiently by the following week to take him to the Cathedral as he had promised.

The triptych of *The Last Judgement* was hanging over the altar in a little chapel away from the bustle of the nave where workmen were still busy.

They stood in front of the painting and gazed for a while in silence.

'I shall be brief,' said Bosch at last, 'because there is a quality of fear and hatred in these places that catches my breath. Look at the left-hand panel. What d'you see?'

'The Garden of Eden, sir. God putting life into Eve, Adam reclining . . . then behind them the tree, the serpent in man's form offering Eve the Apple . . . And behind that again, the angel with the flaming sword chasing them out of Eden.'

'And what behind that?'

'Falling angels, sir. Lucifer, I suppose. Oh, and God in a cloud.'

'What sort of God?'

'Sort of cloudy, sir.'

'Anything else?'

'No, sir. It's very nice and green.'

'Nice and green?' the older man snorted. 'Nice and green? You have not properly opened your eyes, boy. Why are the falling angels falling into the Garden and not into Hell?'

'Well, sir . . . I don't know. It's not what we are taught.'

'Of course it's not what we are taught. But St Augustine himself says that the separation of Heaven and Earth has its origins in the division of the angels into good and bad. This is the First Judgement of God. And there he is, as you say, sort of cloudy. Faint, it is true. Little more than a sepia outline. But then the painting is not about cloudy old God the Father. You must read it, not from the centre, but from left to right.'

'I will, sir,' said Julius, anxious about the noise the old man was making.

'Lucifer's revenge, of course, is the temptation,' continued the old man. 'This Eden will never be recovered. The Paradise of Original Creation is lost forever. But the situation is not quite hopeless. For who do we see in the centre picture?'

'God the Son, sir, sitting in Judgement, with the Apostles on either side ... And the Blessed Virgin, of course ... and one or two souls making it up to heaven ...'

'What else?'

'All sorts of torments and monsters ... and sinners of course ...'

'Of course,' said Bosch, 'it is a nasty place, for that is what man has made of the world. This is the Second Judgement. It is my idea to have Christ judging it. And on the right?'

'More torments and monsters ... a very nasty monster in the centre with burning eyes and mouth and a fire in his bread-basket standing in a doorway ... judging more sinners, I suppose, unregenerate and hopeless with some very unpleasant things happening to them ... for all eternity ...'

'That is the Third Judgement,' said Bosch. 'Do you like the picture?'

'It's very well painted.'

'Pig-shit.'

'Master ...'

Julius tapped at the old man's sleeve, appalled. He had noticed a priest walking over towards them. No expert in heresy as Julius was, he rather thought it would be better if Bosch was not heard giving his interpretation of the painting.

'What is it, boy? Ah.'

He had seen the man, a nasty-looking, sneaky-faced fellow, quick on his sandals.

'*Pax vobiscum*,' said the priest.

Julius mumbled a reply. The priest lingered.

'Anything you need?' he asked. 'Can I be of assistance? Hear your confession? Take alms off you? Tell you about the warning to the lustful?'

'Piss off,' said Bosch.

'Well, really. This is a church, you know.'

'Go and pray, then, that Mr Luther doesn't ever preach here. You'd be finished if he did.'

It was the year of the famous notice on the Wittenberg church-door.

'What? What is your name? I know you, don't I?'

Julius felt it was time for diplomacy. He took the man aside.

'My master has been very ill. He doesn't know what he is saying some of the time.'

'Well, I should hope not. As it is, I shall have to report the matter. What is your ...'

'Please,' said Julius. 'He has a fever, that's all.'

But a larger priest was beckoning sneaky-face to come and look at some masonry. The fellow gave in.

'Oh, just ... take him away somewhere ...'

Julius turned back to his master. Bosch was still standing transfixed by his work, nodding and smiling.

'I think we'd better go,' Julius told him.

'Stay a moment, boy. What was that you said?'

'I think we'd better go.'

'No, no . . .'

The old man started coughing again and clutched at a pillar.

'You said "it's very well painted",' he continued at length. 'Let me tell you, boy, that well painted does not make a good picture. This triptych that you see is an exercise in deception. It is a ruse, a box of tricks that seems to say one thing and in fact says quite another. Come along, boy. Look again. Think about it.'

Julius thought about it.

'The light is interesting,' he said at last. 'It seems in the scenes of Damnation to be coming from a hundred glowing sources, not one central point as most painters would have it.'

'Confound it, boy. You are talking of technique again.'

Julius thought harder. Suddenly light began to dawn.

'If God the Son put life into Adam and Eve . . .'

'Go on, boy.'

'And He knew, as He must have done, that Eden was flawed because of the falling angels . . .'

'That death was already in the Garden when it was first made . . .' the old man put in helpfully.

'And if Christ is sitting in Judgement in the centre, it must mean . . . that Death is not the same as Sin . . .'

'And Original Sin does not exist!' shouted Bosch triumphantly.

Several people in the church, including the two priests, looked round sharply at the noise.

'Shh,' whispered Julius to his master. 'That is heresy.'

'I know,' said the old man with satisfaction. 'Lovely, isn't it?'

Julius was still puzzled.

'But what about Judgement and Damnation? Is your picture not a warning to us?'

'He who hath eyes to see, let him see. My picture is full of hope. You are talking about the man-made, Church-made religion of Sin and Fear, boy. When you are a little older, I will show you the Religion of Love.'

Chapter 8

Soon after his sixteenth birthday, his master sent for him and asked him if he still wanted to go to Italy.

'You have learned enough for the moment here, boy. How do you feel about it?'

'I should like to go, sir.'

'I know a fellow who says he will take you. Name of Father Bartolommeo. He is well regarded. Doubtless he will need, as I have done, the patience of a saint.'

Julius could hardly contain his excitement. He had not thought the old man really meant it. To leave the dull confines of Bois le Duc with its narrow streets, little squares and small society, fusty with provincialism, for the grace and opportunities of Florence; to live in the city of Leonardo and Michelangelo and Botticelli, where more great artists and sculptors had lived than could conveniently be enumerated in a parenthesis – this was the opportunity of an artist's lifetime.

'When shall I go?' he asked.

'In April,' Bosch informed him. 'You will travel after Easter. Meanwhile you are to take Italian lessons from Brother Ernesto, who will also conduct you on some of your way.'

'You are a fortunate young man,' said his old schoolmaster when Julius told him. 'I should have given my left eye to go to Florence when I was your age. Of course, that was in the days of Lorenzo de Medici. Florence was Florence then.'

Three months later, with a passing knowledge of the language and enough money to see him through the journey (after which he would be cared for by the studio), he set out for the Beautiful City with hopes as high as if it had been Jerusalem the Golden.

After several weeks of travel, during which Brother Ernesto contracted food poisoning in the Alps, and he himself had his precious brushes stolen in Lombardy, he arrived in Florence, finding – even as he entered the gates – that the city's reputation had not been over-rated.

Florence was paved and drained. Grand vistas opened up at every turn. Graceful porticoes, elegant pillars, domes, pediments and noble arches, statues, overhanging cornices, balustrades, rustications and finials crowded in glorious profusion upon his northern sensibilities. He had passed through other towns on the way, of course. The transition

26

had been gradual. But now it appeared that he had not merely come four hundred miles but had crossed the very boundaries of time. This city seemed to have been planned. It had not simply grown. The lines of the buildings were controlled, the façades unified. There was an ordered philosophy to the place . . .

The man to whose care he had been entrusted, Fra Bartolommeo, was a Dominican who had entered the reformed church of the Order after Savonarola's death. That much Julius knew from Brother Ernesto, who was himself half-Florentine and who received gossip from the city from his cousins. No one seemed to have told him, however, the studio's exact address.

Finding themselves overwhelmed by thirst – the heat of Florence in April surpassed the excesses of 'sHertogenbosch's August – Brother Ernesto and Julius stopped at a tavern and ordered refreshment.

The Tuscan sun blazed. Bells tolled mid-day. White butterflies fluttered like putti. Pigeons kept to the shadows. Brother Ernesto – a melancholy little man with a big head, a clown's face and a tendency towards hypochondria – sipped his wine and talked about the Medici tendency to gout. He seemed in no hurry to go anywhere. He had come further than Bosch had said he would.

Julius let his ears wander to a table near the door where two young men were having a tense discussion.

'I tell you,' said one, a brown-haired, quick-eyed chap, perhaps very slightly the younger of the two, 'the North has the secret. We have had grace and space, perspective and form. Now we need the fantasy. Look at Dürer. Look at Bosch.'

'Bosch tosh,' said the other, a red-haired fellow. 'Northern goblins. And Dürer had to come to Bologna to learn perspective; old Pacioli taught him.'

'Precisely,' replied his companion, triumphantly.

'Precisely what?'

'I don't say the northern painters don't need such criticizing. But perspective is something you can learn – like mixing pigment. What you can't learn so easily is fantasy.'

'You value the curious and the bizarre above painterliness?'

'Skill without fantasy is nothing. It is sight without insight. The North learns from us. Can we learn from the North?'

Julius could not contain himself. He had to talk to these gods.

'*Scusi.*'

'Yes?'

The young men turned and looked at him, half amused, half irritated.

'I could not help overhearing you. I come from the North. I am looking for Fra Bartolommeo's studio.'

The two men burst into laughter.

27

'You win, I think, Jacopo,' said the red-haired one.

'Come back, Julius,' called Ernesto. 'I am sorry, sirs, for this interruption. He is young.'

'Why are you laughing?' asked Julius, puzzled and slightly offended.

'Well, northerner, it is because you are going for your instruction to a master of form without fantasy.'

'Yes,' agreed red-hair, 'Fra Bartolommeo could make a bubble look important.'

'Or the fistula on the Pope's bottom?'

'And doubtless has done.'

There was another little splutter of laughter.

'Fra Bartolommeo,' the red-haired one continued more kindly, seeing Julius puzzled by their mirth, 'entered into partnership with Mariotto Albertinelli, a man who gave up painting and ran this very inn. Bartolommeo, seeing the opportunity to have the biggest studio in Florence, lured him back and, with form and flattery, they sewed up all the ecclesiastical commissions in Florence – which is about eighty per cent of anything that moves.'

'So should I not go there, then?' asked Julius.

'Hush, Julius, you are obliged to go,' said Brother Ernesto, scandalized. 'It is your master's wish.'

'Certainly you should go,' agreed brown-hair. 'You will be taught to put paint very well upon canvas. After that you must study the works of the masters, to say nothing of those of Rosso and myself. Our friend del Sarto may have something to teach you. And if you wish to stimulate your northern fantasy, seek out his master, Piero di Cosimo. He has a droll way with animals. Oh, and one other thing – Albertinelli and Fra Bartolommeo got too successful, quarrelled and split up. So you won't be going into quite the den of Mammon that it was.'

'Thank you,' said Julius.

'Come,' said Brother Ernesto, 'we must find the studio . . . Could you direct us, gentlemen?'

Fra Bartolommeo's establishment was indeed very much as the young man called Rosso had described. Two senior assistants did most of the teaching while Bartolommeo busied himself on the choice portions of the grander commissions, and on drumming up new business.

They treated Julius gruffly but not unkindly, putting him to work at first on priming canvases and mixing paint – at which he was by now well practised – until he had shown enough experience to be allowed to work on corners of backgrounds for minor compositions. He had, it seemed, to unlearn almost everything that old Bosch had taught him, but by degrees he came to be trusted with foliage and eventually with figures on larger undertakings. He was once even allowed to paint a putto in a Bishop's enthronement.

Meanwhile, he had taken lodgings at the house of a carpenter to which he was recommended by the assistants, and grown to familiarity both with his fellows at the studio (who regarded him, not unkindly, as a northern curiosity who did not have the good fortune to be Florentine), and with the city itself, whose beauties and marvels acquaintance did nothing to diminish. The bronze *David* by Donatello especially astonished him, and he would often go to gaze at it. It was a vision of Man as God. Adam himself would have looked so.

He found also that there was a crueller side to the city. The beautiful squares and churches, even the Duomo itself, had been spattered with blood. He was shown the spot where Archbishop Salviati had been thrown from a window onto the pavement for his part in the Pazzi Conspiracy in which Cosimo de Medici had narrowly escaped murder at the High Mass in the Cathedral – and where his cousin had been less fortunate. He was taken to the Piazza della Signoria and shown the blackened marks where Savonarola had been burnt (tortured by the strappado, forced to confess, recanted, tortured again, and burnt), for heresy ostensibly, but in fact for being a nuisance and unleashing terror. His companions spoke of the dark days when the Medici were banished from Florence, the French were on the warpath, and the fire and brimstone sermons of Savonarola were finding a ready audience among the poor and the disaffected.

Aristotle and Plato, gambling and card games, carnivals and palio races, fine clothes and scent, powder and paint, prostitutes and sodomites, and (worst of horrors) pictures that made the Virgin Mary look like a harlot . . . all these were excoriated and vilified from the pulpit.

A shadow, it seemed, had settled over the city. There was to be no fun any more. Intimations of wrath and desolation hummed in the wind and whirled in the dust around the piazzas. It was as if there had been some kind of rehearsal of horrors to come elsewhere; but here, in Florence, it could not stay. The southern sun, the temperament, the spirit of the place, the people had been too much for it. And they were frightened and angry at the fate that so nearly had overtaken them. So they killed the Prior, burning him and his companions until their arms and legs fell off, and riddling the timber until they were consumed and could be discreetly sprinkled in the Arno.

Julius felt he would always remember the hatred in the voices of his fellow-apprentices when they spoke of those days, fifteen years before, even though they had been so young at the time they could hardly recollect them. It had been a profound shock – especially to the artists – for there had been little work of any kind, and what there had been was grim (naturally Bartolommeo – even though young – had the job of painting Savonarola himself).

Fifteen years later, of course, all was well. There was a Medici on the papal throne and another Medici, Lorenzo, Governor of Florence (albeit unpopular as a man, it was enough that he was a Medici). Michelangelo had returned and shortly afterwards Leonardo himself. To crown it all, there was to be a grand visitation by the Medici pope, Leo X, next autumn, for which a dazzling reception, involving arts and artefacts of all kinds, was already in preparation.

As the city stirred itself in anticipation, two important things happened to Julius. He fell in lust with Lucia, a young Neopolitan prostitute who lodged nearby. And he met a Platonic philosopher, one Francesco Ammanati, who had sat at the feet of the great Marsilio Ficino, friend and mentor to both Cosimo and Lorenzo di Medici. This man – touching on matters that the Jew d'Almagaes and his master Bosch had raised – revived in him an interest in the Platonic principles – knowledge, order, harmony, love itself (whatever that might be), music, enquiring into the soul and its journeyings, and the reduction of all things into the One from which they stem . . .

Chapter 9

Lucia held court in a little apartment that smelt of old mullet in an alley above a fishmonger's. Julius preferred not to think too much about the shameful things that went on there – though the thoughts kept creeping back like cats.

Ammanati held his gatherings at his home, the Villa Rosata (so named after the unusual pinkish hue of the stone), which was situated some half an hour's ride out of the city near Ficino's own villa at Careggi.

Here, to a group of mostly young men, he dispensed the wisdom he had received from the Master.

On Julius's first arrival, he was welcomed by a servant and shown into a generously proportioned chamber looking out onto a splendid vista of Tuscan hills, woods and greenly undulant valleys. (It was later explained that Ficino set great store on surroundings of natural beauty.)

There were a dozen or so people sitting in the room, and a silver-haired man whom Julius knew to be Ammanati was reading to them.

'It is undoubtedly a golden age,' he read, 'which has restored to light the liberal arts that had been almost destroyed: grammar, eloquence, poetry, sculpture, music. In that light, we must search for an accord between the teaching of the ancients and that of Christ.'

'Is there not a deep divide between the pagan world and our own?' questioned a young man with a shock of dark hair. 'Isn't paganism the very antithesis of Christianity?'

'An interesting question, Andrea, and one that the pagans themselves have answered. But let me first ask what you mean by paganism, for there is paganism and again there is paganism.'

'Well,' said the young man, 'I suppose that it means worship of trees and streams and images, gods in the clouds . . .'

'That does not sound so bad. For after all, God created Nature and we habitually put God in the heavens.'

'Well, then . . . beastly practices.'

'Do we not have those too?'

'Mm . . . human sacrifice?'

'You are talking of primitive paganism, Andrea. I am talking of Athens. Hear what Pico della Mirandola says, interpreting Plato, and see whether this cannot be taken into conjunction with the teaching of Christ. "A dog must always behave like a dog, and an angel cannot help but behave angelically. But man has the power so to shape his own development that he can become either bestialized or spiritualized . . ." Ah, Julius, I see . . . welcome to our gathering . . .'

Julius was introduced, murmured his greetings, and was shown to a seat next to the shock-headed Andrea who had still another question to ask.

'But will this goal of self-perfection we set ourselves not make us restless with those who convey Christ's teachings but are themselves seen to be far from perfect?'

'Ah.'

This was a tricky one for Ammanati, since the wrong answer could send an informer scuttling to the Archbishop. You never quite knew who stood where, even at gatherings such as this. But the Master was equal to the occasion.

'If the world were perfect, Andrea, there would be no need of self-perfection. If it were easy, everyone would be good. We must, in our quest for self-perfection, be tolerant of others whose faults we see while admiring the truth which they serve. It is by our example and not by precept or arrogance that we may hope to change those whom we should wish improved . . .'

Julius settled back onto his seat assuaged by the occasion. It was a dream, a vision of the classical ideal that his old dominus had talked about – fine proportions, youthful energy, lucid ideas, fluent language, a grave yet spirited instruction, and, as he later discovered, a fitting modicum of the very finest refreshment.

He visited the Villa Rosata many times in the course of his two years in Florence, and both Ammanati and the shock-head (whom he afterwards discovered was del Sarto himself, some ten years his senior) became good friends. Something of the teaching of the Academietta – as it came to be called – began to infuse his own work. His style grew less cramped.

'Whether it is the light of truth or the truth of light,' said del Sarto one day, looking at some of his paintings, 'you are starting to become a Florentine as well as a humanist, Julius.'

These were the golden days which, afterwards, Julius counted as his life's happiest. He was learning from masters, he was surrounded by friendship and by beauty. The Good Life – on the days when he had not visited Lucia – seemed to be a prize that was infinitely attainable.

Not, of course, that Florence itself was entirely good. In many ways, it was as corrupt and venal as any other place. But the light seemed to shine more clearly there, and the harmonious quality and proportions of the town transcended the physical scurryings of the fallible towns-folk. Like the collected smoke of prayer in a Cathedral roof, the work of the town's artists over two centuries filled the air with accumulated grace.

Ammanati warned Julius about being too severe with himself.

'Do not lose your sense of life or of humour,' he counselled. 'The way to self-perfection does not lie in the path of groans and flagellation and furious frowning like that fool of a Savonarola. If you must sin, sin cheerfully. How is your friend Lucia, by the way?'

Julius blushed. He had not realized that Ammanati knew of the girl. He wished his loins did not heat every time he thought of her. There it was again. She had the most wonderful secret in the world.

'She is very well,' he mumbled.

'She is very beautiful,' said the Master. 'Are you in love with her?'

'What is love?' answered Julius. 'It is a word which I seem colour-blind about.'

'There are many kinds, and passionate or carnal love is the lowest. Love is the love that Ficino teaches, the love of the First Parents. The Love that finds oneness in and with the Beloved . . .'

He did not find Oneness in and with Lucia the prostitute, and there was a ticklish moment when it seemed one and one might make three, but happily it was a false alarm and they were able to watch together the triumphal entry of the Pope into the city on 30 November.

Two thousand men had been set to making decorations, obelisks, statues of classical gods, trophies, emblems and triumphal arches orna-mented with classical quotations, at a total cost, it was said, of some 70,000 florins. One of the artists employed had been Julius himself. In fact, one entire studio had been put at the disposal of del Sarto, who had given the very Cathedral a temporary façade complete with marvellous pictures and ornaments.

The Pope, who loved processions, was made to wait several extra days before entering the town so that every detail should be perfect. When he finally arrived, it was by no means an anticlimax. Julius, who had managed to get himself and Lucia a particular vantage-point, sur-veyed him with interest. He had never seen a pope before.

Riding side-saddle on a milk-white Arab palfrey, his crimson face only equalled by the red of the cardinals' hats, the Pontiff's vast, corpu-lent figure seemed like something out of an Eastern fable. This was no pope. His bloated features, with their affable, self-indulgent mouth, weak jaw and little boar-like, short-sighted eyes, were those of a Mammon. Julius even caught a whiff of something as the procession passed, a malodorous vapour which hung in the heavy air, causing

33

more than one Florentine lady to put a handkerchief to her delicate nose.

'Cor,' said Lucia, 'he farts like a dog.'

'The Pope does not fart,' said a voice behind them. 'Not a Medici pope. That rushing, mighty wind is the exhalation of infinite credit.'

'He farts bullion. He shits ingots,' commented another.

There was a grudging respect in their voices, however.

'He's not a bad old Holy Father.'

'Tell that to the Germans,' said a third voice with a foreign accent that made Julius look round sharply but in vain.

'He ought to have his fistula seen to. That smell's awful. Like they forgot to change his bandages,' commented another.

The Pope passed on his way and the crowd started to get down from its various perches, preparing to make its way towards the Cathedral.

Suddenly there was a cry of alarm and a sound of splintering wood. One of the smaller arches swayed and toppled into the roadway, scattering the onlookers and pinning two little children dressed as angels – they had been part of the pageant – to the roadway. Willing hands lifted the framework and the children were pulled clear.

They were seemingly unmarked and both quite dead. Their little bodies were borne aloft by their distraught parents as the populace clucked and tutted. Then once more closing upon the street, the crowd – its dues done to woe – moved on towards the entertainment.

Julius could not join them.

'Come on,' said Lucia, pulling his arm, 'I don't want to miss the do.'

Julius shook his head. The image of the two little fair-haired children in their angel wings, broken butterflies, would not leave him. A terrible premonition seemed to weigh upon him. So many children . . . wailing and lamentation . . . pain and darkness . . . loneliness and death . . . He staggered in the bright sunshine.

'Oh, for God's sake,' said Lucia, 'not one of your moods. People die all the time. They'll go to heaven, that's for sure, dying like that. More than what old Smelly will. C'mon, northerner. Don't be so soft.'

But he would not go. She spotted a friend and left Julius standing by the wreckage. He wanted to do something, go and help the parents in their grief, cry out, rail against heaven.

At last he walked home through the jocular streets to the carpenter's house where he sat alone until darkness brought the sound of fireworks, music, dancing. And he sat on, his mind heavy with the sadness of things, while the Medicis settled down to a sixty-course dinner in the Palazzo Strozzi and the full moon sailed high over Fiesole.

Finally, he went to bed and lay sleeplessly, listening to the revels; and at dawn he got up and went straight to the studio.

He painted a picture of the two little putti being wafted to heaven by adult angels – a reversal of the usual mode – made a copy, and sent a picture each, as a gift of condolence, to the bereaved families.

There was no reply. Afterwards, he saw the pictures in the second-hand market with a rather shamingly low price on them.

He did not see Lucia again. Fra Bartolommeo allowed him to paint the Magdalen's figure (not her face) in a Deposition he was doing. He painted from memory. It was Lucia.

Three months later, he heard from Bois le Duc that his master Bosch was ill and wished him to come home. This he did with regret but, at the same time, with a peculiar kind of inevitability, for – even though he loved the place, and Bartolommeo offered him money to stay – he sensed that his fortunes lay in the North and that this pleasant, violent, corrupt, easy, dangerous and graceful city represented no more than an instructive and tempering interlude.

He called upon his friend, the philosopher, one evening, to make his farewell.

'You will not come back, I think, Julius,' said the old man.

'Surely I will,' replied Julius, unable to admit the implications of his own presentiments.

'I think not. But I believe you will remember our conversations. That memory will join us just as if we were talking as we do now. You remember our findings on Plotinus's *Scala Mystica*?' The philosopher's eyes gleamed like candles inside a skull.

'That all forms of creation are a step-by-step development and ascent reaching its peak and perfection in man . . .'

'Very good. And what must we look for?'

'The condition of sinless Adam so that there may be a re-birth into the simplicity, beauty and purity of original human nature, for it was created by God in his own image.'

'And what is Love?'

'It is a sacrament, the embodiment of the oneness of our First Parents. Further, it is the cause, Nature and substance of Creation. The divine quality of Beauty stirs desire for itself in all things. Beginning in God, it is Beauty. Passing into Creation, it is love. Returning to unite Creation with the Creator, it is pure desire.'

It was more or less the Prayer of the Academy though he was not by any means sure, even now, that he understood it.

'And what is the purpose of your art? Of all art?'

'It is to kindle in the soul a desire to return to its divine home by presenting sights and sounds which remind it of its divinity.'

'You have learned well,' said the old man. 'Many come to Florence

35

to whore and feast and make money, but Florence is at the end a flower for those with a thirst for wisdom to drink from. What you have learned may not be comfortable but it will be valuable. Go in peace, Julius, my friend. And may you find your soul's desire.'

Chapter 10

Mushroom weather. Muggy mists and heavy rain. The brooks and rivers in flood. Brown waters tumbling down the streams between the furrows and lying in lazy pools, islanded by tussocks, on previously respectable, hard-working pasture. Moisture on the eaves, under the eaves, hanging on eyebrows, dribbling down the watershed of noses, cattle in disconsolate huddles, children kept in too long because of the rain, getting under parents' feet and behaving like turks, the whole land dissolving in slither and bad temper. Too late to do any good to the harvest, too early to do any good to anything except mildew; rain today and, from the look of the clouds, rain tomorrow and the day after that.

There was a glut of chanterelles in Bois le Duc when Julius returned home, but it hardly seemed to compensate for the liquid atmosphere and leaden skies. Perhaps he had been wrong after all to come back.

After the sun, the limpid light, the palaces, the brown-eyed girls, the quick-witted youths, the high minds, the low lapses, Brabant provided a drab backdrop.

It was easier in Florence the Beautiful than in flat Brabant to think of man 'standing in the centre of Creation'.

As Julius sheltered under an accommodating eave, surveying the sodden roadway and the trees which upreared in the fog like standing smoke, he could hear Ammanati again, talking in those mild, calm tones, against a backdrop of brilliant sky and golden domes and arches.

'Man's body consists of the earthly elements, but his spirit is of a heavenly kind. His vegetable life he has in common with the plants, his senses with the animals, his reason with the spirit of the angels. He is considered an image of God.'

But how difficult it was here to see man as such a marvel. Red-nosed, blue-lipped boors bleared by drink and streaming with cold; bloated friars; saddle-hipped farm girls . . . had man slipped so far down the *scala mystica*? What had happened to the Creator's first design?

He found lodgings at an inn – the butcher's house would have been too much for his ebbing resolve – went to bed early and felt a little better in the morning. His first call was on his master. Aleid greeted him at the door, and her welcome was as usual less than warm.

'He has been very ill,' she said, 'we were expecting you sooner.'

'I came as fast as I could.'

'I dare say you did. I must insist that you do not excite him.'

'Is he . . . all right now?'

'He has had a stroke. His arm is paralysed and he is very weak. He wishes to see you but you have only five minutes. He could have another attack and it would kill him.'

Suitably chastened, he followed as she led him down to the passage to his study where he sat propped up in his great arm-chair.

'Here's Martens from Florence,' she said. 'See if you can persuade him to go to bed, Martens.'

'Oh . . . yes, of course,' said Julius.

'And remember what I said,' she told him, giving a stony look.

'What did she say?' asked Bosch awkwardly, out of the corner of his mouth. His face had fallen on the left side.

'She said I have only five minutes, and I mustn't excite you.'

Bosch snorted and motioned weakly with his right hand.

'Come here, boy, into the light and let me look at you.'

Speech was obviously an effort for him. A little froth gathered at the side of his mouth.

Julius moved towards the window. The old man gazed fiercely at him for a while. Julius knew he had grown taller and filled out during his sojourn in the South. He had found the Florentine fare to his taste and had cause to bless Marco Polo on many occasions for bringing the art of pasta back from his travels. He now presented, he knew, a not unappealing appearance. Of rather above medium stature, his dark, golden-brown hair curling a little, and his complexion fresh and mercifully free from eruptions, his eyes a remarkable bright blue (which had excited the Florentine tarts used to the prevailing brown), he was growing to be a presentable fellow.

That, of course, was as far as appearance goes. What he thought and felt about himself was a different matter. The lack of a father can make a young man feel strangely awkward in the world. Everything was to be discovered. There is no daily taking in of information about how a man behaves through, as it were, the pores. Naturally the same goes – in a different way – if there is no mother. You see what other people do, but you have to learn it consciously. As for a loving background – it is hard to know love without it.

Julius didn't understand love. It wasn't that he couldn't observe it in others, watch its influence, marvel at its excesses. He just couldn't feel it. It was a cabinet in his heart which remained resolutely locked. And even when he had wept in front of the Grand Master, it was tears of sorrow for himself which sprang from his eyes.

So, although he was a handsome enough young man and could feel affection, loyalty, courage and many of the admirable virtues, he was still a solitary – isolated and handicapped by this condition of his heart.

Whether or not Bosch guessed any of this, Julius could not tell. Indeed, he was not yet fully aware himself how serious his condition was. For, after all the instruction that he had received, the wise words and the precepts, his intelligence had indeed taken in the information – but his emotions had not. They were not yet open. He was a closed rose.

'Humph,' said Bosch at last, with more or less the same old expression – now slightly skewed – half cruel and half ironic. 'You don't look exciting enough to give anyone a heart attack. I dare say the young ladies thought you a fine fellow.'

Julius's loins still ached for Lucia, and he blushed a little. Sometimes she came to him in the night and he would be lying again in the fragrant slip between her legs.

He blushed and murmured.

'Not really.'

'Not really,' Bosch mimicked. 'Ah, well. Don't want to make any more bastards, do we?'

Julius froze. It was the cruellest thing the old man had ever said to him. He could feel the blood draining from his face and his hands clenching involuntarily. He was about to turn on his heels and walk straight from the room, but something about the painter's watchful expression made him stop. He was testing him. He was damned if he was going to show the pain; so instead he smiled.

'No,' he said. 'I wouldn't want to repeat my father's carelessness. He must have thought so little of my mother.'

Bosch stared back at him unblinkingly; owl-eyed, fierce.

'Don't tell me about Florence,' he said. 'Show me. In your painting. We expect some pretty brushwork from you, I can tell you. Let's get some southern flesh tones going here.'

'Yes, sir,' said Julius.

'Martens.'

It was Bosch's wife calling from the passage.

'Look here, boy,' said Bosch, suddenly urgent. 'I want to show you something out of town. Get a horse and cart. It's just a couple of miles. Next week. All right?'

'No, sir. It's more than my life's worth. Your wife would kill me.'

'I'll look after her. Next Wednesday, right? Nine o'clock in the morning. Remember I showed you *The Last Judgement* in the church? The Religion of Hate? Now I'll show you the other side.'

'Other side, sir?'

The door opened and Bosch's wife stood there like the Angel flaming in Paradise.

'The Garden,' the old man mumbled urgently. 'Light and Life.'

'Time's up, Martens,' said Aleid. 'Time to go.'

39

It was not a request. It was an edict.

'Wednesday, remember,' said the painter.

'Wednesday what?' asked his wife.

'Never mind, wife,' said the old man, with a tone in his voice that made her fall silent. 'It is a matter between the boy and myself. I have a journey to make, as you well know, and I shall make it if it is my last.'

Chapter 11

Miraculously, it had stopped raining. The sun shone and the earth steamed like a mare.

Julius appeared at nine o'clock complete with covered pony-cart as instructed, and presented himself at the Bosch front door with some misgiving. If Bosch wasn't afraid of his stone-eyed wife, he, Julius, certainly was. Nor did he know what he would do if the old man were taken ill on the journey. He didn't even know where they were going. It seemed a venture fraught with disadvantages.

He tied up his pony, and knocked.

The temperature of Aleid's welcome was cooler than tepid today. He could feel the frosting on it as soon as she opened the door.

'I shall hold you personally responsible, Martens,' she said, 'if anything happens to him.'

'It's not my idea, Mistress Bosch,' he protested.

'Don't try and wriggle out of it. You encouraged him in this madness. He is a very sick man, Martens.'

'Nonsense, Aleid,' said the old painter, shuffling down the hall. 'Julius will look after me, won't you, boy? We're taking it very easily.'

'Take this cordial, then, and this basket, Martens,' said Aleid, more or less throwing them at Julius, 'and if you're not back by four o'clock, I shall make life very uncomfortable for you.'

Julius knew she meant it.

'She doesn't mean it,' said Bosch, as he settled down at last on the seat of the trap.

Julius took the reins, and they moved off.

'I don't think she likes me very much,' he said.

It was the first time he had mentioned it.

'She has had much to put up with,' the painter said. 'Her life has not been easy.'

Whose life was? thought Julius, as the trap bumbled over the cobbles.

'Which way?' he asked.

'Straight on.'

They took the road towards Bruges, splashing along in the remnants of inundation. Woods and fields panted vapour on either side. The old man seemed sunk in reverie.

'Why are we going there, Mr Bosch?' asked Julius. 'Wherever it is.'

Although the old man was evidently disinclined to talk, it embarrassed Julius to be completely silent.

'Wait and see,' said Bosch, cryptically.

'Ah. Right.'

They trundled on for a while. Julius tried again.

'When did you paint *The Last Judgement*?' he enquired.

This time the old man was more expressive. He held up all the fingers of his right hand twice.

'Ten,' he said, and then lapsed once more into silence as if already half in another world.

'So, ten years ago,' Julius observed. 'It seems to me that in that picture you were doing something new.'

The great painter turned his head at that and fixed him with a sardonic stare.

'What d'you mean?'

'I mean the painting of St James in shades of grey, in grisaille, that one sees when it is closed. I went and looked at it again yesterday. To paint a complete scene in just one colour, that is extraordinary. It is like Mantegna . . . sculpture . . .'

The old man became extremely agitated on hearing these words – words which Julius had thought would flatter him – but which now seemed to goad him so much that Julius had to halt the pony and clutch at his companion's cloak in order to stop him tumbling off.

'Execution nothing. Content everything,' Bosch enunciated finally. 'Drive on.'

Julius flicked the reins and they proceeded once more in silence. Why should I be saddled with this crotchety old josser? he thought. Italy had made him less of a doormat.

'As for your Hell in the right-hand panel, it's as if you'd been there,' he said rather rudely.

The old man cocked a rheumy eye at him.

'I have,' he said.

They arrived toward noon at a little group of buildings down a lane a mile or so off the main road, grouped around a couple of farms. These were labourers' cottages, a run-down alehouse of rickety appearance with mossed thatch and pocked walls, and a low, barn-like building which turned out to be a chapel. Their approach was watched from the tavern doorway by a wild-eyed man in a tattered red cloak, wearing what seemed like a turban on his head. On the roof of the mean building, sheltered from the wind, a couple of shepherds, one holding a bagpipe, peered glumly at something beyond the arrivals.

'I don't much like the look of them,' said Julius, wishing he had brought a sword.

'They can't see us,' said the old man, indicating that these people

42

were looking for, or at, something altogether beyond whatever reality the two of them represented. 'They've taken the juice.'

Julius had the strangest feeling that he was entering one of the Master's own paintings. The fact that the Master could hardly talk made the whole experience odder and more dreamlike.

Julius, disconcerted, tethered the pony and helped the old man down. He was beginning to feel more and more uncomfortable. Why on earth had the old fossil brought him here?

A man came out with two goblets of spiced wine which he offered them.

'Drink,' said the old man. 'Better than cordial.'

'Who are they?' he asked Bosch, indicating the men on the roof.

'Watchers and waiters,' came the muffled reply.

He seemed to be having more difficulty talking. Julius hoped he wasn't going to have an attack out here, miles from anywhere. Aleid would not forgive him.

'What do they watch for?'

'Wait and see.'

Julius had the peculiar feeling again that he was being drawn into some kind of circumstance whose reality was stranger than the one he inhabited. Was there a drug in the hippocras he was drinking?

'Now we are ready to enter,' said Bosch, putting down the cup and leading him towards the porch of the small building at which the watchers directed their gaze.

He lifted the latch, and opened the heavy wooden door.

Julius could never describe accurately the curious emanation that seemed to waft out of the building. He was reminded of a carol the Burgundians had: 'Whence is that goodly fragrance blowing?'

It was something like the store cupboard that his landlady in Florence kept locked – a smell of spice and baking, honey and herbs, orange peel and raisins . . . But the waft was more than fragrance. He had read in Italy of Marco Polo's account of a treatment he had received in Cathay for a backache, with needles that healed . . .

'When the first needle went into my left foot between the great and second toe, there was as it seemed to me an outflowing of something – a subtle force or flow which I felt must be blood or fine fluid – but, when I beheld, it was not, nor was any to be seen.'

So it was with the chapel. The watchers felt it too. They craned forward, bathing in the flow.

'What is this place?' he asked the old man, wonderingly.

'It is the Chapel of Love,' came the reply. 'Now I must ask you to promise never to communicate what I have to show you to anyone who is not of the Mystery.'

'I promise,' said Julius, suddenly impatient with the old man no more.

43

They stepped inside.

It was a tiny place, hardly big enough to hold more than ten or twelve people, but it was suffused with pearly grey light which emanated from the image on the front of a closed triptych that hung behind the altar. Julius thought at first that it was indeed a stained-glass window, but as his eyes became accustomed to the interior, he realized it was a painting.

It represented a sphere, the earth as it seemed covered by lucent clouds, with soft rain falling upon a land that drank gratefully, a wooded land, with lawns and hills and rivers that ran down to a placid sea. It was a world that was fresh-worked, pristine, expectant . . .

The old man hobbled up to the altar, leaning on Julius's shoulder, and gazed at it with satisfaction.

'There, boy, the Third Day of Creation. "And there went up a great mist from the earth and watered the whole face of the ground." Or as the psalmist says, "*Rorate coeli* . . ." It is the alchemist's egg, the bubble of life, the fertilizing moment of the world. Open it up and man, the Crown of Creation, appears . . .'

With that, with a sudden movement which surprised Julius, he opened the left-hand door to the triptych. All at once, the little chapel was alive with light and colour, tones of such fresh sweetness and delight that Julius almost swooned.

'What is this? Yours?'

'Mine was the hand. I had the joy of it. The plan was . . . another's.'

Julius looked at it again.

The left-hand side of the triptych was a picture of Eden, that he could recognize; but even so it was an Eden that radically diverged from any representation he had previously seen. For a start, the figure of the Creator was again not God the Father but God the Son: a young man in a long, dawn-pink robe, with long fair hair, bearded, holding the pulse of the hand of the newly created Eve to feel the vital flow of her blood. Beside him, Adam stretched out his own feet with an air of wonder to touch the feet of God.

'It is the marriage of our First Parents,' said the old man, 'solemnized by the Creator. Adam born of the Spirit and Eve born of Earth. The double nature of ourselves . . .'

Behind this group were trees and hills, fountains and mountains, half vegetable, half mineral, such as Julius had never before seen. In front and behind also were animals, part familiar, part legendary and part dream. The images danced and swam before him . . . Surely that wine . . . There was something strange here, though . . . he would put his finger on it if he had a moment . . . that leopard carrying a . . .

The old man now reached up to the triptych and opened the right-hand door. The lucent colour that had been half exposed when the first panel was opened now shone out in its entirety, as if it were infused

44

with more than mere pigment, so vivid that it was like a sound. Indeed, Julius thought he could hear, as from a great distance, the call of birds, the sound of many voices, the thud of hooves, the gentle murmur of the breeze, and song, and many waters, all mingled as in a concert of summer.

'Now, what d'you see, boy?'

Julius, even in the midst of his delight, was surprised to hear the old man's tones; there was indeed something more to him now than the teasing, crotchety master he had known. Something hieratic, solemn, profound.

'What do you see?'

The words came out of the darkness like a priest's call to a congregation.

'Speak.'

He cleared his throat.

'I see ...'

One half of him wanted to say, felt he ought to say, so he did say, because at least he could put words to it:

'I see a wondrously painted scene of the lusts of the flesh. Naked people everywhere ... disporting themselves without shame ... People in strange bulbs and gourds ... doing things together ... I see a warning to us all to beware of the lusts of the flesh. I see a disobedience of the Fifth Commandment: Thou shalt not commit adultery ... I see ...'

Julius found the scene quite upsetting; it made him hot between the thighs.

'You are not looking, boy.'

'I think I am, sir.'

'Look again. This panel is equally a Paradise. See, it continues from the first. There is a continuous landscape. The marriage in Eden has been blest, boy. There is a whole throng of the children of Adam and Eve. These denizens of Paradise are frolicking in unashamed nakedness among strange fruits and trees, my son, because here Nature and God are one. Look at the egg-pool, circled by potent animals, look on the grass and in the water, boy. You will find sacred carnality everywhere. *Crescere et multiplicamini.* Look in the air and see soul turned to spirit and wafting towards oneness ...'

These were the words, Julius thought, that I wanted to say if only I could have found them. This is the land where I want to be if only I could get there.

His master stood in front of the picture, rapt, his face glowing with the reflected gratification of his creatures. Julius now heard him sigh and felt his hand lean more heavily on his shoulder, as if some intolerable weight were beginning to drag him to the ground.

45

'Now, look,' he cried, 'look ... ahhh ... at the difference between that scene and its neighbour to the right. The one radiant, fertile, harmonious, pregnant with natural energy, harmony and love ... the other ... it is too painful ...'

The old man seemed genuinely agonized.

'Are you all right, sir? Would you like to sit down?'

'No, no.'

The old man recovered himself a little.

'Gaze now,' he continued, 'at the horrors of the Hell, now, next to it.'

Julius looked at the right-hand panel of the triptych from which he had instinctively, at first, tried to avert his eyes. For, just as the centre seemed to give forth sweet sounds, here was nothing but discord. Its colours were sombre as befitted its subject: cold tones of blue-black, lead-grey and purplish-blue, pools of darkness, lit by fitful spasms of light derived as if from a volcano-side, spouting malignantly through a multiplicity of vents. Nameless creatures which seemed to have crawled out of the slime of nightmare were treating the sinners like living meat. A broken half-carcase, half-eggshell, whose innards housed a vile tavern, rested on tree-feet whose broken extremities lay in boats locked fast in icy water ... Helpless skaters, propelled by some demonic force, whizzed forward towards a hole in the ice, to drown. A satanic bird, sitting at stool, swallowed the guilty and shat the damned. A pig-nun lasciviously caressed a former notary. Musical instruments, lutes and violas, devoured and crucified the wicked ... A sinner slid screaming down a kitchen knife. A huge key, which might have been taken as a symbol of mystery, had turned into an instrument of torture. A lantern which might have given forth light disclosed itself as a prison. Overhead, two huge, waxy yellow ears were sliced apart by a penis-like scalpel ... Julius staggered back a pace. He could bear to look at it no more.

Bosch's voice came out of the darkness beside it.

'What is it you see?'

'I see the punishment of the guilty,' Julius groaned. He felt as if he had been there himself.

'You are right. The word is guilt. For us, indeed, that is one of the great sins. For if we feel guilty, we do not feel love, and we are not the children of that Adam and Eve we see in the first picture. Of course, not everyone can reach that wisdom which sees love not simply as a means but as an End. For ourselves, love – true love – is a religion. Lovers are predestined for each other in order that God's will – "one flesh" – should be fulfilled. Some of us believe indeed what is written in Plato's Symposium; that, before we were born, we were whole; but at birth we were sundered, and we must spend our lives searching for the lost half that we so desire.'

46

'But . . . how do you know when someone's . . . predestined?'

'Oh. You know, all right.'

'It sounds too easy.'

The old man's eyes flashed again in the dark.

'Easy? It is sometimes the hardest thing in the world. And the destination is sometimes too early or too late. It is sometimes . . . damnably . . . hard . . .'

He heard Bosch catch his breath, almost sobbing with the effort.

'Are you all right, sir?' he asked again.

'I'll do, I'll do,' Bosch said at last. 'Now, boy, since we have not much time, what else do you notice . . . about my Hell? . . .'

He was struggling for breath now and his speech was becoming noticeably more slurred.

'Well, sir. It is not finished. Above the carcase, there is a gap. And at the top, behind it, the background is not filled in.'

'Exactly . . . That is why you are here . . . boy . . . You . . . you are to finish it.'

'I, sir?'

Julius was aghast. The piece was Bosch at his very best. He himself was only eighteen. He was good, he thought, but . . .

Bosch cut in on his thoughts.

'You. It has been decided. I . . . I can no longer . . .'

The old man was deathly white in the glow of the Garden.

'Say that you promise, boy.'

'I swear, but . . . what am I to paint?'

The words came out in a cry almost of anguish. It was like being asked to finish a Bible but not having the Revelation.

But the old man's only response was to point at the centre panel with a quivering hand. Then he fell to the ground clutching his side.

Chapter 12

The journey back was nightmarish.

Julius had rushed out of the chapel to fetch help, but none of the watchers and waiters were around. The ramshackle inn was empty, the tapster who had brought the hippocras no longer in evidence. Only the pony, tied to a fence, remained. It patiently cropped the grass and waited for the mad humans to tell it what to do.

'Help,' Julius shouted.

There was a couple dancing louchely to a bagpipe in a distant field. Far off, near a wood, two men seemed to be beating and tying up a third. On a distant hill, a crowd gathered under, could it be, a gallows?

Julius passed his hand in front of his eyes and ran back into the chapel. His master was lying on the floor, breathing strangely and making odd noises. There was nothing for it but to lug him up and drag him out to the roadside – no easy matter, for Bosch was a big man – and harder still to get him up and over the back of the cart and onto the floor. But in the end, desperation lending brawn, it was done, and the old man lay there like a bolster. Julius put a bundle under his head and tried to give him some cordial, but he only bubbled and choked a little.

The patient pony was by no means a fast mover. And though Julius was concerned that his master might die before they reached home, he could have wished the journey twice as long – indeed, he could have wished himself the Flying Dutchmen and amble along for ever – rather than face the wrath of Aleid Bosch sooner than was necessary.

His only consolation, when he pulled up outside the house, was that it was only half past three.

Chapter 13

The old man actually regained consciousness and lingered awhile, asking once more for Julius, though for a day or two Aleid refused to allow a visit. Her husband was in no condition now to exert his formidable authority.

Eventually she relented for, in her way, she loved him – loved him perhaps too much. Now, however, recognizing the inevitable, she sent for Julius once more.

He was surprised, for the roasting she had given him when he brought Bosch home unconscious was only tempered by her desire to convey the old man with all speed to his bed.

'He's sinking fast,' she told Julius severely but not so coldly now. 'You must not tax him. If he does not answer, it is because the effort is too great.'

She led him to the bedside and went out.

Julius was shocked to see how his master had changed. The familiar face was swollen and puffy. The hands that had invoked such wild and gorgeous visions lay useless on the counterpane. The breath came painfully. Only the eyes, like drying pools of life left by an ebbing sea, stirred a little as he came in.

'Julius.' The lips formed the words though the voice barely spoke them.

'Master.'

They remained for a while in silence, but at length Julius had to ask the question that had been tormenting him.

'What shall I paint, in Hell?'

Silence. After a long pause, he tried another question that had exercised him.

'Who is my father? You said once that you knew him.'

Silence again. Julius so much wanted an answer he felt like shaking the old man. But it would have done no good to anyone. He tried another tack.

'About love . . .' he began.

The shadow of a smile crossed the old man's face. He stretched the finger of his right hand, and beckoned. Julius felt encouraged. He had raised the right subject this time.

'Come here, boy,' Bosch whispered. 'What is it?'

49

'The Church says women are inferior to men. Is that so? Priests tell us celibacy is the ideal condition. Your Garden says differently.'

'Men and women . . .' The voice was so low that Julius had to lean over the bedclothes to hear it, but his mind at least was clear '. . . are unequal . . . as earth and water. Different . . . Not inferior. That is easily settled. As for marriage, the Church regards it as a concession . . . a concession to human frailty . . . at best, a convenient legal and financial institution . . . that has nothing . . . nothing within a thousand leagues of being . . . to do with . . . Love.'

He used the word 'Love' as other dying men would say 'Jesus', thought Julius.

'Why then is Love so important if both Church and State ignore it?' he persisted.

'They do not ignore it. They recognize its power. So they have built their temples upon it . . . as if it were a pagan site . . . and tried to hide it . . . They are afraid of it. That is the truth of the matter . . .'

The effort of talking had begun to exhaust the old man. Julius took his hand as a prelude to departure but Bosch held onto it, encouraging Julius to ask his final question – the perennial question, the hardest of all.

'What is Love?' he blurted out at last.

'Ah . . . Love . . .'

This time it was more than a shadow. A radiance, a look of complete beatitude, flowed into his face like a ripple from a distant ocean.

'Ahhh . . .'

The old man closed his eyes, bathing in the word. Silence again as the sea receded.

Julius thought about love but, for the life of him, he could find no answer. He had a dreadful feeling that when he understood it he would find he had known it all the time and never valued it, like some dreadful, rusty old key.

'Love?' he would say. 'Oh, that, I threw it away last week. Don't tell me I needed it.'

'Sorry,' they would say. 'You can't get in without it . . .'

'I think you have answered me,' he told his master.

Slowly, the fingers holding his own relaxed their grip. He kissed the old man on the forehead and made to steal from the room, knowing he would not see him again.

As he reached the door, however, the eyes suddenly opened once more. A spasm of pain crossed the face.

'Ohhh . . . You . . .' The word came out as a bitter exhalation as he half-raised himself from the pillow.

Two days later, Bosch was dead.

The service in the Cathedral was magnificent. The Insignis Pictor was buried in suitable state. Julius sat in the side chapel and looked at *Judgement Day*. Wherever his master was, he was confident he wasn't going in at that door hosted by the demon with a brazier in his belly.

But what was that vision he had so hated on his death-bed? He pondered the strangeness of it as the choir sang the *Dies Irae*, only concluding that he himself would not like to die with such a look of hatred in his eyes.

Chapter 14

Rather to his surprise, Julius was left nothing in Bosch's will apart from items from the studio – pigments, brushes, unworked canvases, a little study of a typically lifelike, impossible nun-witch whose body was a fat-bellied pitcher, and just enough money to rent himself a studio for six months in town.

He had half-expected more, since the old man had so earnestly begged him to finish his Hell. What did he expect him to live on?

And of course there was nothing from Aleid, whose face was now closed to him.

He could not possibly go back to the butcher's, whose only interest in him anyway was as a friend of the famous painter. So there was nothing for it but to find a place and set up as a painter in the town.

Legacy or not, he missed his old master more than he would have thought, and – intent on honouring his promise to complete the picture – he journeyed back to the hamlet with a view to collecting the triptych and bringing it back to the small studio he had found in Duck Lane.

He had of course told the new Grand Master of the Brotherhood – a smallish, rounded man with a pursed mouth and soapy hands – of his instructions but, much to his surprise, the Grand Master declared he knew nothing of the picture.

'It sounds most interesting,' he said. 'But dear Brother Bosch was always giving us surprises.'

Julius had a presentiment that, when he arrived at the chapel, the triptych would not be there. And such indeed was the case. The place was darkened. There were cobwebs on the windows and the altar. The glory had departed. Outside, once again, the hamlet was empty save for a simpleton who lolled at a farmhouse door. There were people in the fields but no robberies or dancing. There was no sign of a gallows.

He returned home puzzled – half relieved, half heavy-hearted.

He asked Aleid but she neither knew nor wanted to know about it. Bosch's 'workshop' was closed; the painters who worked there had all been left generous sums by their old master, and had gone their various ways.

Julius gave up the search and started to look for commissions in earnest. The place to start, of course, would be the Brotherhood itself, but he found it sadly changed since the days of the mysterious Jew.

They welcomed him, of course, and admitted him as one of their number, as had been promised, on his return from Italy. Whatever observances had been practised in Bosch's time seemed to have been curtailed. They now had an almost exclusively religious emphasis of the more conventional kind, though they seemed as possessive as ever. They wanted your money, they wanted your time, and they wanted your talent.

Well, there was a correction here. It seemed they didn't want all his talent. They didn't really want the Italian part of it at all. The flesh frightened them. They wanted him to be a shadow of his master – but a pale shadow. They required the same sort of religious paintings.

'But less controversial,' said the new Grand Master.

And it was no surprise to find that they wanted them almost for nothing.

Of course, one could find excuses for them. Their average age was older now. Luther's activities had made the authorities much more vigilant in pursuit of deviation. There were risks in recruiting the young. A Beghard who had seduced a girl with the promise that the experience would convey her to the gates of heaven had been tried for heresy in the town, and sentenced to be thrown in the river and stoned till he drowned.

It all tended to make the committee more conservative in their atti-tude. Mind you, it was a relief in a way. The idea of naked gatherings – which had been implicit in some of Bosch's remarks – the primal state of our First Parents, and so forth, did not appeal so much when he looked at his fellow Brethren.

At any rate, he painted away for them upon a pittance, trying to interpret the instructions he was given.

'Another Judgement please for the chapel of the Hospital. Let's have a good rousing Hell this time . . .'

It was tricky trying to interpret the symbols he was given, and weave them into northern dreams and nightmares with means that had been so modified by the South. In the end, you risked pleasing neither your clients nor yourself. Oh, they recognized his skill but they didn't like the new-fangled approach.

'Too carnal,' they would say. 'It's really not our idea of our First Parents.'

Or:

'That's not Hell. It looks far too much fun.'

Or:

'I know what I like, and it's not that.'

He would have gone back to Florence for two pins – but he had no money and Florence, it seemed, was going through bad times of its own.

And so he worked on, unhappy with his work and with himself, with few friends – and no nearer the secret of the locked compartment in his heart.

Chapter 15

Years passed with a lamentable lack of change in his life after his master died. As the astrologers and alchemists said, 'As above, so below.' And these were bad years in Brabant and indeed throughout Europe.

The cloth industry was in disarray, Lutherans railed against Catholics and vice versa, whole families were divided, harvests failed, rumours of the imminent World's End multiplied – fuelled by those Last Day millenarians, the Anabaptists, who proliferated in Holland and who were beginning to fall seriously foul of the authorities. An outbreak of plague in successive years added to the general feeling of disseverance. And, ominously, the Spaniards – thanks to a dynastic marriage involving the possessions of the former Dukes of Burgundy which left the Emperor Charles as overlord – began to filter into the Netherlands, bringing with them the shadow of oppression.

These things left their mark on commissions, which were scanty, and on the Brotherhood, which grew more and more like the worthy little order it had only seemed to be before – a religious undertaking with about as much sense of magic as a lardy cake.

When Julius could afford it, he painted pictures for himself and made studies for a work that would one day be a Garden of Love interpreted in the southern manner, but not without a certain northern 'strangeness' – for was he not a product of both schools? The few friends to whom he showed this work were encouraging – but it didn't butter the parsnips. Indeed, the parsnips went unbuttered for many a long summer and winter too. Bread and dripping were the order of the day, washed down with beer so small it was virtually inconspicuous.

Then at last something happened, totally unforeseen, which, while it did not alter the physical circumstances of his life, gave it an entirely new emphasis.

He remembered the day well. He had been working on a tedious commission which had come via the Brotherhood (a bare minimum of whose meetings he now attended commensurate with getting work out of them). It was for a series of the Deadly Sins for a nuns' refectory, and he happened to be working on Lust that day. 'Nothing too disturbing for the Sisters', he had been told.

It was hard, of course, to depict Lust without making it look lustful. The Florentines would have gone to town on Lust and really made it drip lubricity. But not the 'sHertogenboschers (as the gentry called themselves now, since they were no longer Burgundians). Oh no. Lust must look prim and distasteful.

'Could we not have something like a girl – not too bare, none of that Florentine wantonness – with, say, a toad covering her shame? Your old master Bosch was very good with toads. Yes. That's the style. We'll have a toad, please. That'll give the sisters something to think about.'

He remembered even the hour.

It was late in the afternoon of an October day. He paused, brush in hand, and gazed across the studio to where the window showed the spire of St James's Church exactly framed. As he watched, the church clock struck five. The light was beginning to go, and he realized he was hungry – hungrier than usual, for just hungry would have passed unnoticed.

He looked back at the picture he had been painting. He had managed to find a large stuffed toad which he had placed in the required position on the model's pudendum. It had been his fancy – not quite in line with the spirit of his instructions – to make his girl clutch at it as if it were pleasuring her. It was only an interpretation you could put on it, of course. He had learned in a good school. You *could* say she was trying to push it away . . .

He was happy with the toad and with the model, who was a handsome peasant girl – on the thin side for Florence, but as buxom as he dared go up here. They still hankered for small, high bosoms and big bellies in 'sHertogenbosch.

He made a last brushstroke, and stood back reasonably satisfied.

'That is all for today, Anneke. Please come back tomorrow at the same time,' he told the girl.

She put the stuffed toad down with some readiness, and came over stark naked to look at the picture. He was quite disturbed by her proximity. She had rather pretty tow-coloured pubic hair which didn't at all cover her sex. She peered over his shoulder, nudging him with a nipple.

'Coo,' she said, 'you must have a funny mind.'

'Funny? It is a religious picture, Anneke.'

'Warped, if you ask me. Toads on me thingummybob? It's diseased.'

He smiled at her.

'It's symbolic, Anneke. The toad represents the Sin of Lust.'

'Lust's something you enjoy. Toads isn't my idea of a good time,' she said, looking at him sidelong. 'I know what is, though.'

'Good evening, Anneke.'

He had learnt how to deal with models in Italy. Rule number one was never to sleep with a model until you had finished your picture. She became possessive, suggestive and unco-operative if you fell into that error.

'Sure there's nothing else you want me to do?'

Anneke was loitering at the door, waggling her bottom.

'Nothing. Good night.'

She shrugged, huddled on her clothes, made a petulant face, and shut the door with a little slam.

Poor girl, he thought. She'll go and tumble with some oaf out of sheer vexation, get pregnant, marry him, have twelve children and lose her sinful figure. Why shouldn't I sleep with her now when she is as she is? What is so evil about it? Why am I painting a toad and not a panting progenitor?

Just at that moment, there was a knock at the door.

He imagined it was Anneke again so he did nothing. She could come in again if she wished. He waited and nothing happened. He could feel his loins stirring, and wished she would come in. Come in, Anneke.

Still nothing. At length, in a rage, he ran to the door and opened it. There was no one there.

A package fell inward across his feet.

'Anneke,' he called.

No answer.

He opened the package and took out a carefully rolled canvas. It was a perfect copy of his master's triptych, complete save for the top section of Hell. There was also a small bag of money, and a note.

'To Julius Martens, painter of Bois le Duc,' it read. 'It is understood that you agreed with Master Hieronymus Bosch to complete his picture known as *The Millennium*, also known as *The Earthly Paradise* or *The Garden of Earthly Delights*, a copy of which accompanies this letter. You are hereby commissioned to do the same, viz finish the panel called Hell to your complete satisfaction and in accordance with the style of the painting. Until you do this – and for however long it takes – you will be paid quarterly. When you have finished, you will notify, in your own person or by trusted messenger, the keepers of the Chapel. Your acceptance of these terms will be signified by your retention of the money here left in advance.'

The message was not signed. It might have been a government trick. Their spies were everywhere. But somehow Julius thought not. How would they know about the Chapel and what went on in there? There had been no witness.

He investigated the purse. Not much. Just enough to pay the rent for three months. Hardly a fortune, but more than enough to run to a celebration for one whose stomach was rumbling with hunger.

There was a knock on the door again.

He rushed to open it and found Anneke.

'I came back,' she said simply. 'I thought you might be wanting something.'

57

'Go and get us a sausage and some bread and wine, if you please. Then I should like you to take your clothes off.'

She started to take her clothes off.

'Oh, very well,' he said.

It seemed pointless to complain, as he had done so often before, about the order of things.

Chapter 16

But it was not going to be so easy, even though he set to the task with
a will.

For days afterwards, he experimented with ideas, starting to make
copies of the copy to help him.

His Lust fell behind schedule, earning him reproof from the Brotherhood and impatience from Anneke.

'I'm not going to sit here with a toad on my fanny for ever, you know.
This bloody thing's taking root.'

Their relationship, as Julius had feared, had resulted in a more
truculent and possessive attitude on her part.

'You're paid by the hour,' he observed mildly.

'Yeah, but . . . but don't think I haven't got better things to do.'

'What have you got to do, Anneke?'

'Well, there's a painter who said the other day he might want a
Magdalen. Or there's pig-work. I got other fish to fry as well as you,
mister.'

He wished she would use a little more soap and water occasionally
as well as frying fish. She was beginning to smell, rather.

He decided to press on with Lust and get it out of the way. Hell was
temporarily set aside.

But, Lust completed and Anneke out of his hair, another commission
came in. The nuns were so pleased with Lust, they wanted him to
complete the other six Sins.

'It is a signal honour,' said the Grand Master of the Brotherhood
when he told Julius. 'The Sisters can do a great deal of good to us.'

Of course, the money was derisory after the Brotherhood had taken
its cut. Even with the extra money from the mysterious commissioners,
Julius was still in a precarious financial position. His rent had gone up,
food prices had risen . . .

'Oh, all right,' he said.

He sometimes asked himself why he did not forsake the Brotherhood
entirely. Not for the first time, he reflected on what a pale institution
they seemed after the great and mysterious days of the Jew. But one or
two of them were decent old sticks. And it was the only family he had.
Besides, as he had said before, as he would say again, any commission
was better than none. He knew of a couple of artists in the town who

were receiving alms. There was no hurry to finish Hell. The letter had not specified a deadline.

And so Wrath was undertaken, Pride followed, and Envy, Gluttony, Sloth and Avarice succeeded. It pleased him that *The Seven Deadly Sins* was one of Bosch's rawest, earliest paintings. It did not loom quite so large over him, dictating its style to his clients, as a Judgement or a Temptation would have done.

Gluttony was exceptionally messy, but it gave him the opportunity to entertain both himself and the two starving painters on the leftovers.

All this while, Hell was resting upon an easel – draped to deter inquisitive eyes – in his bedroom above the studio. Though hidden, however, it was not hidden from his mind, which, whenever there was a spare moment, kept coming back to the problem.

Above the withered carcase, the broken egg, there was a significant gap. He thought of all manner of things to put into it – obscene, terrifying things – but they did not add anything to the picture. And what about the missing background? Crags and chasms? Volcanoes? Gulfs of fire? He was not so worried about the background. That will come naturally, he felt, when I have solved that central point.

Sometimes he would wake in the night and by candlelight would work on the piece of paper he had pasted on his own rough copy of the copy, over the gap.

He tried devils, a hobgoblin, a snakehead devouring a lustful nun . . .

It was strange how the problem seemed to grow the more he thought about it. It grew to obsess him. He dreaded not having other work to do so that he would be forced to think about it all the time. He accepted commissions that he would never normally have taken.

The money kept arriving, every quarter, in a little bag. He was appalled to note how often it seemed to come. Twelve, thirteen, fourteen . . . Nearly five years had passed, and he still seemed no nearer the end.

'You are pale,' said the Grand Master of the Brotherhood one day. 'You are not looking after yourself. What you need is a wife.'

'A wife?'

The idea had never struck him seriously before. How could he marry if he didn't know about love? He shook his head.

'Love,' he said. 'I don't know . . . ?'

'Love!' cried the Grand Master. 'Who said anything about love?'

Julius was shocked. It was like a bishop saying he didn't believe in the Resurrection. However, there seemed no point in arguing about it with the man. Perhaps he himself was wrong; perhaps Bosch and the Jew had been wrong as well; perhaps the Religion of Love was nothing more than a fantasy and he had, all his life, been pursuing marsh-fire.

60

It was certainly easier to believe in the pragmatic approach of the man in front of him.

Why should he go on believing in something he did not understand, striving at a picture that was causing him near-madness? He was tired. He was poor. Perhaps marriage was the answer. Look what it had done for old Bosch.

'I don't ... know anyone ...' he said.

The only girls he could think of were models and barmaids, girls of the town who would be no good at all.

'There is a young lady ...' the Grand Master began, and then stopped. 'I don't know. She might be too ... good for you ...'

'Too good for me?'

'Yes. She is wealthy and well-born. Her father could do much good to our Order. He is a lawyer of the town.'

Julius was curiously charmed to hear of her advantages.

'Is she ... well-favoured?'

'Very much so. Singularly comely.'

'Could you not effect an introduction?'

'At our next pageant rehearsal,' said the Grand Master, who had clearly thought – or been asked to think – the whole thing out beforehand. 'We thought you might like to do some masks and she ... well ... I believe we could invite her to help with some costume-stitching.'

Chapter 17

She was the daughter of Willem Duynstee the advocate, known for the hectoring nature of his prosecutions. Her name was Blommardine.

As soon as Julius was introduced, she made it clear that she had arranged the meeting.

'You've been to Italy, haven't you?' she asked.

He admitted that this was so, while taking stock of her. She was a smallish girl with a slender figure – they'd like her for a Lust, he thought – and a manner that was both vivacious and engaging. He rather thought he could detect a strong will there too, though now she was going all out to be charming.

'Florence,' he said.

'Florence? Heavens, you're lucky. I wish I were a man and could go charging about.'

'I wasn't exactly charging about,' he said. 'I was learning to paint.'

'Same thing,' she said, smiling as if to say she knew what painters got up to.

'You're an orphan,' she said, 'aren't you?'

He was glad she hadn't said bastard. Not that he hadn't got used to bastardy by now, but he'd rather you didn't bandy it about, if you didn't mind.

'My mother died when I was little too,' she said.

And indeed, he felt as if they had something more in common, but he couldn't place it. There was something both familiar and alarming about her. He smelt danger, which interested him in spite of his natural caution.

They met once or twice after that in church – she had told him she would be there – and very engaging she looked in her Sunday clothes. Later, she had a note dropped in to the studio, telling him to meet her for a clandestine walk along the riverside. They kissed among the shelter of the willows.

He was used to the ways of Florence and of model girls, and it did not strike him for a moment that what he was doing was fool-hardy.

She raised the subject of marriage, in a general sort of way, but Julius was by no means certain that it would be a good thing. He gave a friendly but non-committal reply.

He still could not get rid of the idea of that picture. Hell without its centre. He himself had felt curiously centreless, recently.

He went back to his studio, dodging further rendezvous with her, and thought no more of it, until her father one day sent for him with an instruction to visit him at his house.

Blommardine had mentioned the possibility of a portrait of her father – the Notaries' Guild of which he was a member was keen on such things – so he went along with charcoal and paper in case a preliminary sketch was needed.

Mr Duynstee greeted him unsmilingly – there was no sign of Blommardine – and led him towards a room which seemed to serve as his office in the house. He pointed at a deliberately uncomfortable chair.

'Sit down,' he ordered.

'Thank you,' said Julius, smiling pleasantly, though sensing something wrong.

There was a long silence.

'Would you like a portrait, sir?' Julius enquired at length, indicating his little roll of paper and his charcoal.

The lawyer gazed at him some more beneath stag-beetling eyebrows. He was a very tall, thin man. How came it that such a very tall man should have such a very small daughter? The silence was getting on Julius's nerves. He tried again.

'Perhaps a picture of your daughter? I really prefer portraits to the metaphorical or allegorical scenes we get so often nowadays. I say that just in case you thought I was simply a metaphorical or allegorical painter.'

More silence.

'Though if you wanted a metaphorical or allegorical scene, I could of course do you one of those.'

The lawyer spoke at last.

'I have no interest in metaphorical or allegorical scenes at this moment. Or any other scene for that matter. I hope we have no need for scenes. I was just trying to see,' he said, 'what my daughter Blommardine sees in you, but for the life of me I can't fathom it.'

'Oh,' said Julius.

He was both anxious that the interview should have involved his relations with the daughter, and relieved that the man seemed to have taken against him. This relief was short-lived.

'However, if you attempt to wriggle out of your obligations to her – to which I have reluctantly given my blessing – there will be such a scene as you never dreamt of in all your metaphorical and allegorical philosophizing.'

'W . . . what obligations?'

'Why, that you have proposed marriage to her and that she for some reason has accepted. She tells me you are now thinking twice about the matter. May I add a certificate of my own personal wrath to the suit for breach of contract that you will be facing?'

It was such an arrant lie on Blommardine's part that Julius almost laughed. She had only been to the studio once – she had said she wanted to see if his style was suitable for painting her father.

However, he didn't laugh because Mr Duynstee appeared to be the sort of man who would not take kindly to a giggle on such an occasion. How the devil was he going to get out of this thing?

'I, er . . . I hardly know her, sir,' Julius ventured.

'You should have considered that before.'

A thought crossed the lawyer's mind. Julius could see it moving slowly along his brain like a storm at sea trailing skirts of brume.

'She isn't . . . pregnant, is she? You haven't been playing two-backs? My God. Because if you have I might have to destroy you.'

'Certainly not.'

'Well, that's one good thing to come out of this whole sorry affair.'

The implausibility of the thing was suddenly too much for Julius.

'Sir,' he burst out. 'It simply isn't true. You have to believe me. I never said anything to her about marriage.'

The tall man regarded Julius calmly for a while from under his beetling brows. It was a gaze of well-modulated distaste mingled with menace. Its effect in the courtroom was legendary, causing many an innocent to confess all and be stoned to death in the canal.

'Sorry,' he said. 'I didn't hear that. You were saying?'

Julius could feel a cannonball-size sense of guilt beginning to form. Ridiculously, his eyes were watering. Confessions, real and imaginary, trembled on his lips.

'I must think,' he said. 'I must have time.'

'Certainly you shall have time,' said the lawyer. 'Until next Sunday. But we know what the answer will be, don't we?'

Blommardine was listening at the door when he left. He ignored her.

It had been a bleak day, and was not improved by the reaction of the Grand Master to whom he had immediately repaired.

'You should marry her,' he said.

'But she is not – nor is her father – one of the Brethren.'

'You must wind them in. He is an important man. It would be a most useful connection for us.'

He had already stressed that aspect of the affair.

'What about the sanctity of predestined love?'

'You will find, if you fix your mind upon it, that Blommardine could easily be the pre-ordained partner for whom you have been waiting since the dawn of time. She is said to be rich, well brought up . . .'

64

'Spoilt . . .'

'You will teach her the path. Remember, she is Earth. You are Spirit. Reflect upon it, my son.'

It is hard for those who have never been short of family – perhaps even have suffered from too much – to understand the sensations of someone who has been brought up as an orphan. Brought up without the comfort of love, there is always a temptation to enter or to form a family.

If they said he should marry Blommardine, thought Julius as he walked home, perhaps they were right. It was perhaps hubris in him to feel that he knew better. (As it turned out, of course, it wasn't. It was merely an instinct for self-protection – an instinct that was trying to tell him that someone who displayed such scant regard for his feelings before marriage was hardly likely to make much in the way of sacrifice afterwards. But it is not completely discreditable to learn to trust one's instincts later rather than earlier in life. It depends on the individual; and the instincts.)

At all events, he agreed to marry her. Her father was not surprised.

'I'll let you two young people talk alone,' he said, leaving the room. 'I don't need to hear love's young rubbish.'

Blommardine looked like a cat that, having got the cream, has the butter as well. Julius asked her why she had lied.

'Oh,' she said, 'you'd been to Italy. You knew about love and death . . . Popes . . . and poison. I've never been out of this place. You've seen the world. I'm so bored. I thought you could show me something I didn't know. Oh, and I'd like you to paint me naked. Will you? I can't think of anything naughtier. I'm positively wetting myself.'

He surveyed her small bosom apprehensively.

'Of course,' he said, masking his lack of enthusiasm. 'You can be one of my sinners if you like.'

'I'd like that.'

As it turned out she had a rather good figure in a boyish way – not unlike some of the nudes that old Bosch used to paint – breasts high and small and not much bottom or belly. She was also an enthusiastic and enterprising lover.

These were her good points. Her bad points were just about everything else. No, that was not fair. The trouble was, she was mischief.

It was tough luck she couldn't have any children. Naturally she blamed him for the deficiency.

'I bet your father could only manage one,' she would say, 'and that was out of wedlock. And now I'm married to a bastard and he can't father a legitimate brat. Perhaps I'd better try elsewhere.'

He lived in anxiety that she would carry out her threat – he would dearly have liked a child of his own – but whether or not she did there

65

was still nothing to show for it. Sometimes she would blame the water or the locality in general.

'We must move,' she would say. 'We must go to Bruges.'

'What would I do in Bruges?'

'Goggle at nudes the way you do here.'

'I need commissions. There are many painters already in Bruges.'

He had been to Bruges once. It was Venice without the warmth. He could not imagine himself in Bruges.

'I could not work in Bruges,' he said.

She shrugged her shoulders.

'My father would support us. He might come and live with us.'

Julius shuddered. The idea of living in Bruges, not working, living with Blommardine and her father, was a nightmare beyond the brush of Bosch.

'Not Bruges,' he said again, with that rare firmness which his wife recognized as being bedrock.

'All right, not Bruges,' she said. 'But somewhere.'

Talking of support, he wondered what had happened to the money that had been supposed to attend the marriage. There had been little evidence of it so far. A little easer now and then would not have come amiss.

Chapter 18

After a difficult afternoon with the toads – and an even worse evening with the Brethren who were becoming increasingly impatient about the delivery of their latest commission – Julius returned home to find Blommardine packing.

For a moment his heart leapt as the notion that she was going to leave him entered his head, but she dashed it with her opening words.

'We're going to Rensburg, stupid.'

'Rensburg? Why Rensburg? Rensburg's German, isn't it?'

'Rensburg's German, isn't it?' she mimicked. 'That all you know, face-ache? What difference does it make? We speak their language, don't we?'

Everyone did who lived near the border.

'I know Rensburg has a fine church with some remarkable glass depicting scenes of the Apocalypse,' Julius said mildly.

'Scenes of the Apocalypse,' she repeated again. 'Scenes of the Apoca-ruddy-lips. It's all you can think of, isn't it? Art . . .'

'And music,' he said, for music had been almost an obsession with Ammanati (through its harmonies, based on right proportion, could be discerned that truth which was beyond hearing).

'Art and music . . . All you can think of.'

'It seems enough,' he said.

'Enough? If it paid, it'd be a quarter of enough. But look at us!'

He looked.

'We're not starving,' he said.

'There's more to life than food,' she replied. 'Though, God knows, we're not living delicately. But no, what I meant was, look at us. I married a man I thought interesting. A man who had travelled, who knew things, who would show me marvels and mysteries. What did I find? A man obsessed by toads.'

'And art and music,' he told her.

'Art, music and toads.'

'So is that why we're going to Rensburg? To escape toads?'

'Partly.'

'What else?'

'The most interesting thing in the world is happening in Rensburg.'

'And what is that?'

'I met an interesting man the other day.'

'He'd have to be pretty interesting to make one change towns.'

'He's interesting all right.'

He shook his head.

'I'll believe it when I see it.'

'You wouldn't know an interesting man if he levitated off the ground and pissed in your face,' she told him.

He looked at her closely. He had decided that she was slightly unhinged some time ago; anything that she suggested had to be carefully examined for flaws.

'Is that what he's been doing?' he asked mildly.

She snorted.

'He's an Anabaptist,' she said. 'There's going to be trouble there. They've kicked out their Roman Prince Bishop and let the Lutherans in. And that's just the beginning. There'll be trouble, I tell you . . .'

That, of course, was really what she liked. There was no doubt, however, Julius reflected, that her plan had certain advantages. For a start it would mean that her father and the Brethren would be some convenient distance away. Then again, it would relieve him of further struggle on the pictures that he detested. If there were a new regime in Rensburg, it could be that the ideas of the Renaissance – as well as the Reformation – might have inspired it. Eyes that appreciated the classical and the allegorical might be eager to see what a modern northern artist could do. Lastly, if, as he had heard – he had not communicated it to Blommardine, for it was always wise to conceal such information from her – if it was true that some vision of a new heaven and a new earth were to be made flesh in Rensburg, then it would be madness for one already imbued with ideas of the Millennium not to be present to witness, to record and to experience.

It would have been harder to go along with in Florence, but up here in the misty North it was easier to believe in the imminence of the Last Days. Even the great Luther had lent support to it, in rare accord with his arch-enemy, the prophet-martyr Muntzer. It was only in the area of whether the Kingdom of God should be in Heaven or upon Earth that the two fell seriously out.

Less furiously, the neo-Platonists at the Acadamietta were inclined to support the theory of potential perfection on Earth. Julius recalled many debates on the subject. But it could be, a tiny part of his mind whispered to him, it could just be that in that melting-pot of manners and mores – such as the Last Days would create – he could cast off the shackles of a mistaken marriage and find the true complement and love that was waiting for him as surely as destiny itself.

In finding such a union – like Adam's and Eve's, in the first wing of

Bosch's triptych – he might also achieve the vision to complete his labours on the last.

Of all this he said nothing to Blommardine, for he was beginning to suspect that she was a witch, and though he had developed a mild affection for the toads he worked with, he had no desire to be turned into a symbol of lust himself.

Part Two

I went to the Garden of Love,
And saw what I had never seen:
A Chapel was built in the midst,
Where I used to play on the green.

The Garden of Love
WILLIAM BLAKE

Chapter 1

The Dutchman came during Lent. She remembered it because there was still snow left in little stubborn patches on the road, and the trees were bare and black against the sky.

She happened to be looking out of the window when the man came down the street.

She was often looking out of the window. It was one of the things you did if you were a girl of eighteen in Rensburg. And then he appeared – not hurrying as people of no importance hurry, to fetch a midwife or escape a beating, and yet not dawdling either. He came purposefully as if he knew exactly where he was going and what was going to happen. It was remarkable for a stranger.

'That's him.'

She turned. Her old nurse, Frieda, had come up on slippered feet, and was staring out into the street over her shoulder.

'Who is he, Nurse?'

'Why, he's the Anabaptist, child. You asked me once what evil is, and I said never mind, you'll know in good time.'

Her nurse was a devout Catholic and loyal to the Roman Church – something of a rarity these days in Rensburg – and had found many occasions for expressing her disgust at what was going on in the town.

'What is his name?'

'His name is Legion,' said her nurse, stretching her lips as if the name were a sloe.

'You know him?'

'I know of him. I saw him once when he was here before.'

'Is he not a good man?'

'Good? Why, he is the Devil,' her nurse told her.

Elisabeth watched in silence as the man came up to their door. She did not believe it; yet the old woman did not take the name of the Evil One lightly.

'Why is he coming here, Nurse?'

Again the sloe-sucking expression.

'He's coming to see your father.'

Elisabeth always assumed that her nurse knew everything. It was a belief which Frieda actively fostered; and indeed it was true that the

73

network of crones in Rensburg probably knew more of what went on in the town than the Leader of the Great Guild himself.

'Why would he want to do that, Nurse?'

'Questions, questions. I expect he wants to talk about . . .'

But Frieda stopped.

'What, Nurse, talk about what?'

But the old woman refused to be drawn. Elisabeth's father was a prosperous and important man, and head of his guild; so it was not strange that any visitor should wish to call on Konrad Harting. But why a person her nurse had described as the Devil? It was all very perplexing. Frieda, however, maintained her silence.

'You will discover soon enough. I must go and tell Anna that he has arrived.'

Elisabeth lingered, watching as the man was finally admitted by the serving-girl, Billa, wondering what devilment lurked beneath that tall hat, behind that enquiring eye. She heard the front door close and, shortly after, the boom of her father's voice raised in welcome.

She did not like the idea of her father greeting the Devil, even if it was old Frieda's talk. The Devil was in the house. Though normally not markedly devout – church up till now had seemed as much a social as a religious event – Elisabeth crossed herself.

Apart from his general interest in picking up souls, what could the Devil be wanting with her father?

74

Chapter 2

Elisabeth's father, Konrad Harting, had a little weakness, as it happened.

Not that he wasn't a strong and vigorous man. He was; but weakness is best highlighted in such characters. It is thrown into relief.

Born of a family that had connections with minor nobility but had fallen on thin times, he had inherited a small business and had very soon turned it into a thriving one. Now, at fifty, he had a substantial house in one of the main streets of the town, and three shops and two warehouses at a sensible distance away. One of the warehouses had a still-room behind it where cordials, essences and strong waters were made.

Indeed, distillation was one of the secrets of his success, for it was still something of a novelty, only recently introduced from France, where in the south-west, in Gascony, the Arabs had left the art a century or so before.

Konrad had been quick to recognize the potential of the invention, and had installed an ex-alchemist to supervise the work.

As he sat in his study now, he could feel his energies undiminished. It was as if he were twenty years younger. And yet he was better than he had been twenty years ago because now he was a success. He was recognized, popular with a few, envied by many. You would have thought there was nothing he could not be or do. People would have given their eye-teeth, perhaps their very souls, to have been in his position.

And yet, he thought, and yet there were causes for dissatisfaction in his life. It was all very well for them to envy him but they did not know.

In fact there were two causes for his dissatisfaction. Firstly, his wife, who was sickly, had only given him a daughter; and although the girl was all right as far as daughters go, she was after all only a woman; and there were still serious doubts in some people's minds as to whether a woman was a human being at all. The question had been raised at the Synod of Macon. The Church called them the 'portals of Satan', and the great Hammer of Witches, the *Malleus Maleficarum*, called the whole sex 'diabolic'. He needed a son. In fact, like that Henry in England, he needed another wife.

For that was his other source of discontent. He was a man of great sexual energy. It found relief in a number of little portals of Satan, in the stews, but he knew that this was not properly in keeping with his position.

He used to go to confession, of course. But he was not convinced that the person hearing his confessions was any better than he was. There were plenty of stories about the things the nuns and monks got up to. Besides, what with the current state of affairs in the Church, and the way standards were falling everywhere, you couldn't be sure that the person hearing your confession wouldn't sidle off and blab about it to your neighbour.

It was partly why he had been attracted to the new Lutherans. You knew where you were with them. They didn't presume to come between you and God. They didn't put glosses on the Bible. They encouraged you to think – and pray – for yourself.

The other thing he liked about them was that they didn't set up in business and compete with you, tax-free, the way the Catholics did. It was hardly credible, was it? He was actually paying taxes to have a group of friars steal his business. Of course, there had been plenty of cases of that kind of unfair poaching by the clerics going on, so he wasn't the only one to complain. But it made his blood boil. Setting up in the grocery business with glebe-farm produce!

You heard the same sort of complaint from every side. But still, it was a Roman Catholic prince-bishopric. Over the years, one had come to expect this kind of thing. It had happened before; it would doubtless have blown over and happened again, and again. But this particular Prince Bishop made a stupid mistake, just at the wrong moment.

'Stupid, stupid,' Konrad murmured.

He poured himself another glass of Franconian wine as his mind played over the circumstances leading to the denouement that now gripped the town.

Everyone knew that it wasn't so much the Bishop who was really important in a prince-bishopric. It was the chapter of the diocese which elected him that really mattered. They were the power behind the episcopal throne. The chapter, of course, were local bigwigs – barons and gentry, landowners for the most part, not even priests. They usually simply chose one of their number, whether ordained or not, as bishop – someone who could be counted upon to act in the interest of his own kind and the clergy.

It was well known that most of the chapter had rich prebends and canonries to bring in a juicy income – money that was for the most part provided by taxes which the town had to pay. (Naturally the chapter and clergy were almost entirely exempt from paying taxes.)

Over the years in Rensburg the town had won concessions by bargaining over taxes. The State always needed money and, if you made excuses or simply delayed – particularly in times of good harvest when you couldn't be squeezed – you could make life very awkward for the chapter.

'More wine,' he called.

He was getting slightly drunk – and why shouldn't he? Billa came in and poured the wine. He held her wrist to steady her as she did so – perhaps a trifle too long. Where was he? Ah yes, the chapter and the town, he thought, shifting his haunches.

Recently the game had gone the other way. An outbreak of plague, three crop failures (the price of rye had trebled), an armed insurrection by the peasants against another state in the South . . . this was just the kind of thing that helped put the advantage back with a vengeance in the hands of the chapter. And this time, vengeance was the word. They had taken back all the concessions the town had won, and more.

The height of irony and – it seemed to the citizens – injustice was that every time a new bishop was elected, they had to pay fat sums for the privilege to the Roman Curia. Normally a bishop might last a good twenty years, but a run of bad luck and poor health meant that four bishops had had to be elected in the space of just three decades, and the last bishop had been one bishop too many. As if that hadn't been enough, the latest one was not even a priest.

All this could and would have been endured. The people of Rensburg were on the whole a patient and acquiescent lot; but then this frockless bishop did a very stupid thing. He tried to sell the bishopric to the neighbouring bishop of Paderborn without even asking the chapter's permission.

In a rare instance of unanimity the chapter, for a brief but fatal interlude, now sided with the townsfolk.

As it happened, the Lutheran cause had already been much assisted by a forceful young preacher called Hans Hass, a blacksmith's son whose extraordinary talents had won him a university education. Hass had been filling the churches with passionate sermons on behalf of the Lutheran movement and had pledged himself to bring the town into the Lutheran fold, finding a degree of support from the guilds.

The final *coup de grâce* to the Romans was the resignation of the bishop who had tried to sell his diocese-cum-princedom, and the death of his successor after yet another bout of taxation for the town.

'We can't afford another bishop, who wants another bishop?' shouted the townsfolk at meetings and demonstrations that were becoming daily noisier.

It was the cue for the guilds to act.

Before another bishop could be wheeled forward, the guilds, supported by the people and at least part of the chapter, proceeded to install Lutheran preachers in all Rensburg's churches. The new bishop-designate was unable to force or even persuade the town to abandon its new faith. And that year Rensburg was recognized as *urbs Lutheranorum*.

It had been a difficult year for the town, and the approach of 1533 had made it more so. It had been said by some, for many years now, that 1533 was going to mark the End of the World, or the beginning of the Last Things. The overturning of established order was traditionally one of the signs of the onset of the Millennium. There were those in Rensburg who were already addressing themselves to the prospect of Judgement.

With all this – and the usual problems of a severe winter – Konrad could still have coped. It was the other thing that troubled him. He did his best to occupy himself with business, but the price of sausages and the distillations from the new alembic would never dampen the furnaces of his own blood.

He seemed aflame all day. At night, wild dreams assailed him which provided only transitory relief. He began to think that he was the victim of an incubus, some spell laid upon him – by whom? His suspicions were beginning to centre on old Frieda. She was always grumbling and mumbling when he was near.

He tried a drench from the apothecary but it simply turned his stools yellow. He tried praying but nothing of significance emerged.

It would have been all right if he had been single. He could have found some sprightly creature to wed him and he could have ridden her all night. But he was married. And, though sickly, his wife was still very much alive.

And then one day in early January, a minor official at the Law Courts, one Ignaz Schwenk, whom he had once bumped into in the low quarter of the town, had told him about the teachings of the Brotherhood of the Free Spirit or, at least, of a particular sect of them, called Adamites. They believed, Schwenk informed him (and he had heard rumours to this effect), in the pre-Fall state of innocence; more particularly, in the beauty and sanctity of the sexual act which they named 'acclivity' or 'the path to the heights' or even 'Christerie'.

The notion of what these Adamites got up to worked on Konrad powerfully.

'Tell me more,' he had urged Schwenk at their next meeting.

'Come.' Schwenk motioned conspiratorially. 'Walk with me; it does not do to speak of these things too close to doors and windows.'

There was something sleazy about the little man, but Konrad stifled his distaste.

'What more do you know of these Adamites?' he enquired.

Schwenk gave a disagreeable snigger.

'It is said,' he confided, 'though I have not myself witnessed the truth of it, that they have a special way of performing the act which was that enjoyed by Adam and Eve in the Garden of Eden. It is the lost art.'

The lost art! Konrad could feel the blood pounding in his ears. This was the esoteric garden of delights.

'Go on,' he said thickly, 'speak more of this.'

'For the subtle spirit,' continued Schwenk, nothing loth, 'carnality cannot in any circumstances be a sin.'

'Not a sin?' cried Konrad. 'Why, what is it, then?'

'It is a virtue,' smiled Schwenk, triumphantly. 'Indeed, by such intimacy a woman can become chaster than she was before. If she was not previously a virgin, she can become one again by congress. Indeed, it is one of the surest signs of subtlety of spirit, if he who indulges in concupiscence can do so without fear of God or twinge of conscience. Their creed is *"crescere et multiplicamini"*.'

'Where do the subtle exercise these virtues?' asked Konrad.

'There are meetings,' replied Schwenk with a sidelong look. 'But I beseech you not to ask me more for I am sworn to secrecy.'

'Do not stop there.'

Konrad stood stock-still in the street and shouted at the little man.

'Please, calm yourself,' urged Schwenk, 'there are eyes in this town.'

But Konrad was in a fever.

'I must know where it is.'

'Be patient,' said the fellow, nodding and grinning like a monkey. 'I will lead you to it, never fear. The day will come and I will send for you. But pray do not speak of it. There are spies everywhere.'

Konrad had waited through January and much of February, but the call never came. The rigour of the season merely exacerbated the heat within him. Schwenk seemed to have disappeared.

Chapter 3

Only the other Deadly Sin to which Konrad's character was seriously prone – Superbia or Pride – could offer any temporary diversion from the inflammations of Lust.

Indeed, ambition in him seemed to derive from the same hot part of his identity as Lust itself – a place full of impatient, restless fires, microcosm of the Pit, source of the energy that had already made him a fortune and brought him to the top of his trade. Oh yes, he had made a success of his business. You did not lightly become head of your guild; even though, it had to be said, the Grocers were not in the very first rank. The Judges and Notaries, the Doctors, the Bankers, the Wool, and Silk, even the Furriers; these were the nobility, the Major Guilds.

It had never been known for the leader of a second-rank guild to become head of the Great Council. But to Konrad, as he shifted on his office chair, played with a paperweight carved in the shape of a Rhine Maiden, tried to concentrate on the abacus and re-align the impulses that stirred within, it seemed that with such fire, such energy, no position in the town was beyond his reach. He could be, he should have been, he would be elected Head of the Great Council. There seemed no reason on earth why the Grocers could not be elevated to Major Guildhood. Others had been; the Bankers for instance. What had they been once but moneylenders? They had only recently been promoted. How much more vital to mankind in general, and the town in particular, was his own trade. You could not eat a promissory note.

The idea of it had long exercised him, but now his carnal impasse, the build-up of a scarcely supportable impatience in the blood, had the effect of jogging him into political activity. The election for the new Grand Master of the Guilds was to be held in six weeks' time. The Catholics were out with their taxes and privileges. The Lutherans were in . . .

He began to put into practice certain stratagems for advancement.

Then, suddenly, one cold morning in late February, Schwenk sent a message asking him to meet him in one hour outside the Corn Exchange.

The minutes passed as if time itself had frozen but, at last, when fifty-five of them had gone by, Konrad reached for his hat and cloak,

80

and – almost incontinent with anticipation – hurried off towards the main square. He saw Schwenk right enough, standing out of the wind in the lee of the building, his short-sighted eyes peering greedily forward like a barbel looking for its breakfast.

For a moment, Konrad thought of going back. The man was so deeply unattractive. The whole thing was madness. He was a respectable citizen . . .

But then, he reflected, what if there were a Secret Way? Would it not be tragic to die without tasting such fruits?

'Come, Master,' said Schwenk, motioning secretively, 'I have an invitation for you.'

Konrad was almost speechless with excitement. His cod-piece felt as though it would burst open like a poppy pod. Schwenk led him behind a buttress, looking with almost ostentatious carefulness around to see that they were not observed.

'You have expressed interest in the beliefs of the Brotherhood of Adam, our great Ancestor. This evening there will be a meeting. Do you wish to be present?'

Konrad attempted vainly to show nonchalance.

'Yes,' he said, shrugging, 'I am intrigued by this conventicle. What must I do?'

He licked his lips, leaning his buttocks against the wall. The chill wind was doing nothing to take the heat from his loins.

'Above all,' said Schwenk, 'you must, on pain of the direst consequences, reveal to no one what passes at the meeting, or where it is held. Do you swear to this?'

The little man seemed to have gained strangely in authority, thought Konrad. Why am I deferring to him so? He is but a clerk.

'I do,' he said, with a show of impatience. 'Do you think me a blabber-mouth?'

'There are those who would destroy us,' said Schwenk. 'There are those who would call our gathering heretical. I presume you know the punishments that are available to the authorities under such a heading?'

Konrad indicated that he was aware of them.

'Very well,' said Schwenk. 'You must come at seven o'clock to the cellars here, what they call the hypocaust, where the furnaces are for the hot draughts that heat the building. Here you will be blindfolded and led to the meeting-chamber. Is that understood?'

'It is. What should I wear for the meeting?'

'Your dress is of no importance.'

'Very well.'

'I shall see you at the appointed hour, then.'

Schwenk took his leave, and Konrad walked home in a state close to carnal delirium. So the moment that had exercised his keenest imaginings was at hand! A confused medley of fancies thronged his brain and minnowed round his loins. Returning home, he found his daughter playing the lute and singing. She stopped when he entered the room, but he motioned her to continue.

'Continue,' he said, with rare approbation. 'What is that piece?'

'It is an English song,' she said. 'I am afraid it is profane.'

Normally he might have frowned, for it was Lent, and he felt that he was expected – whatever his own leanings; perhaps indeed because of them – to encourage probity in his family. Now, however, he smiled.

'We cannot be grave all the time when we are young,' he said. 'What are the words?'

'"Come hither to me, my true love sweet",' she said.

'Sing on,' he told her.

The melody and her fine, clear voice pleased him. And were not the sentiments holy according to the teaching of the Adamites? To them, was not the only sin shame? She played on while he sat locked in pleasurable anticipation of the evening ahead, enjoying the sudden snapping of his bands of restraint if not of guilt. It would not, of course, do to tell his daughter about such things. Carnality was too rich a diet for the young. And guilt, if one should feel guilt, was either too piquant a sauce, or too bitter a drench . . .

The rest of the day passed for Konrad in similar reverie and a rare mood of benignity. He even visited his wife in her chamber.

'Konrad? What brings you here?'

How ill she looked, he thought. The pale beauty had grown transparent-grey like one of those bowls travellers brought from the land of Cathay. For a moment, he felt a twinge of guilt at his neglect – the piquant sauce, the insupportable drench.

'I thought I would bring you a spring garland,' he said.

He had seen the snowdrops in the market on his way from the rendez-vous with Schwenk.

'Flowers?'

Her pale face flushed with pleasure.

'I'm afraid I have neglected you of late,' he said. 'You know how it is. Business . . . the city . . .'

'I understand. I am no company. Liserle is very good to me. She tells me things. It is a strange time, I think. People talk of the Last Days. The Prince Bishop has gone. I think I too must . . .' Her voice trailed off.

She had discovered over the years that it was better to say too little.

'Now, now,' he said, with the selfish man's hatred of hearing anything that might upset him.

'It is true,' she continued at length. 'I shall not be long.'

He did not argue with her. The truth was written on her face. After a few more politenesses, he left. He hated the smell of the sickroom.

Chapter 4

When evening came at last, he washed himself, changed his clothes, and walked through the gathering dusk to the Corn Exchange once more. Arriving, he looked around cautiously to see that he was not observed, pushed open the side door which Schwenk had pointed out, and descended the steps within to a vaulted antechamber off which led various doors, all shut and locked. Here Konrad paused. His sense of danger started pricking. There was no one here. It was a trick, a dupe, even a trap. He tried the doors again, and was about to remount the steps when he heard a voice behind him.

'Close your eyes.'

He half-turned, automatically.

'You must obey, or it will be the worse for you. Close your eyes,' commanded the voice.

It was one Konrad did not recognize, but he did as he was instructed. A bandage was put tightly around his eyes.

'Come, I shall guide you,' said the voice.

They set off, passing through one of the doors and traversing a long passage, through another door, up a short flight of stairs, along a corridor, then down a long circular staircase with forty-seven steps.

'Now,' said Konrad's guide, 'you may take your clothes off but not the blindfold.'

For a moment, Konrad thought of refusing. The idea of a possible trick had by no means disappeared. What could be more ludicrous than for a respected member of the Great Guild to be revealed to his giggling enemies in a state of undress, poised as it were upon some adventure whose purport it would not take an Erasmus to guess at.

'Obey the order,' said the voice. 'Absolute obedience is the condition of admittance. There is a chair beside you for your clothes.'

Konrad stifled his misgivings and did as he was bidden. It was pleasantly warm in the chamber, thanks doubtless to the fires of the hypocaust, that relic – peculiar to Rensburg in these parts – of the days when the city had been a Roman camp. Undressing was no hardship.

'Now drink this,' said the voice. 'It is *aqua vitae Edensis*.'

A goblet was raised to his lips, and he drank. The liquid was slightly bitter though not unpleasant in taste. He recognized a spirit in it such

84

as he himself might have distilled; and he felt the suggestion of heat coursing through him as though his veins were fuses that had been torched with flame.

'Now,' said the voice, 'count up to ten and remove the blindfold.'

Konrad took the bandage from his eyes and blinked in the candlelight that shone brightly about him, reflecting from looking-glasses hanging from the walls. He was alone.

He looked at himself – a well-built man, inclining now to a little seemly portliness, observable for the first time in his life in the round. He noticed that the interest of the occasion, perhaps encouraged by the potion he had drunk, had left its mark upon his member. His first instinct – of shame – was to hide himself in his cloak again. It was not politic to be seen like this.

Suddenly, however, the door in front of him, between two mirrors, burst open; two beautiful young women, completely naked, advanced upon him and led him forward. He went with them; bemused, ashamed, covering himself as best he could, his member growing to a full and, as it seemed to him, preposterous erection; and the more he covered it, the more it grew.

It was the most exciting, the most shameful thing that had ever happened to him. At the same time, the aqua vitae seemed to be eliciting a curious passivity in him, so that he could not have followed, even if he had felt it, any inclination of escape.

The room into which he was led was a large circular chamber with a finely vaulted ceiling, warm but not oppressively so, and lined with people he did not know who stood in a circle watching his arrival. They too were all completely naked.

The circle parted as he and his two mentors approached. In the centre of the circle stood a tall man with golden-red hair and piercing blue eyes, holding a beautiful dark-haired woman by the hand. They advanced to greet Konrad.

'Welcome, Konrad,' said the man. 'I am Adam, that is, Christ. And this is my consort, Eve.'

'Or Mary,' said the woman.

Adam-that-is-Christ had a slightly foreign accent which Konrad decided was Dutch. Eve, however, was pure Rensburg.

The whole thing ought to have been absurd, but to Konrad it had the curious logic of a dream.

'Why do you hold your hand in front of you, Konrad?' asked Adam-that-is-Christ.

Konrad blushed in spite of himself. It was difficult enough to hide a monumental erection without people drawing attention to the fact that you were doing it.

'I . . .' he stammered, and stopped.

'Are you ashamed of your sex? We know no shame here. Take his hand away, Magdalena.'

The more beautiful of the two beautiful attendants took the offending hand away and pressed it to her own. In doing so, she brushed against his person – either accidentally or with intent – and to Konrad's total dismay, he started to ejaculate.

He looked around in utter horror and abasement, expecting mirth and derision, but the expression on everyone's face was one of joy and delight. Magdalena herself, seizing a goblet, proceeded to catch his flow with practised dexterity. Adam motioned; and one of the number approached with a pitcher of wine, pouring some into the vessel.

Magdalena thereupon handed it around to the entire company, each one of whom took a sip with holy reverence as if it had been a sacrament.

'An auspicious beginning, Konrad,' said Adam, when he and Eve had completed the ceremony. 'Spontaneity is a sign of the greatest virtue. Later, when you have become used to our ways, you shall truly taste the heights – the *acclivitas* or "Christerie" as we call it – which is the path to God. Let us pray.'

A service followed in which prayers, hymns and a brief sermon featured. Konrad sat bemused – a chair had been brought for him – and listened to Adam extol the sanctity of nakedness and the sublimity of love, since this, he said, was the state of our First Parents before the Fall.

Finally another set of doors was thrown open and a banquet revealed. Konrad ate and drank, sitting next to the Magdalena and feeling his loins once more beginning to burgeon. Songs in an outer chamber profaned chastity and extolled the joys of conjunction. Magdalena took Konrad's hand and guided it between her legs . . .

Adam now stood up and called for silence.

'It is time for the dance and the loving-couch now, my children. For remember, the chaste are unworthy to enter the Kingdom of Heaven. Go, be fruitful and multiply; replenish the earth . . .'

Konrad's memories of the next hour or so were confused. Images of naked limbs, of bright breasts and swollen loins, of damp hair like fountain moss, and warm, open, red, enveloping, sweet, gaping aahs and ohhhhs . . .

He woke in his bed at home, with the knowledge that he had tasted what he had for so long desired, and that his life would not be the same again.

Nothing more happened, however, for several weeks; and Konrad began to think that the whole episode had been a dream brought on by the draught he had been given in the hypocaust. For this he could not help but be relieved. His extraordinary indiscretion could have ruined him. The whole thing had been madness.

At the same time, as the days wore on, he began to hanker again for those forbidden fruits which had seemed so deliciously, so shockingly easy to gather.

Then, that one day in March, a man called at his house, uninvited and unannounced, wearing the high hat of the Anabaptists.

Chapter 5

'Says he has a message from Mistress Magdalena,' said Billa, the servant-girl.

Fear and the memory of desire awoke in his heart at the mention of the name. He had somehow assured himself that all that had passed was buried in the darkness that surrounded the subterranean chamber.

When Billa showed the man in, Konrad did his best to remain impassive, preferring to give the impression of the successful merchant and burgher who had much on his mind and little time to spare for visitors.

'What can I do for you, Master, er . . . ?'

'My name is not important,' said the man. 'Let us not play games, Master Harting. Though we have not met before, I know a great deal about you. Your principal sins are Pride and Lust. You have spilled your seed like Onan in the . . .'

'Shhh . . .'

Konrad was red with embarrassment, and cast nervous glances towards the door.

'Not so loud,' he urged.

'Very well,' the man continued. 'I had imagined you would not wish your exploits underground to be exposed to the light of day or the ear of a servant.'

There was a pause. Konrad fidgeted with a stick of sealing-wax.

'What do you want here?' he burst out suddenly.

He half-hoped the man would say he needed money. That at least would be understandable.

'That's better,' said the man. 'It is much better if we are open with one another. Indeed, after so publicly spilling yourself, we know how open you can be.'

With a sickening lurch in his stomach, Konrad accepted the idea that this man, these people (whoever they were), were not going to let him off the hook.

'What do you want?' he repeated, numbly.

'The Lord has need of you,' came back the reply.

'What sort of need?'

'The Last Days are upon us and the Elect – some of whom do not, even yet, know the nature of the destiny that is to be theirs, and who still, being simple, have been restrained upon the foothills of the Truth, but to whom it will be revealed – they, the Elect and the Elect-to-be, need a haven and a stronghold for the things that are to be. They will be turned out of Holland; yea, cast out and reviled. It has been ordained that they shall come to Rensburg.'

'To Rensburg? But . . .'

'There is no argument, my friend. The last plague here, I am told, has left some houses empty. The Lutherans have furnished the opportunity by replacing the Prince Bishop. Now we need your help to see that they too will be replaced.'

'I see.'

Konrad thought quickly. He was trapped and he knew it. The man, or his masters, would not hesitate to expose him. He considered with a momentary pang the city which he had grown up in, to which he had always professed loyalty. He was going to betray it . . . his family . . . his friends . . . For seconds, he wavered. And then he thought how far his plans were advanced for an assault on the highest position in the town, and how he more than anyone – certainly the spineless Grand Master of the moment – would be able to see that the town was properly served in all this.

The man seemed to read his thoughts.

'It will not be a betrayal. It will be an apotheosis. You will lead your city into the Kingdom of Heaven.'

'And . . . my reward?'

'You will be in a position of the highest authority. You will sit at the right hand of the Saints.'

'In spite of my, er . . .'

Konrad did not like to mention the occasion of his vulnerability again, but he knew that his visitor would not have forgotten it.

'Certainly,' said the man. 'Let him who is without sin cast the first stone. Of course, repentance is essential.'

Konrad thought repentance would not be difficult. Not going to the hypocaust again would be far harder, but that didn't seem to be part of the agreement.

'What do you want me to do?' he asked, wondering again how it was that Adam and Eve practised congress in Eden (in spite of many marvels, it had not been vouchsafed in the underground chamber).

'We wish you to use your good offices with the Council to make sure that our brethren are well received here. They need food and drink as well as shelter. They need freedom of worship.'

Konrad put his hand on his chin, and thought.

'Why are they to be expelled from Holland?'

'For the same reason that they were expelled from Cleves.'

'And why were they expelled from Cleves?'

The man fixed him with a glittering eye.

'Do you question the messenger of the Lord?'

'It is fitting that I should know. I may myself be questioned.'

'Very well, then. The blessed Melchior Hoffmann, the prophet, wandering far and wide through many nations, preaching the Second Coming and the Millennium, chose our northern provinces of Holland for his special sojourn. There he preached to us, speaking of a period of "tribulations" which we now see all around us – as well as many signs and wonders – which will lead to the onset of the Millennium in this very year, being 1500 plus the years of Christ's life being thirty-three. Does that answer your question, Brother?'

'But why were his followers expelled?'

'They began to attract huge crowds. The authorities became nervous.'

'Did they not preach community of ownership?'

'That was much exaggerated.'

'But will the authorities not become nervous here?'

'You are the authority, Brother.'

'I am not the only authority.'

'You will be the one that counts.'

'Will I not become nervous too?'

'Why should you be nervous, Brother? In the days before the Last Things, you will be a Leader of the People. In this world you will be honoured and attended, your wants provided for . . .'

The man paused.

'Ah, yes,' said Konrad. 'Of course.'

'Your every want, Brother,' said the man, stressing the extra word.

Konrad had the feeling that the man did indeed know everything about him, more than he knew himself. The glittering eyes pierced through to the jelly in his spine. His every want . . .

'Ah, yes,' said Konrad again, crossing his legs as he felt the old, familiar stirring.

'You will sit at the right hand of the Messiah in the Second Kingdom,' concluded his visitor. 'That is enough honour for any man. What do you say?'

Konrad thought again about his life. It was comfortable, secure (as secure as anything could be in these troubled times), but . . . could he really secure the admission of the Grocers to Major Guildhood? Was it not wishful thinking to imagine he could become Grand Master of all the Guilds? Had he not perhaps gone as far as he was going? (Where did these thoughts come from?) Hereafter, shortly, must he not expect declining health, the problems attending his lack of male heir, a diminution of his powers . . . impotence? This man, on the other hand, strangely convincing with his piercing eyes and his smileless intensity, seemed to be on the verge of something tremendous – beyond reason but not beyond belief. And then, of course, there was the little matter of the secret way of congress in Eden . . .

'My every want, did you say?' He turned to his visitor. 'Yes. Yes, I will do it.'

Chapter 6

The visitor stayed to share their meal. He made Elisabeth feel most uneasy. For a start, his grace was far too long, more like a sermon than a grace. She had expected her father to look at least uncomfortable if not downright restless, giving his little cough that signalled impatience; but he seemed for some reason to be taking the whole thing in deadly earnest. And when she started to smile, he frowned at her.

The man made no attempt to start a conversation during the meal, though he answered her father's questions civilly if briefly.

She ventured at last some remark about a visit to Holland she had once made with her father during which she had heard about the boy and the dyke; but he made no reply. Thinking that he might not have heard (for her father was particular about the women around him speaking in suitable mild tones), she repeated what she had said, and added a question.

'Is it true that the boy stopped the sea with his finger?'

There was still no reply.

The Dutchman turned his head away from her and addressed her father.

'It is not seemly,' he said, 'among the Saints for a young female to address an Elder of the People unless she is spoken to. Indeed, it is most unusual for such a creature – for you know what sinful vessels women are – for such a creature to be allowed to break bread with one at all.'

Elisabeth blushed like a strawberry. Surely her father would rebuke the man? Konrad, however, bowed his head gravely as if in proper submission.

'We have yet to learn all the ways of the Saints,' he murmured. 'When next I have the honour of entertaining you . . . we shall eat alone.'

It was the visitor's turn to bow gravely. There was a deal too much grave bowing about, thought Elisabeth, stopping eating. (Who wanted to eat with a Saint anyway?)

She could feel the man's eyes now upon her, boring through her, parting her clothes, lifting her skirts, resting upon her body, not so much enquiringly, she thought afterwards, but requiringly – yes, that was it, requisitioning her, and then passing onward to her mind and her soul, which she prayed God she could hide, for he looked like the sort of man who would take everything. What was it Nurse had said?

'He is a devil.'

She began to feel his power now, beating down her resistance. His eyes – bright, humourless, lit from within like windows on a furnace – were making her feel dizzy. In desperation, she said the first thing that came into her head.

'Is it true you are a devil or is it just what they say?'

'Elisabeth.'

Her father stood up, shaking with rage.

'Yes, Father?'

She knew it had been wrong but simply couldn't help herself.

'Go to your room. I shall speak to you later. Before you go, however, apologize to our guest.'

'I shall not.'

Her father advanced as if to strike her.

The Dutchman raised a hand.

'She must be chastised,' he said, 'but later. First, let me answer her lewd question, however. Yes, it is true, Mistress, that our enemies sometimes call us heretics and even devil's spawn. I am proud to be called a devil by some, and doubtless your father will catechize you upon who it was who repeated such a slander to you. As for whether I am or not, let me say this. I am a devil to the unrighteous and a Saint to my friends. I am more. I am God.'

Elisabeth gasped. She felt the man must indeed be struck down, if not by God at least by her father, who had always been very hot on blasphemy. But still her parent offered no rebuke, but gazed mildly upon the man as if illuminated by what he had said.

'You . . .' she gasped at last. 'You are God? But that's . . .'

'Heresy? Blasphemy? Consider. God is in us. Yes?'

'I believe so.'

'If God is in us, we must be God. God cannot be part of something. He is everything. Therefore I am God. And you, even you, a woman, you too could be God if you could but reach up to it.'

'If I am God, I cannot be beaten,' she said. 'You can't beat God.'

'Who says you cannot? They crucified Him, did they not? Go now.'

Elisabeth sat irresolute. She wasn't going to be ordered about by a Dutchman in her own home, even if he was God. But her father added his weight to the matter.

'To your room, Elisabeth. And apologize for your rudeness.'

'I apologize for my rudeness,' she muttered.

The Dutchman inclined his head without emotion, and Elisabeth hurriedly left the room before the tears could start. She wasn't going to let him see her crying.

Later, in her room, she wondered as she wept what had possessed her father. He could, of course, be mercurial; she knew that. He could hector and bully with the best of them; but he had always seemed to be his own man, a leader of men. Now he seemed for some reason to be happy to follow. What had got into him? God? The Devil? It was all very mysterious.

He sent for her afterwards. She braced herself for the beating, though he had not struck her since her childhood. But to her surprise he was smiling.

'He likes you,' he said.

'Likes me? He has a strange way of showing it, Father.'

The news of this success was not merely unwelcome but somehow alarming.

'He is a remarkable man,' said her father, rubbing his chin. 'Do you think you could grow to like him?'

Chapter 7

Ten days and an election later, Konrad went to the meeting of the Council of the Great Guilds. It was composed of the Masters of the Guilds of Rensburg, and Konrad knew that he – even though Master of but a middle-ranking guild – had come within an ace of being the Grand Master of all of them. At the last minute, however, he had been defeated by the Master of the Drapers, and it mortified him deeply. Had not the Dutchman more or less guaranteed success, causing him to relax his own efforts? Or had he been merely showing him that he could not succeed on his own?

'I thought the Grand Mastership was mine,' he had complained to his friend Folz of the Scriveners.

'There was a last-minute rumour that your, you know, private life might not stand too much examination,' said Folz. 'The Grand Master has to be above reproach. I told them, of course, that I knew of no such thing, but I'm afraid the seed was sown, if you'll pardon the expression.'

Konrad wondered whether Folz might be quite as good a friend as he had thought. He had once made the mistake of confiding in him. Folz, of course, was jumpy about his own position. The Scriveners' Guild had been severely put back by the success of the printing invention. In fact, it was rumoured it might be taken over by the Printers' Guild – in which case Folz would be out of a mastership.

Konrad could see it now. Folz had ditched him. Well, he would see who did the ditching when the boot was on the other foot.

Konrad smiled as he met Folz now in the street on the way to the Council Chamber. He must not for a moment show that he knew Folz had let him down.

'How is trade?' he asked him.

'So so. It's never going to be the same, though. Every week sees more books coming out.'

'Printing has caused nothing but trouble,' agreed Konrad, although he didn't mind if it caused trouble for Folz. 'It's putting knowledge into the wrong hands.'

'My point exactly,' said Folz. 'Look at the Bible, for instance. There are some things that should remain a mystery.'

'And yet,' said Konrad, 'it could be said that the spread of knowledge could improve the position of the scrivener.'

'Oh?' asked Folz. 'How is that?'

'The more learning is disseminated, Folz, my friend, the more people there will be who need your special skills. More ledgers to be kept, more records to be inscribed, more rolls to be written up.'

Folz's face brightened.

'I hadn't thought of that.'

'You just have to keep your eyes open and spy the opportunities when they come.'

'Things could hardly be worse now, however. What with the Turkish invasion, the late plague, the famine, the price of ink . . . As if we hadn't had to pay enough without the election of yet another bishop . . .'

'Well, at least that's over.'

'I'd be surprised if we've seen the last of them. Those Romans will come sneaking back.'

'If you ask me, the Lutherans haven't gone far enough,' said Konrad, smiling inwardly and seizing his chance. 'They're still in league with the princes and the dukes. They're not a faith for the townsfolk.'

'You could be right,' said Folz. 'I hadn't thought of that. Maybe these Anabaptists have something after all.'

'Strange you should mention that.'

'How, strange?'

'I understand some of them have been rather unfairly treated in Holland. I thought it might be no more than charitable – to say nothing of commercially beneficial – if we gave them refuge here.'

Folz's eyes lit up. How could he ever have been a friend, thought Konrad; the man was a time-serving idiot.

'How d'you mean, commercially?'

'Well, you know how in the late plague we lost, what, two thousand people. That's two thousand people who needed feeding, clothing, housing and, yes, scrivening. Here is an opportunity to put some people back.'

'Are we to take two thousand?'

'No, no. Nothing like. Say a hundred or two. But what a hundred, Folz! From your point of view, they are ideal. They regard machinery, such as printing-presses, devil's work. They are prime candidates for your trade. Think of the tracts that they will want, the records that they will wish to keep – for, you know, they believe the Millennium is near. Every day to them will be important. And you know how industrious that kind of immigrant always is.'

Folz's face looked brighter by the minute.

'And you, Harting, do you think that the Millennium is close?'

'I keep an open mind, Folz,' replied Konrad, truthfully for a change.

He really did not know what to think. He saw personal gain, of course, in the developments he was mooting; the possible discrediting of the new Grand Master, the probable substitution of himself to the position in the not too distant future, an influential role whatever the outcome, combined with his own personal profit (Saints had to eat) – all in all, however things turned out, he was going to do well. But there was something beyond that. The Dutchman had a power, there was no doubt of it. He seemed to be possessed in some way – perhaps he was even a true prophet. If the Millennium were to be on the cards, or even a remote possibility, it would be as well to be on the safe side. Perhaps all the recent disasters were really portents of the Last Things, as the Saint had told him. The fact that the man was a stranger somehow made the claim more plausible. He would have pooh-poohed a Rensburger who came up with such a tale.

'An open mind! I quite agree,' said Folz. 'So what is to be done?'

'I shall tell the Council of the request from the Dutch,' said Konrad. 'Perhaps I can count on your support?'

He nearly added 'this time' but managed to suppress it. He didn't want Folz to know that he knew what a little rat he was.

Chapter 8

Everyone had always known that the guilds really ran the town –
especially so since the Bishop and chapter had left. There was a show
of having a town council and a burgomaster, but on the whole the guilds
told them what to do and many of the guild officers were also town
councillors. So it was with particular interest that Konrad attended the
Guild Masters' meeting.

It was a close thing, as it happened. The Master who had pipped
Konrad, the Master of the Drapers, was a great moon-faced man who
was not as stupid as he looked. His chief characteristic, that of political
manoeuvring, was to prove his undoing, however. A stronger man
would have stuck out for the unpopular decision; a wiser one would
have realized he could not run with the hare and hunt with the hounds.

The session in a chamber off the Great Hall – a fine building with
a high corbelled roof – was an august affair. The various Guild Masters
assembled in their robes and sat around a long table at the end of which,
on a great oak throne, sat their leader. Their robes, trimmed with fur,
shone richly against the dark panelling. We are like a pack of cards,
thought Konrad, and I will shuffle it.

The Master of the Drapers struck the table with his gavel, and the
meeting started. Certain routine matters were attended to; finances
were discussed; a replacement for the Master of the Vintners, who
had recently died, was commended. All this was expected. And then
the Grand Master dropped his bombshell.

'Next,' he said, 'we come to the matter of the election of the Bishop.'

The Guild Masters all looked at each other, amazed.

'The Bishop? But we are a Lutheran state now.'

'Nonetheless, as a state, we must have a Prince Bishop. It will be a
purely secular function.'

'It always was,' murmured Konrad.

Some of the Guild Masters were on their feet.

'No, no,' they shouted.

'Order,' cried the Grand Master, banging his gavel, his moon-face
peering here and there to see where the advantage lay.

'No more bishops, no more taxes, no more priests,' they shouted.

Konrad stood up.

'Brothers,' he said, 'let us not waste our time in unseemly squabbling.

The decision for us is surely clear. Either we must be seen to have broken away from what – to many of us – seemed the bad old days when we were allowed on sufferance to ply our trades . . .'

'For the benefit of clergy,' someone interrupted.

Konrad looked round and smiled. It was Folz.

'Indeed, the clergy did benefit more than any of us,' he continued smoothly. 'Either we must be seen to have broken away . . . Or, Brothers, we must go back to being little more than merchant-serfs in our own city. Surely we have not come this far to be turned back from our promised land at the last moment. Which is it to be?'

'Freedom, freedom,' they cried.

'Well, er . . .' said the Grand Master, realizing the extent of his miscalculation, 'that seems to be unanimous. We must ask the Chapter of the Diocese of . . .'

'No asking,' said Konrad, 'telling.'

'There is no chapter,' cried Folz. 'This is a free city.'

'The chapter is closed,' shouted some wag.

The Grand Master sighed. The Dean of the Chapter, Baron von Linfeld, had dangled the most intriguing possibilities for his future – a grant of land, a manor house, perhaps even a minor ennoblement – if he could persuade the guilds to return to the old ways. They were clearly going to have to be postponed. He wondered whether the Dean would consider keeping his offer on ice, and decided that he probably wouldn't. He could see himself a knight. It was really too bad. That man Harting must have known he'd bribed Folz to stitch him up at the election.

Konrad rose to his feet again.

'We need some gesture, Brothers, that will bring it home to these former masters of ours that we mean business. Something that will both shock them and be to our advantage. Has anyone any suggestions?'

There you are, Folz, he thought. Let us see if you know which side your bread is buttered. But Folz remained seated, looking attentively from speaker to speaker as various Guild Masters made suggestions.

'Why don't we confiscate all Church property?'

'Too much,' said Konrad. 'Too strong. They would march in with a small body of men and take it back – and the whole town with it. We are weak at the moment. We must be subtle.'

'Why don't we let it be known in the town that the Town Council is going to start raising taxes for another bishop election?'

'There'd be a riot,' said Konrad. 'Again, that would bring the soldiers in. Or it could be directed against us. When was the last time the townsfolk burst in here?'

'1441,' said someone.

'And what happened?'

'Six councillors were killed with knobkerries.'

'I think that answers the question,' said Konrad, evenly. 'You have to be very careful with a crowd. It's like letting a homunculus out of a bottle. You don't know where it'll go.'

'Why don't we just . . . play for time?' said the Grand Master, making a bid for control again. 'It would be more statesmanlike. A lot of people are watching us. We don't want to do anything rash. There may come a time when we need powerful protectors. These are evil days.'

Konrad was dismayed to hear one or two voices begin to fall in with this line.

'The Turks are in the East now,' said the Master of the Goldsmiths. 'Who knows when they may not come north?'

Konrad sprang to his feet once more.

'Brothers, this is not worthy of you. Was any undertaking worth the effort not achieved with a little bravery? Without stout hearts we will simply slide back into servitude. Freedom is not given away. It has to be won. If it was easy everybody would do it.'

He was pleased to hear the murmuring this time agreeing with him.

'Now,' he said, not looking at Folz, 'any other ideas?'

Folz rose slowly and gazed rattily around the chamber, gauging where the majority's wish lay. Then, seeming to make up his mind, he began to speak.

I shall kill him, thought Konrad – and he was both appalled and exhilarated to find that he meant it – I shall murder him if he gets this wrong.

'Brothers,' said Folz, '"though I speak with the tongues of men and of angels and have not Charity, I am become as sounding brass or a tinkling cymbal . . ."'

Konrad started to smile. He knew that it was going to be all right. He hardly listened to the rest of what Folz had to say.

'. . . a charitable act to take in these oppressed people . . . from Cleves and from the Netherlands and Brabant . . . Saintly . . . industrious . . . replacing those who died in the late plague . . . adding to our commercial and, I believe . . . our moral stature. At the same time . . . will be seen as . . . act of effrontery to bishop and chapter who cannot abide Anabaptists at any price . . .'

Finally, Folz sat down. He had done a good job. There was already a great deal of yah-yah in the background. Konrad rose to his feet for the final time.

'I believe,' he said, 'that our brother Folz has hit on an idea of brilliance. It will infuriate our enemies but they can hardly take up arms against it. I second his suggestion and would now like to propose a vote of no-confidence in our Grand Master.'

'I second that,' said the Master of the Printers.

'Now wait a minute,' said the Grand Master.

'For?' asked Konrad.

Twenty hands went up. He had done his homework well.

'Against?'

Five hands showed, one of them the Grand Master's.

'Motion carried. And now I should like to propose that Brother Folz be elected in his place . . . It is, I know, rare to depose a Grand Master. When was the last time we did it?'

'1441,' said a small voice hidden behind a screen.

'Evil times call for strong measures,' announced Konrad. 'And that means strong leadership. For?'

Twenty-one hands went up.

'I declare the meeting closed,' said Folz.

Next day, he made Konrad, at his own request, one of the Great Guilds' representatives on the Town Council. It was a formal appointment. Very little happened in the Town Council these days – much deliberation and scant action – but it was useful all the same to know what flickers of corporate resolve might still reside there. Nothing, even now, could be taken for granted.

Chapter 9

The Saints were on the move. A long line of them, interspersed with several baggage-wagons in which rode the very young and the infirm, plodded down the road from Nijmegen making for the border and Rensburg. The Leader was at the front – David Mosman himself; though still only forty, his silver hair and beard framed his summit like a cloud; he was the man of action – inspiring, upholding, exhorting. Sometimes he would throw up his hands at which the whole procession would stop; and he would break into prayer. At others he would sing hymns of his own making about the journey to the New Jerusalem. He had given up crucial organizational work to be present on this first major pilgrimage.

Bringing up the rear was a man of a very different character, who had slipped back from Rensburg to join him. He went by the name of Enoch. Enoch was reflecting on leadership as he walked. Now, here, the Leader was leader, he thought. But was he the true Leader? He could not say. He was in shadows still. But he sensed, a twitching on the golden thread told him, that there was someone yet to be disclosed, the Chosen of God, who would be the true Messiah. The notion filled him quietly with a fierce delight. Whoever it was could not be far away, for the hour of the Millennium was very near.

All the signs, all the portents, had been manifested. Even now they were still being witnessed. A couple of Saints had even seen a great horse in the clouds only yesterday. Another had drawn blood out of a well. Best of all, in three days' time, God would open the gates of Rensburg to them – a town that had only two years before been celebrating the abominable Mass in the temples of Antichrist. It was indeed a miracle in which he had been merely a humble instrument. Or rather, he had been able to help do it because God was not simply with him, but in him.

Oh, he had wanted to shock the frivolous German girl when he said that he was God. But he had not said it lightly. He was God – God the Son, twining into God the Holy Spirit but not yet God the Creator. For if he were God the Creator he would be able to make the trees bow to him as he passed. None of them could do that. Not even the Leader could do that.

And then he thought: God would not do that either. Of what use would bowing trees be to God? That was the kind of idle temptation the Devil had set for God in the wilderness.

'I am a vessel not a vassal,' he suddenly cried.

It was inspiration. He had not thought those words. The cry was taken up by all around him. The Saints loved a play on words. It passed up the line.

'I am a vessel not a vassal.'

The Leader and he would turn back when they had led the pilgrims as far as the gates of Rensburg. The time was not quite ready for them. The Saints must work like yeast among the wash of the townspeople. Then the distillation, the refining might begin.

'Oh, God,' he prayed as he walked, using an invocation he had written and which would come to be widely adopted. 'What shall I say you are, when you cannot be named? What shall I speak of you when in speaking of you I speak nothing but contradiction? For if I say I see you, it is nothing but you seeing yourself. If I say I know you, it is nothing but the knowledge of yourself. If I say I love you, it is nothing, for there is nothing in me can love you, but yourself; and therefore you do but love yourself . . . O, sweet Lord, let me seek Myself – that is Yourself – through the You-ness in me . . .'

He must argue less, and let the golden thread keep extending.

Chapter 10

A faint wind from the river tickled the lime trees as Pastor Hans Hass walked home, with that customary grave and rapt air which masked self-esteem, after the Sunday-morning service.

He had come a long way from the poor farrier's cottage where he had been born. An innate intelligence and restless temperament had carried him first to university, and from there into the arms of the Lutherans – whose infiltration and conquest of Rensburg he had helped to encompass.

His self-esteem was particularly high this morning. His sermon had been taken from a text expounded by no less an authority than Melchior Hoffmann. It was a risk but it had paid off.

He had met that celebrated preacher, visionary and wandering prophet – himself a disciple of Muntzer who had led the peasants in their brave if disastrous war against the Elector of Saxony – when Hoffmann had made his visitation a year or so back to northern Germany.

Hoffmann had lodged for a while in Cologne, and Hass had journeyed to speak with him, hearing at first hand the prophet's conviction that the Second Coming and the Millennium were imminent. It was Hoffmann who had then travelled on to the northern Netherlands and had been responsible for the spread of that particularly energetic form of Anabaptism (literally, 'baptized anew') which was now making its way back to Germany.

Hoffmann himself had returned, passing by Rensburg, and had sent for Hass again on his way to Strasbourg (where he ended his days hung up in a cage). He had made Hass promise that, when the Spirit spoke to him, he would cast off the mantle of Lutheranism and start preaching for the Anabaptists.

Last night, unmistakably, it had happened. It was Saturday night – which was significant, for he was due to preach next morning, and he knew there would be, as there always was for him, a full congregation.

He had been awakened in his bed by a voice which seemed to come from directly over him.

'Hans ... Hans ...'

'Yes,' he whispered, in some fear, for he knew not what it might be. 'Yes, who is it?'

'Preach the letter of the Lord, Hans. The letter is C. The number is V.'

That was all. Hass had struggled up to light a candle, but when he had finally struck the flint and puffed the tinder – there was nothing to see. He had known there would not be. It was the voice of the Spirit.

There was no more sleep for him that night. The number is V, the letter is C. What could it mean? And then he remembered Hoffmann's enthusiasm for the Fifth Epistle of Clement. He had even given him the new German version of it by the humanist Franck.

He turned the pages and found the passage he was looking for. Ah, this would make the townsfolk sit up and take notice! This would shiver the fat-bellies and shudder the shanks of the thin.

There had been scarcely a movement in the church this morning when he had climbed the pulpit and looked out on the sea of faces – yes, they were expecting something today, there was a feeling in the air, angels had been in the city. How different the churches were now, he thought, from the degenerate concourses the Roman idolaters had permitted, nay encouraged – hawkers selling comfits, lovers greeting their ladies with kisses, prostitutes plying their reeking trade! There was none of that now, not a wink or a smile. When he was quite sure they were giving him their total attention, he delivered himself of his chosen text.

'"Shortly after that,"' he started, and then stopped to look around.

You could have heard a hair drop. He was full of theatrical tricks like that, and why not? (For all his university degree, Hass was more demagogue than philosopher.)

'"Nimrod",' he continued. '"Nim-rod".'

He pronounced the two syllables with equal weight so that they became ridiculous, so that the very man whose name it was became transparently absurd.

Still there was not a sound, not even a stifled cough, from the huge congregation. Hass warmed to his theme. He was enjoying this.

'"Shortly after that, Nim-rod began to rule".'

He stopped again and looked about once more, searchingly, catching a little woman's eye at the back, a youth's, an old burgher's, and making them drop those eyes with abashment.

He now adopted a totally matter-of-fact tone.

'My text today is taken from the Fifth Epistle of Clement.'

Few had heard of the Fifth Epistle of Clement, and few cared. It was, as it happened, from a spurious source, probably a forgery. But, to the congregation, it was gospel.

Hass switched to his emphatic style again.

'"Shortly after that, Nimrod began to rule".'

He stopped once again and reverted to his conversational manner.

'You remember Nimrod, don't you? Nimrod was a great hunter. That was what he liked doing – hunting. He didn't like ruling. Oh, no. Even though he was king, the chase was his idea of a good rule. He didn't mind if there were wars or plague or famine. When they said, "Give us bread", Nimrod would say, "Seems like a nice day for a boar hunt."'

People might have been tempted to smile at this point, if it had been any other preacher. But there was something daunting about this young man with his gift of the gab and his eyes that knew what you were thinking.

Satisfied that he now had their attention, Hass completed his text.

'"Shortly after that, Nimrod began to rule and then whoever could manage it got the better of the other. And they started dividing the world up and squabbling about property. Then Mine and Thine began. In the end, people became so wild, they were just like wild beasts. Each wanted to be better and finer than the other, in fact wanted to be his master. Yet God had made all things common – as today we can still enjoy in common air, fire, rain, sun and whatever else some thieving, tyrannical man cannot get hold of and keep for himself . . ."'

He had paused. There was a sudden concerted exhalation of breath at this unmistakable call to revolution, a noise like a giant bellows being squeezed. It was as if, with the sound, something more than air was being let out – a spirit that until expressed was unformed, inchoate, labouring in darkness but now, like the demon in the bottle, it was out and abroad.

Chapter 11

The next day, Monday, the Anabaptists from Holland arrived at the gates. The guards had instructions from the Great Guild to open up for them, and in they streamed, singing hymns. They were escorted towards the town square where the citizens were gathering excitedly. Oh, they had had refugees before, but it had never been quite like this. There was an inescapable feeling that something wonderful, strange, even a little frightening was afoot.

While they waited for the Saints to arrive, the talk ran on Pastor Hass's sermon of the day before.

''e said the early Church held all in common. There was no silver plate and fat abbots then,' said one out-of-work carpenter.

'No, nor taxes either,' said a stranger in a tall hat with half an arrow stuck through it by way of decoration.

'No effing kings and nobles riding the poor, who takes it all like donkeys,' said a bricklayer who'd been to an alehouse.

Suddenly a cry went up from the direction of the Westgate Street:

'They're coming. The Saints. Give them a cheer!'

'I hear they believe in free love,' said a dyer's man, red as a devil from his trade.

The Saints never faltered. With their wagons in their midst they marched, still singing hymns, to where a space had been left for them before the Town Hall. Here Konrad, with Elisabeth at his side – he had been particularly insistent upon the point – was waiting to greet them on the steps.

While they formed up, the people of the town cheered and applauded them as if they had been a victorious army rather than enforced exiles whose crime was that they had caused too much trouble in their own land.

Elisabeth now had a good opportunity to look at these strange people of whom she had heard so much. It was plain to see a similarity between them and the Dutchman who had visited her father's house. They had the same sombre clothes, grave faces and rapt air as he, though none had perhaps quite his bearing or his chilling air of unswerving rightness. She knew that many of them were weavers from Leyden, centre of the cloth industry. Her father had told her that these people had worked alone in their hovels – wool was brought in and material was taken out as and when it suited the merchants – and at a price that suited them too. They were unrepresented by guilds, for guilds could not operate when people worked in so dispersed a manner, at home. They were desperate. And Anabaptism had saved them and given them hope.

'As it must give us all hope and inspiration,' said her father. 'And help us fix our eyes a little more firmly on Heaven and less on frivolities which are ill-suited to times such as these.'

He repeated these sentiments in his speech of welcome. He described them as hard-working, clean-living, decent people driven out of their own country for faults which appeared virtues in his eyes. He urged his fellow-townsmen to listen to them, to learn from them, and maybe even to come to share their shining hope and faith in building a New Jerusalem. Who knew? It might even be here in Rensburg.

Elisabeth, who had put on a new dress for the occasion to do honour to her father, began to feel slightly conspicuous in her frivolity and flummery, and in her nervousness allowed her gaze to wander. She was conscious of eyes watching from the Town Hall – eyes that were not by any means all as overjoyed as her father's purported to be; merchants' eyes that measured profit and loss. If I were one of those, I'd be thinking more prophet than profit, she reflected. There were plenty of poor, out-of-work and hungry people already in the town. Perhaps it might be better not to take in all these Dutchmen but to try to feed and clothe the poor who were already here – people who had cheerfully accepted next to nothing, but who might with some reason become desperate sharing nothing at all.

She wondered whether she might not put this to her father, but it seemed a little late now.

There did seem to be an awful lot of Dutchmen – far more than the hundred or so the man had said; more like four hundred, she thought.

Her father finished his speech to tumultuous applause. The Saints began to look as though they wouldn't mind finding a soup-kitchen and somewhere to get their heads down.

Pastor Hass stepped forward to say a few words.

Chapter 12

Elisabeth, had she been born into another family of her class, would have had the average education of the day. Reading and writing, of course; grammar; a little logic (unteachable to a woman, her father said); a smattering of French (being so near the border with Burgundy); maybe some music – the lute perhaps, or the new virginals; and perhaps some drawing. But she happened to have an exceptional mother, daughter of one of the professors at the University of Paderborn.

The habit of learning is as dominant as blue eyes in a family; and Elisabeth's mother Hilde made it her business to see that her daughter was educated to a proper standard. Though largely confined to her room – she had an extreme weakness of the blood, the doctors said, which made her subject to fainting-spells and occasioned a permanent physical feebleness – she had taught Elisabeth to read at the age of five, and had built upon her knowledge and understanding ever since. Indeed, it was because her mother was so confined that she was able to do it. A fitter woman would have run the house or buried herself with good works.

Hilde lived in her mind, for her daughter.

'But of what use is all this knowledge?' asked her husband, impatiently.

He had been impatient with her ever since he had first known her. She had liked his energy then. He had liked her extraordinary pale beauty. 'Like a water nymph', he used to say. 'Like a pale creature of the pool.' But that was long ago. It had been an arranged marriage anyway – much against her own mother's will.

'Such a waste of your learning,' her mother had said, but her father had been adamant.

'Harting will go far,' he had said. 'Indeed, he has come far already. In these troubled times it's no bad thing to have a grocer in the family. You academics always have this prejudice against trade.'

It was true, her husband had gone far – far in his business and far away from her and whatever tenderness had passed between them in those early days. Ironically, he was now saying the same things about their daughter as her father had said of her. There was a dreadful little rhyme he would keep declaiming with the fatuous look of one who repeats proverbs.

109

'"Too much Latin and too little tatting",' he would utter, sagely. 'Keep her mind clear and fingers busy.'

She would scream if he said it again, if she could find the energy.

For an ordinary daughter of a merchant, then, the list of activities suitable for a young lady would have been severely limited.

At one end there was needlework; at the other there was the Church. The list included an interest in flower arrangement, home economy, and discreet and modest singing. A modest walk might be undertaken, and the making of cordial jellies was countenanced.

Fortunately for Elisabeth, her mother had given her more to occupy her mind than the average Rensburg girl enjoyed, and she had developed an interest in herbs and their curative effects to the point where she was even planning a herbal of local plants, but she was still expected to indulge in flower arrangement, jellies, needlepoint, madrigals, and religion, and this she did with a greater or lesser degree of enthusiasm. 'Religion' perhaps was the wrong word. 'Church' was better, for Church and Religion meant two different things.

Church under the Catholics had been rather a jolly affair. It was a meeting-place, a centre where the young men ogled the pretty girls – Elisabeth herself had been the recipient of more winks and nods than she had had hot custards. Not that she ever encouraged them, but you could not exactly be impervious to them. And they certainly helped liven up the sermons in which the fat priests used to wallow like pigs in their own trough. It was the place where trysts were kept and letters exchanged.

In fact, in a way, the winkers and the oglers and the prostitutes plying for trade and the souvenir sellers and the games of pitch and toss behind the pillars and the children with their hoops and the crying of the babies and the sparrows in the rafters and the gossip and the scandals and the dropping of scarves and the fluttering of hearts and the heaving and sometimes even baring of breasts all made her feel far more at home in God's house than the haranguing of an Anabaptist, who couldn't wait to see you consumed in everlasting clinkers, in a church so rapt you'd think everyone had come there in a stupor. But she didn't like to say so to her father, because he was the man who had helped to bring the foreigners in, and all the town knew it. She had once ventured a comment on the subject and he had gone purpler than a marsh orchid. So she kept her counsel and returned to her herbals and books – there was a new one almost every month which her mother somehow managed to have smuggled into the house – punctuating her reading with visits to the sickroom and walks in the meadows beside the river where the kingfishers didn't seem to have heard of the world's imminent dissolution and the end of things.

It was a strange time, poised, as it seemed, between two orders, its feet in the muddy past, its head in darkening clouds of wrath and justice. It was a strange time; but it was still full of warmth and colour and that sense of quickening expectation that makes plants grow and young girls wake up in the morning feeling unreasonably happy.

She would get up and fling the window wide, and breathe greedily like a carp, puffing out her cheeks and saying, 'I love, love, love . . .'

What did she love? The town, the world, the unknown ... the everything and nothing. Love, love, love . . .

'I hope your father doesn't hear you,' old Frieda told her. 'He'll marry you off as soon as look at you. Fathers don't like to hear that word. He's got plans for you, no doubt.'

'Plans?'

'To marry you off.'

'Marry . . .'

She laughed. The idea was ridiculous, yet somehow pleasing.

'No one would have me,' she said.

'They would.'

'Not me.'

She laughed again at the thought of it.

'What about that devil?' said her nurse.

'Devil?'

'The Dutchman.'

'My father wouldn't want me to marry him? You're joking. Horrid nurse.'

A cloud, bruise-black, was stealing over the sky, from the west, though the sun still shone. Old Frieda crossed herself.

'I expect I'm joking, my lamb.'

'I'm going to marry for love,' Elisabeth announced.

Chapter 13

The path was not all smooth for Konrad and his friends. There were many in the town who grew alarmed at the way things were going.

Of course, it had been fun to watch the Bishop and chapter being humiliated, to see the old clergy ousted and the new Lutherans installed. How those very people had crowed when they were able to claw back all the hard-earned concessions the townsfolk had won in the days of plenty! How vindictive they had been in the time of famine and pestilence! And yet, were not these at least people they knew, who spoke their tongue and understood the local ways? Were they not, invidious though their past had sometimes been, preferable to a city suddenly full of unemployed and desperate foreigners?

In the face of such feeling, the Roman Catholics and the Lutherans joined forces – an unlikely alliance, as some of the older monks called it, but there it was, needs must when the Devil cracks the whip.

Konrad was, of course, held responsible for the admission of the Anabaptists and was cold-shouldered by many in the Town Council who passed resolutions requiring silence on pain of expulsion from the loquacious Hass, whose sermons grew ever more emphatic. But Konrad remained adamant that they had done the right thing in protecting the weak and helpless.

'"Blessed are they",' he quoted in the Chamber, '"blessed are they that delivereth the poor and needy". I have no doubt in my mind, Brothers, that we shall be blessed for what we have undertaken, and the name of Rensburg will be writ large in the annals of Charity. I make no apology for my stand.'

He had been accorded a special visit to the underground meeting-room after the Anabaptists' arrival in the town. Not perhaps quite such a lavish affair as last time but undeniably exciting. Pleasure was now like a drug to him. He had to keep taking it. They had promised him the secret of Adam's way soon.

'As for the preacher Hass,' he continued, 'I doubt whether his disciples would let you near enough his church to turn him out. He is perhaps over-zealous, but there is no denying his godliness. Is that a crime now in our city?'

The Town Council shifted its bottoms.

It did, in fact, achieve the expulsion of some of the lesser Anabaptist preachers, but it was only a temporary triumph. Popular clamour soon drew them back.

As spring gave way to summer, excitement mounted. Fittingly for such a fever in the body politic, the summer turned out to be exceptionally hot. Day after day of blazing sunshine did nothing to cool the ardours of the Anabaptists or allay the anxieties of the more conservative towns-folk. Something was going to happen – you could feel it. A kind of hysteria gripped the city. In the rougher quarter of town, fights broke out. Fanatics rent their garments and prophesied.

It was at this point that the first of the Dutch apostles arrived to take up residence in the town – two men sent directly by the Leader, by David Mosman himself.

Chapter 14

The Anabaptist movement in northern Europe, gathering momentum with the century, had at length become unstoppable. If one leader was overthrown, another immediately took his place – and the prophetic baton of Hoffmann, caged in Strasbourg, had been passed two years before to this Mosman, an erstwhile fishmonger, of Haarlem.

Mosman, however, was a very different creature from Hoffmann. Whereas Hoffmann had preached acquiescence, encouraging his followers to await the Last Days in a state of quiet resignation, Mosman, with his youthful face and white hair, was a firebrand.

'The righteous,' he preached in Haarlem, 'must take up arms. They must fight and hack, hew, slay to prepare the way for the Millennium. It has been revealed to me that the earth must be cleansed of priests and princes. We shall scour the ungodly, Brethren. We shall dash them in pieces like a potter's vessel.'

From Haarlem, he sent out the Apostles to all who believed that the Holy Spirit had descended upon the Anabaptist communities. In each town they baptized huge numbers of adults and ordained bishops with the authority to baptize. Then they moved on, while from the newly converted town, more Apostles sprang to still more communities. It was like Pentecost – or a contagion, depending on how you looked at it.

One of the two Dutch prophets now entering the town was a man known as Elijah. He was a fine, impatient, commanding fellow with a carrying voice and penetrating eyes and a great, black sweep of beard and hair. There were a number of officers like him among the senior Saints – hard, forthright, unforgiving men.

The other man was a Saint apart – not that he couldn't deliver a hell-fire sermon to rival anyone's – but you had the impression that, among the Holy Ones, he was a Watcher. His eyes did not so much look into you as beyond you.

He was a man who had already appeared and reappeared in the town, and would appear and reappear again, for that was the way of him.

Fierens was not his real name at all. That was a name he read once in an alchemical treatise translated from the English on the properties of fire, and had selected for its resonance. Fire, after all, was both consuming and purifying.

His original name, though – which he had long discarded – was

Uitwaarden. He had left it behind many years and miles back. It was an awkward, provincial name and ill suited to a man of destiny.

As he re-entered the Westgate, however, with Elijah at his side, he gave his name once more as Enoch, the name he had used when escorting the first train of immigrants to the appointed city with the Leader.

Brief formalities over, the two newcomers were directed down to the warehouses, where many of the immigrants had been temporarily quartered.

Rumours began to spread.

The significance of the two names was not lost on any who knew their Bible. Elijah and Enoch were the prophets who, according to tradition, should return to Earth as the two witnesses against Antichrist, and whose appearance would herald the second coming.

Nothing happened for a week – and then the pot began to boil. First at one church and then another, communal baptisms started to take place. Hass was one of the first to be rebaptized, and his church featured prominently in subsequent mass events of this nature. Nuns, prosperous laywomen and, in the end, at least a third of the entire adult population, particularly the women, were spattered with holy water and given a new start in the True Way. Hass was made a bishop.

Some of the more impressionable townsfolk started to distribute their goods.

Chapter 15

It was one of the ironies of that time of confusion that aspects of the Religion of Love – particularly its emphasis on sharing and community – should have become so associated with the religion of enmity. For discord was the prophets' game. Although they would, in their milder moments, expostulate that theirs was a crusade of the spirit, that it was *souls* they were about in the run up to the Millennium, there was little doubt that their picture of an earthly kingdom (where all would share the riches of the world) made a direct appeal to the poor, the dispossessed, the simple, the shiftless, the violent, and the criminal; and that force was going to be their means of bringing it to pass.

It was hatred which they stirred up – the hatred of the oppressed (and those that felt themselves oppressed) for their masters. It was hatred that would fuel their machinations . . . hatred that stretched the web in the name of the Almighty . . .

It was still too hot by half and the harvest was parched. Signs of confusion manifested themselves in the city. Fires broke out – not serious, but worrying; fighting around alehouses, disturbances in the stews, break-ins down at the warehouses by the river; dust, a hot and irritating wind, and no sign of a break in the weather . . .

Rioting erupted one evening near the town square. It had begun simply enough with a stall-holder in the market belabouring a gipsy whom he had caught thieving, but it developed into a confrontation between some of the remaining local Catholics and the new Anabaptists. A mendicant monk who happened to be passing by, probably on his way out of Rensburg, became caught up in the fighting, was badly beaten and died. The justices never got to the bottom of it.

The cost of living had gone up as some of the machineries of commerce in the town became disrupted. Those who had money found it was worth less, and those who had little or none simply became more desperate (egged on, of course, by the new preachers).

The local constables found it increasingly hard to cope and made urgent representations to the Council for more recruits. Further fights erupted as the more ruffianly section of the immigrants sought to extend their views on the girls of the town.

Shops started to shut, businesses to go bankrupt. By some stupid oversight, there was, one day, insufficient money in the vaults for the

Town Hall to pay its servants. It was soon rectified, but the rumour spread that the very city was insolvent.

In contrast to this volatility, a general air of sluggishness permeated the working life of the place. People would not work because there seemed to be no point. There was no regeneration of business – why open a shop if the Last Days were in the offing? Interest rates from the usurers went up. Profit went out of the window. Morality declined. If people did not fully understand some aspects of the new creed, they understood enough to know that 'Do what thou wilt' absolved them from most obligations. All the old values seemed to be vanishing. Those who cared, despaired. And those who had been contained by the manners and mores of the past fell into crass apathy or excess. The Church offered no comfort, the State little protection.

Only the Saints remained locked in prayer, seemingly unaware and unconcerned about the perturbations which increased daily around them – or, if they were, taking the disturbances to be proper indications of the world's last chapter.

Chapter 16

Summer appled into autumn, and with the passing of the hot weather, some of the fever seemed to leave the town. The harvest was brought in – a poor one again. Michaelmas came and went. The Anabaptists settled into their quarters and the townsfolk – the many that had remained, either because there was nowhere else to go or because they saw no reason to leave – slowly grew used to the high hats and the nasal ranting and the funny goings-on between some of the extremer members of the new community, although the talk of 'holding all things in common' disturbed a number of the burghers.

Behind the scenes, though, it was anything but quiet. The leader of the two Saints, Enoch, visited Konrad daily, and Elisabeth used to glimpse them talking earnestly over documents and maps spread out in the study, where they were closeted for hours.

It was as well that Elisabeth did not know what they were talking about for, amongst other subjects that were raised, Fierens had indeed expressed interest in herself.

'She is a proper vessel,' he told Konrad, 'such a one as would make a fitting spouse for a Saint. I am preparing the way for the Leader in this city which, it has been shown, shall be Jerusalem, our blest abode . . .'

Konrad swallowed. There was no mistaking what the man meant. He was conscious that his own weakness had led him to expose his daughter to this situation, and he experienced a pang of concern which he quickly stifled. He fixed his mind on the financial side of fatherhood. His ideas on the subject were no different from most of his peers. However much you loved your child, and he did love her (though his love was to some extent merely an extension of his own compulsive personality, his self-obsession), you had, with a daughter, to be stern to be kind. 'A woman is there to serve and bear', his own father used to say. It was no good bringing them up to be wilful. Dynasties were not founded on affections.

'You do not agree?' asked Fierens, looking at him quizzically. 'You think that she is unworthy of a Saint? Or perhaps that a Saint is unworthy of her?'

'Oh, no, not at all,' said Konrad. 'It is just that she is young.'

'So much the better,' replied Fierens. 'She will not have had time to be corrupted. Has she been re-baptized?'

'Ah, no,' said Konrad.

'Then we must make arrangements for it. Bring her tomorrow to St John's Church at noon. Elijah will perform the office.'

'She may not wish to . . .' Konrad floundered; for all his usual arrogance he found it impossible to express his misgivings in the face of Fierens' steely gaze. 'She may not feel ready for such an important step.'

'You must make her ready.'

I shall not feel guilty, Konrad thought, for guilt is the only sin. It may well be that re-baptism is exactly what Elisabeth requires; and what could be more honourable than a match – if that is what the man has in mind – with one of the great men of our time, a Leader of the Latter Day? After all, what is the alternative? That popinjay son of Heinrich the Draper? That oaf of a Ludwig? That pipsqueak of a Peter? Thinking about it made him feel better. He smiled at the Dutchman, fixing his mind on the next meeting of the Adamites.

'I shall see that she is in the church tomorrow even if I have to drag her there kicking and squealing.'

The roughness of the image pleased him, obliterating any sense of weakness.

'Spoken like a Saint,' said Fierens. 'And now let us discuss our stratagem for your appointment as Leader of the Great Council.'

Chapter 17

Elisabeth was aghast when she was told of her impending re-christening. She surprised herself by feeling so strongly on the subject.

'But, Father,' she said. 'I have been christened once. The Church only requires one baptism. I am called Elisabeth after the mother of the Baptist. I have been confirmed.'

'Silence, Daughter,' said Konrad. 'It is your father's will. That is enough.'

'It is your will. It is the Dutchman's will. But is it God's?' she asked, desperation making her bold.

He lifted his hand and struck her on the face. She reeled back, her face blind with tears.

'You dare to argue with me?' he said. 'Go to your room and ask God for forgiveness. I know more about God's will than you do, headstrong girl. See that you are ready for church tomorrow or you will be beaten.'

She stumbled desperately out of the room, leaving him hitting the table with rage. She had seen him in a fury, but never like this. It was as if the Devil had got into him. And yet she remembered him quite clearly playing knucklebones with her and jumping out of her cupboard in the nursery like a jack-in-the-box.

An hour later, he heard a knock at the door. Thinking it might be his daughter come to apologize, he called to her to come in. To his surprise, his wife entered on the arm of Frieda, the old nurse. She looked deathly pale and clung to the lintel for support.

'You?' he exclaimed in surprise. 'What are you doing downstairs?'

He was astonished that she had been able to make the journey at all. With some ill-grace, he rose and helped her towards a chair. For a few moments, she was too exhausted to speak. Konrad gestured to the nurse to leave them, but his wife shook her head and held on to Frieda's arm.

'Well?' he asked, impatiently. 'I am sorry but I am extremely busy at the moment. What with all these new people in the town, I am finding it hard to keep enough supplies. The bean position is totally inadequate. And the Council's meeting at all hours of the day and night.'

He was careful to say night because it covered his nocturnal excursions. He did not have to feel guilty, but there was no point in provoking gossip.

'It is about Elisabeth,' his wife said at last.

His brow darkened.

'What? Has she run snivelling to you?'

'Certainly not. She always comes to me at noon. I saw that she had been crying and asked her why.'

'She told you I wished her to be baptized?'

'And she replied that she had been. It was a good answer, Konrad, and you did wrong to strike her.'

'What?'

He rose to his feet again, his eyes blazing.

'Pray do not exercise yourself, Konrad.'

'Have a care, woman. I know you are sick, but by God I will not be spoken to like this.'

'By God you will, sir,' broke in the nurse. 'This has gone on long enough. The town has gone mad and you along with it. You too were christened and baptized.'

'And re-baptized, woman. Since you are insolent enough to interrupt, you may as well hear it too. I would not ask my daughter to do anything I had not done myself.'

'You?' asked his wife, shocked.

'Some weeks ago. See, I am none the worse off. I have not grown horns.'

'No horns,' muttered the nurse, 'but I dare say a tail.'

There was something in her remark that made him sense she knew something. Had he been followed?

There were eyes all over this town and the old crones' coven oversaw them all. He suddenly grew icy-calm. What was the use of bluster? The world was coming to an end. His household must do as they were told or they must cease to be his household.

'If Elisabeth is not at the church tomorrow,' he told them quietly, 'you will leave my house and take lodgings where you can.'

'You cannot do that,' cried the old nurse. 'The mistress will die.'

'You must make your choice,' said Konrad. 'It is little enough to ask of my daughter. If you take her part, I must simply say I do not wish to live with you. And now, I'm afraid, I have business to attend to.'

Chapter 18

It was to this disturbed city that Julius and Blommardine had come some weeks before on a torrid day of late summer with a cart full of belongings and a trail of dust like the tail of a comet – a portent Julius found both suitable and disquieting. He did not mention it to Blommardine; but then he did not mention very much to his wife. She, unexpectedly, was in high good humour.

'It is here,' she said, as the wagon paused giving them a sudden prospect of the place. 'I can feel it. You'll have to take me out of here feet first.'

He had gazed at the broad river, winding between water meadows, lapping at the wall of the old town with its towers and spires, workshops, warehouses, watergates and weathercocks. Flanked by low, wooded hills, the city of Rensburg looked a sleepy sort of place, and not at all the kind that would evoke Blommardine's enthusiasm.

'Feet first?' he said at last. 'If the Last Days are in the offing, I shall not be in a position to take you anywhere. On Judgement Day, we shall all be in the same boat – or whatever vessel the Almighty sees fit to put at our disposal. The Ship of Fools, perhaps.'

'All right, clever dick. Why do you always have to be so literal? The point is, at last I know what I want to do.'

'What do you want to do?'

'I want to be here.'

'Good.'

They trundled on in silence.

As they neared the city gates, they met several wagons and some riders who had evidently just left the town. They reined up as one of the horsemen approached them.

'Where are you bound?' he asked. 'And whence do you come?'

He was an elderly man, spare and lean, yet with a look of substance about him. Julius guessed that he was some kind of cleric who, for whatever reason, was not wearing the dress of his order.

'We are going to the city,' Julius replied. 'We came from 'sHertogenbosch in Brabant.'

'I should go straight back there if I were you,' said the man.

'I fear we cannot,' said Julius. 'We have sold our house and have made arrangements in the city here.'

'That is too bad,' said the man. 'Are you Roman Catholic?'

'Yes,' said Julius. 'I suppose we are.'

Blommardine, who could put on the most irritatingly plausible display of female modesty, was peeping shyly out at the man and now smiled downward at him, ducking her head like a nun.

'Tell him to stick his head in a hog's turd,' Julius heard her say in his ear.

'The city is lost, at least for the time being,' said the man. 'As far as I can see, it has gone mad. It is a mystery to me why God does not send a thunderbolt to destroy the godless place. It is Sodom and Gomorrah with a smattering of Babylon.'

'Thank you for the warning,' said Julius. 'Where are you going?'

'As far as we can. At any rate as far as Paderborn where I shall make representations to the Prince Bishop. The talk in Rensburg is all of the Last Days. I am not at all sure that they are not right to do so, but not for the reason that they suppose. Such heresies cannot be allowed to remain unpunished.'

'It is a free city, sir, I believe,' chimed in Blommardine, sweetly.

'Free or not,' said the man, 'there is such a thing as evil. The Turk is free, yet he must be chastised. The Albigensians were free, yet they merited a crusade. The Taborites . . .'

'For pity's sake,' said Blommardine, 'we don't need a sermon from a priest who's hocked his robes. Come on, Julius. We don't want to waste half a Last Day talking to this old has-been.'

'Sorry, sir,' said Julius.

'Look to your wife, sir,' said the man. 'She has the demeanour of a witch to me.'

'It's a free city,' said Blommardine pertly. 'I can say what I like.'

'There is no such thing as freedom,' said the man. 'We have the freedom to discover the walls of our prison and you will shortly see what a prison that is. Good day to you.'

'Silly old fart,' said Blommardine, as they watched him ride off.

'It's bad luck your hating people so much,' said Julius.

'It's not my bad luck. It's theirs.'

He wished that she wasn't so ingenious in bed.

Chapter 19

They had put up for a night at an inn and next day took lodgings in Bear Lane near the Church of St Michael. It was not difficult to find accommodation of the better kind in Rensburg, since a number of the wealthier families had moved away. Indeed, one of the advantages of the city which Blommardine was quick to point out was the comparative cheapness of that kind of accommodation. It was only in poorer areas that rents did not diminish.

Soon Julius found a studio, not too close but nearby, up a little side alley over a joiner's shop, with a good north light from a side window giving onto the churchyard, and here he started painting again. It was not the painting that he knew he would soon have to embark upon once more – the riddle that sat at the back of his mind like conscience itself – but work that loosened his arm and exercised his art. The church; mourners among the graves; angels; a portrait of the joiner and his wife, for rent.

Later, he thought, there will be time. I shall unpack the Garden and copy it here upon the wall. For the moment let it lie there in its wrappings.

Even so, now and then, he could feel the power of the thing, blazing under its sackcloth; a light behind a bushel, waiting . . .

Blommardine, meanwhile, made it her business to work her way into the town. Soon she was a complete repository of its recent history and its present politics. She had encountered the black-bearded Dutchman, the prophet Elijah, and appeared favourably impressed.

'I met him in the square,' she said, 'and I asked him to bless me. He noticed the way I talked and asked where I came from. I told him and he said, "Ah, you are Dutch. Then of course you are re-baptized." And when I said no, he told me to come to church tomorrow and he would do it himself. Now there is a man . . .'

She told Julius how impressive, how wise, how burningly brilliant Elijah was, how like Christ he seemed, how completely unlike Julius he appeared to be. Julius, who had been thinking that perhaps the man they had met before the gates was right and that Blommardine really was a witch, was relieved to hear of her new interest. Whether it was in religion or, as he imagined, in the man who propounded it, he did not really care. Blommardine interested was a great deal better than Blommardine bored.

'You should get out and see what's happening here,' she told him. 'Show a bit of interest. He's changing the world.'

'I thought he was finishing it,' said Julius.

'Change, finish, it's all the same, isn't it? Finish is change. Anyway, you can't ignore it.'

'I'm not ignoring it,' said Julius. 'I'm open-minded about it, that's all.'

As a matter of fact, the more he heard about it, the less he believed in this northern End of the World. He could see his tutor in Florence shaking his head and laughing. They had discussed this very subject once. Julius had told him that it was popularly supposed to be billed for 1533.

'Why should it be fifteen hundred and thirty-three years after the birth of Christ? Why not one thousand and thirty-four? Or one thousand? Or two thousand? Or five million and nineteen? Or any number you care to think of? God is not confined by symbols and arbitrary numbers. If he wants to end the world, my guess is he'll shut it up like a book – snap! And there won't be anything anyone can do about it,' said the old man.

'But what about the prophecies, the Bible?'

'Scaremongering. Personal aggrandizement. Propheteering. Anyone can foretell the end and they'll always find reasons why it doesn't happen. And then they say the end will be next year. Or the year after. But I do not understand this need for an end. We are all going to die some-time. That is the end of the world for us. Who needs more end than that? The whole point of our perfectibility is that we should go back to the One our own way, in the time that we have available. If God gives us notice of his intentions in such an obvious way as the catastrophists indicate, it makes it all too easy. The End of the World? Pish. Anyone can be good with a pistol pointed at his head. Do you think God works like that?'

Julius, not for the first time, or the last, wished he were back in the sanity of the South.

There were times, even in his early days here, in this northern fast-ness, surrounded by crazed, gnarled northern people, when he fancied that the very light of Reason was going out. Sometimes he felt that he simply must leave, that he had to escape to the new world of the South again. At other times, he realized that, for whatever reason, his future was here. There was something waiting for him, amongst these extra-ordinary events – Perfect Love, merging and fulfilling – which he would discover nowhere else.

Perhaps Blommardine was right. He should, after all, get out more.

There were sights to be seen, matters to be met, maybe even a commission or two stirring . . . Perfect Love was not going to be encountered in a solitary studio.

Chapter 20

'I'll wager you won't do it,' said Blommardine, a few weeks later. 'Bet you haven't got the balls to do it. You're much too heathen.'

She always referred to his schooling in neo-Platonism as heathen, not that she had ever had the slightest interest in religion. Church, yes, that had always been a favourite diversion. But the intricacies of faith had never been her concern – until now. Now her obsession with the prophet Elijah, a majestic figure (she said) compared with his more shadowy colleague Enoch, had rendered her adamant in the new faith.

'As a matter of fact you are wrong,' replied Julius. 'I'm keenly interested in the rigmarole of these people.'

'It's not a rigmarole. Re-baptism is one of the essential pre-requisites for salvation,' she quoted.

'It is one of the essential pre-requisites for my sketches of the town and record of the times. I intend to be baptized tomorrow.'

'Who needs a record when there will be no history?'

'Suppose you are wrong? Then it will be a record of futility which will be most instructive.'

'I'm not sure I should let you be baptized after all,' said Blommardine. 'It seems to me your attitude's all wrong. It seems to me you're thoroughly disruptive. Elijah told me to look out for people like you.'

She was really throwing herself into this thing, but she didn't carry out her threat to tell the prophet, and next day at noon Julius formed up with forty other people – 'forty for the days Christ spent in the wilderness'; everything had to be symbol-perfect – in the aisle of St John's Church beside the ancient Saxon font wreathed in stone curlicues and serpents which spoke of earlier victories over devils.

Surplices had been distributed and the candidates presented a rather pleasing picture, he thought.

Many of them, by their demeanour and haircut, seemed to be nuns, or ex-nuns (for many had recently been leaving their convents). A minor Saint busied himself up and down while they all waited for Elijah to come from the vestry.

'There is one missing,' he said, 'it is a vexation. We cannot begin until we have forty. Forty for the days Christ spent in the wilderness. Come along, come along. Elijah will blame me if I know Elijah. Ah, there you are, child. Quick, now. You are abominably late. It is wicked to keep the prophet waiting.'

Julius turned to see who had occasioned this outburst, and saw a pale girl with golden hair, wearing a white dress, hurrying towards them from the doorway. There were dark rings under eyes as blue as alkanet which betokened sorrow and perhaps sleeplessness. His first instinct was pity for her. She obviously did not wish to participate in the ceremony but was doing it under duress.

His next instinct was one of recognition. He smiled at her without thinking, but with a tremendous sense of relief. She stared back at him, blue eyes widening, and then looked back at the chivvying little man holding out a surplice – unnecessarily, for she was in white already, but she put it on.

Julius could hardly contain his excitement. All thoughts of his mental record of the ceremony were gone. There was only one reason that he had been brought here. It was to meet the Love for which he had been created and to which he must inevitably incline and cleave until they were one flesh and one soul, the perfect marriage of earth and spirit, lily and dragon (as the alchemists had it), which Ammanati, so many miles away in Florence, sitting under a golden arch with the sunshine of Tuscany streaming behind him, had extolled for him as being the highest state of human happiness and, more, the very End of human existence.

'The Universe was created and is sustained by love – not the love of the brute for that is all earth, nor the love of the Saint for that is all heaven – but the love of the soul which is the perfect bond, partaking of both in due proportion, between the two.'

Hardly daring to look, for happiness, Julius turned again and saw that the girl was standing almost opposite him among the other women. Her eyes were cast down, but he had the impression that she had noticed him. Were the same thoughts stirring in her? Had she experienced the same bright shoot of recognition?

Any further enquiry was interrupted by the arrival of Elijah, who swept in like a thundercloud. He was a proud prophet and, as his acolyte had foretold, he did not like to be kept waiting.

'Who among you was late?' he asked, beetling his brows.

The girl was about to answer, but Julius raised his hand.

'It was I, I'm afraid. I do apologize.'

Sensing that the acolyte was about to contradict him, he launched into a story about a portent he had seen on the way, a cruciform cloud which seemed to be standing over the city while the other clouds moved on.

He told the story with such conviction that the other candidates seemed quite to believe him. He had, after all, been last but one. If people hadn't been so willing to believe, they wouldn't be here now.

The prophet cut him short.

'Very well, then. A vision is a vision. It was doubtless sent to spur you on rather than delay you. Let us now proceed with the reality of re-baptism, for you are all at this time in a state of ungrace. If you died now, now at this moment, you would go to Hell. Quick, then, sharp, then, and let us to the business of salvation.'

The girl stole a little look at him as the service commenced. What did it mean? Puzzlement? Gratitude? Did she now know who he was – the One?

The thought tormented him while Elijah went at it hammer and tongs. His head buzzed so loud with conjecture he thought it would be heard above the singing and the prayers. He sat when he should have kneeled, stood when he should have sat.

'Pay attention, visionary,' snarled the acolyte, yanking at his surplice as the preaching started.

'Thus saith the Lord,' said Elijah, furiously. 'Kings, priests, lords, great ones, must bow to the poorest peasants. Rich men must stoop to poor rogues or else they'll pay for it. Howl, howl, ye nobles, howl honourable, howl ye fitting prelates and rich livers for the miseries that are coming upon you ... For our parts, we that hear the prophet, we will have all things in common, neither will we call anything that we have our own, for we are come to the Last Days when only the elect shall be saved and the remnant shall slide like ordure to the Pit...'

There was more in this vein and it went on for half an hour until suddenly, almost in mid-sentence, he stopped.

'And now,' he said, 'to the ducking-pool.'

A gasp went up from the candidates. What kind of talk was this? Had something gone terribly wrong? Were they betrayed to the torturer? Even Julius blanched slightly. You didn't joke about such things.

'Ah, I see you twitch,' said Elijah. 'You are puppets at the end of the string of sin. Guilt makes you stir and jump, or else of what are you afraid? Any witches here?'

There was no movement. The surpliced ranks seemed carved out of candle-wax.

'Very well, then,' continued Elijah, 'do not then be alarmed when I speak of the font as the ducking-pool. For as the ducking-pool proves or disproves guilt, so will this holy water find out your heart, and you will discover, as it touches your forehead, that it soothes you like balm of Gilead or burns like squill, eating into the very fabric of your soul. Come forward, then. Ladies first...'

There was something so grotesquely styleless about his 'ladies first' – had the man been reading Castiglione? – that Julius almost burst out laughing. It revealed the official under the Anabaptist carapace. What had he been before? A town-hall witch-ducker? He noticed the girl looking at him again, a slight frown wrinkling her fine brow, making a little pucker above the line of her nose. He looked back at her, communicating devotion. She moved forward to be splashed.

He wondered, for a moment, when it came to his turn, whether the water would indeed scald his guilty, unbelieving spirit – all the guiltier because he was married and had no business to be in love with a young girl. But the holy liquid merely dribbled down his cheeks, leaving one drop which clung tentatively to the tip of his nostril, which he did not like to brush away in the face of Elijah's baleful glare.

It was true, one candidate, a nervous young man with a face like a sheep, did fall to the ground clutching his head and uttering the most piteous shrieks, but Elijah did not seem to take him seriously.

'It is the Devil coming out. He will be well enough by and by. I bid you be gone, Beelzebub,' he admonished. Julius had the feeling that the youth had been briefed to enliven the proceedings in this manner.

When the ceremony was over and another hymn sung – the tune and words were unknown to Julius and seemed to take the form more of a popular song than of the good old hymns that he had been brought up on – the Saint dismissed them with a threat and a blessing.

Julius could understand Blommardine's obsession with the fellow. He was her father over again – rigorous, fierce, utterly insensitive to her armoury of subtle shafts and barbs, bullying, straight as a stock-pot, a long, hard, cruel, stern, tyrannical, exacting, bearded, glittering-eyed, bone-crunching, gab-gifted quintain of a fellow.

Julius walked out of the church into the late-autumn sunlight. Elijah had for some reason delayed the fair-haired girl and was talking to her in the porch. Julius could not deduce the reason. She had seemed to grow paler still, and swayed imperceptibly as the water had splashed her – perhaps the prophet had noticed and was proposing a course of special instruction. Julius shuddered at the thought. It was like a moth instructing a Clouded Yellow.

Finally, the preacher seemed to ask a question. She shook her head, and they set off together through the churchyard.

Julius pretended to be deeply involved with a gravestone as they passed though, again, he knew she was looking at him. When they were safely out through the lych-gate, he set off in direct pursuit. Surely, he thought, she can't be going back to his quarters. It would be insupportable. I should have to do something.

Their steps turned, however, towards the more prosperous quarter of the town, and he sensed that the prophet would not be living in these parts. His place would be with his people.

As the little procession progressed, the follower, as so often, had the feeling that he himself was being followed. It was absurd, of course, but he turned round once or twice to make sure he was alone.

Quite soon, the girl and her companion stopped outside a large house in Broad Street. Julius had the distinct feeling during the walk – it wasn't, he told himself, that his soul's desire was clouding his judgement – that the girl wanted to be rid of the man. And now he knew it to be true; with a quick shake of the head and a polite little bob, she opened the front door and almost ran into the house, shutting the oak in the man's face.

The Saint paused for a moment and then walked back down the street. Soon he began to wave his arms about, fending something off that seemed to be bearing down upon him.

'Wail ye nobles and ye rich . . . wail . . . give all away . . . let nothing be hoarded . . . Crouch ye before the Judgement . . . blood on this wicked city . . . Repent and re-distribute . . .'

One or two heads appeared at windows but distribution seemed to be slow in coming.

'Wonderful, isn't he?' said Blommardine, appearing beside him.

So, it had been his wife who had been following him. He might have known. He did not answer her for a moment. He was still too dazed by the vision of perfection, of his own perfectibility. At least he knew where the girl lived. He could find out who she was and do great deeds for her. He felt like singing.

'"Come hither, love, to me",' he warbled.

'You don't have to be sarcastic,' Blommardine said. 'I saw you following them. You're jealous, aren't you? But why should a sparrow be jealous of an eagle? You're in a different class, dear. Relax. Don't try so hard. You'll get a rupture.'

'He seemed to be . . . interested in someone else,' Julius ventured, to annoy her, though even the suggestion made him shudder.

'That little tart!'

Blommardine tossed her head contemptuously.

'She didn't seem like that.'

'All women are tarts when they want to be.'

'Oh.'

'Anyway, don't get the hots for her. Elijah's only interested in her because Enoch's got his eye on her. Enoch's going to get his holy rod up that one, fish-face.'

An icy hand, colder than font-water, gripped Julius's heart, but he dared not show his concern to his wife. She would never let him forget it.

'You do have the most obnoxious way of putting things,' he said, lightly. 'I should put you in the stocks for a scold.'

'Chance would be a fine thing,' she said. 'Anyway, if you did, I should probably turn you into a cockroach.'

When she said these things, he had the curious feeling that she was not joking.

What was he doing here in this place, this life? It was like a dream that could slide at any moment into nightmare.

Chapter 21

Events had taken the Guild Council by surprise. It wasn't used to moving fast and its leader, Folz, was patently not up to the pressures of the moment.

'I keep getting these headaches,' he told Konrad. 'I really don't think I can take very much more of this. My wife says she never sees me.'

'It must be a tremendous strain,' murmured Konrad, sympathetically.

He had been told that certain decoctions had been put, as he had instructed, into Folz's wine. Many other leading members of the Council had had similar refreshment. There was a general feeling of panic about. Subsequent to the expulsion of bishop and chapter, much extra administration had fallen on the Council. This could have been coped with, but recent developments in the city had put extra pressure on its system and on its controllers. There was undoubtedly going to be a shortage of food, due to extra mouths, brigandage and bad harvest. This much was certain. Worse still, however, was all the mess, legal and fiscal, that resulted from the egalitarian preaching of the Anabaptists. Their creed appealed in varying ways at different social levels.

There were guild members who suddenly recanted their usury and cancelled all debts that were due to them. There were others who welshed on all money that they owed. Some prosperous people, inspired by a daily regime of impassioned precept, began to live as loving brethren, sharing all that they had, abstaining from luxury, donating all excess to the needy. Very soon, in this way, many became needy themselves – and rejoiced to do so – though it put an extra burden on the city.

At the same time, news of the events in Rensburg spread far and wide among the homeless, the drifters, the unemployed and the unemployable.

'And so they came, the Dutch and the Friesians and scoundrels from all parts who had never settled anywhere . . . fugitives, exiles, criminals . . . people who, having run through the fortunes of their parents, were earning nothing by their own industry . . . who having learnt from their earliest years to live in idleness, had saddled themselves with debts; who hated the clergy not for what was told of their religion but for what was told of their wealth, and who themselves pretended to practise community of goods like the Apostles – until, growing weary of poverty, they thought of plundering and robbing the clergy and richer burghers.'

That was an exiled monk's description of the scene.

There were still some people in the city too who could see only too clearly what was happening, but none appeared able to put a stop to the madness. And, of course, the majority of the population now regarded the developments more and more favourably. In their view, the rule of the Saints could not start soon enough.

As Christmas – or Christ-tide as the Anabaptists insisted on calling it – approached, the government of the city resembled more and more the antics of a headless chicken, now scuttling this way, and now that.

The brain and nervous system simply could not cope with the problems that were daily heaped upon it. Some Heads of Guilds called for a return of the Bishop, any bishop. Others envisaged a town council with more draconian powers. It was at this stage, with the first snow falling, that Konrad (with Fierens ever quietly at his elbow) made his move. It had been noticed by the more orderly-minded of his colleagues that his particular province – the city's Commissariat – had been especially well run. (It had been decided some weeks earlier that certain people, versed in specialist areas, should take over civic responsibility in those departments.)

It was known that food supplies were short, but Konrad, by ingenious purchasing and careful husbandry, had been able to build up at least sufficient stocks of bare essentials to last them through the winter. Where he obtained them from and where he kept them were his own secrets. Indeed, it was sometimes said that Konrad held the city by the stomach. His colleagues did not necessarily like it, but they were grateful that there were any supplies at all. The idea of food shortages – and consequent riots – with all these people in the city, simply didn't bear thinking about.

'Brothers,' said Konrad, standing up in the Great Guilds meeting, after a particularly feeble discussion about the risk of cholera breaking out due to the influx of refugees, 'it seems to me that our Council is having too much demanded of it. We are guild members, businessmen, not politicians. Wouldn't we all, if we could, go back to our shops and our trades and let the city be run by such as enjoyed talking of water supplies and drains and leper hospitals? I know I for one would gladly forgo this everlasting headache . . .'

'And I . . .' echoed Folz.

'And I . . .' agreed another recipient of the tincture.

Soon most of the Council were nodding their heads and vowing that they were thoroughly sick of the responsibility for all these new people in the town. It was unfair. It was not what the Great Guild was about.

'I agree, Brothers,' said Konrad, 'and I think we should accept Councillor Folz's resignation as Master . . .'

'What?' spluttered Folz. 'I didn't offer my resignation.'

134

'Oh, but you did,' said Konrad. 'You said you would gladly forgo it. I have heard you say so many times, and now you stated it quite clearly. I think we should let him go, Brothers, with the greatest reluctance . . .'

'Hear, hear,' said the Master of the Apothecaries, who had never liked Folz and to whom Konrad had given some medicinal spices. 'With the greatest reluctance.'

Others joined in. Folz looked both indignant and relieved.

'Well, really, I . . . don't know what to say.'

'Say nothing, thou good and faithful servant,' advised Konrad. 'We all know the sacrifices you have made. And now we must think of an alternative. No . . .' He raised his hand. '. . . not simply an alternative Leader but an alternative Council. We know what a cipher the Town Council has been in our recent troubles. The guilds have run the town. But now we must open our Guild Council up to deal with this emergency. Some of us, of course, must be on it. We need to safeguard our interests. Perhaps indeed we should have one of our fraternity as Leader. I would be very happy to do that. It will be a burden but I feel responsible for bringing these poor people into the city and I must shoulder that responsibility to help bring good out of it for all of us. Our Master must step down – he has been looking unwell – and I shall replace him. It is fitting that the Master of the Great Council should also be a Grocer at this time of shortages. Are we agreed?'

It was unheard of for a prospective Grand Master to propose himself. The Masters of the Guilds looked at each other helplessly. They had more or less lost the power of decision.

'I think we should do as he suggests,' said the Master of the Apothecaries, thinking about the consignment of Grains of Paradise that Konrad had proposed for him. 'And I will gladly serve on the new Council at considerable personal inconvenience.'

Others nodded.

'But of what else shall the new Council be formed?' asked the Master of the Skinners, a small, vole-like man with a penchant for Franconian wine which Konrad had taken the trouble to gratify.

'It seems clear to me,' said Konrad, 'that we must have some of our new friends with us. Some of those who speak so eloquently from the pulpit should be given the opportunity to be heard in Council. Not that we want them to have a majority, for we of the Old Rensburg do not want to lose control. But I fear that if we do not give them a voice, it will become a source of grievance, even of civil disturbance amongst their followers. Now, shall we have a vote? I may say that, in the event of an adverse outcome, I shall have to stand down from my responsibility on the Commissariat, not that I would in any way like to influence the decision.'

He did not need to explain the threat that was latent in his words. If he stood down, some of the supplies that he had in secret store might mysteriously not manifest themselves at the moment of need.

The vote, however, went his way. The Guild Council was re-formed with six Guild Members (four of them Konrad's men), four minor nobles who had always resented the fact that they had not been members of the erstwhile chapter, and five representatives of the Anabaptists.

What the guilds did not know was that four of their appointed members and two of the nobles had already been re-baptized.

Nobody thought to inform the Town Council or the Burgomaster, as a courtesy, of the formation of the new Guild Council; let them wait; it was a measure of the impatience with which their office was now regarded . . .

Chapter 22

It was time at last. He could put it off no more. The picture wrapped
– no, not just wrapped, swaddled like a baby in careful cloth – lay against
the wall where it had been stowed when he first arrived, and where it
had been quietly but insistently calling to him every day for attention.
Now, he thought, touched with this love, I can do it. He could feel
parts of his mind, his heart, unfolding like a rescued rose. Once I can
understand the happiness, he thought, I shall comprehend the
unfinished desolation.

He set aside the self-portrait he'd been working on and picked the
picture up, setting it on a table and removing its covers. At last it lay
there, glowing up at him, warm with life.

It was only a copy, he knew; but it still had that remarkable living
quality he had first noted in the chapel. This was not a picture; it was
an existence.

He knew what he was going to do with it. The wall had already been
prepared. He was going to paint it as a mural in the studio – larger
than life-size – so that it would be part of his every day. Then, surely,
the secret would be borne in upon him.

He gazed at it again, breathing it in. It seemed incredible that so
much detail could have been so accurately reproduced without losing
either intricacy or that sense of portending presence. But it had been
done with that same strange facility that had been so much a part of
the old man's later work. Indeed, it had been said 'he had angels and
devils working for him'.

Here it lay now, faithfully transcribed and looking to him as he gazed
at it as though it were pristine, never before seen.

He peered at the central panel as the witches do, shutting out all
thought, letting it fill his mind.

It seemed to him that there were three stages to the panel. First, the
foreground, where a curious kind of tranquil carnality reigned and where
– apart from a bright-eyed man in the lower right-hand corner who
was, it seemed, the only clothed figure in the picture, peeking out and
pointing to the beautiful bubble-mouthed girl reclining in a trance in
front of him – women were generally predominant.

Women – crowned with fruit; naked apart from the occasional curious vegetably, feathery integument that enwrapped one or two of

them; cartwheeling, comforting, tender, carnal, innocent, adept, experienced . . .

There were birds in this first stage, too, a procession of them – a robin, a duck, a bullfinch, a kingfisher, seeming almost to come from the Paradise to their left, one of them feeding refreshing grapes to the man beneath him in the throes of death.

There was a huge tortoiseshell butterfly sucking at a great thistle, which held in its bell-shaped root another group of people in which another dying man was being tended by two companions, one of them feeling his pulse.

Again, thought Julius, stealing a glance at the left-hand panel, that pulse which Christ in the first panel is feeling on his newly fashioned Eve. And butterflies, didn't they feature in Ovid's *Metamorphoses*, studied so earnestly in the Academy in Florence? A butterfly with its strange life-history, was it not a symbol of immortality?

Another image caught his eye. A young man was sticking a bunch of flowers up his companion's anus. It should have been ridiculous, and yet it seemed curiously natural, as if bearing out what his master Bosch had told him about the human body.

'Forget what the preachers tell you,' he had said, 'about the body with its functions. What is that woman you so lust after? A stinking bag of slime and ordure. That's what they tell you. But I tell you, boy, the body is wondrous, alchemical, a curious engine which produces fire and thought from dead meat, grass and water.'

Julius had attended, at first with some queasiness, an anatomy lesson (which included a rare dissection) in Florence, and had indeed come to marvel at the bulbs and bladders, the filaments and bellows, the tubes and valves that were necessary for thought to function . . .

And here, in the picture, as if to echo the idea, were strange edifices, portals, bulbs, barrels, strange swollen-veined fruits . . . a fish, heavy with roe, beside a third expiring man.

The men expired. There were no women in decline. And because they dominated the foreground, they dominated the picture . . . although behind them, in the middle ground, the men on their strange animal steeds surged about and about the pool . . . there was the force of life, the energy . . . and the girls were playing in the water . . . while beyond . . .

His concentration wandered and he found himself thinking about Elisabeth. Where was she? How was he going to arrange a meeting? Why did he have to be married?

Come, come. Enough of whining, he told himself. And enough of puzzling, for today. Some painting now, and perhaps a glass of wine later – if I can find one in this godforsaken town.

Chapter 23

She had noticed him, of course. How could you fail to notice someone who looked at you as if you were more important than the Last Thing itself. And when he had made that excuse for her lateness, taking the blame on himself just when she was almost fainting with anxiety and mortification . . . it had been unbelievably chivalrous. Of course, her tardiness had been entirely her fault. She simply could not make herself hurry for such an invidious ceremony. And yet she had to do it because she could not bear to see her mother so distressed. To be threatened with eviction by your own husband! It was disgraceful. She hated her father for what he had said. And, though her nurse had used more circumspect language, she knew that Frieda was disgusted with him too.

So when this young man had stood up and offered himself to the preacher's wrath, her heart had gone out to him. It was gallantry of a quite Round Table kind. And then he had followed her home while the terrible Elijah had catechized her about her mode of life . . . And he himself had been pursued by a small shadowy figure in black . . . It was all most mysterious – perhaps a little disturbing – but on the whole she felt pleased by such interest. It was better than being lectured on the Revelations by a wild-eyed baptizer.

She had the strangest suspicion that her father was going to suggest her betrothal to the other prophet, Enoch. Things seemed to be pointing that way.

Normally, girls of nineteen in Rensburg could have expected a marriage to be arranged for them, but somehow Elisabeth had never imagined it could happen to her. She had half-thought of becoming a nun for, in the convent, she could have continued her studies – and, though she was a healthy girl, with a figure that had already excited admiration among the young men of the town, and given her some private pleasure, she was fastidious when it came to the notion of sharing it with Tom, Dick or Hairy, and rather than that she would go to a nunnery.

This escape route, however, had been cut off by the latest events in Rensburg. The convents had either been closed or taken over by the Anabaptists. She could hardly run to such a place to evade one of the heads of the movement.

The best thing would be an alternative candidate – someone of whom she approved and who could not be faulted by her father; or, if he did object, someone with whom she could run away. But then, again, she couldn't run away and leave her mother lying sick and helpless. After her father's latest outburst, she did not trust him to continue in kindness towards her. Perhaps he would behave like the English King, and try to shuffle her off. At least he wouldn't have to change his creed to do it. It was changed already!

Her mother, as if in recognition of her plight, now relieved her of that care by suddenly growing very much weaker. It was clear now that the end, so long delayed, could only be a matter of a week or so away.

Elisabeth spent most of the days and half the night in the sickroom, taking it in turns with old Frieda, to sit up and watch over the dying woman.

'Don't die, Mother,' she implored once when she thought she was sleeping. 'What will I do without you?'

But the eyes opened wide and a little smile played on her pale lips.

'I'm pipping the Last Days to the post,' she said. 'Who knows what will happen if it's the End of Everything? Maybe we'll all meet up a day or two later and watch Frieda eat dumplings in Paradise.'

Frieda's fondness for the delicacy was a standing joke between them.

'But supposing there isn't anything? Not anything at all?'

She looked round furtively. Such speculations weren't encouraged whichever Church you belonged to in Rensburg.

'Then they're all going to look rather silly,' said her mother, sinking back on her pillow and closing her eyes again.

'Mother,' said Elisabeth, softly, urgently. 'Mother, I think I'm in love.'

But the tired mind was drifting away, washed further and further out by each faint ripple of a heartbeat.

Chapter 24

Fierens had not enjoyed success in early life. His parents were a peasant-girl from Bois le Duc and the mayor of a local village. They were not married, although his father had a wife.

His father soon died in a local outbreak of fever; his mother suffered from delusions, and took to mopping and mowing, and the boy was placed in the care of the parish, and sent to school.

Though developing a keen interest in the stage, he did not take kindly to instruction and began to play truant. He was beaten several times, but at length, by luck and plausibility – he could be extremely persuasive when he wished to be – he wheedled his way into the favours of an old pastry cook and his wife who took him on as one of their apprentices.

He was unpopular with the other lads for he was always stirring things up – everything that was, except the pastry; he did not seem very keen on that. But he was already adept at politics, setting one faction against another and making sure he was on the winning side. He had no capacity for friendship and esteemed people – rather too obviously – merely in terms of how much value they could be to him.

Perversely, the old pastry couple regarded him as their favourite. They had no son and it seemed they might very well have left the business to him; but one of the other boys, happening to find a journal that he kept, showed it to the old dears and Fierens was out on his ear that afternoon. It seemed that he referred to them as the Old Pratsy Cocks and, in a memorable passage, made a burlesque of their bedroom habits.

It was unwise perhaps of Fierens to keep a journal at all; but a man who confides in no one is tempted to intimacy with that best friend of the solitary, a sheet of paper. It was his folly to leave his best friend somewhere where it might be found and used to destroy him. But he was young. And though he continued to keep making notes, he never made the same mistake again. He had his revenge on the Old Pratsy Cocks by inserting, before he left, a dollop of pig-shit into the mix for the custard delights. It amused him to hear it pronounced more than usually savoury.

For the next four years, he scratched a living, sleeping in cheap lodgings and jobbing by day in the less particular pastry shops of the area. He would not have been a good pastry cook even if he had been diligent. Food, for him, rather like people, was there to be used. It was not required that he should like it (though he drew the line at eating pig-shit himself).

This was hardly the attitude of an incipient meister of his craft. Finally, at the age of twenty-three, he set up in business himself. Not surprisingly, he failed. He blamed a conspiracy of the rich. He was out on the street again.

Nothing seemed to go right for him. And yet and yet . . . There was always something waiting in front of him; he knew it. It kept him going when his next employer threw him out. It kept him going when his tart became pregnant – not that he normally cared, but she was the boss's daughter, which was why he was ejected.

Not his fault. He was a handsome fellow. The girls liked him. But he found that kind of thing much too limited. 'I love you, shall we get married?'

No, we shall not get married if we can help it. There is something more which will wind me out of this custard pie of a life.

And then he rediscovered the theatre. At school, he had always liked watching the mystery plays and the pageants, the floats in the guild processions, the mummeries and the charades, the dances and the antics, but he had to give all that up until one fine day a master-baker pointed at him and said, 'You', 'Who me?', 'You've drawn the short straw', and told him he'd got the job of putting together the Bakers' Diversion in the annual procession.

It was a world of its own – a land of otherwise – complete with dispensable costumes and props, characters and acting, laughter and tears (especially he liked tears), murder and mayhem . . . above all it was a world that, however prone to panic and unforeseen catastrophe (the wheeled stage collapsed halfway through the bakers' offering, marring what was otherwise judged to be a hit), could for the most part be ordered to your will. You could play God in the theatre – sometimes literally, of course, for many of the themes were biblical. You could feel on very close terms with God if you were writing, directing and playing Him, say, in your version of *Lubber the Sheep-Stealer*. You could begin to understand what it must be like to be God Himself . . .

It gave him a taste for something he could not express, but it made pastry cooking seem flat indeed; and yet there was nothing else to do. He had to make a living. At the same time, it was this very business of making a living which imprisoned a man, made him just another little ratchet in the mill. He would have liked to have gone on play-writing and acting all his life, because there he could feel free. He could feel invention taking him like a leaf and whirling him up in the air. What use was it when his only duty was to mix the dough and prick the biscuits? He knew he could order these people, bend them and shape them like gingerbread.

He was soon sacked by another and then another master-baker, and once more he walked the streets.

It was during this rootless existence, in Leyden – a town that was experiencing a depression – that he began to hear wild talk in the estaminets about property and money and food being the right of all, not just of the rich, and that it was the duty of the faithful to appropriate such things as and when they should want them. This was the kind of talk that he had been waiting all his life to hear. It sounded just the sort of trouble he could use.

'Excuse me, Brother,' he said one day to a young man who had been discussing such matters with a couple of friends, 'where do you get all this clap-trap from?'

He didn't want to sound too interested in case there were informers around. A man had been thrown off the bridge into the canal only two days ago, and prodded until he drowned, just because he said, over a pot of ale, that he didn't believe in Purgatory. That was the way things were in Leyden. Fierens had no intention of ending up waterlogged. He was a vessel waiting to be filled. A cause, a purpose, a calling, that was his predestined bellyful, not muddy canal water.

But there was something stirring here, he could sense it.

'It's not clap-trap,' said the man. 'Who asked you, anyway?'

'All right, it's not clap-trap. Where can I find out more?'

'Here. You're not one of them informers, are you?'

'Put it like this,' said Fierens, sizing the man up, 'I don't believe in Purgatory. Do you?'

'No,' said the man. 'I'm blest if I do. It's just a trick to line the pockets of the clergymen. Here, you ought to go and hear old Mosman preach – he's the leader of them. Hear him read the Dutch Bible. He's a regular bibellezer.'

'Where?'

The man gave him the address of a warehouse used for such meetings.

'Thank you. I shall go there now.'

'Here,' said the man. 'Don't I know you from somewhere?'

'Never met you before in my life,' said Fierens, congratulating himself for having grown a beard.

His companion, by some significant coincidence, was the boy who had shown his day-book to the Pratsy Cocks. On his way to the warehouse, Fierens dropped into the Bishop's office and reported the man for heresy.

'Doesn't believe in Purgatory,' he said. 'Can't fail to spot him. He's a pastry cook. Doublet's all white down one sleeve where he's rubbed against a flour barrel.'

Not half as white as his face was going to be when he felt that hand on his shoulder, or when he'd been bobbed about in the canal all afternoon, thought Fierens. A good scene that would be. It was already written in his mind.

The service was in full swing when Fierens arrived at the building. He was surprised to find that it was packed. The congregation was singing an unfamiliar hymn in Dutch. He stood at the back and pretended to sing too. The singing stopped and a preacher with a young face surrounded by silver hair began to mount a makeshift pulpit.

'Your name, stranger,' said a voice beside him. 'We don't want snoopers who aren't going to join in.'

Fierens opened his mouth but the man in the pulpit spoke first.

'Faith,' he said. 'F ... A ... I ... T ... H. A single word. An enormous word. What does it mean? I will tell you. It means all the difference between Hell ... and do I have to tell you about Hell? The torment of the fire that never dies, the constant and bitter regret, the loss, the absence, the darkness, the longing that can never be fulfilled, the hopelessness, the despair, the horrible cold, the loathsome worms, the stench, the hunger, the filth, the desperate cries, the gnawing misery, the sight of loved ones ... your children ... little ones, consumed and never burnt ... No, no. You know about Hell ... And you are bound for it. You, and you, and you. Each one of you. And you know about Hell for it is good to know where you are going. Faith ... it means all the difference between Hell which you know about ... and salvation ...'

'Your name, stranger,' said the voice again.

'Oh, Fierens,' he told him impatiently, not even bothering, as would have been prudent, to give a false one. (Uitwaarden had long since disappeared.)

He was rapt, enchanted, overmastered. Here was the fire that would fill the belly and burn on. No wonder his life had seemed so vacantly pointless. He had been waiting for this moment, this revelation, this point of power. Acting, his highest joy, was low beside this God-talk.

'Save us,' cried a woman in the congregation.

The cry was taken.

'Save us, save us.'

'I cannot,' cried the silver-haired preacher. 'I cannot. Nay, I would not if I could. For only by yourself can you be saved. Only by Faith shall you reach Heaven. F ... A ... I ... T ... H. And what is Faith? Can anyone tell me?'

The crowd in the packed warehouse was hanging on every word. Fierens could feel the strength emanating from the man, controlling and holding, turning this way and that, every one to his one way. But Fierens could see something else which moved him more than the harangue. He could see an invisible thread of silver that came down from the roof, entering the preacher's head just behind the cranium. If the crowd was composed of puppets pulled on wires of silver sound, the preacher himself was an angel. It was to angelhood that he, Fierens, must now aspire – a straight line to God. His study must be to spin and extend his own thread – somehow he knew it must be a golden one. He must become God's spider and draw the little flies into the golden web of salvation.

All this came to him instinctively. He did not have to think it out. It happened in an instant, even as the people were blurting out their definitions of F ... A ... I ... T ... H. His moment of inspiration passed, leaving him dizzy. He leant against a beam and heard the more educated members of the crowd – there were some of monkish appearance who had, it seemed, broken their vows – showing off their Latin.

'It is *credere deum*,' said one. 'It is a belief in the existence of God.'

'It is *credere deo*,' said another. 'It is the acceptance of the Holy Scriptures.'

'Above all,' cried a third, 'it is *credere in deum*, which is the saving faith itself.'

The rest of the crowd fell silent at these evidently learned suggestions, but the preacher, it seemed, was not impressed.

'Pig-shit,' he shouted.

The vernacular rebuke impressed the crowd. There was a momentary ripple of laughter. Fierens took the particular form of excreta mentioned to be a sign.

'Silence,' called the preacher. 'The Scriptures say Jesus wept, but we never hear of his laughter. Laughter is the Devil's work. Groan, if you like, weep by all means. Prostrate yourselves on the floor and gibber with terror. But keep your laughter locked and your silly simpering to yourselves. For the time is very near ... nearer than any of you imagine ... when all must be called to account. We have had the year 1500 *anno domini*. There is only allotted the extra years of Christ's life on Earth; that is thirty-three. We have but two years to prepare ourselves. Now, will you close your faces and be earnest? Do you want to live or do you want to die?'

'Live, Master,' shouted the crowd. 'We want to live. Tell us of faith.'

'Credo this, credo that, credo my sainted backside. This is Popish obscenity to cloak the truth with lewd Latin. Until now you have not had a faith ...'

He looked very hard at the ex-clerics, who cowered in their clogs. Their neighbours also turned to stare at them.

'Sorry, sorry,' they mumbled.

'Until now, you have not had a faith. You have been in despair. You couldn't be saved with the sort of faith you've had up till now. Oh, holy faith, you have been slumbering. Your *credo in deo*, your creed – is that your faith? It's a sham, it's an historical faith . . .'

And so he went on for an hour – exhorting, bullying, menacing, cajoling and wheedling until the crowd was in an ecstasy of faithfulness. But still the preacher wasn't satisfied. It was a performance beyond any that Fierens had witnessed.

'Oh, I know you,' he said. 'You're full of it now. Dripping wouldn't melt in your mouth. But you'll go home and you'll start thinking foul thoughts, you will cog and croak and snort, and your faith will drop away. You will take it off like your best clothes and get into your greasy ways again for everyday. But I tell you, get yourselves ready. Stay in your best clothes. Wear your faith like your skin, for the Bridegroom cometh. Meanwhile, as we see, Antichrist himself stalks the land. Rains of milk and blood, stains, famines, plagues – black death and French sickness which, I remind you, started here in 1500 (in case you think that date is not significant) – monstrous births, a veritable plague of them we hear from Germany, open graves, witches, wars, invasions of infidels . . . these are all the precursors of the End. Make haste. Be ready. Watch and pray. Keep the faith. Look very closely at the unrighteous. Mark them. Their days are numbered. The Path of the Second Coming must be smoothed. Ignore the law if it is not God's. Mark the enemy. Sharpen your swords. Look to your shield and buckler. Blood must be shed before tears can be dried. Our next meeting will be held here at six o'clock tomorrow. And now let us sing "God is with me, God is in me" to the tune of "Old Zeeland".'

As the gathering dispersed, Fierens waited for the preacher to detach himself from the little knot of admirers who lingered around him. At last the moment came. He stepped forward.

'I am Fierens,' he said. 'I have come to save and be saved. I am both text and word.'

The preacher, Mosman, stared at him from under beetlingly dark eyebrows – all the darker-seeming under that silver hair. He was a very tall man, half a head higher than Fierens, and of martial presence. His whole demeanour was that of a John the Baptist.

'"A Jew",' he said at last, '"begets the Beast on his own daughter . . . it circumcises itself . . ."'

'"It circumcises itself",' responded Fierens promptly, the words forming from somewhere on his tongue, '"and triumphs over those who deny it as they are sawn, burned, crucified or buried alive".'

'It is good,' said Mosman. 'You know the Enemy. Now we must prepare you for the Battle.'

In the days that followed, Fierens devoted himself to the study that Mosman prescribed. Although in the past he had had little interest in religion, it now filled his life. He was soon as adept at a text as the

Leader himself, and could slug it out in disputation with the best of them.

Four weeks after that first meeting, it was considered that he was ready for re-baptism. The service was conducted by Mosman himself and, as Fierens emerged dripping from the water, you could almost hear the endorsement on the Leader's lips: 'This is my beloved son.' There was, however, no dove in his church – only one of the old town ravens sitting up in the rafters and croaking in ominous response.

There was little jealousy among the Saints. Fierens was so clearly predestined for greatness. And all the time he could feel the golden yolk of his destiny beginning to multiply, to form, to hatch . . .

Chapter 25

Winter fell early and with exceptional severity that year. The river froze. Birds dropped dead from the sky.

Thanks to Konrad's careful husbandry, there was no immediate shortage of food, but the cost of keeping the Anabaptists and their followers warm and victualled was becoming an increasingly irksome burden.

Grumblings began to be heard, and scuffles broke out as irate shop-keepers refused to take the tokens that the Great Council had issued to the visitors.

Julius and Blommardine were sheltered from many of these pertur-bations, being comparatively prosperous as well as citizens of another state. Other countries' problems, like their police, seem in a curious way not really as serious as those of home.

Blommardine was especially light-headed about the situation.

'Elijah says that a few hardships are inevitable,' she told Julius. 'We have been living in the age of Antichrist. Travail won't simply disappear in the twinkling of an eye. Heaviness may endure for a night. But what he doesn't want is gloom-merchants like you spreading alarm and despondency before the joy that cometh in the morning.'

Julius said nothing. It was always wiser to bite one's tongue when Blommardine talked of Elijah. A week later, the blow fell.

She burst into his studio one afternoon as the light failed, in disarray, a tear freezing on her cheek, her lips trembling and a little bibble of moisture working back and forth in her nostril as she breathed.

'No wonder you've got a cold if you go around like that,' observed Julius.

She didn't bother to correct him.

'Elijah's going,' she said, and flung herself on the couch in a tantrum.

Julius was used to such outbursts and waited patiently for some minutes, finally advancing with a clean paint-cloth to wipe her face when the tempest subsided.

It appeared that the Saint was needed elsewhere and would be departing in the New Year.

'I'm sorry,' said Julius.

'Fat lot you feel sorry,' sobbed Blommardine.

'Perhaps they'll send another Saint,' said Julius.
'There'll never be another Saint like Elijah,' she sniffed.
But there she was wrong.

Chapter 26

Elisabeth's mother confounded all predictions by rallying; so much so that within a week she was able to take solid nourishment and when Elisabeth looked in after breakfast, she found her sitting up in bed reading letters.

'Good morning, darling,' she smiled at her. 'I'm just going through one or two things. I found this letter my mother wrote just before I married. We were living in the same house but she wrote me a letter. Funny, wasn't it?'

'Let me see,' said Elisabeth.

'I'll read it to you,' her mother told her. 'The writing's blotchy.'

She held the letter in front of her and read in her small, clear voice.

'"My dear Hilde, I thought that, since we will not be seeing so much of you now, I should try to tell you what a pleasure it has been to have you as a daughter. Marriage, like life, is a puzzling and not altogether satisfactory affair but it seems to me that you have two attributes that will help you on your way.

'"One you have acquired – that is, learning. Learning is a two-edged sword, of course, for the more you know, paradoxically, it seems the less you know. But without it we are worse than the brutes, for at least they are not capable of doing more than plod or beg or bark. There are some men who think only of hunting or fighting, robbing or killing. These should be avoided or, like the knight in the story, should be covered in oil and hung up in a cupboard until they are needed. These men hate learning because it is like a burning brand to a beast of the dark. Nevertheless, do not allow them to put you off it, for without that light you will never find any kind of path. In Italy they understand these things more. Up here in the North, we are still in the shadows.

'"Your other great virtue is good humour. I do not just mean laughter, for that can be merely spiteful or cruel. I mean the easy enjoyment of what life has to offer without the continual nagging pain of what might be. I can think of no greater advantage in the matter of marriage; for a husband, whose business it is to hold the sky up, is often of much more restless disposition. I suppose it is understandable.

'"I can see you smiling now and wondering why I bothered to write all this down, since you know it already. It is perhaps for my own benefit – for which I hope you will excuse me. Thoughts have a way of slipping down the sides of time and leaving nothing behind but a little dust. The written word is a scratch in the wall that you can return to.

'"It says your mother was here. She loves you. Wherever and whenever you may read this – now or in the future – it will bear that unalterable message. I hope it brings you as much joy as you have brought me, my little one, big girl, grown-up, and about-to-be-married daughter."'

She finished reading, and Elisabeth found that her eyes were full of tears. She looked up at her mother who was smiling at her.

'I wish I had known Grandmother,' she said.

'Now you do,' said her mother, putting the letter away. 'She was exactly like that letter, only prettier. Now hurry, it is Advent and you must go to church. Just because we have these strange preachers in town, it does not alter the story.'

Elisabeth kissed her and rose to go. Something made her bend down and hug her again. The shoulders seemed terribly thin in her hands, the warmth of the pale cheeks hardly perceptible.

'What was that for?' laughed her mother. 'It must be my lucky day.'

When Elisabeth came back from church, she found the house in turmoil. Billa the maid was drying her eyes in the hall and the doctor was coming down the stairs.

'What is the matter?' she asked.

'It is your mother, I'm afraid,' said the doctor. 'She had an attack. It could have happened any time. I tried leeches but it was too late.'

'Leeches?' shouted Elisabeth. 'Her blood was thin as water anyway.'

'Calm yourself, Elisabeth,' said her father, coming out of his study. 'It is a merciful release.'

Chapter 27

Had he been a roadsweeper or a soldier or even an alchemist's drudge, you could perhaps have found origins for the fires of Fierens' fanaticism. But the pastry shop ... What passions – with its shortcrust and its marzipan – could such a place have aroused? Nevertheless, certain tricks of finesse, light-of-hand and the art of presentation, were well learnt by Fierens and had been soon pressed into service by his new mentors.

What they did not comprehend – how could they? – was that his mind was like a thread reaching up to heaven; or a Jacob's ladder upon which angels descended.

Sometimes then he spoke with the tongues of angels. He found himself uttering sounds, beautiful words which he had never heard before. This always happened when he was alone. He understood that it was a sign, and that he should as yet reveal to no one the extent and implication of these developments.

He mentioned to Mosman, however, that he was anxious to preach, since he had had visions of sermons written in blood upon the clouds, and Mosman had been impressed, securing him a congregation and church to preach in, and thumping good sermons they were too; so good, in fact, that Mosman promoted him to bigger and even bigger congregations. He next instructed him to undertake certain delicate missions to Rensburg, later charging him with the duty of leading the pilgrims to the city, and finally commissioning him to mastermind the complete conversion of the inhabitants. For Fierens was a curious mixture of the visionary and the Machiavel, and apt for all these kinds of work. His remarkably handsome appearance made him particularly suitable for a mission in which women were to play so crucial a part.

Of more than medium height, he was of sparse frame with a fresh face and straight golden-red hair, but he was transfigured – if that is the word – by his eyes, which were large and so brown as to be almost black, glistening like olives rubbed with oil. These had a curiously mesmeric quality which, as he spoke, seemed to grow bigger, pulling you into their centre. His voice too was an extraordinary instrument which, as it wore on, seemed as insistent as an organistrum, winding its sound into your head until you were quite caught up with it. He had a knack, too, of knowing what you were thinking – a trick he had learned from the angels, or from the days in the pastry shop when customers would talk freely in front of him because he was just a pastry cook, no more than the furniture of the place.

With these attributes, his political career now advanced in Rensburg while in his head he silently stoked his vision of God the Son whose Age it now was, after that of the Father and the Spirit, each lasting 750 years, which had passed – and whose Self it was man's opportunity and destiny to become.

He himself, he could sense it, could be the Man. He could topple emperors and re-cast the world. There was still much to be done; but he could feel his mind, with that curious pressure upon it, squeezing its golden web up and up, streaming higher every day.

In the New Year, which was to be the Last Year, that would be the time. Meanwhile he must complete his negotiations in the matter of betrothal, for it was certain he must have a Bride, and he knew who it would be. She filled the twin functions of being ideal regenerate Eve-Mary and daughter of the most influential man in town. There must always at this time be the spiritual and sublunary dimension. As above, so must it be below.

Of course, there was still Mosman to consider. Mosman had come before him. There was no question of strife or contest; it was out of his hands and Mosman's too. Mosman, whether he knew it or not, was his Baptist. God would provide the Interpretation in His own good time . . .

Chapter 28

Christmas was a gloomy affair that year in Rensburg. Many of the Lutherans and all the Anabaptists deplored the celebration of a festival they saw as Popish, and most of the traditional amusements were curtailed. As for feasting, what with all the new inhabitants of the town, and the drain on the civic purse, and the Bishop's Tax of last year, and the bad harvest of this year, there was precious little to feast with. Some of the older families in town did what they could to provide seasonal cheer, but there was a sense of impending event hanging over the town – whether of doom or glory it was hard to discern; either way it made bobbing for apples and hitting people with bladders seem rather superfluous.

In the Harting household, things were especially quiet. The death of Elisabeth's mother had cast a shadow which even in normal times would have made celebration impossible to sustain. It was strange what an influence the woman who never left her bedroom seemed to have possessed. The servants seemed almost as distraught as Elisabeth herself, and old Frieda was inconsolable. Only Konrad appeared unmoved by the event. Of course he went through the motions of sorrow, but it was clear to Elisabeth that his heart was not in it.

When Christmas was over, he gave her a short talk on the self-indulgence of grief and the necessity of carrying-on with life. He even mentioned marriage as being something she should look forward to.

'Marriage!' she exclaimed. 'But that is the last thing I want.'

'How so?' he asked. 'What else had you in mind?'

'My mind is full of my mother's death,' she told him bitterly.

When she had looked for the letter that her mother read out to her, she found it was in her mother's writing and addressed to herself. It made her cry all the more.

'Mind your tongue, girl, and be grateful that you yet have a father,' said her father.

'A cruel father who talks of marriage when his own wife is still fresh in her grave,' she exclaimed.

He sprang up with an oath, upsetting an inkstand. The dark stain spread across the table like a rage.

'By God,' he said, 'you talk to me like that and I'll lay a strap to you, young lady or no young lady.'

She suddenly did not know him any more. She had seen him in a temper, of course, many times before. But it seemed that there was something else riding him now, that he was no longer in control but lumbering on all fours, a bull bridled by a toad. The shock of the image placated her. She almost felt sorry for him. He looked so red and cross. Perhaps she should try to give him some tincture of meadow-sweet.

'I'm sorry, Father.'

'I should think so.'

'I don't want to quarrel with you – not with Mother only dead a month. There's just the two of us now. I will look after you.'

'I thought I told you to stop harping on about your mother. Mourning is considered self-indulgent by the Anabaptists. Life must go on. Your poor mother was half-dead anyway for ten years.'

'She was more alive in her sickroom than most people are in the street,' said Elisabeth stoutly.

'There you go again. Contradict, contradict.'

'I only mean,' she said desperately, 'that I loved her. You would surely not take exception to that?'

'It is time you learned to love a husband,' said Konrad heavily, 'and, as it happens, I have found one for you.'

'Found? But . . . surely you mean to ask my opinion in the matter?'

'I see no reason. It is a decision that rests better on a parent's shoulders.'

It was true that arranged weddings were the general rule, but some-how Elisabeth had always expected a more enlightened outcome for herself.

'My mother would never have wanted it so,' she said, fighting her tears.

'Your mother's marriage was arranged like everybody else's.'

Elisabeth fought back the obvious retort that it didn't seem to have made her happy.

'Am I to know the name of this lucky fellow?' she asked coldly.

'Certainly,' said her father. 'It is Mr Fierens.'

'Fierens?' she gasped.

She had had warnings enough, but it was still a shock to hear it baldly spelt out.

'He is the one.'

'Oh, my sweet Lord.'

She sat down on a chair as if pole-axed.

'Good,' said her father. 'I see you are overwhelmed with the honour. You are right to be.'

Her mind scuttled about looking for excuses.

'I will not do it. He is a priest.'

'He is a preacher not a priest. If he were, it is allowed by the Lutherans.'

'It is too soon after the funeral.'

'You will be married before Easter. It seems to me a decent interval.'

'But I do not love him,' she burst out.

'What has that got to do with it?' replied her father calmly.

'I do not even like him.'

'Ah. So at least you have an opinion. You must at least have taken an interest in him. He has taken an interest in you.'

'He does not know me,' she said. 'It must be lust. He is enflamed by mere trappings.'

'Do not speak disrespectfully of the flesh,' said Konrad, heavily. 'It is God-given. We must use the gifts of Nature.'

'Just so long as they don't use us, Father.'

'What . . . what do you mean?'

Surely no one had been blabbing about his visits to the hypocaust? Her next words reassured him.

'I just mean, Father, that I do not wish to be betrothed to a man who is merely pleased to look at me, when my dear mother spent so much time improving my other faculties.'

Elisabeth was almost crying with the effort of being reasonable.

'He will like your mind well enough,' said Konrad impatiently, 'just so long as you have a mind to like his. Now enough of talk. There are great things afoot in this town, and one of the prime movers, one of the princes of change, wants you as his consort. Could there be in all Rensburg a more suitable match?'

She had a sudden vision of the man who had lied for her in church, with his gentle, amused, melancholy eyes and his perplexed, intelligent face. Where was he now? What was he doing in this town? It was a place that, if she had been a stranger, she was beginning to feel she would leave in rather a hurry.

She sighed exhaustedly. Grief and argument had made her weary. Perhaps it would be all right in the morning. Perhaps she would wake up and find it had all been a nightmare.

Chapter 29

He had copied the triptych onto the wall in the extraordinary space of three weeks, but there he had stuck. The images whirred and thrummed in his ears, but Love still did not tell him what he needed to know. He looked about again for other work.

As he went about the town, trying to ignore his hurting heart, it began to become clear why his master Bosch had sent him to Florence. It was not simply to ape the Florentines. There was an equation to be arrived at, a mingling of the South and the North, of the Gothic and the classical – two poles represented by his master's style and that of his teachers. In the past, he could see, he had been over-influenced by Florence. He had turned his back on his roots. It was necessary for a while but it had gone on too long. There was something about this town of Rensburg that demanded, deserved, an understanding of the North. There were gargoyles here walking in the street, preaching in the churches. There were monsters to be discerned, disguised in human form.

He could feel a capacity for this northern world now stirring again in him, rising like a mist, dimming but not totally obscuring the Florentine light and the sun of reason.

He began to find customers for his portraits. One of his new subjects was a prosperous butcher's wife who had a face like a little pink pig. He flattered her, making her features more human but retaining something porky in the expression which escaped the butcher and his lady. Julius was paid good money for the work, and garlanded with sausages. There were other sitters and further emoluments.

It so happened that it was the practice of the Great Council to have its leader's portrait painted: the butcher put forward the name of Julius as a candidate for Konrad's picture, and this was duly approved.

Of course, it was not purely accidental. Julius had done some research and found out exactly who the beautiful girl's father was and who his friends might be. The butcher's name was among these. Good fortune deserves a little push and shove.

So it happened that on a clear, bright morning in early January, Julius found himself knocking at the front door of the house in Broad Street. He had dreamed of it many times. How the door would be opened by the maid, the father would be busy for a while in his office, how the daughter would entertain him, how well they would get on . . . What

157

would happen after that his dreams did not specify. Reason of course told him that even dreams were madness. He was married. The girl was of good family. There could be no possible grounds for optimism. It did not, however, stop his heart thumping like a rabbit under his heavy cloak.

He raised his hand and knocked smartly at the door. Footsteps approached, the latch was raised, and the first part of his dream took form: the maid, in black, appeared, framed in the lintel. He had heard that the girl's mother had died and now he wondered whether portraiture was the thing when you were in mourning. The maid admitted him, however, without demur.

'Come in, sir, we was expecting you like but Master's busy just now. Will you step this way?'

She led him into a small chamber furnished with a couple of heavy chairs and an oak table.

'The young lady will be down in a moment,' she said.

'Thank you.'

She curtsied and left him hugging his good fortune. It was all going according to plan.

Five minutes later, there was another set of footsteps outside, lighter than the maid's. The latch lifted, the door opened, and she was there.

Elisabeth, in mourning, presented a delightful vision. The black of her dress set off her fresh colouring, her astonishing pale-blue eyes and her golden hair, almost better than if she had been wearing brightness. Her breasts made nonsense of the black material. Her little feet twinkled in dull slippers.

Even she did not really believe that men should be unimpressed by her appearance. Indeed, she had gone to some trouble to look her best because she too had dreamt of this meeting. Old Frieda, who had been peeping, had told her that the painter, just arrived, was no less than the man who had saved her bacon in church, who had followed her respectfully on her afternoon walks.

Perhaps, Elisabeth told herself, by some miracle this man could save her from the future that her father had planned. Would he like her, though, when he met her?

Her heart, also, was beating like the Drummer of Niklashausen.

They exchanged long glances, lost for words.

Finally, they both opened their mouths.

'I...'

'I...'

They both burst out laughing. It was love at first syllable.

Elisabeth tried again.

'Won't you...'

'Will you...'

She hadn't laughed since her mother died. She raised her hand like a child at school, signifying that she wanted to speak.

'Please go ahead,' he said. 'Sorry.'

'I just wanted to say sorry.'

'No, I'm sorry.'

The conversation seemed to be heading for stalemate. She took a deep breath and started again.

'My father's busy at the moment,' she said, very quickly. 'But will you take some wine and put up with me for a few minutes, because I'm all there is otherwise?'

'Gladly to both.'

She fetched a jug from a cupboard and poured him a measure. He sipped appreciatively. It was good wine. He supposed you would expect it from a grocer.

'I know what you do and what your name is,' she said, looking him over. 'What else is there to know?'

'A great deal of very little,' he told her.

She had not been wrong about his face – watchful, intelligent, something of unhappiness and yet also of humour. He was well built, almost tall, graceful in his movements; his brown-gold hair curling about slightly pointed ears gave him an air of a creature of the woods, a faun. She had a sudden image of him dancing on the lawns.

'Do you dance?' she asked him.

'Not in this town,' he said. 'I don't think the Lutherans are keen on that sort of thing. But in Italy I did.'

'Italy,' she exclaimed with pleasure. 'You have been to Italy?'

'I studied in Florence,' he told her.

'Ah, Florence,' she said. 'My mother used to speak of it. It was the one place in the world she wanted to go.'

She wanted him to take her to Florence – now – out of this town.

'I must tell you,' he said, 'since there is no time, and who knows when I may have the opportunity to say this to you again, that you are the most beautiful girl I have ever seen. I love you hopelessly and if you ever need anyone to die for you I beg you to consider me for the office. Have you heard of the Adamites? It is the Religion of Love.'

Before she could reply there were heavy footsteps outside and the door opened abruptly, revealing the figure of Konrad.

'Ah, Painter,' he exclaimed. 'Carousing with my daughter, I see. Is it quite seemly, my dear?'

'Seemly, Father?'

'You are about to announce your betrothal. Should you be pouring wine for a young man we do not know?'

Julius tried to come to her defence.

'She was merely doing me the civility of . . .'

'Silence, Painter.'

Konrad smiled like an Etruscan, mirthlessly, to show there was no ill-feeling.

Painter ha!, thought Julius. Why does he not call me dauber, and have done? The reality of what the man had said, though, was beginning to sink in. Julius looked in horror at the girl. Was she really on the verge of betrothal? She had not given that impression – although, it had to be said, there had not been time for her to give any impression at all. What, for instance, had been her opinion of his declaration of love? Did she know he was married? He thought not. Her reaction had certainly not been unfavourable, or he would have taken that in through the pores. Yes, colour had suffused her cheeks. Her eyes had sparkled. The beginnings of a smile had played on her lips. But why was he thinking like this? The news of her betrothal had dashed his hopes. And his hopes, at the best of times, could be no more than empty shells. He must tell her the truth. At the same time, he could hardly bear to break the enchantment that had so unexpectedly been granted.

A change had come over the girl in the presence of her father, he noticed. Her gaiety and naturalness had retreated like Mrs Noah in the mystery play, and out had come Melancholy and Unease.

'Since you were busy, Father, I thought it my duty to entertain your guest.'

'Well, well. Enough said. To business now, Painter. You had better come to my shop where you can discover me amid my trappings, eh? A portrait should have a background, and what could be better for a grocer than a chunk of cheese or a flitch of bacon. You shall surround me with butter and split peas, Painter. You shall spice me and pickle me if you wish.'

The man, after his bad entrance, was becoming positively roguish. But there was still something in those eyes that Julius did not like; the smile never reached them. It would be there in the painting.

'Well, well,' said Konrad, 'what are we waiting for? Let us proceed. The light will be failing soon and doubtless you are charging by the day. I know you painter fellows.'

They hurried out into the snow, huddling on their coats as Elisabeth watched them from the door, hope and tenderness filling her heart. The painter loved her! There must now be a way of escaping from the Dutchman. Whilst there had been no alternative, she could not find the courage to go against her father's wishes, but now . . . Well, if the worst came to the worst, they could run away together . . . If indeed love was his religion, he would do it. It was like something out of the *Roman de la Rose* . . . Love would find a way, it was well known . . .

Meanwhile she must prepare herself for the meeting with her

unwelcome suitor this evening. She turned away from the door and ran upstairs with a light step and lighter heart.

Old Frieda, who overheard everything, sighed as she saw her go. There was trouble in the house and trouble in the town, and what the Almighty was up to was anybody's guess.

Chapter 30

Fierens was in high good humour. Things in Rensburg were going so well that Mosman was already planning to come and join him. It was a signal mark of his success, for the Anabaptists had cells in many towns. It meant that the Rensburg operation had been more successful than anywhere else, and Mosman clearly felt that he, Fierens-Enoch and not Elijah (who had already been given his movement orders), was responsible for the triumph. Of course, Fierens knew that to be true, but it was important others should also.

It would mean that Rensburg would now be seen as the headquarters of the movement and that he, Fierens, would be its second-in-command. No, no, he thought, correcting himself; not second-in-command, but leader-in-waiting.

Before this could happen, however, before even Mosman could come to the city, certain things had to be set in motion. The takeover of the city had to be completed. It was to discuss this – as well as to obtain the hand of his Bride, the grocer's daughter – that he was now on his way to the house in Broad Street this evening. As he walked, his mind was full of his plans. It was a curious attribute of his that he could so quickly slip down from his ladder and his debates with the seraphim, and make stratagems that were intricately and ingeniously rooted in things of the ground and below the ground.

Thus it was that he had established from the earliest days a network of information and deception in the city, using Saints and perverts, the disaffected, the trouble-makers as well as the genuinely crazy for his cause.

The people who gathered underground in the heating-cellars of the Town Hall belonged, in fact, to a pagan off-shoot of the Cult of Love, of which there were a number in the northern cities. The coiffed Eve-Mary was high-priestess of Ashtaroth, the White Goddess. Adam served Attis. These and their kind had been only too willing, in return for protection, to take part in the deception of Konrad. They would naturally be punished for their vile practices in due course.

It was simply one of the instances of his God-given genius for domination. He would play now on this weakness and now on that. He made it his business to sniff out foibles at every level. What good fortune it was for Rensburg and for mankind! A mere Machiavel could perhaps have been contained; but a Machiavel with a vision of godhead was as implacable as he was irresistible . . .

And so Fierens walked on, cloaked in thought, nodding mechanically at one or two of the Saints or prophets who passed him, and ignoring the stony looks of those townsfolk who knew him and deplored his influence. They would come round in due course. He despised them for not having the energy or organization for resistance; in fact, even if he had met with concerted opposition, he would still have despised them. What was afoot in this town was not just history but the End of History. They would be crushed under Time's wheel.

Fierens' brow momentarily clouded when he saw Konrad walking down a side street from the direction of his shop in the company of a youngish man he did not recognize. He did not like strangers to mingle with Konrad. He did not like strangers at all. He liked to know everyone: what they did, where they worshipped, whether their wives were happy, what sort of food they enjoyed, whether they drank too much . . . His mind was full of files.

Konrad greeted him.

'Mr Fierens, well met. Let me introduce Julius Martens who is doing my portrait.'

Ah, so the man was a painter; a dangerous breed full of dreams and phantasms; things were never what they seemed with a painter. They were ruled by light and yet they were not of the light.

Fierens stared at him hard and the man stared back. Neither liked what they saw. The Saint saw trouble: I don't like the look of you, Painter, he thought. I know you. I'll have you on file. Julius saw something worse. He too had a sensitivity for faces. There was something about this one that he recognized and did not like.

'This is Mr Fierens who is to be married to my daughter,' said Konrad, heartily. 'I hope that is not jumping the gun, Fierens, for I know the formalities have not yet been agreed.'

'If it is the Will of God,' said Fierens, meekly.

Julius gave the man another look – of horror this time – which Fierens did not miss. It was bad enough that anyone should be betrothed to the only love of his life, the one for whom he had been created – since this was now Julius's happy conviction – but that she should be betrothed to one of these canting, secret, high-hatted nose-voices seemed to him the height of infamy. And then he remembered who he was. The years had fleshed out a face he had to admit was now handsome. Envy and pride had lined the sides of the mouth. But it could only be Uitwaarden. He almost ribbed him, but stopped. Uitwaarden had given no sign of recognition. Perhaps he did not remember him. It might be better not to remind him of their last conversation in 'sHertogenbosch all those years and miles away.

If he should cause offence now, Konrad would immediately dismiss him, for it seemed he was unaccountably in favour of the fellow. In that case, he, Julius, would not easily be able to see Elisabeth again; and it was of the utmost importance to him that he should do so.

'You were going to say?' asked Fierens, with his almost supernatural – he regarded it as seraphic – instinct for what was in people's minds.

'I was going to say the Will of God is the only will we can put our faith in,' said Julius, scrabbling for an alternative to the rudeness that had already begun to curl his lip.

'That goes without saying,' said Fierens, rudely, and turned to walk off in the direction of the Harting household.

'Tomorrow at ten o'clock,' said Konrad to Julius.

'I shall be there,' he replied.

It would only be the office of her father's shop, but it would be better than nothing.

'Are you sure that you can spare the time for portraiture at this juncture?' asked Fierens, loudly, as he and Konrad walked away. 'It seems to me to smack of vanity. It is altogether little.'

'The Council wishes it. It might not be politic to . . .' Julius could not hear the rest of the explanation. He suspected that vanity was one of the vices of the Master of the Great Guilds, but not the one that Fierens had particularly hooked onto. As the two picked their way along the snowy street, one after the other, it seemed for an instant – Fierens threw up his hands to steady himself – as if he were riding like a demon on Konrad's back.

'Oh, God,' prayed Julius, 'let it not be Your will. Let her not do it, God. Let there be a way.'

Or was He tired and thinking of turning it all in as these people seemed to believe?

Chapter 31

Blommardine had recovered from the loss of Elijah, but she had not found a new outlet for her interests which now, for want of anything better, reverted to her husband.

When Julius returned she was pacing about like a caged weasel. The cold weather did not suit her temperament. She liked to be out and circulating, nosing into things that weren't her business, making sly digs, spreading rumours and innuendo, gathering weaknesses.

She would be a much better wife for Fierens, thought Julius. She's absolutely made for the man.

'Where've you been, spindleshanks?' she said as he came in. 'Out all day and never a thought for your little wifie.'

Oh, God, thought Julius, she's going to be amorous.

'I hope you haven't found some little tart in town. I'll tear her eyes out.'

Why did I have to get into this? he thought. I took the easy option. Easy option's a soft gate into a hard field.

'I'm going to give you some broth and then we're going to go to bed,' she told him. 'I've been thinking of one or two new things we can do.'

'I'm . . . a little tired,' he said. 'It's been a long day.'

'Oh, fuck me,' she said. 'Don't tell me it's your time of the month. Are you man or hermaphrodite? Why don't you go to one of those Attis rites and castrate yourself?'

Julius bit back his reply – that he wanted to be alone; that he wanted a divorce like Henry of England had from Anne of Cleves; that their whole marriage had been a mistake which she herself had master-minded but he couldn't blame her because he had gone along with it.

All he knew now was that he didn't want to rock any boats. His only hope of seeing Elisabeth was to preserve the status quo – at least for the moment. If Blommardine suspected his attachment to another, she wouldn't rest until she had blown the whole boat out of the water. And, within her lights, he had to admit, she'd have every right to do so.

'Very well,' he said as pleasantly as possible. 'Wheel on the soup.'

'And for afters?' she queried, hand on hip, hitching up her skirt.

'For afters,' he said, 'I think I'll have a little roly-poly pudding.'

It wouldn't have been so bad if he hadn't enjoyed it so much.

It is hard to resist pleasure when it is expedient; but it doesn't stop you feeling sick about it next day.

Chapter 32

Fierens sat in Konrad's study, staring at the hearth, well pleased with the way the conversation had gone so far. His host did seem to have dwindled in dimension since his first conversation with him months ago. There was a hollowness to him. He was being sucked out – literally, if the reports from the hypocaust were anything to go by. So much the better a vessel he would be for the works of God. Must not, of course, appear weak; that would never do. He must be a leader of the people with God in his head and Fierens in his understanding.

There was nothing incongruous to Fierens about the manner of Konrad's suborning. The end justified the means. Moreover, the sin of Lust, though anathema to the Papists, did not figure so large in his own black book. He had known many women formerly, and the pleasure the act of sex had given him was incidental. It was the power that he had enjoyed.

To him, sex had always seemed no more sinful than a sneeze, and the archangel Amiel had confirmed this privily.

In the Book of Ezekiel, it was suggested that God Himself sneezed, scattering the Egyptians 'with a blast of the nostrils'. If God could sneeze, He could also engender, said Amiel. Had He not spawned the world? Sneezing was an excellent parallel: a spasmodic flatus of power. He would keep the revelation hidden from the Saints for the moment; it might distract them from their immediate course. But just as a sneeze could let in the Devil, so perhaps it was that God could be admitted through the organ of gender.

As he reflected on the matter, and as he considered his forthcoming betrothal to Konrad's comely daughter, he thought: I am not a carnal man, that is the man in me that is yet on the ground. The pursuit of the New Jerusalem is an infinitely greater matter, and Godhead is the greatest matter of all; but it would be perverse to hold back when the pepper is, as it were, under the nose. I shall sneeze with the best of them. It is good, hot pepper.

And yet there was something about her which denied that kind of thought ... something bright and cold and burning which made one turn away ...

He looked up as Konrad came in again with some papers. I won't be peppered-out like this fellow, he thought. If you can't take the pepper you should keep out of the hypocaust.

'Well,' Fierens said. 'You have our plan. Do you think you can now take care of the Town Council, Nose?'

Konrad pointed to a list of names. Though the Saints viewed the town councillors with contempt, there were still those among the towns-folk who looked to them for stability if not for leadership.

'These fourteen are on our side. There are six doubtful whom I have marked with a cross. And this list here shows the opposition: Catholics or firm Lutherans. There are eight of them.'

Had the man called him 'nose'? Or had it been 'no' with a question mark. No?

'Then it is fourteen all,' said Fierens, frowning. 'Not quite good enough.'

'I believe one of the doubtfuls is for us. This man Backhaus . . .'

'Even so, should one of our persuasion fall ill, we should be in some danger. Could you not do something about the other doubters?'

'Well . . .' said Konrad, doubtfully. 'It's very difficult.'

'I understand one of the members of your society . . .'

'Which society?'

'You know the one I mean. I understand she wishes to tell the authori-ties of the goings-on. A sudden attack of chastity. Too bad. I fear she will pepper her report with names.'

'I thought you told me it was safe.'

'It is safe. As long as you can prevail upon that list. It is all connected; wheels within wheels. This town is like a clockwork toy. Wheels spin; figures dance. You should know that.'

'I suppose I do.'

Konrad gulped some wine noisily.

'Think again. Can nothing be done?'

'Well . . . This man, Hessing, a Lutheran, owes me money.'

'Well, then . . .'

Fierens made a tightening gesture.

'But he is an old friend.'

'So he should be loyal. Good. That is one.'

'And this man, Stumpf, has suffered from the bad harvests.'

'He is vulnerable? Squeeze him.'

Fierens made a strangling motion. Konrad gave the ghost of a sigh. Such practices were bad for business. Business needed give and take.

'You are a hard man, Fierens.'

'Hard for God, Mr Harting, hard for God. There can be no let-up. Well, now, that is excellent. We have seventeen on our side and the most they can raise is eleven. You have three weeks to make your dispositions.'

'Very well,' said Konrad.

'And now let us see the maiden. I trust you have told her of her suitability?'

'I have.'

'And is she honoured?'

'She is young, Mr Fierens. Her mother has only recently died. You must be patient with her.'

Konrad lifted a silver bell and rang it peremptorily.

'Patient? When the end of the world is upon us? You are sneezing too much, Brother Harting. I fear it has shaken your brainbox.'

Konrad gave the man a startled look. Every now and then he said these things that made you think a voice from far away, from a far country, was speaking through him; a voice that, being foreign, had not got all the words right. It was part of the extraordinary effect he had on one. Sometimes it seemed to be the voice of God, sometimes – could it be so? – of a devil.

Where was that girl? He had told her to look her best and to come down when he rang the bell. He rang again. Fierens looked heavenward as if taking in more messages. Finally the door half-opened, revealing Elisabeth in an unbecoming black smock with her hair scraped up in a cap.

Konrad frowned.

'I thought I told you to wear your best dress, Elisabeth. This is disrespectful to our visitor.'

Fierens lifted a hand. Elisabeth looking her worst looked better than most girls looking their best, he thought. He could feel a perceptible tickle in his nose. And yet – what was it about her that had that other effect on him? . . .

'Sit down, Elisabeth.'

She sat, not raising her face. Fierens spoke to her as if to a child.

'You are a pretty maid.'

'Thank you, sir.'

'Has your father told you that we shall be betrothed?'

'Yes, sir. He has spoken of it.'

'And what do you think?'

'I think I should rather die, sir.'

'Elisabeth!'

Her father sprang up, grimacing with rage like a face on a corbel. But Fierens lifted his hand again.

'Please, Mr Harting. The maiden has a right to her opinion. She would rather die, she says. I hope that won't be necessary. I wonder why she is so extreme. Perhaps there is some pretty young gentleman who has taken her fancy?'

'By God, if there is, I'll . . .' Konrad started to bluster.

It was strange how his daughter brought out the worst in him these days, as if she were a mirror in which he could see things that were lost.

Again, Fierens cut him short.

'Let her speak.'

'Indeed,' she said. 'I am in love with no man I know.'

It was true enough, for she did not know him.

'Well, there you are,' said Konrad, deflating.

'And yet,' Fierens told him, 'there is something. I will find it, never fear, for I mean to marry you, Maiden. And you must surely give your consent to it. The wedding, I think, shall be in March. Or April – a cheerful month for a wedding. If it is not too late. Come, now. I have much to attend to. Look to your lists, Harting. And, Maiden, to your heart. Good evening to you both.'

Chapter 33

It was no good going to the shop every day. It might have served if you were in love with food and the object of your veneration was lentils. But sitting in the office painting an impatient father brought him no nearer the daughter than if he had been painting the Antichrist's bottom.

It was true the father sometimes talked about her. Indeed, he raised the subject by asking a question that almost made Julius drop his brush.

'You are married, Painter?'

'Er . . .'

What should he reply? If he said yes, it might get back to Elisabeth before he could explain himself. If he said no, he might be exposed as a liar. But then it would get back to Elisabeth anyway. Better play for time.

'. . . no,' he said.

'You seem unsure. Is there some doubt in your mind?'

'No doubt. I was just wiping off some oil. Don't move . . .'

His sitter was beginning to crane round.

'That's the way. Don't want too much oil,' said Konrad, turning back. 'There's too much oil in this town. You oil me and I'll oil you.'

He was one to talk, he thought. But he didn't have to like what he was becoming, even though he was powerless to stop becoming it.

Julius, recovering from the shock, decided to bring him back to the subject of marriage. It seemed, on reflection, a promising area after all.

'You asked me if I were married, sir. Why was that?'

'Oh, nothing.'

He tried again.

'I was nearly married once.'

'Nearly, eh? What happened?'

'I got cold feet.'

'Ah, wise lad.'

'She had a great deal of money and a tongue like a ratchet.'

Konrad laughed harshly.

'That is often the way,' he said, 'and most often without the first of those attributes. Woman's tongue is always there. Take my daughter . . .'

Was this an invitation?

'Gladly,' he murmured.

'What, Painter?'

'I said, really? Does she really have a tongue on her?'

'Not so much tongue, but a will like the Devil. I wheel on the best man in town, but will she agree to a betrothal?'

'Will she?'

'Will she blazes!'

Julius's heart leapt up only to be subdued again.

'Fierens thinks she has some other interest which she denies. But he'll wed her yet. I've never known such a man for getting what he wants . . .'

An apprentice came in.

'Yes, Christoph, what is it?'

Julius sighed. There had been many interruptions. Boys asking the price of cheese, wanting to know about an order of pickles . . . It was becoming impossible to get the man to hold a pose.

'There's a Mr Hessing to see you, sir, urgent. A private matter he says.'

Konrad made a sound of irritation.

'I'm sorry, Painter. He'll have to come in here. Do you mind waiting outside?'

Julius did mind, rather a lot. The flow of the thing was hard enough to sustain at the best of times. He moved his easel to one side and made to leave the room. As he opened the door, a pleasant-looking, slightly sheep-faced man in his late forties brushed past, arms outstretched to Konrad in a gesture of comradeship. This was Hessing, Master of the Masons, in trouble due to non-payment by exiled ecclesiastics.

'You wanted to see me, I gather, dear friend. What can I do for you? Still plenty of people eating, I see. Maaarvellous. So sorry,' he said to Julius.

Julius closed the door and waited outside in the passage, sitting on a sack of beans. In the shop beyond he could hear bustle. From within came the rise and fall of voices. Adjusting his buttocks on the beans, he settled down to a frustrating delay. Time was short. Fierens was out there looking for trouble.

There must be a way to see Elisabeth alone again. He was becoming obsessed by her. Every minute of his life spent away from her was life lost. It was as if the Garden which his master had painted, that mysterious place of warmth and colour, fragrance and fertility, where everything could be happiness and fulfilment for ever, could only be opened when their love was perfectly joined. She had the lock; he had the key.

As he reflected on the matter, stirring on his bag of beans, he became conscious that the voices in the office had now become raised. He heard the bleat of entreaty and the bark of denial. Finally, the voices subsided again. The door opened, and Hessing came out looking ashamed of himself. He passed Julius without speaking. Julius waited for a little and then went back into the office, where he found Konrad sitting balefully at his desk.

'Business is a hard world, Painter. You're better off sticking to your art,' he said.

'Art is business too,' replied Julius. 'And I won't get this commission finished if we keep being disturbed. Could we not work in your study at home? I won't need you there all the time . . .'

Konrad turned it over in his mind. The notion did seem to make sense. And he had the interview with Stumpf still to organize.

'What about the background?' he asked.

'I have some record of that,' replied Julius. 'And I can fill that in later. It is the face I must have. It really won't take long.'

'Very well, Painter. Let us do as you say. The house will be more convenient. We shall not be disturbed there.'

Julius, however, did find it disturbing. To know that Elisabeth was so near made it almost impossible to grip the brush. He was in a fever.

'What is it, Painter?' said Konrad, irritably, as the brush fell for the third time. 'Got some kind of ague?'

'No, no. All is well. Just working fast. It is coming on splendidly.'

And so it was. The urgency of the moment, the tremulous quality in the air, somehow communicated itself to the brushwork. His hand might be febrile but it had a lively touch. Konrad's fine head and vigorous expression were perfectly caught – and yet there was something behind the cold eyes, a curve to the mouth, that indefinably hinted at other qualities: an air half-cruel, almost wild, yet regretful, as if there were some kind of struggle going on in the man.

Julius hardly saw Elisabeth for the first two days. She tiptoed in once.

'May I look?'

'When it is finished, child. We are in a hurry,' said Konrad.

His daughter's presence, there was no doubt, made him restless, thought Julius. She made both of them restless. He personally had had no rest since he first saw her. It was the promise of rest in her that was paradoxically so disturbing. And yet, thought Julius, did she represent that to the world – or to herself – before I saw it in her? Was rest her gift? Does love give qualities and dimensions to the beloved that before were lying rolled up, unused, behind a curtain? Is she already doing the same to me? Are we ever unfolding and blooming like those fantastic flowers and fruits in the Garden? So Julius worked and dreamed, happy in the nearness of his love, unhappy in her absence, until Konrad suddenly broke through his thoughts.

'Enough for today, Painter. I have to go now.'

Now, Julius thought, now I can do it.

'May I do some finishing, while there is still light?'

'You may. And do not let my daughter disturb you.'

He could hardly believe his good fortune as the grocer left the house and the door latched shut behind him.

Now, where was she? Would she come to him? He peered out into the hallway. He could hardly go creeping round the house. Somebody would see him – the maid, the nurse – and report him to Konrad. Where was she? She must have heard her father leave.

Suddenly a voice spoke behind him.

'Here I am.'

He turned and was dazzled; she stood framed in the doorway; she had changed into a blue dress; her hair was down; if he had thought her beautiful before, he now found her almost too lovely to be looked at; his heart gave a great swoop.

'My heart is a kite,' he told her. 'Please hold on tight to the string.'

Frieda, who was listening behind the door to the stairs, looked grave. The servant-girl Billa, who was listening behind the door to the kitchen, gave a little smile.

'We had better go into the study,' Elisabeth said.

They moved back into the room and she looked at the picture while he shut the door.

'It is good,' she told him. 'There is something in the eyes that I thought no one else could see. You have found it.'

He kept peeping at her like a small boy who has discovered where his present is before his birthday.

'I love you,' he said.

'I think you should tell me about it,' she said.

So he told her: about his bastard childhood, about his famous master, about Florence and his studio there, his teachers and his friends, of his master's showing him the chapel and the Garden of Love, of the Grand Master of the Brethren, of his continuing inability to paint that last unfinished part of Hell, of his coming to Rensburg in search of commissions. He told her of his faith in the Adamite belief, partly because of his master's teaching, partly because it coincided with the ideas of his teachers in Florence, and mostly because he felt that he had always known its truth in his heart. The world began in Love and was sustained by it. And as Adam and Eve were Spirit and Earth bonded in perfect proportion by Love so that they became One, so every man and woman must look for his or her perfect complement in another, which would make each of them whole. He had always known that somewhere that other person existed. Now he had found her.

'You are that One,' he said simply, coming to an end.

She looked at him for a while, her eyes not resting on the surface but looking into him.

'That is the whole of it?' she asked.

He could not bring himself to tell her at that instant – he would later, not now. The mention of Blommardine would absolutely destroy this moment. There would have to be explanations, disclaimers. The very words 'married man' would put a gulf between their understanding. When their love was just a little firmer, when it could stand it, then would be the time.

He did not mean to be deceitful. It was the same little weakness

175

which let him slip into marriage. It was pragmatic. It was optimistic. It was inexcusable. He had already named it 'the soft gate'. And he knew where it led. He knew all this but he told the lie.

'That is the whole of it,' he said.

Still looking steadfastly towards him with eyes whose pale-blue brilliance seemed to shine now through him and far beyond into unknowable eventualities, she rose and took his hand and placed it under her left breast.

'Take my heart,' she said, 'and me with it. I trust you completely. We must leave this town at once.'

He was overwhelmed with the joy of her; but at the same time alarmed by her urgency. He somehow had to tell her about Blommardine; but not today.

'At once?' he asked, doubtfully.

'If not sooner.'

He knew she was right. But what about Blommardine?

'We must make some dispositions,' he told her. 'We simply can't just go with nothing. We have to think where to go, what we should take with us. Whether your father would pursue us. We must have time to think.'

'You are wrong, Painter,' she said, sadly.

He knew that she was right – but all he needed was another day. Just one more day to digest the fact that she loved him; just one brief absence to let love take more weight. The mortar was not yet dry . . .

'Come tomorrow,' he said. 'We will talk about it then. I will say I can do no more painting until I have mixed and tried some new pigment. I shall have plans tomorrow. Trust me.'

'I do,' she said, 'with all my heart. But I am afraid. Afraid of this town and of that man . . .'

'And of your father?'

'I am not afraid of my father. I am afraid for him.'

'Come, my dearest love,' he said, 'let us kiss and part. I must not be found here when your father returns. It is already dark.'

He took her in his arms and felt her melt into him. They hung together, spinning, like dew on a single strand of gossamer.

At last they broke off, breathlessly. Her eyes remained fixed on his as if they were operated by some reciprocating Florentine clockwork.

'Now I must go,' he said. 'Will you come tomorrow?'

'I will try,' she said. 'I should like to see the Garden that you speak of.'

He gave her directions as to how to find the place.

'I am still afraid,' she told him. 'I am even more afraid.'

'Come,' he said, 'you must take heart. I will let nothing bad happen to us. What harm can possibly happen in a day or two?'

176

As they left the room, they heard a slight scuffling noise from the direction of the back of the house.

'Who's there?' she called.

There was no reply.

'The cat,' she said. 'It gets out of the kitchen and plays with the scarves.'

'Goodbye,' he said, holding out his hand formally, in case anyone should hear. 'I hope I was able to show you some of our painter's art.'

'Oh, yes,' she told him, looking at him with those lucid eyes again. 'I think I have a better understanding now.'

Out in the street, the night air was bitter. A full moon shone from a cloudless sky and the snow bounced the light back from a field of silver crystals. Only under the overhanging roofs were there corridors of darkness. As Julius crossed the street, he turned back to look at the house and thought he saw a deeper darkness move in the shadows there.

'Who's there?' he called.

No answer. It was getting late. He pulled his cloak about him and made for home.

Chapter 35

Rumours in the city, counter-rumours, whispers in taverns, meetings in deserted warehouses, sidelong looks, assertions, counter-assertions, prophecies, runs on the banks, signs in alleyways, scribbled messages in church, portents in the heaven – a conjunction of Mars, Saturn, Venus and the Sun in Aquarius (sign of revolution as well as philosophy) in opposition to Jupiter – hurried Council meetings, calls on loans, every stable and barn in the place full to bursting and still throngs of beggars, out-of-work indigents, dissidents, criminals and malcontents streaming into the city from every quarter of the compass, crowds like flocks of birds gathering mysteriously and then as mysteriously moving on.

There was beginning to be, especially among the newcomers, a noticeable trimming of rations.

An epidemic of measles broke out.

Strange women started to appear – nuns who had broken out of their convents inspired by the eloquent Hass. He now preached, for the Anabaptists and Spiritual Libertines, that only those who received 'the living Christ' would be saved. He made the clear distinction between the Christ of history – who had made a great contribution by pointing the way to salvation – and the 'living' or 'inner' or 'spiritual' Christ – whom he depicted as being born in the individual soul. It was this latter Christ, he said, who possessed the power of redemption. But first this Christ must suffer the afflictions of 'the Cross': sickness, poverty, persecution, all of which must be endured with patience; intense mental anguish, world-weariness, hopelessness, despair, fear, horror. Only when this had been achieved, when the soul was totally naked, could direct communication with God begin. But once the 'living Christ' entered the soul, it would be for ever and ever; he or she would become a paracletic being. Hans – rapt, superb, some said even suffused in a golden glow – spoke of the possibility of 'becoming God'. Given perfect insight into the Divine Will, and living in full conformity with it, such spirits would be perfectly qualified to roll up the map of history and preside over the Last Things, he said.

The more excitable nuns snapped their vows like carrots and poured from the nunneries, casting aside their habits and coifs and finding what alternative garb they could lay hands upon. Some even stripped themselves naked, following Hass's instructions to the letter, enduring derision and sometimes rape as being no more than the necessary humiliations and suffering. Others, their sisters in the Living Christ, stumbled about in outsize or undersize cast-offs, repulsive or pathetic spectacles, hungry, homeless, chilblained, sometimes frost-bitten, always revelling in their misery.

Chapter 36

She had opened the door at the top of the stairs just as she had been told.

The room was in near-darkness when she entered. Light, stealing in through a chink in the shutters, revealed a sliver of wall and floor, merely accentuating the blackness beyond. She was surprised and a little frightened; but a fire, crackling in the grate, threw a little cheering glow upon a chair drawn up beside it.

'Come in,' his voice told her. 'My dearest. Thank God you could come.'

Her eyes now began to take in the general shape of the room – a rectangle barely furnished with couch, table and easel. So this was where he spent his days, thinking about her, he said.

'Keep your cloak on if you like,' he told her, nervous in his pleasure at seeing her. 'I'm afraid it's rather cold. I only just lit the fire. Some wine? A biscuit? My . . . landlady, you know. She cooks so rarely . . . They're not bad in a strange sort of way.'

It had indeed been an unusual gesture of Blommardine's to pack some for him. He felt guilty offering his wife's cooking to Elisabeth, but it was all he had. She reached out her hand, took one and nibbled.

It had a peculiar but not unpleasant taste.

'Shut your eyes for a moment,' he said, walking to the window.

'What shall I see?'

She could hear the sound of the shutters opening.

'Now,' he said, 'open again.'

'Oh,' she exclaimed. 'What an extraordinary place.'

There on the left by the right-angled wall were God and a slightly familiar-looking Adam and Eve. God – God the Son for he looked like Jesus – was holding Eve's wrist, feeling and rejoicing in the new pulses of her blood. And there was Adam, sitting on the grass with his toes outstretched to touch the hem of God's flowing red garment as if the life-flow joined them all and made them One. But all around them – in front, beside, behind – what astonishing creatures, what birds, what salamanders, what hippogriffs, what pools with what a strange fountain – with its bells and pinnacles and peaks – what mountains, caves, what trees, yes, and The Tree too.

'But that's only the Beginning,' he said. 'Come, my love, look over here.'

And he led her on a little to where she could see the background of hills and countryside continued . . . but in front, above – what wonders, what enchantment, what bells, shells, gourds, glasses, crystals, caverns, what strange fruits and, more than all, what people! Naked people, people admiring themselves, eagerly glancing, peering at each other, touching, exploring, fondly making love to each other, even to themselves. People prancing, riding in cavalcades, revelling, bathing, boating, balancing great red, luscious fruit on exuberantly splay-legged bottoms; creeping, peeping, nestling up to great birds who fed them berries. People made out of fruit or fruit made out of people. People all naked – except one – and all innocent and happy, however exercised in what most people she knew would have called shameful, indeed unmentionable, excess.

To a nicely brought-up girl it was shocking. To a nicely brought-up girl it was irresistible.

'What does it mean?' she asked. 'I never saw anything so beautiful in my life.'

'It is a copy of my old master's last painting. It is a mystery. Everything in it has meaning which I am working at. But principally I believe it contains the key to the Adamites' belief.'

'That is . . . explain it once more . . .'

'Through Love – and right Nature – we can achieve the highest earthly bliss. And, if we can find the one that is truly ordained for us, like Adam and Eve – made out of One, our First Parents – we can become one in God and return to the ultimate Oneness that is God Himself. That's what they believe.'

'And do you believe it?'

'I did not.'

'Now?'

'Now, yes, I am beginning to think I do.'

She let her eyes wander over the scene – almost as if she could step into it herself. First, the soft greens of the foreground, peopled with slim white – and black – bodies. Then on across the lake into the sweet greenish-yellowish pasture where the cavalcade rode joyously round in a ring. And finally on to the background of the lake, in which fantastical mermaids and other figures swam, where from its shores strange eggs spilled seed into the water and astonishing fruit buildings, with shapes that should have made her blush, puffed birds like ejaculated seed at a sky of the peacefullest blue, in which marvellous flying things and angel creatures like dragonflies wafted and sported in the gentle undulations of the breeze.

With difficulty she wrenched her eyes away from the wall. It was almost painful to come back into the winter world of Rensburg with its cold light and its harsh cries. She could still almost hear the sounds of that other place: laughter, proud hoofbeats, pleasant discourse, birdsong that would have shamed a nightingale, so sweet it was, the plash of water and the murmuring of a multitude of loves.

But he was there still. It redeemed everything.

'It is the most beautiful place in the world,' she told him.

He took her hand and they kissed.

There was no doubt in either of their minds that he was her Adam, she was his Eve. It seemed that they had been together since that Day of Creation; parted by something that was almost an irrelevance, and now together again.

'Look harder,' he said, taking her back to the first scene where Adam and Eve touched God.

The woman indeed had *her* face and body, and as she looked she saw that Adam was Julius.

She was not shocked to find that he knew her well enough to paint her naked, even though he had never seen her unclothed. There was indeed a little mole on her breast which he seemed to have known about. She was not even surprised to find the two of them in this central position in mankind's affairs. He was in love with her; she with him. It was Love that had brought them back to its and their origins.

He took her hand again and led her back to the far end of the picture. A man looked out at them: bright-eyed, alert, strong in will and learning; a face that seemed to stir unknowable memories; his finger pointing enigmatically to a reclining woman who again seemed to have *her*, Elisabeth's, features. Next to him was a glass cylinder in which stood a black and white bird.

'Look,' she said. 'He is the only one clothed. The only one except God.'

'He is the Grand Master of my master's day. He disappeared after my master's death, and his place was taken by a lesser man. This man was a magus. My master said he was a Pythagorean, may even have been the great Egyptian magician, Hermes Trismegistus. He could change shapes. You see that hooded crow beside him? It is also in the Beginning. My master said that that was one of his metamorphoses. He was there on Creation's morning. It was his pre-existence. I still feed hooded crows when I see them.'

'This is witchcraft,' said Elisabeth. 'Are you not afraid?'

'It is magic but not witchcraft. I would be afraid if there were no magic.'

'Why is my face on that woman?'

'It is Eve again, Eve redeemed.'

'Look,' said Elisabeth, suddenly.

'What is it?'

'I saw him move.'

'Who?'

'The man in the picture.'

'A trick of the light,' said Julius. 'I am no magician.'

'You may be wrong. Come closer, hold my hand.'

They walked up to the picture and looked hard at the man who continued to gaze out at them steadily.

'He cannot move,' said Julius. 'I created him. He is only paint. I painted this room to remind me of you, and Love, and of my master and of this picture which has yet to be completed. And to practise painting in this style because I find it hard. When I have done it, I shall be free.'

'Free?' she echoed.

How much she too would treasure such a freedom!

What happened next, Elisabeth could never satisfactorily explain, but it seemed at the time the most natural thing in the world. The magician looked at them and motioned with that pointing finger, beckoning them in.

The fresh green lawn appeared to spread towards them, the sounds which she had thought she had heard when she first looked at the picture began to enfold her once again, and the fragrance of a thousand fruits and flowers wafted in the air like church incense.

From the coldness of the room, hand in hand, they stepped into the warmth of the Garden, their clothes seeming to drop off them like butterflies' pupae.

They looked at each other's nakedness with joy and tenderness. It was as natural as the perfumed air they breathed that they should make love somewhere in this wonderful place, but there was no hurry, no feeling of brutish impatience. This was a world of innocence and tenderness. Tenderness and ripeness were the secrets of the Garden.

The magus did not speak to them. He did not need to; his look expressed everything – invitation, welcome, acceptance. Nor did any of the others – engaged, as they were, in contemplation, conversation, acrobatics, fruitful playfulness and the rituals of love – interrupt their activities to comment on their arrival or question their passage through their midst.

And so they walked, watched the bright colours of the birds and the butterflies, tasted the fruits, smelled the odours dropping from the trees, bathed, touched the wondrous gourd-shaped pods and carapaces that lightly bobbed on the water, peered – without prurience or shame – at the ingenious and indefatigable antics of the lovers, stroked the deer and the unicorn, and came at last to a bank where a boy carried a great blue mussel, its huge shell opened to disclose a silk-soft bed of mother of pearl, which he laid down for them upon the ground – and they crept in and lay down together, the shell discreetly sheltering them from view.

All their senses seemed to have been sharpened in the course of their progress through the Garden. The very breeze seemed like a caress, the smell of the flowers like waves in a sea of fragrance. And as they turned and touched each other, it seemed that their skin was of gossamer fineness, so that every sensation upon it went straight to the centre of their being. And it did indeed seem as if their being were one. He could feel his touch upon her – upon her bright breasts each crowned with strawberry, her white neck, her thighs, her rose which shed its dew in bright stream to the pearl below – he could feel all this as if it were upon his own body.

And, as she held his manhood, and tongued, and sucked and slid her hands around and under, and licked the drops that oozed like plum tears, these astonishing feelings were happening to her too.

And as they joined at last and became one, all self merged, it was as if One were riding round and round, up and down, in and out, in that extraordinary, fierce, sweet cavalcade of pleasure and plenty that was now entering, up and up and up, don't let this ever stop, and up and up into that red, taut, stretched out as far as one can go, bulbed, horned, veined, huge, yes, ah, ahhhhhhh, whooosh of birds flying away in mad, sweet, seeded delight to the very limits of perception while the dragonfly angels swooped and whooped with the everlasting rapture of being.

An eternity later, it could have been a minute, she found she was clothed, standing with Julius in front of the picture, looking at the magus who remained motionless.

'My master was an important man,' he said, 'honoured in his lifetime for his art. But I am not sure he ever knew Love. And I thought I should be the same. I was brought up without it. It is a sad thing to be a bastard.'

Did he not recall what had happened? She could not bring herself to ask him.

'It is not so sad now,' she said.

He looked at her. She was so beautiful it pained him.

'No,' he said, 'you are right.'

And he thought to himself, something has passed between us that she knows and I know not. She perhaps knows more of Love than I do. It is a sad thing to be a bastard.

Why does he not speak to me, she thought. Did it happen? Was it a dream?

'What is that gap for?' She ached to cover her sudden strange anxiety, and pointed towards the top right-hand corner of the wall.

The whole section had been draped when they had entered the Garden, but now the covering had fallen. She was pointing at the area that remained unpainted.

'That,' he said with a sad look. 'When I have done that, I will be mightily relieved, for I cannot yet think how it should be filled. The Brotherhood, which owns the original of this painting, pays me good money to labour at it, for it completes the third panel of my master's unfinished work. It is a matter of finding the idea for it, and copying the whole panel so I can send it back. But it has been a long and painful search.'

'What will it be?' she asked, looking at the wall more closely. 'I cannot believe that you would find it hard to imagine more joy. But all I can see here is horror.'

'No more joy,' he said. 'This is Hell. It is punishment for those without grace – and my punishment, for what I do not know. I cannot do it yet, but I am working upon it every day. There is plenty in this town to furnish inspiration.'

A shadow had fallen between them. The horrible images on the wall pressed down upon her. Why couldn't she ask him if he remembered being with her in the Garden? It was either too foolish – you did not walk into paintings – or too important to ask questions about. She felt ashamed.

In his turn, a mist of self-pity, seemingly out of nowhere, drifted across his unimaginable joy. His soul drew back. Why could he not tell her about Blommardine?

'Until Monday,' he said. 'Then we shall work on our plan of escape.'

Chapter 37

Hass was in his element. He loved to see the rows and rows of upraised faces turned towards him, still as sunflowers, as they sat rapt; and then to hear the gasp as they responded to some well-timed jab . . . It was all he wanted. To stir, to wheedle, to cajole, to coax, to arouse, to tickle, to whip, to wound, to drive it into a kicking, mindless frenzy. He loved to feel the crowd moving under his touch, he loved to stroke it and lead it and put his tongue between its ears. Hass was not a sexual man at all in the normal sense of the word. This was his delight. Oh, he believed in the Millennium with a passion, but an objective observer would affirm that it was an End to his means. He sometimes found he had an erection after a good sermon.

Fierens had, of course, noted his talents and his tendencies. They were no threat; quite the reverse. They were there to be used, just as Konrad's wealth and power were.

He spoke to Hass in the vestry after a particularly fine harangue which had lasted the best part of an hour and a half. It was the morning after Julius's interview with Elisabeth.

'The moment is coming shortly,' he said. 'I will give you a precise date in the next day or so. Your sermon this morning was excellent. Keep in that vein. We must wind and wind until . . .'

'Until?' questioned Hass, adjusting something under his tunic. 'Until what, Mr Fierens?'

Fierens looked at him. He had a big head like a booby covered with straight black hair atop a round, white face. It was marvellous how one with such an unprepossessing appearance could so move the multitude, but it was the way God worked. Away from the pulpit he was really quite a meagre little man.

'Until the spring breaks, Mr Hass.'

'The spring? You mean spring? Springtime?'

And they say he went to university, thought Fierens.

'Until the spring breaks, Mr Hass.'

'Ah. And then . . .'

'And then the Last Days will begin. You know the prophecies.'

'Hallelujah,' said Hass, hoping they would still need sermons.

'Oh, and another thing. I shall shortly be asking you to arrange a wedding. It will be before Easter, in three weeks' time.'

'A wedding? For whom?'

'For myself, Mr Hass. Who else?'

'Oh. Right,' said Hass, then went on after a pause. 'Do we still believe in church weddings?'

'For the daughter of the Master of the Council, we do. There is still a place for ceremony. It will mark the indissoluble marriage of the Anabaptists to the town.'

Chapter 38

It being a Sunday, Elisabeth had accompanied her father to the church where they had listened to Pastor Hass's eloquent delivery.

She found it difficult, indeed slightly disgusting, to be swayed by the little man in the same way as the people all around her. There was something absurd and yet at the same time disgusting in the way that they moved as a group, now down, now up; now ecstatic, now weeping. She had never been very keen on group anything; particularly today, for what she had to think about was anything but communal. It was about one and one making One.

However, the long sermon gave her an opportunity to reflect upon her conversation with the painter. She freely admitted to herself that she felt drawn to him in a most special, most particular way; but still she felt that there was something left unsaid; that, having given her heart to him, their love was not on hardening bricks and mortar but on thinning ice. It disturbed her to feel it because, even if she had a total instinct of trust, there would be many more hazardous obstacles to be surmounted – not least her father's implacable opposition. Her father was for Fierens, that was for sure. In some way they were bound up together. Her betrothal to him was more than a mere whim of conjugality on the part of the Anabaptist. It was to do with an alliance.

She would see him now, turning his head, observing that she wasn't listening to the sermon, giving a little imperceptible nod to her; not of love, not even of reproof, but a nod of 'I see you, I know what you're thinking, I know something you do not'. It made her blood run cold.

Why had Julius not agreed to go away with her yesterday? They wouldn't have done it, of course. She knew it would need planning and provisioning. But the simple affirmation would have been enough. There was something he was holding back; not his love – she could sense that was sincere enough – but something just as important without which love could not really be love at all. Could it be that he was not telling her the truth?

When the service had at last ended, she was afraid that Fierens would offer to walk home with them; but she was relieved to see him slip round towards the back of the church.

Her father lingered outside the church door, nodding and bowing to friends and colleagues. He enjoyed the little prerogatives of his position in the town. As Master of the Great Guilds' Council – even if some said the Council was not what it was – he was entitled to expect esteem and respect.

It was noticeable that rather more of the newcomers to the town than of the old families were among the esteemers on this occasion. But if Konrad had noticed it, he did not show it, and he walked back to the house in Broad Street in the best of humours.

'See, Daughter, the influence we have in this town?'

'Yes, Father.'

'And that,' said her father, 'is only the beginning.'

Chapter 39

Later that afternoon, a small figure could be seen walking along the frozen Broad Street so fast that she was almost skating. Old Frieda saw her coming. That looks like trouble for someone, she thought. And when the figure – which turned out to be that of a small, energetic young woman with a high colour – drew nearer, she gave a little nod to herself of recognition. She had seen this woman before, hanging about the other so-called prophet, Elijah. She rolled her eyes heavenward at the thought of it. Elijah! I ask you. It was a wonder they didn't all drop down dead of blasphemy.

She pondered where the little witch was going; and when the woman stopped and knocked at the Harting front door, Frieda's face puckered into an expression of concern as well as distaste. Wherever that creature went, no good would come of it. The cronies were going to have to keep an eye on that one.

'Open up,' the woman shouted. 'I want to see Harting.'

'Whatever's the matter?' asked Elisabeth, joining the old woman at the window.

Other faces appeared at other windows across the street.

'Come out, Harting. Stir your stumps.'

They could hear the latch being lifted, and the maid trying to quieten her.

'Well, what is it?' came Konrad's voice.

'You'd better let me in or I'll tell the whole street.'

Frieda and Elisabeth looked at each other, concerned and mystified. The woman crossed the threshold and disappeared from view. They heard the study door close and there was silence for a while.

'What can it mean?' asked Elisabeth.

'Nothing good, you can be sure of that,' the old nurse replied. 'This whole town needs to be stood in the corner with a dunce's hat for all the world to see.'

Chapter 40

Konrad had woken from his afternoon sleep to hear the knocking and shouting, and it had been a terrific shock to him. He thought that someone from the underground meetings had come to expose him. Of course, when he came to think about it later, he realized that such an event was almost impossible. It would not be in Fierens' interest to have him held up for general contempt. He was too important, too instrumental to the plans; but just for a moment he had panicked. There were things he'd done – had done to him – he wouldn't want anyone to know about.

'Well,' he said, looking at the young woman wildly, still not completely recovered. 'What is it you want?'

'Your daughter.'

'I beg your pardon.'

'Your daughter. Stealing the affections of my husband.'

'Your husband? I don't know what you mean, woman.'

'There.'

She pointed at the unfinished portrait in the corner of the room.

'That's me,' said Konrad, still not comprehending.

'He painted it, you silly old codger.'

Konrad looked at the painting, and looked at the woman, and slowly comprehension dawned.

'Penny dropped, has it?' said Blommardine. 'Charming when the Guild Master's daughter seduces a visitor's husband.'

'I know nothing of this,' said Konrad slowly, then he shouted, 'ELISABETH.'

'Hold me back,' said Blommardine, 'or I'll scratch her eyes out.'

Upstairs they heard Konrad's shout.

'What have you been up to, darling?' asked Frieda. 'Anything I should know about?'

'I'm in love, that's all.'

'I thought as much. That painter man?'

'Yes.'

'Why couldn't you love a nice Rensburg boy?'

'It doesn't work like that.'

'ELISABETH. COME HERE AT ONCE.'

A suspicion began to form in the old nurse's mind. She had heard through her network that Blommardine was married but she hadn't heard to whom.

'Oh, my Lord,' she said. 'She's wedded to him.'

'Who? Quick, Nurse.'

'Your painter. He's a married man.'

'I don't believe you.'

'Go on, darling. Down you go. Face the music.'

Elisabeth went slowly, a terrible dread gnawing at her heart like the serpent at the roots of the Tree of Life.

Her father was waiting grimly at the foot of the stairs.

'Well, miss,' he said. 'You've been up to some pretty tricks.'

He led her by her ear into the study like a small child.

'Bitch.'

Blommardine sprang at her and pulled her hair. Konrad held them both at arm's length.

'Control yourself, madam,' he said to Blommardine, 'and let us hear your accusation.'

'Can you or can you not deny that you have seduced the affections of my husband?'

'I have seduced no one. Who is your husband?'

'Julius the painter, worse luck.'

So it was true, thought Elisabeth. He was holding something back after all. She felt suddenly faint. She couldn't breathe. Konrad caught her roughly and almost threw her onto a chair. The brusqueness helped to revive her.

'Her guilt has caught up with her,' said Blommardine.

'She is ill,' said her father, anger vying with annoyance. 'Stand back. Give her air.'

'Shock, was it?' said Blommardine, a little more kindly. 'You ought to be more careful who you make eyes at.'

Elisabeth couldn't think who could have told her. And then she remembered the noise at the kitchen door. Billa! She had seen her on one or two occasions talking to Fierens. So that was how it was; spied on in her own house. She was not going to cry, not in front of this woman; besides, mere tears seemed totally inadequate. She had lost love, faith, respect, dignity, her father's trust . . . There was nothing she had not lost including her virginity, though doubtless they did not know she'd lost that too.

She stared blankly in front of her.

'I didn't seduce anybody,' she said. 'It was love, that was all. It doesn't matter now.'

'Well, that's all right, then,' said Blommardine. 'Just so long as you know. You keep your claws off him. He's far too susceptible. Plausible too, though, I grant you. You're not the first. There's a devil of plausibility in him. You'd think butter wouldn't melt in his mouth.'

Konrad showed her out, gracious, apologizing, as if he were canvassing for a guild vote.

'So sorry you've been put to this trouble . . . I regret . . .'

He was rather attracted to her. She'd be like a ferret in bed. When he'd finally waved her on her way, he returned to the study.

'Well, miss . . .'

'I'm sorry I embarrassed you.'

'Embarrassed me? You embarrassed yourself. "I am in love with no man I know",' he mimicked. 'The story will be round the town tomorrow. How you let a married man trick you into . . . It's the oldest one in the book.'

She did not think it would be round the town. Fierens would see to that.

'I didn't let him trick me into anything, Father. I . . . liked him. We talked. He told me about himself. He has been to Italy. That is not a crime.'

'He did not tell you all about himself.'

'No . . . no, not all.'

She suddenly found, in spite of herself, that she was crying; hopeless, heavy tears for the passing of a dream.

'Not all, not all, not all,' she wept.

'Well, at any rate, one thing is settled,' said her father in a milder voice.

'What is that?'

'Tomorrow you can announce your betrothal to Fierens.'

She did not have the energy to argue.

He picked up his portrait and threw it on the fire. As it burnt, paint melted and flowed from his image's forehead, dripping in a stream of carmine across his cheek.

Chapter 41

Blommardine seemed unusually quiet that Sunday afternoon. He wondered whether it was her time of the month, which habitually made her behave like a boiled egg, but a quick calculation told him this was not so.

There was no conversation over the cold and meagre supper she slapped down in front of him, nor afterwards as he sat in front of the fire thinking of one and one making One, for which he was considerably grateful. The last thing he wanted was her shrill abrasions interrupting his vision of completeness. However, as the evening wore on, her silence began to have a menacing quality. He had known such silences before, and they tended to precede a storm.

'Everything all right?' he ventured at last, looking over to where she sat furiously sewing something that looked like a dishcloth.

'All right?' she replied, sewing on, without looking at him. 'What's that supposed to mean?'

'Just asking,' he said mildly. 'Simply interested.'

She made a noise like a retching cat, but offered nothing more in the way of comment.

He shrugged and continued his study of the flames. He could see in their leaping mime-show all manner of bright possibilities now he knew that Elisabeth could be his. The only thing that remained was to tell her of his inconvenient state of matrimony. It would be difficult, he knew. She was bound to have objections. But when he told her of the Adamite belief that Love was the Sacrament, not marriage – a fact that he sensed she knew instinctively – then all would be forgiven and they could elope at their leisure. Well, not too much leisure. There was the loathsome Fierens to contend with. The slightest hint of preparation or packing and the man would move before they could be off. He must speak with her tomorrow, arrange some stratagem so that they could be alone; yes, he would pretend that there was more work he could do on Konrad's coat while the Guild Master himself went to his office . . .

Julius stirred in his chair. Blommardine had presumably gone to bed. He supposed he must have dozed off. There was a deathly cold in the house as if winter itself had taken lodging. He leaned forward and riddled the fire. A little flash of ember suddenly caught flame, flared, leaped and sank again into ember like the soul returning to its Maker.

An altogether jollier life-history, Julius thought, than most souls around here. What a difference there was between hopeful humanism and that dire view of wicked humanity whose only hope was a vindictive God, peddled by these appalling preachers. It seemed clear that if you believed people wicked, they would be wicked. But that, of course, was what the preachers wanted – wicked people afraid of their wickedness.

He suddenly saw, with a sizzle of insight, a new side to his old master's view of Hell. Those dark visions of his weren't Satan's Hell, they were man's Hell, preachers' Hell – evil humanity without faith, disnatured, deserted by God, separated from each other, ridden by devils. Not one of the damned was doing anything to help his fellow. Sin, it seemed, was a selfish business . . .

A last spark flared and died. Julius shivered, rose, and went upstairs. The bedroom was bolted on the inside and a note was pinned to the door.

'DON'T COME NEAR ME', it read.

Julius shrugged. It suited him. He found an old blanket in a chest and settled down in front of the fire, huddling on his cloak for extra measure.

It was not a comfortable repose. He rose early with the feeling that, somehow in the night, a furniture-maker had got hold of his joints and glued them rigid. The fire refused to respond to his ministrations and needed four applications of the tinderbox. When Blommardine finally appeared, she reacted in like manner – only in her case she would not even ignite. They breakfasted in silence by candlelight on small beer and dry bread. He could not face the mutton around which the fat had turned a particular, almost greeny yellow.

'It is like a disease,' he said, 'this mutton of ours. You should put a cross on the larder door and bury it secretly this evening.'

No reply.

Presently a little light seeped into the sky, and Julius rose.

'I must go to the studio and prepare my paints for the day,' he said. 'I know you will excuse me.'

Blommardine turned her face towards a repulsive figurine of the Virgin Mary which she hung on the wall to annoy him. Little he cared now what she did. Let her peruse her repulsive figurine until she was blue in the face or as green as mutton fat. He was going to see his Complete Love; nothing else mattered. Picking up his cloak, he strode out into the morning.

The sun was rising now in a clear sky, touching the snow-decked streets with Botticelli hues of pinkish gold. It was as if Nature had wiped out at a stroke all the hatred and ugliness that had collected in the town. He decided to take a roundabout route. A sense of ungovernable hope seized him. He started to caper and run for joy; skidded, tripped and

195

almost fell; laughing uproariously, he ran on. It was partly the pleasure, the relief of not being with Blommardine; but mostly it was the knowledge of his imminent meeting with Elisabeth.

He started to sing the old Christmas carol: 'There is a rose new-sprung . . .'

He had missed the old songs at Christmas. Why not now?

A window flew open and a deluge of slops nearly caught him.

'Drunk so early? For shame,' called a woman's voice.

'It was Christmas, wasn't it?' shouted back Julius. A Saint, passing, frowned and came over to him.

'Who are you, talking about Christmas? It is Christ-tide if it is anything. Mass is an abomination. And anyway, Christ-tide is well past. Your name, sir?'

'I am Eros,' said Julius, happily. 'I am Love. Do you not know me?'

'Catch him,' shouted the Saint. 'He is a devil and a lover of devils.'

He ran after him with surprising speed in his bony knees, so that Julius was hard put to it to outpace him. Several other Saints – they were everywhere these days – joined the chase, but Julius, knowing the streets better, was able at last to elude them.

'You shan't escape, Love,' cried the first Saint, frustratedly. 'You may get away now, but I shall have you, Love. I never forget a face.'

Julius turned and made a rude gesture before he darted into an alleyway which took him – through a little series of other passages – at last to his studio door. He turned to make sure he had shaken off his pursuers, but the alley was silent.

Opening the door quietly, he crept softly upstairs.

Once in his studio, he set to work hurriedly. He had spent more time than he had intended on the way. Idiotic capering about at your age, he thought. You could have got yourself into trouble. Mix the paints, put out the brushes, clean the palette . . . Bustle, bustle. The familiar disciplines calmed him. It was good. He must think clearly now.

At last he was ready and within ten minutes presented himself, panting slightly, at Konrad's front door. As he knocked, he looked up, hoping to catch sight of his beloved, but there was no dear face or shadow at the window. Doubtless she would be tripping downstairs, hurrying to the door to beat Billa to the happiness of letting him in . . .

But it was not Elisabeth who opened the door, nor was it even Billa. It was Konrad himself, and he appeared to be out of sorts.

'So,' he said to Julius, 'it is you.'

He made no immediate move to let him in.

'Yes,' said Julius at last. 'I cannot deny it.'

'It would be better for you if you could,' said the older man cryptically.

'I'm afraid I don't understand,' said Julius, though a terrible unease was beginning to gather in what old Franciabi in his anatomy class called the *viscera minima*. What manner of good morning might this be?

'Come in, then, Painter,' replied Konrad unpleasantly, 'and you shall receive enlightenment even if I have to drum it into you.'

'I hope that won't be necessary,' said Julius, awkwardly. 'Something you don't like about the painting?'

Konrad threw open the door of his study and revealed Elisabeth sitting white-faced, holding the blackened frame of the canvas from whose centre her father's features had been replaced by a charred-edged hole. She did not look up as they entered.

'Something you didn't like about the painting?' Julius repeated, stupidly.

'Something I didn't like about the painter,' explained Konrad heavily.

'Oh.'

A tremendous blow caught him just above the small of the back. It was so sudden, so unexpected, that he dropped automatically to his knees. The worst thing about it, though, was the noise Elisabeth made – an awful in-drawing of breath that sounded like a shriek – as though she herself were suffering the pain.

He thought he must have had a heart attack. He had heard people describing the sensation as a feeling like a blow behind the ribs.

He looked at Elisabeth again. It was as if the whole of Nature had slowed down. Nothing seemed to be moving. Suddenly the ruined canvas she held slid from her grasp and clattered to the floor. Her expression of pain and fear did not alter, and her hands continued to grasp the empty air as though the canvas remained.

Pain flooded through him as the shock subsided. He turned to ask Konrad for assistance, to try to explain that he must be having some kind of attack.

'Help me,' he said. 'Having an . . . attack . . .'

And then Julius saw the heavy knobbed stick in the man's hands. Surely Konrad had not struck him?

'Yes,' the man smiled horribly at him, 'attack is just what you're having.'

And he struck him again, this time across the shoulders. And again Julius fell forward, this time onto his hands.

'What? What?' was all he could say.

'You have been discovered in your beastly stratagem. Seduce my daughter, would you?'

Another dreadful blow fell, this time across his buttocks. He could not, would not crouch here like a boy and be beaten in front of his love. He scrambled up, red-faced, tears of pain oozing from his nose and eyes.

'I did not seduce your daughter. Who says so?'

'Never mind who says so. It's what *you* said or rather didn't say that I'm interested in.'

'I said I loved her. I still love her.'

He turned and looked again at Elisabeth. Her expression had not changed. She was locked in her own private nightmare. Another dreadful blow rained down on him, cutting across his thighs as he turned. He fell again, halfway across the arm of the chair.

'It's what you didn't say, Painter. Bad enough to pay court to one who is your better. But worse, far worse, Painter, to pay court to such a precious jewel . . .'

He paused. Julius struggled up again. He was not a coward – or only sometimes, but not now. He was not going to let this bully treat him in this way, to humiliate him, without opposition. He looked around for a weapon. If the man wanted to fight, at least he would defend himself. The poker by the fire looked to offer some means of resistance. But Konrad had not yet finished.

'. . . when you are already married. When you lied to me and said you were not married. But you are, aren't you, Painter? You are married . . .'

Elisabeth gave another of those terrible inward, involuntary groans, and all the fight went out of Julius. So she knew! What a fool he had been not to tell her at once! What weakness, what vapid hopefulness, what stupidity not to know that malice would find him out. He deserved whatever punishment was meted out to him.

'Married, married, married . . .' cried Konrad, beating him every time he repeated the word.

Julius turned like an ox and let the blows rain down upon him, and he wept not for pain but for the shame and stupidity of the thing.

'And there was something worse even than that, Painter. You know what that was, don't you, Painter? Don't you, Painter? Don't you, Painter?'

The questions and the blows rained on.

'I know, I know,' he shouted. 'I know, I know, I know, I know.'

'What was it, Painter?'

'I didn't *tell* her I was married.'

Another tremendous blow which knocked him to the floor. Another terrible sound from Elisabeth who still didn't move. Konrad started to kick as well as beat.

'Why, Painter? Why did you not tell her? Tell her now.'

'Because I was weak . . . I wanted to know that she loved me . . . before I told her . . .'

'And do you still love her?'

'Yes. I would die for her.'

'That you shall.'

Julius was beginning to lose consciousness. One eye was half-closed.

A rib felt as if it had been broken. Blood poured from his head. The blows continued to fall.

'And now let us hear from your true love. Tell him, Elisabeth. Do you still love him after all his deceit? Do you? Quick, girl. Coo if you will.'

Konrad's stick was raised again as if he would strike her. Hurt though he was, Julius half-rose and turned a look of such hatred upon him that the older man thought better of it.

'Do ... you ... love ... him?' he repeated, striking now at Julius again.

The question hung in the air, unanswered.

'Yes ... N ... no?' Konrad reiterated, smiting with every syllable.

Suddenly, shockingly, after her prolonged silence, Elisabeth broke down.

'Stop, stop, stop, stop, stop.'

'Yes ... or no? ...'

'No.'

The sound seemed drawn out of her like the cracking of a tree.

All at once the beating ceased. Julius swam in and out of consciousness.

'You are sure?' asked Konrad. 'You wouldn't like to change your mind? I think you would! I smell weakening.'

'I could never love him. He has betrayed love. I never want to see him again.'

'Hear that, Painter?'

Julius groaned, swimming in, swimming out.

'It is just as well, then, isn't it, that she has come to her senses? It would never do if she still loved someone else when she was actually going to marry Pastor Fierens in the Cathedral at Easter.'

'Beat me more,' mumbled Julius. 'I deserve everything. More ...'

This time, he passed out for a longer spell. He came to in a heap of snow rather redder-tinged than the dawn's offering – more Pontormo than Botticelli, he thought, inconsequentially. Every bone in his body – including his skull – seemed to throb, pang or ache – mostly all three. His face was a mass of contusions. His nose was bleeding, and his eye had now completely closed up. His left arm didn't seem to work.

Two crones were standing over him.

'You been in a spot of trouble, sonny,' said the taller one.

'I should think he knows that, Irmgard,' said the other. 'Where do you live, dearie?'

Julius opened his mouth and tried to speak but his lips kept getting in the way.

'It's cruel what they done to you,' said the one called Irmgard, 'but cruel's a way of life these days.'

She dabbed his lips with snow, and they helped him to his feet.

'Feeling better now, dear?'

'Not much,' he managed to say.

'That's right. Well, at least we've got you up and talking. I thought you'd never move again. Where did you say you lived?'

They took him home through the quieter streets. Few people were about, but one or two looked at them curiously.

'He had a nasty fall,' said Irmgard to an inquisitive Saint.

Groggy though he was, Julius was aware of the kindness of the old girls. It had demanded courage as well as strength for them to help him.

Arriving at his lodgings, he thanked them as best he could, telling them that they were the two just women for whom God would spare the town.

'Don't count on it, dearie,' said the shorter one. 'Who knows how long we shall be here. Will you be all right now?'

He nodded, clinging to the door as he watched them shuffle off down the street, benign old blackbirds in a city full of crows.

'Don't expect me to have any sympathy,' said Blommardine when he staggered in. 'How d'you think I feel?'

Chapter 42

The following days were more painful to his mind than to his body, though God knew that was painful enough. The physical assault was over, but in his heart and soul the punishment went on. Why had he been such a fool? All the precepts of common sense could have told him that honesty was the necessary currency of affection – let alone of love. Why had he been so fearful? If this were the pre-ordained partner of his life, if it were the sacrament that superseded marriage, why, then, he might have trusted it to communicate itself to her as much as to him. But he had not, and as in some ghastly parody of some old Romance, he had failed the Test and the magic could not work. He was Sir Gawain; her father, the Green Knight. He was Tristan; she was Iseult.

February, the darkest month of all, was over at last. 'The dark before the dawn' his tutor in Florence had called it in their last days together, when their conversation roamed from Art to Nature. 'A short, blind month, bleak as a Norse dwarf.' They were finally into March, but it seemed they were locked in a perpetual February. He recalled how Ammanati had wrinkled his mouth at the month whose very mention tasted sour and bitter.

Now Julius felt keenly the absence of his, or any other's, counsel and friendship. He could not expect it nor did he obtain it from Blommardine. Exactly why she resented his broken heart so much was unclear to him. After all, she had flaunted her own obsession with the Saint, and he had not been the first of her fancies. She did what she liked and had always done so, and he had not cared so long as she didn't bring back the French sickness. It was sweeping the country like the plague. (Some said Luther would never have got started if it hadn't been for the bone-ache looking like a visitation of God.) But enough of that. Why should she care?

He asked her about it one day, not expecting an answer, more for something to do. He could not yet go out. If he walked far, he felt dizzy. So he pretended to read the Bible by the fire, and occasionally addressed the ceiling which sometimes seemed very low, and always appeared attentive.

'I wonder why she cares, ceiling,' he mused. 'That's what I can't understand. Oh, I wouldn't have expected her to warn me. But what is extraordinary is her vindictiveness. I never did her any harm that I can think of. One doesn't harm witches unless one is very sure of one's ground, ceiling.'

'Stop talking to the fucking ceiling,' said Blommardine suddenly, throwing down her dishcloth. 'It's not that I care a damn about what *you* do. I didn't marry you as you . . . I married you as an idea, a passport to something, the land of lemonade. Do you know what I mean?'

'She's speaking to me, ceiling. Don't go away.'

'It's the principle of the thing. Understand?'

'Not in the least,' said Julius.

'Of course you don't. Always been short in that department, haven't you, ducky?'

'You never use the passport anyway,' he observed after a pause, 'it's not taking you anywhere. We're not going anywhere.'

'What happened to the travels, the meetings with the famous, the *insignis pictor* honoured by all? Look at van Eyck, knighted by the Duke of Burgundy. He did all right. What happened to the artist's life?' she asked.

'What happened to the artist's wife? We could have been happy in an unexceptional sort of way. Children . . . neighbours . . . geraniums . . . But you wouldn't have any of that. You wanted mischief. That is the witch's pabulum.'

She looked at him with green eyes behind which he was astonished to see a moisture forming.

'I wanted Life,' she said. 'And you have found it. That is the mischief. I can't forgive you for that.'

You never knew a woman, however long you lived with her, ceiling, he thought.

Chapter 43

As his headaches diminished, he was able to take to the streets. He visited his studio and tried to paint for a little, but his head swam and he was forced to stop. It was too cold anyway. A bitter wind had started to blow from the north-east, and snow was falling again. He went out once more and made his way precariously – his left arm was still in a sling – round to Broad Street, where he stood in an alley and looked hopefully towards the Harting house.

It had come to this. He, who had stood at heaven's door, reduced to lurking on windy corners. He contemplated throwing pebbles at her window but decided against it. Once he thought he saw a movement in one of the upstairs rooms and he waved, desperately. There was no answering response. He retired into the shadows of Blue Boar Lane, feeling his loss like a cold wound, never to be assuaged.

It was foolish of him, he knew, even to have thought of it, but he was beyond everything save desperation. The wedding with Fierens was due to take place within a month. The revenge he had promised Julius as a boy could not be more exquisitely exacted. Somehow the thing had to be stopped. If all else fails, he thought, I shall have to kill him. But this caused him a further surge of doubt.

At the Acadamietta it had once been debated whether killing could ever be justified. He could not quite remember their eventual findings, but recalled that it had been argued in More's *Utopia* (published in the year of his master's death) that the assassination of the head of a neighbouring (warlike) state was preferable to war. War, after all, was what Fierens and the Saints were engaged in. War against order, war against law, war (this was the most serious charge) against Love. The finding must be, then, that Fierens should indeed be despatched. Could he himself do it? He was not a warlike man. He had once been instructed to kill a chicken and he had made the most fearful mess of it. And yet he could not possibly get somebody else to deputize for him in such a desperate undertaking – even if he could have found someone to trust.

It looked as though he would indeed have to be executor as well as beneficiary. The fact that his arm was in a sling didn't exactly help, but doubtless Roland or any one of a hundred heroes would have managed it.

On the positive side, it did seem that Fierens was a shadowy figure.

He came and went secretly. Such a stealthy comer and goer might be assailed in an alleyway.

He set himself to watch the man, and the shadows of Blue Boar Lane seemed as good a place as any to start. As it happened, his watch was well rewarded. Fierens, drawing on his resources of mummery, threw at least part of himself into the role of bridegroom-to-be, preparing the way for that greater Bridegroom in his heart. His golden thread floated after him as he scuttled back and forth between Broad Street and the Anabaptist headquarters.

Sometimes he would sit with Elisabeth, reading to her from the writings of Thomas Muntzer or David Joris or one of the other approved apocalypsists. At others he would walk out with Konrad, long promenades which would take in the city walls, its towers and gates; or to the warehouses where food was kept; or to the Great Guild Hall where they would sit in long, deliberately drawn-out meetings designed to drive all moderate members from the room with boredom.

Wherever he went, Julius, an incongruous figure with his pale face (now losing its scars) and his slinged arm, would follow.

As if to complement his own sense of urgency, there was a strange feeling in the air which could be sensed more and more about the town. Something was going to happen. The city, like Julius's heart, seemed full now, almost to bursting point. Outside the walls, the pent-up river creaked and grumbled, as if it too sensed the universal tension.

And still Julius haunted the streets, waiting for the opportunity and nerving himself to meet it.

One day, as he walked back after watching Fierens go to ground in an interminable Council meeting, he came across some Anabaptist boys throwing snowballs.

'Ah, well,' he reflected, 'some things don't change. Children will still be children even if their parents have gone mad.'

Approaching, he noticed that the object of their aim was a little bundle of black lying in the snow. Drawing nearer still, he saw that it was not merely a bundle, but that there was one withered arm sticking out of it.

'Stop it,' he shouted to the boys. 'What are you doing?'

A snowball packed tight as a stone hit him squarely in the chest. Suddenly wild with rage, he picked up the old woman's stick (for old woman it was) and ran at the youths. They fled, still throwing balls. One turned and shouted back.

'What you get so mad for, mister? She's a witch, ain't she? Papist witch!'

But they ran on to find more mischief.

He went back to the old woman, who was now sitting up. Apart from a cut on her cheek, she didn't seem too hurt.

'They were breaking windows,' she said. 'I told them not to. Then they set about breaking me! You don't recognize me, do you, dearie?'

'No,' he said. 'Should I?'

'I'm the one who found you when you was lying in the snow.'

'Why, yes,' he said. 'You are. Thank you again. I would have died.'

'One good turn deserves another,' she said. 'We'll need more good turns and all if we're to get through this lot.'

She gestured not at the boys or the street or even the town but at the world.

'I've seen war,' she said, 'I've seen drought and war and failed harvests. I've seen flood and the black death, but I've never seen anything like this.'

Julius helped her back to her door. One or two other heads were now peering, sheepishly, from neighbouring windows. The old woman was a known Catholic. They didn't want to be involved.

'We must pray to St Jude,' she told him.

He walked home, under a sunset which bloodied the edge of huge clouds rearing up from the horizon like Antichrist himself.

Chapter 44

Night was always a fearful time, even in a city as large as Rensburg.

Screams went unheeded. You never knew if they were genuine or merely a ruse to lure you outside and cut you into pieces as a prelude to stealing your chattels and raping your wife and servants.

People barred their doors. In winter, wolves roamed the suburbs. You did not go out unless you had business of the most urgent kind.

With the arrival of the Anabaptists, and the motley crew of ruffians, thugs, petty criminals, dispossessed, desperadoes, and every kind of madman who followed in their wake, things became significantly worse.

Even Julius – and he was desperate enough – did not try to dog Fierens after dark. So when, one night, he heard wild shouts and hallooing in the street, he hardly bothered to stir. Halloos were a common thing. If you got up to look out of the window every time someone caterwauled you would never finish your supper.

As it happened, he was sitting up by the fire half-reading one of the translations of Plato that he had found, actually printed in the town. He was still wrestling with the problem of taking another man's life. Could he do it? Should he do it? Plato did not provide any really concrete answers. Murder had not featured in any of his descriptions so far of the Good Life. And what would Elisabeth say? Would she ever forgive him anyway? To her gentle soul, the killing, even of a monster, would surely be repugnant. And yet what else could he do?

Blommardine was in bed. It was where she seemed to spend most of her time these days. Her fires were banked.

'Wawoo, wawoo,' went the cry in the distance.

'Wolves?' he said to the ceiling. 'Not in the middle of town?'

'Raapaa, raapaaa . . .'

No, there was definitely a human tone to the sound. Was someone out there being raped? He prepared, against his better judgement, to go out and see.

'Raapaart.'

The sounds were coming nearer; and, as they approached, he could hear that they were accompanied by a murmur of voices. Some kind of tumult was certainly afoot. Was there trouble on the ramparts?

'Raapaaant.'

This was no ordinary case of drunkenness or brigandage. He put down his book, dowsed the candle, and peered out of the window. He had a sudden ghastly feeling that the crowd might be coming for him. Could it be that the Saint who had chased him had tracked him down? He peeped out discreetly – trying not to show his face.

'Repent, repent! Repent of the filth and faeces that are your sins! Repent! Follow me! Come to the Cathedral now and repent!' cried a voice he thought he recognized.

'Come to the Cathedral. The Lord is coming!' repeated the crowd. 'Come now, everyone. To the Cathedral . . .'

Reassured that the summons was not especially personal, he looked out further.

To his astonishment, he saw Konrad and Fierens running wildly in the snowy street at the head of a rapidly increasing multitude. Because he was curious to see what might be the outcome of such a summons, and there was always the chance that Elisabeth might be (or be obliged to be) among the crowd, he put on his cloak and hat, and was just about to go out when Blommardine appeared fully dressed at his shoulder.

'Don't think I'm going to miss the fun, do you?' she said. 'This is where it starts to get serious.'

They emerged together and were soon engulfed in a running throng whose numbers were substantially made up, Julius noted, of women – some of whom, especially those who bore the signs of being ex-nuns, were already throwing themselves into the snow and experiencing the most profound exaltations.

'Repent, repent,' the cry went on ahead.

'Sweet Jesu, come, take me now,' called the visionaries, 'fill me up. Make me as thou art.'

Some even shouted, 'He has come into me. Oh! Oh, no! Aaaaargh. I am He.'

Gap-toothed, heavy men on the edge of the crowd, their faces sweaty-red in the torchlight, followers of the Anabaptists but believers only in brutishness, smiled deviously at the women and fingered their cudgels.

The multitude poured like a landslide into the Cathedral, and when it could hold no more, at last the momentum stopped and the people fell silent, save for their panting, which propelled their breath upward in a mist so that it hovered above them like a group halo. All faces now turned upward eagerly as Fierens and Konrad climbed into the pulpit.

Konrad was the first to address them, his chest still heaving with inspiration.

'Brethren and Sisters, many of you are Rensburgers and know me. I am, until the time comes (as it will shortly) when such things will mean nothing, I am Master of the Council of the Great Guilds of Rensburg. To those who do not know me, this purely temporal and temporary title

207

means that you can trust me. I am not some cogging, teasing impostor on the make. So when I say that Rensburg has been chosen as the Seat of the Elect, you can take it that I am not trying to deceive, but that I am uttering the fact as truth. As sure as I stand before you, time is running out for the world. Antichrist is abroad. The Great Day of the Millennium is upon us. And only those who repent then of their sins, only those, here in Rensburg, will be saved. And now I will hand over to the prophet whose presence in our midst both proves the imminence of the crisis, and yet points us to the path of salvation. Brother Fierens, talk to the people.'

Fierens stood impassively, arms folded, looking out at the vast concourse.

'Talk to the people, Brother Fierens,' entreated Konrad.

Still Fierens gazed upon them, his head turning this way and that, searching out the wickedness in each and every heart.

'Brother Fierens, will you not speak? Ask him to speak to you,' Konrad urged the crowd.

A murmuring arose which quickly gathered volume.

'Speak to us, we beseech you. Help us. We want to be saved. Spare us . . .'

'He cannot hear you,' shouted Konrad. 'Ask again.'

'SPEAK TO US, GUIDE US, SAVE US, HAVE MERCY,' yelled the people.

Suddenly Fierens moved. His arm shot straight out at the angle of forty-five degrees from the horizontal. Silence fell like a curtain. It was an impressive performance.

Julius looked round for Blommardine and found her, to his surprise, beside him. Her familiar look of sardonic discontent had vanished and her countenance expressed nothing short of rapture. But she wasn't looking at Fierens. She was gazing at a new arrival, a tall stranger with a face that seemed younger than the cloud of white hair that surrounded it, who stood like a prophet staring down from a little gallery that over-looked the entrance to the choir.

'Down on your knees,' said Fierens in a terrifying voice. 'Every one of you. Down.'

And he pointed the outstretched arm towards the floor. The whole congregation sank without question. It was a feat requiring considerable adroitness in such a close circumstance. They knelt there, trembling, expectant, dreading the lash. It did not come. Silence again.

'Speak to them, Brother Fierens, for God's sake,' cried Konrad.

'Why should I speak to those who are so deep in sin?'

'See! They repent.'

'That is show, mere sham. It is the clothes of repentance. Take off your clothes,' he shouted suddenly.

The people looked up at him uncertainly. It was cold. Surely he didn't mean . . .

'You see,' said Fierens to Konrad, almost conversationally. 'They will not take off their clothes. That is how deeply they feel repentance. They cannot even be bothered to take off their outward and visible clothes. If they will not take off the clothes that we can see, how much less likely they are to remove the semblance of repentance, and show their real shame and sorrow . . . They will put on another cloak tomorrow, I'll warrant. I think I shall go home.'

Fierens gathered up a book and turned in the pulpit, but Konrad held him back.

'See what you have done,' shouted Konrad to the people. 'Oh ye of little faith. You cannot even do as our prophet asks. He wishes to see if you are truly prepared to strip yourselves naked of sin. What is the matter with you?'

By now, certain ex-nuns were already stripping off. This was just the kind of thing they had left the nunnery for. Pretty soon nearly the whole congregation was ripping off doublets and tearing down hoses. Dresses were flapped over shoulders, shifts unlaced and shoes kicked off in a wholesale pell-mell of disrobement. People at first ashamed of their nakedness began to display it proudly. Never in the Cathedral's history had such a scene been enacted. Hairy white buttocks, sloping bosoms, dainty breastlets, stubby red organs fringed with fuzz . . . to Julius's eye the picture was one that only those masters of the multiple in the true late Netherlandish tradition, van Eyck or indeed his master Bosch, doyen of the bizarre, could have painted.

But his reverie was rudely interrupted.

'There are still some of you who do not want to put off sin,' shouted Konrad, looking hard at Julius. 'The prophet will not speak until you are all stripped of your pride.'

Eager hands reached out and grabbed him. His hat and cloak were torn off and a myriad of arms – especially women's – reached underneath.

'Come on, Brother. Get 'em off. Nice 'n' easy.'

'Who does he think he is?'

He could smell the sweat and reek of their nakedness around him. It was pointless to resist.

Next to him, he noticed Blommardine, already naked, nipples stiff with cold (at least he supposed it was the cold), staring up and up at the prophetic figure in the gallery.

'Mind my arm,' he urged, stepping out of his hose as gracefully as he might, though he couldn't quite divest himself of the leggings, and felt them flapping about underneath his nakedness like ducks' feet.

Others in the Cathedral, who had come out of interest rather than

209

belief and who had no intention of stripping to the buff, were being offered similar assistance with varying degrees of compliance or outrage. One member of the watch, a plump old josser known to generations of Rensburgers, who had come to check on the proceedings, very nearly had apoplexy as his doublet got stuck over his head, and stumbled out like a bare-bottomed anthropophagus. It was a sight – the whole Cathedral was a sight – that would have had any normal spectator in stitches. But there was no laughter. No one dared laugh. It was not a laughing matter. Anyone who had experienced mirth would have been severely dealt with. This was a matter of eternal Life or irredeemable Death.

Finally it was done, and the whole of the vast congregation was, as the prophet had commanded, mother-naked and meekly kneeling. The prophet now spoke.

Fierens could feel the golden wire glowing and guiding him as he opened his mouth. He did not need to choose the words.

'Look at you,' he said. 'Just look at you. No, don't look round. Look at yourself. Do you like what you see? Smell yourself. Yes . . . go on . . . You are rank. The stench of your sin rises up. You are shame. You are shards . . . Why should anyone love you? Why should God love you?'

He paused for the congregation to let out a groan. Then he held up his hand again.

'But,' he said, 'and there is a but. God can make you sweet again. Yes, you that truly repent can be made sweeter than the waters of Abana and Pharpar. God can make you beautiful – yes, even you down there with your bandage and your sores – beautiful beyond the contemplation of angels. You are naked now. But God will clothe you in glory. For this town . . . alone in the world . . . has been appointed to be saved. SAVED! Only this one. Do you know what that means? Not a city, not a town, not a village, not a hamlet, not a house, not a hovel will remain. But you . . . you have the chance to win Eternal Life. Darkness will cover the earth. And destruction on such a scale and of such horror that the very contemplation of it presses on my heart so that I can barely speak . . .'

Here he paused, clutching his chest. The congregation waited, poised on its naked knees.

'It will come at Easter,' he continued at length. 'Those who truly repent and wish to be saved must be in the town. The rest must make what shift they can. If there are any unrighteous left, this town itself – like all the rest – will be utterly consumed . . . No, no,' he cried, clawing at the air. 'Do not ask me to speak to you of this destruction. The ground torn asunder, serpents uncoiling from the pit, cacodaemons, winged chimaeras, harpies, gorgons, monsters whom but to name would make you run mad, rivers of fire, babes torn from their mothers' breasts, children trampled, men and women eyeballs bubbling, skin crackling, bowels ripping, bones flying apart ... and above it all ... Antichrist ... scaled, tailed, horned, hoofed, high as a mountain, and spitting skulls like grape-pips ...'

He drooped and seemed almost to faint. Konrad supported him. The congregation screamed and moaned.

'This is the dissolution of things which I have been privileged to see,' he went on in a calmer voice. 'Get dressed now and go home. The call will come. Be sure you answer it.'

It took some time for them all to leave the Cathedral. Blommardine turned to Julius, eyes shining.

'Did you see him? I'm in love,' she said. 'We can be friends again now.'

'Oh, good,' said Julius.

He had seen Elisabeth, naked, in the crowd.

Chapter 45

Early next morning, men could be seen leaving the Anabaptist quarter in twos and threes, casually, and making their way towards the market-place where one of their number was setting up a stall.

It looked like a stall for woven goods such as some of the Anabaptist craftsmen, refugees from the textile towns of Holland, used to sell – with some success – to their new neighbours in the city.

But on this occasion the stall – though normal on the outside – contained a supply of weapons; and when some hundred of the Anabaptists had arrived at the market, they seized the swords, daggers and even a few arquebuses that lay hidden under the jerkins, surrounded the market-square, and stormed into the Town Hall. The fact that there was no one in it at the time did not worry them in the least. It was the place they wanted, not the people. What was a burgomaster without his office?

When the officials and, later, the Burgomaster arrived, they found they could not get in.

'Sorry,' said the heavy, red-faced man at the door. 'Under new management.'

'What . . . what's the meaning of this?' stammered the Burgomaster. 'Out of our way, fellows.'

'You can't get in, cock, that's what.'

'But this is outrageous . . .'

'Outrageous,' echoed some of the other Council officials.

But nobody seemed to be inclined to tangle with the armed occupants.

'Finders keepers,' said the armed occupants. 'This is an Anabaptist Council now.'

A meeting of the Great Guild was called, and Konrad summoned from his office, where he was sampling the latest concoction of his alchemist distiller.

'Well, what is it?' he enquired testily, when he had taken his place under the canopy. 'I hope it is important. In these troubled times, time is money. We businessmen are holding this town together, it seems to me.'

'The matter is grave enough, Master Harting,' said the Master of the Cutlers, an honest man of the old religion. 'It seems these scoundrels have taken to arms and barricaded themselves in the Town Hall. We have asked the Town Council to join us in our session.'

'It is not strictly guild business even in our wider constitution,' said Konrad. 'But we shall be delighted to help. Taken over the Town Hall, have they? Are you sure?'

'Of course I'm sure,' interjected the Burgomaster, who was a weak sort of fellow behind his bombast (had he not been, the city would not have found itself in its present state). 'I myself was turned away and insulted.'

'It is an insult to the town,' said the Master of the Cutlers.

The words were taken up by many others. It was indeed an affront to civic pride, and Konrad knew it. The fact that many of the Guild Masters and councillors had also heard of the desecration (as many thought) of the Cathedral the previous night did not contribute to a mood of compromise. But Konrad had been prepared for the outrage – and indeed had more up his sleeve.

'Gentlemen,' he said, 'Brothers,' making peaceable stroking motions with his hands, 'this is not an armed insurrection.'

'I tell you it is,' shouted the Burgomaster.

'Sir, you are mistaken. It is not an affront to the city. More, it is an appeal to the city.'

'Damn funny sort of appeal,' snorted the Master of the Girdlers, another straight-laced old fogey who would have to go.

'It is not an invasion, it is not an affront, believe me.'

'What is it, then?'

'It is a protest.'

'A protest?' said the Burgomaster, bouncing his eyes off the rafters.

'Damn fancy sort of protest,' said the Town Clerk, a long, drippy-nosed fellow.

'How would you protest if you were outnumbered, in a foreign land, Israel as it were in Egypt ... how would you make yourself heard, if not by taking a stand?'

'But with arms?'

'How else other than with arms? If they came on their knees to you ... and they have ...'

'They never,' said the Master of the Cutlery. 'Never did they once come on their knees ... Besides, we are not Egypt.'

'I speak figuratively, Masters. They have been supplicants in all manner of ways. We have given them food ... We have given them drink ...'

'You can say that again,' said the Master of the Brewers.

'... but what we haven't given them is the sweetest thing of all.'

'Our daughters,' said a wag somewhere down the hall.

It was common knowledge that Konrad's Elisabeth was to wed one of their number.

'Who said that?' said Konrad, sharply.

There was silence. No one came forward.

'By God,' said Konrad, losing his temper. 'If this is to be an occasion for cheap repartee and personal innuendo, I shall leave you to it and let you get rid of your "invaders" by yourselves. But I warn you. If you go about this the wrong way, you will indeed have a battle on your hands.'

There was a gratifying flutter of anxiety down the chamber. They had got used to letting others do the work. He would nail that wag.

'Oh no, Master. I am sure there was no offence meant. The Master of the Coopers has a bad habit of letting his tongue run away with him.'

So it was that little rat. Very well, Master Cooper, we shall tub and drub you out of town.

'Pray continue, Master. You were saying . . .'

'The sweetest thing of all is liberty.'

'Liberty? They have liberty,' said the Burgomaster. 'They can come and go. On the whole, they come. What else do they want?'

'They want you to recognize the principle of Liberty of Conscience.'

There was an in-drawing of breath in the chamber. Liberty of Conscience! What did they mean by it? Where would it end? Apart from a minority of Anabaptist sympathizers, most of the Council were Lutheran with a smattering of quiet Catholics. The notion of complete freedom for the individual conscience was as anathema to Luther as it was to the Pope. To Luther's emphasis on the Word, these people were opposing their emphasis on the free spirit . . .

'But, but . . .' spluttered the Burgomaster. 'We, even we, don't have that.'

'I told you it was a protest,' said Konrad. 'If they'd come on their knees, that would have been your answer. That is why they have taken up the sword. What is your reply going to be now? War? Will you raise the armed bands and drive them out by bloody force? Or will you give them their soul's desire and show the magnanimity for which this town is famous throughout Germany?'

'How can we give them what we do not believe we should have ourselves?' enquired the Master of the Cutlers.

'Then, if it is wrong, they will be damned for it. If it is right, we will be blest. Well, Masters, what is it to be? I give you my word – and you may take up arms against them if I am wrong – I give you my word that, if you accede to their humble petition, this protest will dissolve. The occupation of the Town Hall will cease. And they will return to their quarters as peaceably as lambs.'

'Just one thing, Master,' said the Burgomaster. 'Do I hear that you were running through the streets last night, calling sinners to repentance? And that you had everyone stripped to the buff in the Cathedral?'

'It was the most moving experience of my life, Burgomaster. Yes. I am on the side of repentance. And those people . . . nakedness? I saw no nakedness . . . only people casting off their sins. These are stern times, Burgomaster, and I for one consider the Anabaptists' resoluteness and their determination to shoulder the burden – each one personally – a far more responsible and dignified attitude than some of the squalid tergiversations that pass for religion which we see in some quarters.'

There were several cries of 'hear, hear' (he detected both Stumpf's and Hessing's voices amongst them) in the chamber, and a general lightening of brows. This was the kind of talk they half-understood. It reminded them of why they had originally given the Prince Bishop the elbow.

'Shall we take a vote on it, then, Masters?'

It was agreed by a sizeable – though not overwhelming – majority to let Konrad talk to the Anabaptists and ask them to leave the building without riot or bloodshed.

This, in the course of the afternoon, he did. The red-faced men moved out without demur, accompanied by some of the more serious Saints, who heard the news of Liberty of Conscience from Konrad with the greatest enthusiasm, and broke spontaneously into their hymn 'Prepare the path, wash clean with Blood', to the tune of 'Gathering Osiers'.

Upon this successful conclusion, it was agreed that the two Councils – of the city and of the guilds and their colleagues – should now merge, and that Konrad should be elected Burgomaster over the head of the present incumbent.

Part Three

I will show wonders in heaven above, and signs in the earth beneath; blood and fire, and vapour of smoke. The sun shall be turned into darkness, and the moon into blood, before that great and notable day of the Lord come. And it shall come to pass, that whosoever shall call on the name of the Lord shall be saved.

Acts 2, 19–21

Chapter 1

The Bishop who had no bishopric was a fussy little man with a dominating sister. He was not a cleric, and had bought the bishopric with money he had made from a silver mine on his family estate. He was not altogether a bad man nor altogether a fool; but like many members of his class he had had, up till now, little experience of sharpening his wits.

At the moment, he was staying – not, as he should be, in the Bishop's Palace in the town – but in the castle of a neighbouring lord, his sister's husband, where he had been forced to take refuge. He realized, of course, that he was a laughing-stock. And, if he hadn't, his sister would have told him about it; which she did, every five minutes.

'It's so humiliating,' she said. 'I feel so ashamed. I can't hold my head up anywhere. Theo says we have to do something.'

Theo was their brother-in-law, a man who lived for the chase, drink, food, his dogs and seducing peasant girls – in that order.

The Bishop had heard it all before.

'Anyone seen my best cod-piece?' he said. 'I know I left it somewhere.'

Ornate, aggressive cod-pieces were all the rage, and even secular bishops were expected to wear them, especially secular bishops who had lost their bishoprics and needed to show a display of oompah (as his brother-in-law insisted on calling it).

'Show 'em your oompah,' the Baron said again that evening after dinner.

'Yes, yes,' said the Bishop. 'Quite.'

'It's the only thing they understand,' his brother-in-law told him.

The only thing the Bishop understood was that he could not go on living with his brother-in-law much longer.

'I suppose you mean a show of force,' he said.

'Get out there and kick 'em where it hurts. I'll come with you. Hunting's been awful recently.'

'There are rather a lot of them,' the Bishop demurred. 'They have made it very plain that they do not want me in the town. I did what I could; though it went against the grain, I recognized the Lutheran community. But even that wasn't enough. I could see the Council wanted me out. And then those Anabaptists came along, and the writing was on the wall.'

'Loonies,' said Theo. 'Brigands, criminals, ravers and ranters, God-wallopers. A turd in their teeth, I say.'

'I tried to warn them. God knows we have all heard tales of their excesses in Holland. But I never thought it would take root here. I wish I was back in Lippstadt.'

'The Peasants' War, the Peasants' War,' rumbled Theo, pulling on a tankard of Rhenish. 'All that talk of Judgement Day when all they wanted was puddings and pies and our estates. That should have told us.'

The Bishop wished Theo's wolfhound would not piss on the rushes. It made the room stink so.

'I can't just go in there with soldiers,' said the Bishop. 'They wouldn't let us in.'

'Kick the door down. They kicked *you* out soon enough.'

'I was not kicked out. I left,' said the Bishop, huffily. 'My position was untenable.'

'Harrumph,' snorted Theo.

He knew what he would have done.

The Bishop, however, had not given up. Though not naturally brave, he had a certain tenacity, and he hated to think of all that wasted money he had spent on his election. Yes, he had been elected; by the chapter, but where were his electors now? Kicked out – position untenable, as his had been.

There was just a chance, though, in fact more than a chance, that the Anabaptists would go too far. Let them overstep the mark, and he would go in at the head of some mercenaries (Theo knew where to get them) and relieve the town of its sufferings. To do that, of course, the town would have, as it were, to invite him back in. It would be a moment to savour. The Bishop bided his time.

Sure enough, quite suddenly, the opportunity presented itself. A page ran in with a letter that had arrived from the town. The Bishop read it eagerly.

'This is it, this is it.'

He was almost dancing.

'What is it?' said Theo. 'Cod-piece too tight?'

'An armed uprising. They've gone too far – taken over the market-place with armed bands. We can go in now. The town will welcome us with open arms.'

'I'll get the men.'

There were enough around the castle to provide a reasonable troop, and when the townspeople saw them they would swell their number . . .

That at least was what he thought. But when, taking advantage of a sudden spell of milder weather, he arrived at the gates of the town, they were shut.

'What's this?' asked Theo. 'A welcome? Open arms? Is your town a woman who says no when she means yes?'

'Open up,' shouted the Bishop in his reedy tones, 'open up to your Prince Bishop.'

'Open up your arsehole,' shouted a derisory voice from one of the towers.

'I demand to see the Burgomaster.'

'Buggermaster coming up. Don't go away.'

There was a long pause in which Theo became increasingly restless.

'Let's go and get some cannon,' he said. 'That'll bring the buggers down.'

'They have cannon in there too, you know,' said the Bishop. 'They have all manner of things in there.'

Some of their armed band were looking at the fortifications appreciatively, others with apprehension.

'I shouldn't like to lay siege to that lot,' said one old soldier. 'They've got a lovely curvature along that wall. And do you see the gun mountings? Why, they've got every inch of ground covered whichever way you look.'

Theo rode around the town as far as the river and had to agree that there seemed no obviously weak spot.

'It's that damned river right up to the walls round there. Almost a half-circle. It saves them having to put cannon all round. Good siting, whoever built this town.'

Finally Konrad appeared wearing his burgomasterly gown and chain of office.

'I am the Burgomaster,' he shouted. 'What brings you with a show of arms?'

'We come as friends,' shouted back the Bishop. 'We hear there has been an armed uprising. We came to protect you. Open up.'

And he spurred his horse forward to the gates which, however, remained obstinately closed.

'You are the so-called Bishop?' Konrad shouted down.

'I am the Bishop.'

He beat on the gates with frustration.

'We have no need of help, Master Bishop. The Council does not want your interference. We thought we had made that plain. You have no place in this town. However, we would not like you to go on your way without some kind of tribute. Since we have not paid our quarterly taxes to you, may we offer you this late tithe instead?'

The Bishop looked up expectantly, and a great bucket of chicken entrails and unspeakable etceteras was emptied in his face.

Spluttering and malodorous, he rejoined the ranks of his companions. Some of the soldiers started to snigger, but a furious look from Theo put paid to the more obvious hilarity. There was still a discernible heaving of shoulders. A cock's comb still stuck to the Bishop's hat, nodding to the step of his mare. Theo picked it off disgustedly and threw it down like a challenge.

'You realize what this means, don't you?' he said.

'What does it mean?' asked the Bishop.

He was never going to get rid of the smell of rancid chicken. Thank God his sister had not been there.

Theo rode on a pace or two, and turned to him dramatically.

'This means war,' he said.

Chapter 2

The writing was on the wall for those Lutherans and such of the Catholics as were left who chose to read it. Every day the power of the Anabaptists was growing. They now had legal sanction for their excesses. After all, what was freedom of conscience? Freedom to do exactly as you pleased: to steal, to appropriate, to fornicate, to rape, to ravage, even to murder. All these things (at least theoretically) were acceptable as long as the spirit moved that way.

It was not long before the spirits of many of the well-to-do burghers were moving them out of town with what valuables they could carry with them. Had it not been said in the Cathedral that the unrighteous must depart? If they were unrighteous in the eyes of the people, it was surely better to do it now, voluntarily.

Fierens watched the preparations for departure with the large red-faced man whom he had appointed as Provost of the Immigrants and who soon achieved a wider function. This man had formerly been a gaoler in Utrecht.

'Do you think we should stop them?' asked the former gaoler.

'Let them go,' said Fierens. 'We don't need them. They would only cause trouble.'

'The valuables would be useful.'

'It is not yet time,' said Fierens. 'Let them go,' he repeated.

They stood in silence observing the preparations. A box burst open unleashing a shower of silver upon the street. The hapless owner descended from his cart and flapped his hands at the Anabaptists who swarmed around pocketing like bees. Fierens spoke at last.

'When the Leader comes . . .'

'He is here. I have seen him,' said the Provost.

'When he announces himself, then it will be time,' replied Fierens.

He knew Mosman had arrived. It was Mosman's habit to sniff around on the edge of things before making himself known.

'It is nearly time,' declared God suddenly, giving Fierens the golden resonance, the quickening in the reins of his soul.

'Easter, you say, Lord?'

'The End will come before Easter.'

The train of carts started to move. Fierens noticed the Masters of the Cutlers, the Silversmiths and the Brewers amongst the departing luminaries.

'That silversmith's carrying a lot,' he said, regretfully, and then, 'I feel it.'

The golden wire was glowing with sudden thoughts and words. People watched the prophet jerk like a marionette. The spirit took him like this:

'To the brethren, to the Saints our neighbours, wheresoever they are, summon them to come now with their families to Rensburg. Tell them, the earth to be destroyed before Easter but Rensburg to be saved. Rensburg the New Jerusalem. Food, clothes, money, lodging to be ready for them. But to bring arms. To bring arms . . .'

The Provost was scribbling on the slate he habitually carried, so useful for noting down names and reckoning wealth but indispensable for catching the irruptions of inspiration.

The inspiration suddenly stopped. Fierens looked round, blinking, his handsome face and body moving curiously back to mortality.

'Did you get that, Provost?'

'To tell the righteous to come to Rensburg and to bring arms.'

'Ah, yes. See that it is done. I wish the message to go now. There is not an instant to waste.'

'I shall see to it, Prophet. We shall have a manifesto written, copied and despatched within the hour.'

'You are a necessary man, Provost. You have earned salvation a hundred times.'

'If it is God's will.'

'It is God's will,' said Fierens a touch testily. 'Have I not just told you?'

He turned and watched the long line of carts begin to move forward as the gate opened and the departing families took their chance upon the road. Some of them, he had been told, did not even know where they were going. The weather had turned again. It was bitter cold for such a venture, there were children and old people among them, but Fierens felt no pity. They were not the Elect. They would perish soon enough, shelter or no shelter, for these were the Last Days.

Chapter 3

Answers to the summonses started to come almost immediately. It was as if there had been (and there had been) encampments in the woods, cold bands of hopefuls braving wolf and weather, waiting for the call. Frieslanders, Brabanters, Dutchmen, Danes began to stream into the town in such quantities that they began to outnumber even the original Lutheran influx.

Fierens had organized his men to receive them and they were all found quarters – some in the houses that the prosperous merchants had vacated, some in the stores and empty warehouses, and others in lodgings commandeered from those too frightened or too committed to depart.

Fierens did not trust the townsfolk. They were too comfortable. He put his faith in the dispossessed. The date of their arrival was not coincidental. In fact, he had calculated their advent to a nicety. With Konrad now in office as Burgomaster, he could start to move.

The Deputy Burgomaster was a cipher, a little notary called Heinrich Blaeber, who kept looking to see what Konrad would do, and then doing it a second or so later. His candidature also had been arranged. The whole thing, thought Fierens, was unfolding as he had planned – a pageant to end pageants, each scene, each actor coming in pat on cue.

Mosman would shortly proclaim himself. Then the drama would move into a new act. How that would go, Fierens could not see. The golden wire did not tell. It would be revealed to him in due course.

Meanwhile there must be a shock – that was always good – and the act should end on a celebratory note.

Chapter 4

He had covered the picture on the wall with a hanging, partly to hide it from prying eyes – it was, after all, a Mystery and should not be unduly exposed – and partly so that it should not too much overwhelm him as he worked upon other subjects. Other subjects he must have or he would have to turn to Blommardine for money, and that would never do.

Even now he was thinking about that Hell of his master's – suffused with light from no obvious source, a trick that Leonardo himself had played – thinking about Hell when he should have been preparing a canvas for that Notary's daughter, thinking about the Hell that he had made for himself.

A hooded crow, black and white, perched on his window-ledge, hunched against the cold, tapped once against the window as though he would join if he could the light and warmth from which he was debarred; white for love, black for impossibility.

Oh love, love, love; why have you forsaken me?

It is because you were married, said the crow.

Our First Parents never married. Marriage is an economic and legal institution devoid of love. It is a sin if it is devoid of love, Julius replied.

The crow looked up at him, head on one side.

Then why did I marry? I married because I did not know what else to do, because I was homesick for the South, because I was afraid of the commission, because I did not care for the new Grand Master, because my witch wanted it, because everything seemed like a dream until I loved.

Tap-tap-tap, went the crow.

Love, you see, changes everything, Julius went on. That was what I was taught, but I didn't really believe them. I thought in the end my job was to get by, to survive. I was offered the ship of glory but I chose a cockle. They told me in Florence that Dante himself had said Creation first arose and was sustained not by laws, not by money, but by pure love – I thought, what? Me? Poets say these things. And then . . . it happened. It was like stepping from grisaille into a rainbow.

Give us a crust, said the crow.

Julius rose, went to the cupboard, extracted some bread that he was saving for his own repast, and threw it out to the bird, which accepted it gravely.

'Well, well,' said Blommardine, coming in. 'We must be feeling flush if we can afford to feed the crows. You been paid for a commission, or something?'

But she was in a good mood. The identity of the prophet in the gallery was still unknown to her, but every instinct told her that it would be revealed. She liked this town with its tensions and its revelations. Indeed, a little bird – not a hooded crow but a little street sparrow – had told her there was something afoot this very night. Whatever it was, she would be ready for it. She thrived on mischief, and there was every chance that the great man (as she was sure he was) would be in amongst it, pulling at the strings, standing in the gallery.

'Going out?' Julius asked her, noting her cloak.

'That's right. Sharp, aren't you? Mind you don't cut your cods off.'

The door closed with a bang behind her. Julius found to his surprise that he did not dislike her any more. His own love had transformed his feelings. He felt sorry for her. There was something quite brave about her.

And then again, as he remembered Elisabeth's too-imminent marriage, he felt sorry for himself.

There was nothing he could do. He had thought wildly of abducting her but – apart from practical considerations such as her accessibility – the hue and cry that would follow such a move would swiftly result in their recapture. A late blizzard had swept in from the north-east. The roads were foul again, the woods dangerous, the river unfordable, the paths snowbound. There would be no swift escape. As for hiding in the town, every nook, every niche in the place was full to bursting. You could hardly open a rabbit-hutch but you would find an Anabaptist crouching inside.

Again, there was no guarantee that, even if he did manage to escape with her, she would like it. In fact, he rather thought she wouldn't. Why should she wish to escape with someone who had despicably lied to her? Who had been humiliated in her sight by her father?

No, he could quite see her point. He would need time to explain himself, to let love work – as he knew it could, but only in time. And that couldn't be achieved with a quick snatch at a doorstep. That was a case for come let us sit upon this grassy bank and talk. And meanwhile the clock devoured the hours.

He wrote her a letter, at last, that told her what was in his heart, and gave it to one of the old women who were still to be found in the town (though some had joined the exodus), urging her to pass it to the nurse and not to let the master of the house see her doing it; but whether it reached its final destination he did not know. There seemed nothing more he could do.

He had had the chance to enter Paradise and he had lost it through an exceedingly hackneyed sin. At least, he thought, Eve's exit had the virtue of being original.

He withdrew to his cold studio, took the cover off the wall, and started to try to paint again, nerving himself once more to find the idea, the figures, the design. The first two panels bore down on him, sharp as ever – too sharp if anything; that was the trouble with it, the thing was so well done. The very skill with which his master had painted it – the limpidness of colour, the exuberance of idea, the discipline of design – held him back. How could he complete such a vision? A false note would ruin everything.

He recalled again the teaching of Ficino, relayed by Ammanati.

'The purpose of art' – and Julius could hear the calm, poised tones, almost as if the Florentine sunlight were flooding the room and the smell of ripe peaches was wafting from the wall below – 'the purpose of art and music is to kindle in the soul a desire to return to its divine home – by presenting sights and sounds which remind it of its divinity.'

What sights and sounds could be composed in any contemplation of Hell that would recall such a thing to his own tattered spirit, let alone anyone else's?

At length he gave up once more, put wood on the fire, poked about the room, and found an unfinished canvas of the marshes and water meadows across the river with the bridge in the background that he had started in the summer and for some reason discontinued. It looked good now. A landscape – one of the things the northern painter had been able to teach the southerners! The wind on the grass. That was not a bad effect. And the sense of space across the fields, the perspective ... old what's'isname in Bologna, Pacioli, he would have given that a thumbs-up ...

He started to work on the discarded canvas. There were one or two sketches for it in a folder somewhere ... Yes, there they were. He had not been wrong about the grass: long, marsh-grass it had been; silver-brown on one side, grey-green on the back. It was like the mane of a great windswept animal.

Once more the completion of Hell had had to be put aside. One day he would do it, that was for sure, but now, even in this savage cold with despair biting his heart, there was light and colour to attend to.

So the artist painted on, the water meadows of summer rippling under his brush to the gusts of a former breeze, while the snow fell outside – thick, implacable, disfeaturing, like the dust of Time itself.

228

Chapter 5

Noise again at night, this time in the distance, a baying, breaking noise like pandemonium – and even from afar, the sound of malice, of resentment, of ugliness attacking beauty, and that particular noise that attends the burning of books. Low shapes, flickering smoke, sudden spurts and tongues of fire, breaking glass, tearing fabric, yelps of crass triumph, gloating cries, splintering wood, shattering marble, the thud of axes on doors . . .

Julius awoke with a start from a dream of vague violence. He felt across the bolster towards Blommardine but she was not there. He sat up, huddling the bed-clothes around him, remembering now that he had gone to bed early, tired with painting, before she had returned.

Hearing a confused hubbub far off, he now supposed that she might be caught up in some trouble. It did not greatly worry him. There had never yet been a situation of which she had not been mistress, if not principal.

He got up, reached for his cloak, and hurried out into the street, joining others who had been similarly awakened.

The snow had stopped. The night was still. Only in the distance there was the sound.

'What is it, neighbour?' a man asked him.

Julius shrugged helplessly.

'It's the Cathedral, I'll be bound,' said another man. 'I heard a rumour of this. Our beautiful Cathedral. How can they do it?'

'How can we let them?' yet another voice cried.

Julius peered at him. It was a big man called Mattheson, a saddler, whom he knew slightly.

'Hush, neighbour, if you want to keep your clothes on this cold night,' someone said.

'If you want to keep your head on . . .'

'I'm going back inside. Keep your head down, that's my advice . . .'

Julius and some of the others walked through the streets towards the noise. Sure enough, it was coming from the Cathedral as his neighbour had said. When they came within sight of it, they could discern capering shadows cast by fire and torchlight inside, and smoke billowing from broken windows. From within came the crack and scatter of stone and glass.

'That's as far as you come, masters,' said a threatening voice.

One of the heavy red-faced men approached them from the corner of an almshouse.

'What's going on?' said Mattheson.

'None of your business,' said red-face.

'But it is our business,' said Mattheson, loudly. 'That's our Cathedral. What are they doing?'

'Heini,' the red-faced man called softly.

'Yer,' a voice came out of the shadows.

'Fellow 'ere says it's his business what's going on in there.'

''e wot?'

'Says it's his business.'

'Well, well, well.'

Out of the darkness an even larger red-face came towards them.

'Wants to know what's going on, does 'e?'

He affected to ignore Mattheson.

'That's about the size of it.'

'Wants to join in, I shouldn't wonder.'

'Sounds like fun,' the other agreed. 'Couldn't blame 'im.'

'Is that it?' said the giant, suddenly, to Mattheson. 'Is that what you want to do? Go and give them an 'and, like?'

'Certainly not,' said Mattheson. 'That's sacrilege going on in there. It's desecration. That's our Cathedral. Two hundred and fifty years old. It belongs to the town.'

'Oh yer?' said the giant. 'And that sounds like blasphemy, because I thought it belonged to God.'

Julius thought that Mattheson was shouldering too much of this. Perhaps his beating had made him braver; he spoke up.

'Of course it belongs to God, but it was built and made beautiful by the town.'

'Ooo, 'ark at nancy boy,' said the first red-face.

'Shut yer gob if yer know what's good for you, arsehole,' said the giant, and gave Julius a shove that sent him sprawling across the snow, hurting his bad arm.

'Any more comments, gentlemen?'

'I still don't think it's right,' said Mattheson.

There was a barely audible murmur of assent from the others.

'Well, I tell yer what, then,' said the giant. 'Why don't yer come with me and we'll have a little look-see. No, no. You lot go home. Just clever-dick here. 'e wants to see, let 'im see. 'e who 'ath ears to 'ear, let 'im 'ear.'

He seemed pleased with his grasp of Christ's teaching.

'Don't go, Mattheson,' someone said.

'He said go home and he means go home,' warned first red-face. 'I wouldn't like to see him riled.'

'Go 'ome,' shouted the giant, and he thwacked the ground with his staff, sending a plume of snow in a silver cascade like an iced firework across the square.

'All right, all right.'

They began to retreat. Julius picked himself up, holding his bad arm, and followed them.

'Now, clever-dick,' said the giant reasonably to Mattheson, 'just step this way if you would be so kind.'

It was the last they ever saw of the saddler.

In the morning, every single statue in the Cathedral – some of great antiquity and many of extreme beauty – was either defaced or utterly destroyed. Much of the stained glass was irreparably damaged. There was not a picture that had not been slashed, stabbed or burnt (at least two new Dürers and a van der Weyden perished in this way). And all the Cathedral's books – a priceless library of illustrated manuscripts as well as rare printed volumes – had gone up in smoke.

The Anabaptists were well pleased with their work.

'Thou shalt not worship graven images,' they sang (to the old dyke-workers' tune of 'Opening the Floodgates').

In fact, so pleased were they that, for the next few days, they occupied themselves with performing the same service for all the churches and monasteries in the city. And very soon Beauty was a rare commodity indeed in the town of Rensburg.

Blommardine came back, very late, cold but enraptured, and Julius pretended to be asleep. Next day, he did not ask her where she had been.

He was sickened by the destruction of so much goodness. Had not the great Cosimo de Medici believed that beauty in the physical world would fire men with desire for spiritual beauty and so to discover their divine nature? Destruction of such things argued a very different direction.

Julius suddenly began to be terribly afraid. Perhaps, after all, the world was indeed coming to an end. Was the Antichrist here, in Rensburg? If only he could carry Elisabeth far away from here.

Had it not been for her he would have joined the now rapidly dwindling train of departures, and put as many miles as he could between himself and this appalling place.

Chapter 6

Elisabeth received Julius's letter, faithfully delivered from crone to crone, but it brought her little comfort. She knew that he loved her, and now he was explaining why he had been weak: he was too human, frightened that he would lose her. But it did not help. His references to the Religion of Love did not help. This was the real world. Religion didn't seem to be helping anyone much just now. He was married. She was to be married. That was in the nature of things. Love had nothing to do with it. She even admitted in her heart that she still loved him, but it was like admitting that you had an in-growing toenail (which she had not). It was unfortunate but you had to get on with other things.

True, her mother – brought up on the old bible of romance, the *Roman de la Rose* – would have told her that the most delicious trials of love lie in its unattainability; the rose is a besieged fortress that must not, in practicality, yield, though it can inspire art, poetry and endless intellectual diversion. But Elisabeth herself had never really been in sympathy with the *Roman*. All that sensuality and opinion and allegory seemed out of touch with the times. They belonged to the dark, huddled past and had no place in the light of the new learning. She had said as much to her mother who had laughed.

'Even if we must agree that the thing is a game, it is a game that strives to make life more civilized than the brutal, dangerous affair it can sometimes be, whatever the new learning says. And if its heaven is no more than the rose itself . . .' Here she paused.

'What is the rose, Mother? Is it love?'

'The rose is our sex, child. And, God knows, if that is the way to heaven, it's a curious avenue.'

Elisabeth had waited for her mother to continue, but she remained silent for a while longer.

'And what is Hell in the book, Mother?' Elisabeth asked at last.

'Ah. Well, now, Hell is interesting. Hell is reserved for those who do not observe the commandments of Nature and of love.'

It was just as well now, thought Elisabeth, wiping away the tear which always formed at the corner of her left eye when she thought of her mother, that she herself had rejected the whole rigmarole of the *Roman*. Otherwise she might have considered herself to be in Hell at this moment.

Her dressmaker entered the room. Elisabeth was seldom alone in these last days. It was either dressmaker or father or husband-to-be or the Anabaptist preacher Hass who would keep explaining about the Anabaptist wedding service.

The dressmaker, who was an Anabaptist from Antwerp – chosen by Fierens because she was a stranger – was harmless enough with her mouth full of pins which stopped her babbling about the Last Things, but her father seemed as alien to her as Hass, and Fierens himself seemed hardly to be human at all.

'Do not be alarmed,' he told her. 'I shall make you not just my wife but something infinitely more glorious.'

He did not expand on this promise. His eyes these days seemed fixed on something distant which completely absorbed his interest. It was like being in the room with a tree. She didn't mind. It was better that he wasn't thinking about her. In fact, she rather hoped that he would continue to be like this after they were married.

He would get on with his life, and she with hers – not that life in Rensburg seemed very promising at the moment, but her expectations, previously so high, had been reduced to nothing more than the ground beneath her feet. It was an attribute her father had commended.

'You are not hungry, are you? Not in pain? You have a roof over your head? Clothes? Books? Music? What else do you want? Young people these days don't know when they're well off. Fix your eyes on Heaven and pray to God for gratitude. If what our friends here say is true – and I believe them – we are on the verge of the greatest moment in man's history. The Last Days are upon us. How small is it then of you to quibble, to murmur and to look wan!'

With these and similar precepts, her father had induced in her a dulled acceptance which, if sometimes breached with a flicker of life or a memory of happiness, would be drowned once again with the bitter waters of hopelessness and guilt.

Chapter 7

Mosman now declared himself in town. The tall figure with its sweeping silver beard appeared one morning in the market-place and started to preach a sermon on the Apocalypse.

The word flew around, and soon there were a thousand, two thousand people listening to the famous preacher in the square. He had sent a message to Fierens before this manifestation so the occasion had been well prepared. Anabaptists poured from their lodgings to hear again the message of their Leader.

'Famine, War, Pestilence, and Death stalk the land,' shouted Mosman, 'and none shall be spared save the Elect. Go quickly now, you and you and you, those of you who have not received the new Baptism, and prepare to open your souls to God, to be one with God, for surely God will not destroy His arm, here in this town. But outside . . . oh, my Brothers and my Sisters . . . in what dire straits shall they be . . . what boils, what toils, what sore afflictions shall be heaped upon them as the earth opens and the mountains spew fire . . .'

Fierens at the back looked down upon the scene; half-involved with every movement, every quirk of every expression; half up in the empyrean infinite leagues away, following the action in his Book.

Everything was going according to plan; Mosman was not even ad-libbing. He had his lines word-perfect.

Hans Hass was the first, at the end of the sermon, to come up and introduce himself to the Leader.

'Welcome, welcome, you are well come,' he kept saying. 'You must come and preach in my church.'

Mosman let him babble on. In fact, that was what he said at last.

'Babble on.'

Hass misunderstood him.

'Babylon? You mean . . . Babylon? You are right. I have said it myself. I have preached many sermons upon it. Babylon the Great, the Great Whore, the . . .'

'Silence.'

Hass was utterly confused. No one had ever told him to be quiet before. Quite the contrary, he had usually been begged to continue. He stood there with his mouth agape. One or two of the bystanders, red-faced men, started to snigger.

'I . . . I don't understand . . .' he said at last.

'I did not say Babylon. I said babble on.'

'Yer, babble on,' said the red-faced men. 'Gabble on. Get it?'

'Babble? . . . I do not babble. I have never . . .'

'You are seduced by your own voice. Your own voice is a harlot. You have committed vocal fornications.'

'I don't see . . . How? Why?'

'Your church? You said your church. That is beastliness. That is filth. That is pride.'

Hass saw his mistake and tried to retrieve the situation.

'It was a manner of speaking, that was all. It is not my church. It is God's church. It is the church I look after for God.'

'No "thine", no "mine",' thundered the prophet, 'only ours.'

'Ours and God's, surely,' corrected Hass, looking for a way back into the discussion.

'How can it be ours and God's, when we and God are one. It is ours, I say. Only ours.'

'Only ours.' The red-faced men took up the cry, and the crowd responded.

'Ours, only ours, all, all is ours.'

'Come, Brother Hass,' shouted Mosman, so that all could hear now that the man was truly discomfited. 'Come, tell me about the town. Is it a good town? Is it an evil town? What sort of town is it, Brother Hass? I have heard it said that you are wise in its ways.'

Mosman smiled as if to show he could flatter as well as browbeat.

'Well, let me see . . .' said Hass, brightening. 'I do believe it is a . . .'

'But first tell us,' interrupted Mosman, 'of God the Father, God the Son and God the Holy Spirit.'

'Tell you?'

'Which one?'

'Which one what?'

Hass was shouting with nervousness. A pile of snow fell off an overhanging ledge and he almost jumped into Mosman's arms.

'Which one is it that we are one with?'

'We are one with them all.'

'We are not.'

'I do not understand.'

'Tell him, Brothers,' Mosman called to the crowd, 'tell him with whom we are one.'

'One God,' the crowd shouted back. 'One God, one people, one thousand-year rule.'

'You see,' said Mosman, speaking now in a lower tone. 'We are not one with three. We are one with One. That jealous and exacting Father

235

of infinite power with whom we shall overthrow Antichrist and establish the rule of the Saints. The hour is very near.'

People pressed about them, touching the prophet's garment, a long, rather disagreeable-smelling black gown. One young woman in particular seemed especially attentive. She began to try to wash Mosman's feet – a useful office, for they were extraordinarily dirty as well as being red-blue with cold.

'Is that not blasphemy?' asked Hass, rather jealously.

He was only slowly getting used to being less important.

'How blasphemy?' enquired Mosman.

'Well, it was the service that the Magdalen performed for our Saviour.'

'Have I not told you, have I not repeated to you time and time again, oh wretched man . . .'

'You wretched man,' repeated the crowd.

'Oh ye of little understanding . . .'

'Of little understanding.'

'. . . that there is but one God and it is Him we serve.'

'We serve, we serve . . .' The crowd was starting to sing.

'Well, I . . .'

Hass floundered. There really seemed no answer to the tall man with the glittering eyes. He could feel his knees beginning to shake. The crowd surged about him. Yes, he could see it now.

'You are right,' he said. 'One God. Not One in three but One in One.'

'One in One,' the crowd repeated. 'One, one, one, one.'

'You are a good woman,' said Mosman to the foot-washer. 'What is your name?'

She looked up, radiant.

'Blommardine, sir,' she said.

'Diligent Blommardine,' he told her. 'Blessed art thou among women. You may follow us.'

Blommardine threw him a look of rapture. Mosman turned to Hass.

'And now,' he said, 'tell me about the forthcoming wedding you are to conduct for the prophet Enoch. He assures me you are the best preacher in the town and most energetic in our cause . . .'

Hass blushed.

'That's very good of him,' he said.

'Oh, he is good, have no fear of that. And you too are good, I can tell it, in yourself. You have the makings of a prophet in you.'

Hass blushed again. He could work with these people. Oh, he had had doubts. Who hadn't? But there was no denying their authority. What a sermon he would preach in the Cathedral for Enoch and his bride! How they would sway and swoon to his tones! No, no, he must beware of verbal fornication. But even so . . .

'Come, Blommardine,' said the Saint. 'There is much afoot.'

Hass wondered for a moment whether it was a joke but immediately dismissed the idea.

Chapter 8

The water meadows were once more put aside, and Julius stood again before his wall, poring over the picture as he had a thousand times. What had begun as a duty had become an obsession. He had started to feel, now, that only by solving the riddle could he achieve his own heart's desire.

(That morning, the quarterly payment, the little purse at the top of the stair, had arrived again. As if he needed the reminder!)

To work, then. And work surely meant understanding. There were clues in this picture which must be read.

The left-hand panel seemed the simplest. This was where to start. But already there were puzzles. Why was God the Creator portrayed as God the Son? Why was Eve not being formed from Adam's rib?

Why was there, for instance, death in the Garden? That big cat carrying away a strange, long-tailed creature in its mouth, the ferociously beaked bird devouring a frog . . .

'Without life, death could not exist. And vice versa. The first thing you have to get rid of is the idea that death is not part of God's original creation.'

Had he said that? Who had said that? Where did that leave Hell? Were not Sin and Death inextricably bound together, whatever his old master had told him?

What was that strange pink fountain-head – half plant, half crystal with a suspicion of mill-wheel thrown in – from whose central aperture an owl looked out? An owl! Was that deceit? Or wisdom?

What creatures were those in the foreground? The ibis, bird of death – but with three heads? What was the dark pond from which strange forms were crawling? And behind, beyond God's head, in the limpid fountain-pool, what other oddities – a salamander with three heads, a creature peeping out of what seemed like an animated amphora . . .

And those strange hills behind . . . One that looked like two mill-stones pierced by a great tree-trunk. Mill-stones were supposed to mean gender, he recalled – the male on top, the female underneath – here, side by side. And what of the birds whizzing out of the rock in a mad curlicue, fizzing out like notes of music and coming back slowly to roost and rest, in solemn procession, towards a great broken egg under the baleful eye of a shrike, bird of death?

'Tell me, wall, what it means,' he called. 'Haven't you given me enough trouble? Show me the key. Unlock the gate. There is a sweetness in there I have to taste. What are these shapes, these fruits, these cavalcades and somersaults, these birds and butterflies and haddocks, these sighs and whispering kisses . . .'

The wall remained silent, as it tended to on these occasions. It was odd, Julius thought, that the landscape of the Garden of Eden was so similar to that of the Earthly Garden – almost as if it were the same place . . .

'I wish with all my heart, wall, that I could awake there with Elisabeth.'

In the world, outside his window, suffering wandered in the streets pursued by madness; and yet here the answer, if he could find it, seemed so peaceful, so blissfully simple.

Chapter 9

The golden wire had reached God.

Fierens suddenly felt it – a tremendous shock and surge rushing down his back.

As he looked down at the town from where he stood on the ramparts, he realized that he could climb upward on it. Yes, there it was, the town getting smaller and smaller. It was like a child's town that he had once had, made in wood, when his mother was alive. Well, he would play with it now. God will play with it through him. Or he through God. For God was coming down the wire to meet him. It was most apt. He-God would play the world. He-God would save or destroy these people.

He had always wondered how it would feel to be the Great Author – now pairing, now repairing, now killing, now conceiving. And now the power was his – his to write and his to play.

And yet, the revelation still could not be made public. The mystery must stay wrapped awhile. For everything there is a season. He-God could wait. Had He not waited for untold millennia?

Chapter 10

Konrad, ever since the episode in which he had given the painter his drubbing, found that the taste for violence lingered on. It was the first beating he had given anyone in twenty years and he wanted more of it.

He explained his need to the Adam at the next meeting in the hypocaust (the attendance was much diminished of late). It was one of the rules of the conventicle that you should speak your mind without dissimulation. Konrad, however, made sure that Adam was alone when he raised the matter.

'You wish to beat?'

Adam raised a quizzical eyebrow. Nothing surprised him.

'Yes.'

'There are some women who enjoy it,' said Adam, reflectively.

'I don't want them to enjoy it.'

'I see. That is harder to arrange.'

'And I do not wish them to be women.'

'Ah. You wish to beat young girls?'

'I wish to beat young men.'

For the first time since Konrad had met him, Adam shook his head.

'Ours is the pursuit of Venus, not of Mars.'

Konrad thought about it. He was not going to let this go.

'Surely Venus and Mars were married,' he said at last. 'They must have had something in common.'

Adam sighed.

'It might be arranged, my son. But you may have to wait a week or so. Things are difficult at the moment. There are those who wish us ill. Meanwhile, let me introduce Gerda . . .'

Gerda liked to be tied up, but it was not the same. Konrad could feel the violence brewing inside him as if it were his very seed, produced by some angry new gland he had grown. His workers began to find him impossible, his daughter, terrifying. In the Town Hall it was all he could do to refrain from striking the clerks.

Sitting now in his study with a jug of wine, nursing his wrath, he was startled by a sudden tap at the door.

'Yes?' he shouted, springing up guiltily and scattering wine. 'Now look what you've done.'

'Miaaaooww.'

It was Billa; sly, feline. He had had Billa. It was like pleasuring a panther. Sometimes he had the feeling these days that she was working for somebody else.

'Now look what you've done,' he cried again.

Billa looked at him sidelong, bent down and wiped the table with the cloth she was carrying. There were a number of such spillages these days.

'It's Mr Fierens and another gentleman at the door. Most particular they are to see you.'

She found another little pool of wine and gave the table another rub, her work-hardened hand shockingly, flagrantly red against the white of her arm. She knew what he was thinking. This was no good; he must pull himself together.

'And take that smile off your face,' he told her.

'I'm not smiling, sir. That's my natural expression.'

'Well, change your natural expression.'

'Shall I show them in, Mr Harting?'

'Of course, girl. Don't just stand there rubrub, don't just stand, don't stand rub, get on with it. Show them in. Oh, and . . .'

'Yes, sir?'

She straightened up slowly, brushing against him with one of her breasts.

'Bring more wine,' he said thickly.

Fierens and Mosman were shown in and Konrad greeted them warmly, too warmly. He had, of course, been introduced already to the Leader, but this was the first time he had been favoured with an interview.

'Sit down, my good sirs. Will you take some wine?'

'Wine is the Devil's juice,' announced Mosman, grimly.

'Take the wine away,' Konrad told Billa, who stood there hovering. 'What is it doing here anyway? It is an affront to these good people.'

'And cover your paps,' said Mosman. 'I had not thought to see such collops in a godly house.'

Billa left the room, carrying pitcher and goblets, and her paps, looking as though her natural expression was under considerable strain.

Konrad could hear her outside, even after she had closed the door, making a noise that could have been laughter, could have been tears.

He looked at the two men. Fierens' handsome face was cloaked; you could not tell what he was thinking or even where his mind was. His expression was watchful, attentive, but his usual decisiveness was now in abeyance as if in deference to the older man. Konrad was suddenly reminded of the young Christ and John the Baptist.

'What can I do for you, gentlemen?' he asked.

'Brothers,' said Mosman.

'Brothers,' Konrad corrected himself. 'What can I do? Ask and it shall be done.'

His anger and his lust – were they the same thing? – resolved into a single attentiveness. It was the effect these people had. They were talking about the most important thing in the world. Later, when they had gone, the shameful thoughts might, would, return. But now he was their man.

'What is this town?' asked Mosman.

He knew very well what town it was, thought Konrad, but nothing he said or did was without its purpose.

'This is the city-state of Rensburg,' replied Konrad evenly.

There was a pregnant pause. Perhaps the stranger needed amplification.

'Founded on the site of an ancient Roman encampment beside the river Renn, it stands on the main route west to . . .'

'Is it fit to be the New Jerusalem?' asked Mosman, louringly.

'The New Jerusalem? Such an honour . . .'

'It is not for the honour of Rensburg. Such a temporal purpose would be meaningless. It is in order that the children of God may serve the Father in unity without distraction.'

'I see,' said Konrad, feeling the honour nonetheless.

'I doubt if you do. For to serve the Father without distraction, they require a town purged of all uncleanness.'

'Of course,' said Konrad, thinking of the chamber under the Town Hall. 'We have closed the brothels.'

'Silence.'

It was Fierens' turn to speak. He had risen halfway out of his chair, eyes blazing.

'Don't dare to speak of such places in front of the Saint,' he hissed. 'Don't contaminate his ears with such faeces.'

'I am sorry.'

Konrad did not apologize often. Even now it sat awkwardly in his throat.

'Though great among men, you are of limited understanding. And even your greatness is not entirely of your own making.'

Konrad knew what he meant.

'No,' he admitted. 'It is with your help.'

'It is with God's help,' came the thundering reply.

Fierens sat back once again in his chair, drawing inward.

If his future son-in-law lacked something in respect, Konrad thought, he had to concede that he deserved it. He was two people – overground and underground.

'How then shall we proceed?' he asked at last. 'To make the town fit for the children of God, what must be done? Tell me, and I shall do all I can to put it in motion.'

243

Whatever he had anticipated as a response, he was unprepared for the recommendation that followed.

'Kill,' said Mosman.

'Kill?' he asked, his voice squeaking in surprise.

'Kill,' repeated Mosman.

'Kill who?'

'Kill everyone.'

'Kill?'

Konrad could hardly believe his ears.

'Everyone.'

'Everyone who is unworthy?'

'Every one.'

'You mean the criminals, the, the . . .' He didn't like to say prostitutes for fear of contaminating the Saint's presence. '. . . the publicans and sinners.'

'I mean no such thing. I mean kill those who have not been re-baptized, kill the so-called Lutherans, kill the Romans, kill all those who cleave to the lewdness of the past. They shall not be saved in the Judgement, nay, better they die now and serve as an example.'

'You can't do that.'

Although both power and participation in things forbidden had coarsened him and impaired his sense of morality, Konrad still had some human feelings left in him – human, yes, and practical too, for morality and practicality often went hand in hand.

'If it is God's will, we can do anything,' said Fierens from far off. 'Nothing is impossible to us.'

'Yes, but is it God's will?' asked Konrad desperately. 'God tells me something different. God says we might be making a very big mistake.'

'God has not spoken thus to me,' said Mosman.

He seemed put out by the omission.

'If we kill those you mention,' continued Konrad, 'we shall unite the very forces whose enmity to each other first put the town into our hands. We shall then have formidable enemies ourselves – and not simply those who have lost by our presence here, but many, many others who will be shocked by a massacre. Philip of Hesse, the Elector of Saxony . . . why, the very Emperor himself, recently in Germany, may return with that army he never used against the Turks. He can't wait to see action. It would be the excuse he has been waiting for . . .'

He stopped, surprised by his own logic.

'Let him come with a hundred thousand men, nay a million million. What chance has he against the Almighty?' announced Mosman.

Fierens came down from wherever he had been and was very much in the room again.

'Perhaps, Leader,' he said, 'our friend Brother Harting is right. Not

244

because God, as you say, could not destroy the hosts of Pharaoh with one breath of his nostrils – but because, at the last, there are mundane reasons, beneath your contemplation, which would make such a course untimely. It would take time to kill them which would otherwise be spent in prayer. There would be many bodies to dispose of, and the ground is hard . . .'

'And,' Konrad broke in, 'there are among them those who may yet be saved. Let us decide to expel all those who are not with us after your wedding with my daughter. Such a joining of the town's chief family with one of your leaders . . .'

'Second,' murmured Fierens, meekly, 'always second.'

'Such a tie with one who is second among the Saints may encourage and inspire those who have so far been laggard.'

Apart from anything else, he wanted his enemies in the town to see his triumph. There is no pleasure in strutting before the dead.

'Very well,' said Mosman at last. 'But mistake not. God could tumble the captains and the hosts with a blinking of His eye. The earth would swallow them as if they had never been. God cares naught for kings and emperors.'

'Certainly not, Leader,' said Fierens smoothly. 'But God looks with favour on those who do not always beg assistance. I think that Brother Harting has a point.'

Chapter 11

Fierens sometimes recalled the life that he had left behind as a pastry cook – just occasionally the clouds would disperse and he could look back into the house of the baker in Leyden, take its lid off like a doll's house, and see himself working there alongside Dirk and Pim.

It reminded him that, like Christ, he had taken on a mundane form. It helped him to understand, if not to condone, the men and women that he saw around him.

It is a people that do err in their hearts, he thought. They need to be watched, to be herded. But I must not confuse their need for a sheepdog with the role of the Shepherd.

It is the Shepherd who knows that the road lies through the Valley of the Shadow, and up, up, over the stormy wastes and solitudes, to the Pass of Despair, before it can at length wind down to the rivers and pastures of eternal peace. I have dogs enough to snap at them.

I am wrapped in cloud and pillared in fire.

The people cannot see where they are going. It is no matter. If they could see they would be affrighted. The End of the World is a dreadful matter. It will not be easily accomplished. It will not be the mere deposing of a tyrant, a flash of steel in a throne-room. Antichrist is as gigantic in deceit as he is in destruction. Frogs spring from his mouth, a black dog snarls from the back of his head, his breath is pestilence; his is the power of the wind and the wood; his club is the false cross, his shit is sulphur, his vomit brimstone; his glance is perdition; his sting is death. But I am he that is Faithful and True, and out of my mouth goeth a sharp sword. And though the kings of earth with their armies rise up with them and gather against me, I shall dash them in pieces and cast them with their host into the burning lake. And when all is accomplished, the righteous shall live and reign with the Saints a thousand years . . . and I . . .

Fierens was conscious of someone knocking gently at the door.

'Yes?'

It was Konrad.

'Some of the people have been discovered hoarding chattels, even money. What shall we do?'

Fierens rubbed his mouth. He felt his hand begin to bleed.

Chapter 12

The wedding was held on the twenty-ninth day of March.

Spring, which had flirted earlier, had teased. Winter had come back, it seemed, to stay. The weather still had not broken and it was bitterly cold; but as Konrad had anticipated – and Fierens had arranged – a large concourse turned out to attend the union. Gone were the days of high jinks and barrels of beer in the street, but it was the nearest thing to a celebration the town had had for many weeks.

Normally the Anabaptists disapproved of making too much of a marriage. It smacked of earthly matters; there were always those faint but infinitely regrettable overtones of ribaldry. On this occasion, however, it had been decided to make an exception. A longer service had been devised around the basic Anabaptist prayers, sermon and exchange of rings – it consisted essentially of more prayers, another sermon and a number of Anabaptist hymns, along with a period of extempore 'inspiration'.

It had been made known to those Lutherans and Catholics who remained unbaptized in the town that they would be especially welcome. But this particular invitation had a disappointing response. The honest, industrious burghers who remained in the town were either too old, too sick or too stubborn to be tempted by a two-hour service in a cold Cathedral without benefit of organ (that too had been destroyed in the violence). Besides, it hurt them to see their beautiful church beaten up.

The people who came along were the poor along with the loutish, the brutish and the gogglers – and of course the Anabaptist visitors and their police.

The church clock struck twelve. Fierens and Mosman entered and took up their positions by the rail in front of the bare altar (it too had been stripped). Hass hurried to greet them, giving Fierens last-minute – and quite unnecessary – instructions, for Fierens had already written the whole scene and had it word-perfect.

Somewhere in one of the side chapels Julius huddled, heart pounding, stomach leaden, weather-eye open for the man who cried 'Love'.

A few of Konrad's colleagues from the guilds – the Master of the Apothecaries, the Master of the Dyers – sat despairingly together in the south transept, unable still to believe what had happened to their Cathedral, what was happening to their town.

'Can nothing be done, Master Schumacher? It is worse than the sack of Rome by the Visigoths.'

'It is too late, I fear,' said the Master of the Dyers. 'The die is cast. No joke intended. But die seems a word I can't shake off for some reason. Funny about that saddler being found like that in the river. Such a big man.'

They sat for a while in silence watching, their breath floating up like a soul leaving a corpse.

'D'you see what they did to the Sermon on the Mount window? I could kill the scoundrels,' said the Master of the Apothecaries.

'An interesting sentiment, Masters,' said a low, cold voice behind them. 'If you say that in church, what can you be saying outside? You shall be arraigned for sedition. Form up to my office after the service. I know who you are. Come to the Town Hall and ask for the Provost. We can't have you running around plotting murder. I'd haul you off now for two pins.'

'But . . .' expostulated the Master of the Dyers.

But Elisabeth and her father were entering the church and the choir and congregation raised the roof with the Anabaptist marriage introit to the tune of 'I'll pot a little duck tonight'.

> Come, my Soul, the body's Bride,
> Take a partner to thy side –
> Two together, 'tis well done –
> Two indeed with God are One.

There were a number of verses in similar vein, and when they had finished they started again, because it took Elisabeth a long time to walk up to the altar. She was feeling extraordinarily unwell. Deathly pale, almost fainting with cold, in her severe white dress, she however presented a most beautiful picture, and there was many an 'Ahh' and an 'Isn't she lovely?' as she made her way to the front. Even Fierens eyed her with relish – had he not written this part for himself? He was not immune from such matters (God had after all made women beautiful in the interests of propagation).

He simply did not waste very much time on them. It was not in the script. Beautiful as she looked, however, he was still conscious of a strange, indeed unique reluctance in himself to touch her. Absurd, of course. Doubtless the bridal bed would resolve the matter.

Julius watched her with so much love he thought it would overwhelm him. Standing where he was – there were no seats here, all the better to move around – he swayed slightly and made to loosen his tunic.

'I hope you're not making no sign of no cross, Brother,' said a man next to him with a Flemish accent.

'No, no. A little faint, that's all.'

'I could have sworn you was about to genuflex or something.'

'No, no. Please. It's all right now.'

'You been baptized?'

He had a mind to say something dismissive to the man, but he wanted to look and listen, not to bicker or catechize. Suddenly he thought of a way to establish his credentials.

'I was baptized with her. Here, by the prophet Elijah. I'm a friend of the family.'

What happiness he had known that day! How desolate he was now!

'Oh, well, then, that's different, innit. Elijah did you say? Lovely baptizer.'

'Thank you.'

Julius inched away and took up a position beside a pillar. The man kept looking at him. Julius moved to the pillar's further flank. The service droned on. Hass gave the first sermon. Somehow he seemed to have lost his fire. People began to cough and shuffle. His theme was Heavenly Love and how different it was from gross earthly passions. The audience had heard it all before. They wanted stronger meat than this. At last he stopped. Another hymn was sung. Still Elisabeth and Fierens remained standing at the altar. Julius could see her shivering.

Now Mosman climbed the pulpit. His text was taken from the first hymn.

'Come,' he barked. 'My Soul, the Body's Bride.'

The shuffling and the coughing ceased. The light in the great ravaged building grew darker. Flame seemed to course from his eye, and a cloven sword from his mouth. His face seemed framed in silver.

'Take me, push me, bend me, shove me,' he cried. 'Oh, God. Fill me utterly. I am open only for you.'

An ex-nun somewhere at the back started having a fit and had to be carried out.

'How many of you can say that? Open only for God? You miserable God-teasers . . .'

Julius hardly heard the words. The sound was as of a rushing mighty wind that roared about the head and whistled into the very crevices of the heart. He had to shake himself. He was almost seduced. The whole vast building was spellbound. Finally Mosman stopped.

It was time for the marriage vows, the exchange of rings, to begin.

Julius shook his head. The sound of the sermon was still roaring in his ears. It took him a moment or so to realize that the only persons to be unmoved by Mosman were Fierens and Elisabeth.

Oh, Fierens seemed to have been moved. He wore the right look, the appreciative, slightly rapt but modest look of a regular prophet-bridegroom, but Julius was good at expressions and he could see something else. Was it arrogance? Was it even boredom? Was it vacuity?

Elisabeth simply continued to shiver.

The sight encouraged Julius and filled him with a wild desire to do something, anything, that would stop all this. He felt the cold emphasis of the little knife at his waist under his cloak. Hass was speaking.

'If any know just cause or impediment why these two should not be joined together in holy matrimony . . .'

Evidently the Anabaptists believed in at least some adherence to the norm, he thought. It was at this point that God spoke to him. He could only account for it like that – a shaft of divine inspiration, of certainty that Fierens too was already married. He would speak out now and tell the congregation. And in the last resort there was the knife.

'. . . speak now,' said Hass, 'or forever hold your peace.'

Julius took a deep breath and stepped forward.

Chapter 13

He had not travelled more than a quarter of a pace, in fact hardly that, merely that tightening of the tibia that preludes action, when a firm hand reached out and stopped him.

'What are you doing, my son?' a voice whispered.

He looked around; shocked, desperate. The place was so densely packed that he could see no obvious whisperer or restrainer.

'Come to the other side of the next pillar,' said the voice, 'I will meet you there.'

What should he do? Continue with his endeavour or follow his (as he supposed – but was it a trick?) unknown friend?

'You would have no chance,' the voice urged. 'Do as I say.'

There was such urgency as well as reason in the words that his first mad impulse evaporated. He could prove nothing if he made a scene. And he would end up like the saddler. Better to wait and come back with the evidence. The marriage would still be void. As unobtrusively as he could manage, he wormed his way up to the next pillar, there the crowd thinned (for little could be seen from the position). It was on a level parallel with the altar and some dozen yards away to its right. Vision was anyway blocked by the choir-stalls. At the back it was blind.

Here he rested his hand and put his head on his fingers as if locked in contemplation. The voice spoke to him again.

'Do not be alarmed. There are some of us still here though we must not be seen. You are not one of these people, I think, my son.'

'I am not.'

Julius inclined his head slightly and saw a little man with a face like a church-mouse and that unmistakable priest-look, dressed in the garb of an ordinary townsman.

'Good,' said the little man. 'But not so good is that one of them has seen you and doesn't seem to like you very much. Do not look round. Keep contemplating. If they find a knife on you, you are as good as dead.'

'I had to do something,' said Julius. 'I could not let her marry that man.'

'Save yourself,' said the little man. 'You can do nothing if you are beaten senseless and found floating face downward in the river. Now, when I have gone, make your way past the altar-screen in that side chapel behind you, and press the centre panel on the eastern end of the second tomb, now sadly defaced. It will open. You must descend. I shall go now. Be sure you do not reveal our hiding-place. Your man will come round the pillar presently.'

Julius slowly turned his head and looked behind, but the priest was gone.

Back he now looked across the chancel – he couldn't help himself – to the altar. He saw the glint of gold as Hass took the ring. He started to move forward again. Whatever his new-found friend had said, Love called the tune now. Then two things happened almost at once. A voice from somewhere at the back of the pillar called very softly.

'Stop . . . You . . . Love.'

And Elisabeth turned (how could she have heard?), saw Julius and fainted. He looked at her falling body, helplessly. Konrad and Fierens somehow caught her before she hit the stone steps. Concentrating on her, they could not have seen him. But the Saint who had pursued him in the snow, who now stepped out from behind the pillar, he saw him all right. Luckily the man was obstructed by a little eddy of enthusiasts from Westphalia.

Julius turned tail and ran. Darting past the altar side-chapel, he did as the priest had instructed him and pressed the stone. The tomb opened, revealing a narrow stone staircase going down into blackness. Already he could hear the sound of padding feet the other side of the altar. Although he had a horror of being shut in, there was no other recourse. He stepped inside and pulled the stone sarcophagus over him. It shut tight, noiselessly.

He could hear outside the sound of feet running past, and cries, and muted confusion. The sounds faded away towards the north door, which led into the graveyard, a perfect place for escapees to hide.

He addressed himself to the stairs and found himself in a chamber furnished with table and chairs, where the little priest and a Lutheran pastor were standing waiting for him.

'Thou shalt not kill,' said the little priest, when Julius had explained his idea of speaking out and stabbing Fierens at the altar, 'that is what I think about that. Especially in God's house. Nor do I consider Love to be a sacrament, though I have heard far more dangerous talk in this town.'

'It might not be construed as killing,' said the Lutheran. 'There might be a case for calling it a necessary accident.'

'Typical casuistry,' said the priest.

'Pooh,' said the pastor.

It was evident that they enjoyed their debates.

'If I were to be responsible for this necessary accident, I thought I should do it before they were married. I don't think I could bring myself to give him an accident once he's her husband, however odious he may be,' said Julius, and then, bitterly, 'But anyway, he probably is now, and I didn't.'

'These are terrible times,' said the priest, 'when we have to talk like this. May God forgive us.'

'Amen,' said the pastor.

'Actually, I don't think I could have brought myself to stab him, anyway,' said Julius. 'There must be some other way. I do so love her, you see.'

'I see that,' said the priest.

There was a pause.

'Have you been here long?' asked Julius, at last.

'Some weeks. Since it was made plain we were *personae non gratae*, in fact. There are a few more of us left in holes like this, and other secret places,' said the Lutheran.

'Who feeds you?'

'Black birds,' they said in unison.

Julius knew who they meant. It was no accident that he had been found in the snow by the two old women. He suddenly thought of Elisabeth's old nurse, Frieda, and his heart gave a little leap. There was at least one friend in that dark house. And then he felt helpless again.

'What can we do?'

'We are an odd little collection,' said the priest. 'A Lutheran, a Roman and a pilgrim of Love. We are up against a most terrible and implacable foe – for you know who it is, don't you?'

'It is the Devil,' said the pastor and Julius together.

'It is the Devil,' repeated the little priest, 'in the ultimate blasphemy of masquerading as God's messenger – even as God Himself, since these people say, as God is in them, they must be God. It excuses anything they do since God can do no wrong. If he is already married, as you suspect, it would not make the slightest bit of difference to them. They would say his wife had not been re-baptized, the marriage had not taken place under Anabaptist auspices. It is very easy to wriggle out even in the Catholic Church. Look at the King of England . . .'

'We must watch, and wait. There are only a few of us now. There will perhaps be more. But there will always be many more of the enemy. We must somehow get help – at least some word to the Prince Bishop,' said the pastor, 'though it pains me to say it.'

'That ass?' snorted the priest. 'He'd put you Lutherans to the sword.'

'Who else is there to help?'

'He will not move into the town. He would have to lay siege. A siege is a terrible thing.'

'All we can do is wait. And pray.'

'What good will praying do?' said Julius, bitterly.

'You would be surprised,' said the little priest. 'We set a lot of store by it in our business. And now we should let you out.'

'Back up there?' Julius asked nervously.

'Not into the Cathedral. There are other avenues. We have quite a choice of exits down here. A mausoleum, perhaps? Or why not one of the water-gates? You had better wear a different cloak, perhaps a hat. We have such things. Please help yourself.'

Julius did as he was bidden, and his new friends led him out through another chamber, down a tunnel, across another room, and finally out through an iron grille which looked like a barrier but turned out to be a door, to where he could see the glimmer of cold light reflected on water.

'What a warren,' said Julius as they walked. 'Who built all the tunnels? Where do they go?'

'Monks,' said the Lutheran. 'It's not the first time there's been trouble. They go to the abbey and the granary, to an underground well, even to a nunnery . . .'

'Here we are,' said the little priest. 'Now you are on your own.'

'Who are you?' asked Julius. 'I don't even know your names.'

'Pastor Joachim,' said the pastor.

'And Father Berthold,' said the priest. 'Those are not of course our real names. Do not contact us unless you are in extreme danger. We shall be in touch if the time is right. Good luck and God go with you. You will need Him. Things will get worse before they get better.'

'It is surprising, isn't it?' said the pastor. 'It is as if, given the choice of a couple of straws, each of whose lengths he is encouraged to see, mankind always seems to draw the short one for himself.'

Julius walked out onto the river-bank and looked cautiously around. The sun was already setting and shadows filled the little ravines that ran up from the water.

Seeing no one about, he turned to bid his new friends a last goodbye, but the passageway was already empty.

Chapter 14

Elisabeth had been revived. It had been the shock, Fierens explained later, of her proximity to the emanations of Awful Power coming from Mosman which had been too much for her.

After a short interval for fanning and cold water, the bride, half-conscious, supported by her father, took her place once more at the altar and the marriage service proceeded to its conclusion. Later she collapsed with a fever. She had caught a chill in the church. Fierens agreed with her father that it was better she should stay at home where she could be nursed. The rigours of an Anabaptist Leader's wife were not yet for her, for these were rigorous times and doubtless would be more so. He did not visit her that night, or on the succeeding ones. She was sick. He was occupied. He noted the lack of conjunction, as he went about his work, as a peculiarity. It was almost a relief to him; almost as though there were something in her that was proof against him. Impossible, of course, for he could enter where he would. Perhaps it was His will that she should be intact. At all events, he had much else to attend to.

At a meeting three days after the marriage, Fierens and Mosman with Konrad and one or two others, including their Anabaptist Provost and the Leader of the armed bands (none other than he who had chased Julius in the Cathedral), debated the result of the mass turn-out for the wedding. It had been forecast that it would help kindle enthusiasm for the cause.

'There were a few more for re-baptism yesterday,' said the Provost, 'but not a landslide. Conversions have fallen right off.'

Konrad felt personally mortified by the news. He was, after all, the leading citizen. His daughter's marriage should have inspired hundreds. Did they need drubbing to salvation?

'They will landslide soon enough,' cried Mosman. 'Cataclysms unthinkable. Mountains shall spew sulphur and the fire that clings . . .'

'Your patience is exhausted, I can see, Leader,' said Fierens smoothly. 'The marriage was supposed to cement the town and the Brethren. We have done all we can.'

'Certainly we have,' said Konrad.

'It is time we put our plan into operation – that is, if our Burgomaster hasn't *beaten* us to it.'

He smiled icily at Konrad.

'Beaten?' Konrad stammered.

There was Fierens again, with just a hint of an underlining of the word 'beaten', which raised the possibility of something he would rather not think about. He had, he knew, too many enemies now.

Konrad swallowed.

'I am sorry,' he said. 'I have had much to attend to. My daughter . . . your wife . . .'

It was true that Elisabeth's condition was giving cause for alarm. A congestion of the lungs had set in. The apothecary had been called but she was treating herself. Old Frieda was running up and downstairs with cordials of elderflower and lungwort every five minutes.

'My family is the righteous. My wife is the Congregation of Saints,' said Fierens. 'Do not confuse the spiritual issue with temporal matters. Continue.'

'What do you mean by *beaten* you to it?' Konrad mumbled, red-faced, expecting exposure, back to the wall.

'Why, man. Put into action the plan we discussed the other night. Purge the town of uncleanness.'

Konrad's relief was discernible and, naturally, discerned.

'I have not beaten anyone to anything,' he said. 'I was awaiting the result of our meeting here.'

'Well, it is perfectly plain,' said Fierens. 'If people wish to stay they must be baptized. Otherwise they must be put out.'

'Put out?'

'This day,' thundered Mosman. 'The place is shite. God will not have it. Out with them, I say.'

'But it is hard weather. Surely in humanity we should give them time to prepare themselves.'

'They have had the time. If they are not prepared they are unwise virgins and must suffer. They have forfeited their place at the feast. Whom have they to blame but themselves if they are cast into outer darkness?'

Konrad swallowed. Violence had always been an angry matter for him. Violence in cold blood took a little learning. He was sure that he could do it.

'Very well, then,' he said. 'If it must be done, it must be done.'

'It must be done,' said Mosman, 'and there's an end of it.'

'Amen,' said Fierens. 'Hallelujah.'

'I wish I could put my finger on that Love fellow Brother Jeremiah saw,' said the Provost. 'There's something about him I don't like. And the way he disappeared like that. Guilt written all over him.'

'Don't worry about that,' snapped Fierens. 'Get your men ready for tomorrow morning and look sharp about it.'

He was the only man who talked to the Provost like that. He could swoop like a spider when he chose.

Chapter 15

Names had been taken, faces noted, addresses listed in the course of the previous weeks. There was no shortage of spies. Indeed, the Provost, at the instigation of Fierens, had made a special point of welcoming all those who bore a grudge or were by nature resentful or envious. It was amazing how many there were in a German town.

So it was with no difficulty at all that, early in the morning, hardly past cockcrow – when only the first glimmering of light trembled in the east through bands of palest cornelian clouds beneath darker shadows, illuminating a town that lay eiderdowned in snow, as pristine and innocent-looking as anything outside Eden – the armed bands started to spread through the streets and form up at the appointed doors.

It was another bitterly cold morning – absurdly cold for early April; the very seasons themselves seemed out of joint. The bands waited. They had been warned to keep silent until the signal. Only their breath, cauliflowering upward, would have warned the citizens within that this was to be the last day they would spend in their homes.

'Eh eh, time to get up, I suppose,' said the Deputy Master of the Coopers (a minor guild), to his pretty little, heavily pregnant wife.

'There's not so much work to be done with these loonies and their no-drinking ways, but I don't like to sleep late all the same; I want to talk to Father Berthold if I can find him. You lie in bed and I'll see that the little ones have something to eat.'

Their maid had left to be an Anabaptist.

'You're a good man,' his wife smiled at him, which he was, and that was to be his undoing.

Just as he had assembled his three little boys and his even littler girl, and was cutting the loaf for their breakfast, a distant bugle sounded and there was a tremendous bang on the front door. One of the little boys actually fell off the bench.

'What the . . . ?' exclaimed Master Cooper, picking him up and hurrying to the door shouting, 'All right, all right. You don't have to knock the door down.'

His wife called down from the bedroom.

'What is it?'

Another blow hit the door; it actually fell in on top of him, hitting him in the face just above the brow. Holding his hand to his eye and looking through the trickling blood, he saw a small troop of grim, red-faced men waiting for him in the snow. One of them had an axe.

'What . . . what's going on?' the cooper mumbled. 'What do you want? There must be some mistake.'

He was too shocked even to be angry.

'No mistake, Cooper. Get your wife and children and bring them out into the street.'

'What?'

'You heard.'

'But . . . this is my house.'

'It was your house.'

'There's some mistake. You've come to the wrong place. Consult the records. I am a freeholder.'

'You are shit.'

'What! Now see here . . .'

'Now you see here, Cooper shit. You are a shitty Roman, right?'

'I am a Roman Catholic and proud of it. I intend to remain that way.'

'You are shit. Your wife is shit. Your brats are shit.'

'Nobody says that to me.'

By now the cooper's wife and children had come to the door behind him. The east wind was tousling her hair, blowing drifting snow crystals down the hall, making the little girl's teeth chatter.

'So what are you going to do about it, Cooper shit?'

'No, Franz,' shrieked his wife, as the cooper took a swing at the Leader of the red-faces, striking him a glancing blow on the shoulder as the man stepped back.

The man with the axe turned the blunt end round and tapped the cooper, not all that lightly, on the head. He fell and lay motionless, face down in the snow.

Another of the red-faced men started to kick him dispassionately. The cooper's wife let out a terrible cry and rushed to his side.

'Don't you dare,' she said to the men. 'Don't you dare, that's all.'

The man dispassionately kicking her husband turned round and gave her a shove, tumbling her into the snow. Her eldest son now rushed at the man who cuffed him on the side of the head, picked him up and threw him beside his mother.

'Bad man,' said the little girl, who had just learned to speak. 'Bad, bad man.'

'And you can shut your gob too and all,' said the red-face, barely restrained by one of his colleagues from giving her similar treatment.

Just then Mosman – yes, the Leader himself; he had been at prayer all night, receiving guidance on this very exercise; gaunt, merciless, straightforward – came shouting down the road with a band of followers, making his rounds. He took in the scene and showed stern if strident approval.

'Get out, you godless ones,' he called at them, not even stopping, 'never come back, you enemies of the Father.'

The wind, which had been steadily increasing since dawn – unlike the light whose early palest yellow had darkened to a brimstoney lead – now started to bring snowflakes riding like white galleons on its back.

'Get a cloak, missus,' said the Anabaptist who had restrained the kicker, 'get a cloak for your man and blankets for the little 'uns. You're to come with us. I'll give him a hand.'

He gestured at the cooper who was dazedly trying to sit up. His skull was fractured and he did not look at all well. The snow was falling faster now.

'Are we then to go?' asked the woman. 'You see I am with child. The children are small. Are we to go in this storm?'

'That is the will of God,' said the man, not altogether happily.

'Not my God,' answered the woman passionately. 'Not Sweet Jesus. "Suffer the little children", He said.'

'It is the will of God the Father,' shouted the Leader of the troop. 'Get on with it. Do as the man says.'

'What about our things? Money, valuables, my rings. I must bring them.'

'Bring them out, then,' said the man.

'And some food at least for the journey . . .'

'Aye. Bring it out too.'

The woman went back into the house, fighting back her tears. All the children were crying now, except the little girl, who was trying to hug her father. It was a scene that would have melted the heart of a Caligula, but it did not impress Fierens, who now came stalking round the corner.

'What? Still dawdling? Bustle, bustle,' he cried. 'The Kingdom of Heaven does not wait for laggards, Brother.'

The more helpful of the Anabaptists became sterner.

'Just coming, Brother. Hurry up in there,' he shouted at the house.

The cooper's wife appeared, her arms full of clothes. She knelt and quickly dressed the children as warmly as she could, and ran over to her husband with his cloak and hat. He dimly tried to help her.

'He is not well,' she cried at the men. 'You hurt him.'

'He'll be better soon enough. A walk in the cold will wake him up.'

'Have you no pity?'

'No pity for the unclean. Of course, you could always be baptized. Then you could stay. We'll put the door back on and you'll be snug as snug. What d'you say?'

It was the Devil's own temptation. You could see the woman was torn.

'No,' cried the cooper. 'I'd sooner die. But let my wife and the children stay. Have pity.'

'Come one, come all,' said the woman.

'Get the valuables, then,' said the red-face. 'Bring the food.'

The woman went back in and presently returned with two bundles.

'I'll take those,' said the red-face.

'You mean . . . ?'

For a moment she thought he was offering to carry them. And then she realized he was simply going to take them.

'I curse you,' she said steadily, 'from the bottom of my heart. You will not live the year out.'

The man shrugged.

'Have a care, mistress, or we'll do you for a witch.'

She took one side of her husband, the kinder red-face took the other, and the little group made its way slowly – with many a backward glance from the children at the little house where they had grown up in a happiness so unkindly shattered, a dream invaded by nightmare – towards the town square where a hundred other families in similar plight were gathering in the storm.

For indeed, the same scene had been played out with a hundred individual variations all over town – here a mother, newly delivered, forced from her nursing bed with her child at her breast; here a consumptive coughing his lungs out; there a great-granny whose wits had gone with the shock, telling her guards she would 'walk as far as the baker's' and then she would 'go back and have her gruel'; a musician and his family with the children pathetically carrying their broken viols . . .

Mostly they came from the more prosperous areas of the city, but now they presented a spectacle of destitution. Money, belongings, food, even spare clothes were taken from them. And as they stood in the whirling snowflakes, Mosman mounted a podium and began to preach. He told them they were going because they were defiling the New Jerusalem. They were wedded to their filthy ways and there was no more room for them in the City of God. They must fend as best they could and sup with the Antichrist.

Standing there in the blizzard, with his mane of hair and his beard shaken by the wind, his cloak flying behind him, he did indeed look like a prophet of the Old Testament.

The crowd of the faithful which had gathered to watch these preparations of expulsion sensed it too. He was not merely Isaiah or Zachariah or Ananias, he was Moses the Law-Giver.

'Mosesman,' they began to shout. 'Mosman is Moses. Break sin with thy rod, Mosesman.'

Indeed, he did belabour the wretched faithful Catholics and Lutherans; but he did give them one last chance.

'Out there,' he said, flinging his arms, 'you will find cold, filth, ordure, wolves, fiends flying through the woods, worms, mountains of fire, abysses, chasms, terrors and the Death that is everlasting. Do but stay, accept re-baptism in the one true way, and you will find friends, warmth, food, comfort and the infinite benignity of eternal life. Make your choice, for it is now or never.'

Some of them had no stomach for it. In a lull in the storm, they suddenly heard the howling quite possibly of a dog outside, but it could have been a wolf.

There was a small but perceptible trickle of candidates for benignity. Others, including many of the old crones (though not Frieda, for she was nursing Elisabeth and had been spared), were firmer in their faith and stood their ground.

'Open the gates,' shouted Mosman, and the massive iron-studded portals yawned wide.

Beyond lay the bridge and the road, marked only with a few poles, which ran past the meadows and on into the woods.

'Go,' shouted Mosman, 'and Death go with you. Before harvest, the weeds must be plucked from the vineyard . . . Out, out, I say.'

The miserable group straggled slowly forward, urged on by red-faces, who beat them, and by others who laughed and jeered. One of the Lutherans suddenly started singing Luther's own hymn.

It was totally unexpected. Not even Mosman could stop it. Others joined in; even the Catholics. As they passed the gates, their voices could still be heard – the sturdy voices of the men mingling with the quavering notes of the very old and the piping trebles of the little ones.

'A sure stronghold our God is still . . .'

(Julius, who had come to watch and to sketch – he had determined to record as best he might the trials of the town – suddenly found tears pouring down his cheeks.)

The cooper was the first to die. Indeed, he was only just alive when he left. His wife and children would not abandon him. Indeed, his little girl never did, dying quite suddenly of cold in her dead father's arms.

The mother herself died, prematurely delivering her dead baby in the shelter of a ditch with only the freezing stars – the weather had cleared – and her little boys for company.

The boys, however, survived. They were taken into the care of a kindly and childless shoemaker.

One of the boys eventually became an Inquisitor.

Chapter 16

The Lutherans and Catholics left in town moved around sheepishly now. Oh, they had renounced their faith for various reasons – fear being the principal motive and a perfectly good one – but not the sort of thing that makes one feel very creditable. Other explanations for trimming were: love of family, love of town, chronic indecision, and weak faith in the first place. Or perhaps it was faith in the last place which explained all the others.

However it was, they were all obliged to stand in the cold and be baptized in the market-square. Many of them felt like idiots. Others desperately attempted to achieve the same kind of elevation that the Anabaptists themselves displayed in similar moments of incipient rapture – and some of them, particularly the young, did indeed manage to reach 'inspiration'. There was genuine falling to the knees and raving, but not a very great deal of it. There was also a cynical contingent which shrugged its shoulders and got on with things because it couldn't see what all the fuss was about. It was all one God, wasn't it? (Though in this the contingent was wrong.)

The ceremony in the square lasted for three days, and at the end of it, over one thousand people had been baptized. Hass, who was still anxious to retrieve his position as Best Preacher in Town, lost his voice. Julius, growing a beard to disguise himself from his pursuer, recorded scenes absurd, sinister, profound and distressing.

Everyone now dispersed to his or her home, but not in happiness. An increasing shadow was falling over the town, an ominous cast which people, even the most cynical, could no longer ignore.

It had been officially declared that anyone found unbaptized in Rensburg would henceforward be summarily executed. Now this indeed was a shocking declaration to the ordinary townspeople. Oh, there had been capital offences before, but for crimes that were almost exclusively crimes one understood – treason, murder, and (very occasionally) witchcraft or extreme repeated heresy. But to be unbaptized! A sin of omission when all was said and done! For that to be a capital offence struck at the very root of what a decent town should be about. But it was too late to do anything about it now. Resistance should have been organized earlier. Rensburg, in the eyes of those Rensburgers whose fortune (or misfortune) it was to remain in town, could no longer be called a decent town.

For the Anabaptists, on the other hand, Rensburg could now indeed call itself the New Jerusalem. It was purged of 'misbelievers' and peopled now exclusively by the Children of God, who were instructed to call each other only 'brother' or 'sister'.

They understood that they could now live sinlessly, in a community drawn together by love alone. Many of them, of course, particularly the younger ones more able to endure the cold, the shortage of accommodation, the scarcity of rations, believed wholeheartedly in this novel mode of living. Others were less dedicated, but enjoyed Mosman's sermons and the promises of plenty that he made for the righteous. If the great were cast down, it must mean that the low would be raised up. In the new dispensation, the use of wood, water and pasturage, the right to hunt and fish, would be all theirs. There would be no service, no dues, no taxes. The earth would give forth her abundance and the trees would drop honey and fragrant gums.

There was no doubt in anyone's mind that the last few days had marked a turning-point in the affairs of Rensburg.

Meanwhile, Fierens moved about the city casting and re-casting, drafting and re-drafting, waiting with a planner's patience for the moment when he would show himself clothed in Glory. He had the feeling these days that he was becoming two people – author and performer, God and man.

Chapter 17

Elisabeth's congestion had turned into inflammation of the lungs. Her lowered state of mind before the marriage had not improved her powers of resistance, and she had fallen and lain there like a ninepin. At least that was what Frieda told her when the fever showed signs of wearing off.

'You've got to be happy, child,' Frieda said, as Elisabeth lay with her forehead in a flannel and her mind in a spin. 'You'll never get better if you mope.'

'I'm married,' Elisabeth gasped. 'That won't get better.'

'Yes, but consider, child. And don't talk. Listen. Just rest. Consider, it's an ill wind that blows no one any good, and this fever of yours, it's a godsend on two counts. We can spin your sickness out for goodness knows how many months, and he won't be able to come near you.'

For the first time, Elisabeth smiled.

'I'll spin it out,' she said. 'If it doesn't spin me out.'

'Spin you out,' Frieda tutted, 'what a notion! You're as strong as a horse if you put your mind to it.'

'What's the other count?' asked Elisabeth.

Oddly enough, she was feeling better already.

'The other count is I'm here to look after you. Otherwise I'd have been turned out of town like all the rest of 'em.'

Frieda told her of the choice of enforced baptism or exodus which the townsfolk had had to take.

'That's terrible. What's going to happen to them? What's going to happen to all of us?'

'One thing at a time, darling. Yes, they've gone into the woods and fields, no shelter, no money, begging for food. Most of my old friends have gone. Ingrid Heer and Irmgard Rohm, all gone. I shan't be seeing them again, I shouldn't wonder. Just one or two have stayed – not because they're cowards but because they're needed.'

'Needed?'

'Never you mind about that. We didn't all go mad in this town, that's all. Anyway, the good thing is, I'm here to help you. And help, it seems to me, young lady, you're most certainly going to need.'

'What . . . what d'you mean, Nanny?'

'You know what I mean.'

Elisabeth, already a little flushed with the slight fever, blushed a deeper red. She had thought at least she could hide her predicament a little longer.

'How . . . how did you know?'

'Come on, girl,' the old woman said. 'I wasn't born yesterday, you know.'

'I'm sorry, Nurse. I should have told you. It doesn't show, does it?'

'It doesn't show now, not to most folk, but it will. All the more reason for you to seem an invalid. Your poor mother being the way she was, well, it helps now, doesn't it? Makes it more believable. Your father's got used to a sick woman in the house.'

Elisabeth blessed her mother. She could feel her presence now, in her sickroom, smiling at her, calming her. It gave her strength to voice the fears that had been tormenting her for days.

'My father . . . Fierens . . . I don't know what they'd do if they knew. I was so worried . . .'

Her eyes filled with tears and she hugged the old woman.

'There, there, darling,' said Frieda. 'Don't take on.'

Elisabeth thought of something else.

'And another thing. I don't want him to know.'

'The painter?'

'The painter.'

'That wicked man. If your father hadn't given him such a drubbing, I'd drub him myself.'

'Father didn't even know that we had . . . done anything . . . He would have killed him if he'd even thought of it.'

'You must have been mad to . . .' the old woman burst out, and then checked herself.

'Say it,' urged Elisabeth. 'It's no worse than I've said to myself.'

'It's no use calling back thistledown. What's done's done. It may surprise you to know I once did the same, though with not such obvious results.'

'You?'

'Yes, I.'

'I thought we were in Paradise,' said Elisabeth, with such a face of happiness at the memory that the old woman quite forgave her and thought she would have done exactly the same – as she had long ago with that silly boy called Peter on a river-bank hidden by reeds as high as houses. It was a shame he had died so soon after, doubling up and dying in a day.

'Perhaps he should know, after all,' said Frieda, gently.

'No, no. He . . . is not . . . fit . . .'

'You sound like those Anabaptists. He was weak because he was frightened. He loved you, that's for sure. You can't expect perfection.'

'We felt like . . . gods . . .' Elisabeth said, strangely.

'Well, you weren't and you aren't. You're a silly girl and he's a naughty boy.'

'But I won't have him told, d'you hear?'

'You're the mistress, darling. But you may need him more than you think.'

'Who is his wife?' said Elisabeth in a small voice.

'She is a small woman. I think she is mad. Perhaps that is why she gets on so well with the loonies.'

'Gets on?'

'She is besotted with their Leader. Would you believe she publicly washed his feet? What impudence! Blasphemous, I call that. He treats her like the Magdalen herself.'

'The Magdalen was a whore, wasn't she, Nurse?'

'Before she took up with Jesus, she was. But we don't use words like that.'

'Poor old painter,' said Elisabeth. 'What a time he must be having.'

'Don't think of him, think of yourself, young lady. We have to find a way of getting you out of this mess.'

'What about Billa? Won't she tell?'

'You leave Billa to me.'

It was true. The old woman could frighten a gargoyle off a church roof if she was minded.

'If I'm to get better, I'll need more coltsfoot and elderflower,' said Elisabeth. 'They'll be in the cabinet in my mother's room. Oh, and some elecampane.'

Frieda moved off busily. Elisabeth stopped her as she reached the door.

'Thank you, Nurse,' she said, her eyes full of tears.

'Don't thank me yet, silly. Best thanks is you getting well again.'

Chapter 18

Before the disaster of the chicken entrails, the Bishop and Baron Theo – upon due consultation at home and encouragement from the Bishop's sister – had already been in touch with many of the neighbouring towns and principalities. After the entrails, these activities were redoubled.

'We need more clout,' Theo had said, and he was right.

There seemed to the Bishop now no other recourse. The madness had gone too far. It had to be stopped. Besides, there was his investment to be considered.

The neighbouring towns and principalities had problems of their own: bad harvests, unruly populaces (many of whom had mercifully gone to Rensburg), taxes, hard winters, humanism, more taxes, disobedient children ... Few of them were in the mood to cough up when the Bishop suggested a contribution of arms, supplies and mercenary soldiers.

'It's not my problem,' said the Prince Bishop of Magdeburg, 'if you can't look after your patch properly.'

But the ex-Bishop of Rensburg had an answer to that.

'It is your problem, Prince. It is everybody's problem. Because if these Anabaptists are not defeated once and for all, they will turn the whole country upside down. They will spread like a contagion. Don't underestimate them. I've seen them at work and mighty plausible they can be. I don't suppose the poor of your town would turn a deaf ear to the prospect of sharing out the contents of Your Excellency's larder or his muniment room for that matter.'

'Oh, well, I suppose you're right. Trouble, trouble. You'd better have a company of those idle ruffians that call themselves soldiers I keep seeing around the place – and paying for, I may add. Oh, and I think I might have a couple of spare cannon somewhere. You can have those, if you like.'

And so it went on. A cartload of arquebuses here, a dozen barrels of flour there, a troop of horse, a rusty siege-engine – grudgingly, stintingly and inadequately supplied by the Count of This and the Bishop of That – started to accumulate at Theo's castle, waiting for the moment when it was adjudged substantial enough to encircle the town and impress the inhabitants sufficiently for them to take one look and fall flat on their faces with terror.

And then one early evening in long-delayed spring, just as the Bishop and his sister and Theo were sitting down to supper, there had come a desperate clanging of the bell at the castle gates. All the dogs in the place started to bark.

'What the Devil? . . .' spluttered Theo.

It was a councillor of Rensburg with his sick wife and four children – one of whom nearly died that night – bringing the story, slowly over the flooded fields (the thaw had at last set in), of their expulsion from the city.

'That does it,' shouted the Baron. 'To arms.'

'Tomorrow morning,' said his wife.

'I'll go along with that,' said the Bishop.

And that was how it was. Two weeks later, as the Anabaptists changed guard on the city walls, they saw the file of soldiers, led by a plumed knight, and followed by cannon, engines and baggage-train, approach from the east and take up a position, out of gunshot, around the perimeter.

In the city there was immediate and orderly activity. The arrival of the enemy came as no surprise to Fierens. He had been expecting it. Indeed, as soon as the little army appeared, he arranged that leaflets should be distributed both in the town and outside – for he had organized secret means of egress – among neighbouring Lutheran towns of a wavering Anabaptist persuasion, proclaiming Roman Catholic aggression against the peace-loving, peacefully loving company of Saints.

As it happened – as it had been planned to happen, as Fierens had conceived it; for nothing occurred that he could not conceive, even if he was not conscious of it as yet; he was only gradually sloughing off mortality; there were still areas which were dark to him; the sunlight of Eternity was gradually lighting every dusty corner, every soiled crevice, and would in time show all – as it happened, he had already decided who should take charge of the town's military operations.

It had been plain to him for some while that Konrad, with his rage of energy and his administrative capacities, would make an excellent choice as General. Of course, he had awakened in the man this violence, just as he had from the first called up his lechery. God had played on him as on an organ. Sin, as ever, could be used to promote virtue. Now, if Konrad had a desire to beat anyone, he could beat the enemy.

He watched him now, inspecting the besiegers who were already throwing up earthworks at some distance around the perimeter of town. He would soon return and start giving orders. The people needed orders, thought Fierens. They were milling around in some confusion, reading the pamphlets, wondering whether they had bargained for all this when they had left their flea-bitten homes, their soup-and-vegetable lives, to become Children of God.

There was some murmuring in the square.

'It is sinful to take up arms,' said one whey-faced, long-nosed, tall-hatted fellow. 'Love them that hatefully use you! I say we should go out and embrace the visitors.'

Some of the women, particularly the ex-nuns, seemed to be agreeing with him.

Fierens decided that the Provost should have a word with the little group. How weak was mankind even in the hour of its greatest opportunity. Why had he not made angels to rule over the world, beings who would never stoop or lie or envy or cog or evade or overween or spread their legs or deceive? But he knew the answer, even before he had finished his litany of man's shallowness. To have put angels on earth would have been to turn the performance into a mere tableau. Without man's weakness there would have been no Play. Without Error there could be no Trial.

He looked down from the unmeasurable height of his pinnacle and addressed the crowd through the voice of Mosman, whom he had now summoned by a thought to put backbone into the doubtful.

'Are you afraid?' said Mosman, who did not realize that his part had been written. 'Are you smirching your breeches because you think the big boys have come and will beat you with a stick? Is your faith so weak that the first obstacle makes you curl up like a kitten? Are your minds so low that they cannot see the enormity of joyfulness which is waiting for you round the corner? Perhaps you thought eternal life was to be handed to you on a plate! What gave you that idea? If it were easy, everybody would have it. There would be no Elect. Everyone would be swilling at the trough of joy. Do you think that is what the Father wants? My poor loves, for I do love you in spite of your weakness, the Father wants fighters – stout hearts and high minds, a resolute will, unshakeable faith. He knows that Antichrist must first be brought low before you can taste the sweet, sweet fruits, the infinitely succulent joys that hang, beckoning the faithful, like golden lamps from the boughs of Paradise . . .'

He continued in this vein for some while until the crowd was almost uncontrollable with militancy.

'Go forth,' Mosman concluded. 'Each one of you. Be not afraid. The Lord is with you. His arm is swift, his buckler is broad. He will not be slow to strike and to shield. But you must show Him what you can do. Go now – the strong to the fight and the weak (in frame but not in spirit), the weak to work, to fetch and carry, and gather and mend. So that, when the Hour of Danger comes, it will be seen that we are one. One will, one force, one indestructible army of the Father. "At them, at them, while the fire is hot! Don't let your sword get cold! Hammer cling, clang on Nimrod's anvil! Tumble their towers to the ground!"'

270

This last quotation from the great Saint and martyr Muntzer, executed by the authorities only eight years earlier, aroused tumultuous enthusiasm, and it was all Fierens could do to stop them opening the gates and streaming out to do battle on the instant.

Chapter 19

Next scene.

Konrad Harting, grocer, lecher and newly appointed General of the Chosen, assembled all able-bodied men and addressed them in his turn, exuding competence and military discipline from every pore. His talk was short and to the point.

'The troops out there are few in number, badly equipped, low in morale, far from home, out in the open, cold as monks' charity, and no match whatever for the Company of Saints,' he said.

Hurrah! Huzzah! Caps in the air, etc.

'But don't underestimate the mercenary. That's his job, soldiering. So if he lacks conviction, faith and a willingness to die if need be for his cause – whoever heard of a mercenary willing to die for a cause? [Laughter and jeers] If he lacks willingness to die for a cause, he certainly does not lack practice, skill and a willingness to make you die for yours. [Groans] The way to beat him is to be better soldiers; for, if we are better soldiers, and we have our faith, who is to stop us? [More huzzahs] Now, what we are going to do is this. You, you and you ... take a dozen men each, get every shovel and barrow and pickaxe and cart you can lay hands on, and start building earthworks. I will show you where they are to be sited ... Meanwhile, the rest of you, divide yourselves into ten equal companies, and I want the following people – one for each company – to be Officers in Charge ...'

Konrad read out his list, prepared beforehand with Fierens, and began allotting individual tasks to each officer's command: the construction of dug-outs and trenches for the town's cannon, the placement of anti-siege devices, even the organization of a fire service. Day and night watches were instituted, working by rota.

It was as if all his life he had been waiting for this hour. There were no more thoughts for the moment of subterranean meetings or beatings or the secret of paradisial congress.

Soon every man, woman and youth in the town had their appointed task. And soon, indeed, under Konrad's able direction, sorties were even being undertaken outside the wall against the besieging troops and, in one minor engagement, the Saints notched up first blood.

Chapter 20

Old Frieda, watching these comings and goings from her window, sighed and prayed in amazement and alarm. There was a sort of horrible momentum to the thing. It was out of control. The only good thing you could say about it was that it kept Konrad and That Man (she could not bring herself to mention his name) from bothering her poor young lady.

She kept receiving letters from the painter but she did not pass them on. There seemed no purpose in it now, not at the moment. It would only have disturbed her mistress. The first thing Elisabeth had to do was to get well, for the baby's sake as much as for herself.

Let the painter stew a little, she thought. If he's worth his salt, he'll keep true; and if he does not, why, so much the better for her.

One thing at a time. She is married, she is having a baby that is not her husband's, the world is going mad. That is surely enough for one woman with child . . .

Down in the kitchen, Billa flickered her tawny eyes at the ceiling and smiled her crafty smile. Secrets, she knew, were as good as money in the bank, however much the old crow might caw . . .

Chapter 21

Blommardine had a natural tendency towards hero-worship, even if at first one might have thought she seemed an unlikely candidate for such a trait. But her acerbity and her impatience actually stemmed from the fact that she could never find anyone to live up to her expectations. It may have been something to do with her father – an otherwise cold and violent man who doted upon her – so that she looked in men (especially since her father's death) for another who would inspire the same fearful interest, respect and sense of security. It was an almost impossible equation. Julius, of course, had been an early aberration from what came to be her norm. She had had other affairs before she came to Rensburg, but here at last she was discovering her archetype.

The first prophet, Elijah, had inspired in her some of the feelings from afar. A figure of authority was obviously an object of interest if he was large and stern and preached love of a rather violent kind. But Elijah was a second-class Saint, and had never had the imagination to see what it was or *be* what it was that she saw in him.

As for Julius, of course, he had been a disaster in many ways – the last thing she wanted was a dreamer – but he had seemed to represent an escape from her surroundings, perhaps even from her father, in whose presence she sometimes experienced sensations which at the time had surprised and disturbed her. And then, of course, there was another reason, which she sometimes felt ashamed about, sometimes amused or even aroused about, in her choice of Julius . . .

At any rate, the general consensus of advice had been: better to get away from home and marry a well-travelled man who could teach her a thing or two. It had not worked out. Her fault – she had no illusions about her responsibility for instigating the marriage. Her father's very fury with Julius had made her think that perhaps he too was experiencing the same guilty sensations in her presence. But there it was, it was done, and if it had been a mistake, it had at least brought her here to meet the man who represented everything she had ever hoped for in the male sex – well, not everything, because she had not yet hoped for his male sex; it was too much to hope for, nor was it proper that she ever should; but if she did it would be the sternest, finest, grandest male sex in the world, and it would carry her up to Heaven on a mast of pure pleasure, kicking and writhing like a wild burgee.

Meanwhile she was his assistant, his awareness, his ears and eyes and hands. For while Konrad and Fierens (she didn't like Fierens; no one could *like* Fierens) were organizing the defences – at least, she supposed that was what Fierens was doing; you never knew what he was doing, appearing and disappearing and not putting his shoulder to the wheel; all the same you did have that curious feeling he could see right through you, undress you to the soul with his eyes, which she never felt, more was the pity, with Mosman – while they were doing that, the Leader (with her help) was busy turning Rensburg into the New Jerusalem.

'You have the list of those expelled,' he said to her. 'It is the Lord's wish that the goods, property and houses of the godless ones should be taken into the keeping of the Saints. I shall now pray for guidance. You will see meanwhile that everything is removed and placed conveniently for the Saints' use in warehouses. All accounts, contracts, leases and financial transactions such as IOUs and guarantees are to be burnt. Do you understand?'

'Yes, Leader.'

'I am going into my quarters now to pray. Do not disturb me.'

'No, Leader.'

He turned without a word and went towards his lodgings. She loved him for not seeming to care whether she was there or not.

To the rest of the Anabaptists, however, she did not present any semblance of weakness. They regarded her with awe because she was the Leader's confidante, though inevitably her position had caused some jealousy among the Anabaptist females.

'Get moving, then,' shouted Blommardine, as she organized the women to start shifting stuff out of the houses. 'Everything goes – clothing, bedding, hardware, furnishings, food – everything down to the last onion. Move yourselves, Sisters.'

'Hark at the busy bosoms,' said a little ex-prostitute from Delft to her neighbour, 'who does she think she is? I'll shove a pickle up her you-know-what if she shouts at me like that.'

'Stop griping and get on with it. Wide mouth and wide legs . . .'

Blommardine was more than a match for any street-slanger.

The ex-prostitute made a face and shouldered a flitch of bacon.

Some of these people had not tasted meat in three months or ever seen such domestic luxuries as were now disclosed. Blommardine, even with the aid of the Provost and his red-faces, was hard put to it to stop looting and wholesale destruction.

'Now you see,' shouted Fierens, suddenly appearing like a stage devil, almost popping up from the floorboards, 'now you see how these miserable bags of worms have been living while the righteous starve. Now you see how they've been hogging and snorting while you chew on a mouldy crust and suck mud. But do not fall into their trap. These luxuries have been sent to tempt and seduce you. Oh, yes. They've left them here to turn your minds from God. What's that, Brother Provost?'

'There's one who's eating a sausage, Brother.'

'Bring her here.'

The wretched Anabaptist, a simple woman from Haarlem who had forgotten even what a sausage looked like, was wheeled forward.

'Give me the sausage.'

Simpleton handed it over. It was a shrivelled enough little thing.

'Cut two thin strips from the sausage and leave the rest,' Fierens ordered the Provost.

It was done.

'Now,' said Fierens, 'order one of your men to tie the woman's arms. Put each strip up the woman's nostrils and cram the rest in her mouth.'

The poor woman started to heave at the restraining arms but to no avail. The pieces of sausage were inserted and, this being done, the creature could not breathe.

'There,' said Fierens, 'enjoy your sausage, and let it be a lesson to all who would steal from the Community of Saints.'

The woman was making the most dreadful noises and turned first red and then almost blue.

'Let her go,' said Fierens. 'Where is your greed now? Eat your supper, villainy.'

She fell to the ground thrashing and kicking, her skirts up around her waist. Nobody moved.

'Look to her, cover her,' he said at last. 'Her shame is exposed. Now you see the weakness of the flesh – the poor, kicking houses of meat that are our souls' hutches here on earth. But oh how glorious shall we be at the last.'

Someone threw a sack over her. Another started to pull sausage from her nose.

'Is she dying?' said Blommardine, appearing on the scene and going to the woman's side. 'An attack? What happened?'

'You must ask her that,' said Fierens. 'She will not die.'

It was true. The woman gave a great choking cough and started breathing again.

'Now get on with your work,' he said. 'Antichrist does not stand gaping.'

There were no other cases of theft reported that afternoon. The incident had a profound effect on the Anabaptists. To be suffocated with a symbol of plenty! Indeed, it passed down into Rensburg vernacular, and to this day you may still hear Rensburgers exclaim 'Well, suffocate me with a sausage' as an expression of astonishment.

Chapter 22

Mosman now suddenly came out of his room – haggard, emaciated and looking even more like Moses – refused Blommardine's offer of soup, and read out a list of seven deacons who had been chosen by God to administer the stores accumulated by the confiscation.

God had sensibly composed the list of men who were too old for military service.

'The needy,' thundered Mosman, 'only the needy may apply to these deacons for whatsoever they lack. Let the destitute, the sick and the suffering sup at the rich man's table as it is written in the Scriptures. "The rich He hath sent empty away." But let me hear of no malingerers or scroungers who are in health and have no lack, for by God they shall feel the whip and sting of my wrath. We are on the threshold and we raise our eyes to God and He judges us even as we stand here. For do not imagine that simply by calling our town the New Jerusalem we have as yet attained the heavenly city. Jerusalem must be built. Jerusalem must be earned. Jerusalem must be fought for. The time of struggle precedes the time of peace. So if I know of any of you – any of you – wasting the Saints' commodities or throwing burnt offerings falsely to that idol that is your belly – the punishment will be hard, swift and terrible.'

There were, as might be expected, few candidates for the supplies. Even the sick and feeble were nervous of being accused of wrongful application. Suffocation by sausage had done its work.

Those that did apply were on the whole gratified with the re-distribution of wealth, though the pickings were far from liberal. Still, a new blanket or a jugful of beans were all to the good when you were sitting in a draughty warehouse coughing your lungs out or living out the Last Days in a converted hog-pen. (The actual houses of the wealthy tended to go to the Leaders and officers of the saintly army.)

But there were others, residents of the town, who were less sanguine about the development. True, some of them were mere turncoats and would probably have gone along with anything. The ones who started murmuring and causing trouble ('Oh, I can see you, I can see you,' crooned Fierens from his pinnacle, 'I will wind you in') were the ones who didn't have much time for religion but did understand about property.

277

They didn't like the idea of this foreigner coming and carving up the town without so much as a by your leave. Who did he think he was? Some of them had exiled friends and relatives who looked to them to care for their houses.

At a public meeting for residents only, their feelings were forcibly expressed by a blacksmith called Grundmann.

'Who are these people, who is this man?' he exclaimed. 'We take them in, we give them shelter, and how do they repay us? They boot us into their baptism. Yes, neighbours, we were the weak ones, the time-servers. Can you honestly deny it?'

There was a general shuffling and hang-doggery.

'But as for the strong, the faithful, our good friends, yes, what did they get? They got booted out altogether. And what had they done wrong? They stuck up for their religion, as I should have done if I'd felt strongly about it. As it happens I didn't and I don't, but I respect those who do. Well, we put up with their expulsion – and the manner of it – which makes me sick at heart every time I think about it. And now we're asked to stand by while this Dutchman, this high-hatted scavenger, this cuckoo in our nest, carves up the spoil and commandeers our poor friends' houses and homes. I tell you, neighbours, it makes me mad. And what's more the writing's on the wall. Today, it's exiles' houses. Tomorrow, it could be ours . . . Now, this is what I reckon we should do . . .'

His audience, afire now with indignation, had not noticed that the ferrety Schwenk, one of the time-servers, had slipped out early on in the proceedings. And now, just as the blacksmith was going to elucidate his plan – which involved rushing the gates and opening them to the besiegers – the door burst open and Mosman himself appeared at the head of the armed troop of men.

'Seize him,' he cried.

The troops were out-numbered and some effective resistance could have been mounted at such close quarters, but the opportunity passed. The blacksmith was a big man but – now surrounded by swords and pistols – it was plain that resistance would have been futile.

'To the market-square with him,' shouted Mosman. 'And you, all of you, can follow to see how we treat God's traitors.'

They tied the blacksmith's hands behind his back and shoved and jostled him through the streets to where a crowd had already mysteriously gathered (not so mysterious to Fierens who had already written the scene) in anticipation of something either holy or gruesome or, as more and more happened these days, both.

Trumpeters were now sent out to ensure the entire populace's immediate attendance.

Satisfied at last that he had the whole town's attention, and refreshed by the soup which Blommardine had finally forced upon him, Mosman now mounted the podium – taking the precaution to surround himself with a bodyguard in case there should be any more gestures of insurrection.

Dwelling shortly upon the manner and matter of the arrest, he now told his audience how deeply hurt the Lord was.

'He is outraged, Brothers and Sisters. He is heavy. He hangs His head. He cannot bear to see His servant, His chosen prophet, insulted and slandered by those He thought were friends. It is too much for Him. See how the clouds lour. He has vowed to show His wrath and I fear, yes, He is terrible in His anger, that all His vows to us – the promised Victory, the time of plenty, the golden Eternity that we crave – all these will be cut off . . .'

A groan went up from the Anabaptists.

'Yes,' continued Mosman, 'it will be withheld from all of us, if this godless smith is not cut off from the body of the Chosen.'

A wailing and a howling went up from the crowd.

'Cut him off,' they cried. 'Let us live forever, Lord.'

It was a horrible noise. The Anabaptists were actually baying for blood. Even so, there were a few Rensburgers still who had some fire in their bellies.

A former burgomaster, an old man now, a couple of former councillors and the Master of the Bakers approached the podium. Their way was blocked immediately by the bodyguard, but they spoke up.

'Get back, you.'

'We wish to speak.'

'What is it?' demanded Mosman, sternly. 'Who interrupts the Lord's Chosen?'

'I,' said the ex-burgomaster.

'We,' said the others.

'Speak, then. The Lord inclines His ear. You wish to make an apology?'

'We wish to say that this smith has been wrongfully arrested. As for what you are saying, "cut off", there can be no "cut off". There are laws in this town.'

'Do you hear that?' cried Mosman to the Anabaptists. 'These are the people we are to share our New Jerusalem with. These are the ones we have baptized. And what do they show us in gratitude? Teeth! Stings! They are serpents in our bosom. Talk of laws! There is only one law here. It is the Lord's law and we are both his judiciary and his executive. Away with them to prison!'

'You can't do this,' exclaimed the Master of the Bakers, as they were hustled away, the ex-burgomaster nearly falling as he was pushed, 'he is an old man.'

279

'He will not be old much longer,' said Mosman grimly.

The crowd enjoyed his repartee.

'He won't be old much longer,' they cackled.

'And now, Smith,' said Mosman, 'kneel and make your peace with your Maker.'

'I will not. First, I want to hear your accusation.'

'It is this,' said Mosman, stabbing him in the stomach with a dagger he produced from beneath his robes.

The smith stood for a little while, reflecting on the blood and muck which started to spurt from his tunic, unable quite to gather what was going on. Was this gore his? Was he made of this?

The crowd crowded around, eager to catch every drip.

At last, with a look of horror, the smith sank to his knees.

'Oh, no,' he said. 'Oh, no . . . I don't see that was . . . necessary . . .'

'Well see this, then,' said Mosman.

And, taking a pistol from one of the bodyguard, he shot him through the eye.

The smith pitched forward, dead, but still twitching.

The crowd let out a ghastly 'ahhhh', a sound of almost carnal relief.

'We will now sing a hymn and disperse,' said Mosman. '"Darkly kind and wisely fierce, Blood shall wash away our tears" to the tune of "Thread the Bodkin". All together now.'

Chapter 23

The flat expanse of ochre-coloured turf covering the middle-ground of the Garden bore as many enigmas as the front of stage.

He had scanned it many times with a painter's eye. There was much to admire, and something for a Florentine eye to criticize. This was not the southern idea. It was too Gothic, too unruly. And yet, wasn't that exactly what Verrocchio had praised?

He brought himself to order. This was not the moment for a critique of style. He must look for content – or, as a cryptographer, for signs and portents.

There were two major differences, then, in this middle delight. For one thing there was a sense of exuberant energy instead of dreaminess and innocent sensuality. And, for another, almost all of the energy was coming from men.

There was, it was true, a pool in evidence in which beautiful maidens disported themselves. But around them paraded a whirligig of manhood – triumphant, rampant, feral, and yet strangely ordered, as if moving to the rhythm of an unheard dance.

The anti-clockwise cavalcade reminded Julius, as he looked at it, of water going down a hole – with an energy that was both wild and governed by natural laws. Or the sun itself . . .

The male force, yes – generating, generative, working towards and with and through the female; hence the foreground and the central pool of maidens . . .

All the riders on their strange steeds – boars, bulls, jackasses, stallions, unicorns, stags, goats, tigers, panthers, camels – all of them were male – sometimes flagrantly so; one young fellow was standing on one leg on his steed, arse in the air, having his backside nibbled by a bird – all male except one . . .

There was a bride, sitting in front of a man, on a white palfrey, both partly hidden by a great red bell-flower. They were preceded by a youth on a tiger bearing another great fecund fish. It was at the central part of the picture; both the vertical and the horizontal crossed here. It was at the same level as the Fountain of Life in Paradise next door.

All right, then. Three sections, three panels, three divisions of the fingers in the magical hand-sign that the girl at the front was making – that the Brethren had made at the Feast of the Swan, three-headed ibis and salamander . . . three upon three . . . but what did it mean? Father, Son and Holy Ghost . . . Three in One . . . It could not be a coincidence. But the picture was more than a conventional religious one. It had meanings within meanings like those Italian cabinets he had seen, where you never knew what might not open, however solid it looked.

Wasn't there something else he was missing?

Come, come. Florence, the Academy, Plato . . . yes, that was it. The three stages of man's existence . . . what did they call it? The *Scala Mystica*. Body, Soul, and Spirit. That had to be it for, look, the last section of the picture, the background, was dominated by a limpid sky where strange creatures floated into the ether.

The three sections, then, must correspond to what the neo-Platonists called the realms of the Sun, Moon and Earth. 'With every act of generation, the Sun sows spirit into the cosmos. It is conceived by the Moon which gives birth to the Soul; which Earth clothes with substance and glory.'

Yes, yes, but what did it mean? And all those groups of people on either side up there, clumping like insects around carapaces full of silvery bottoms; splayed legs holding up a mermaid; bulb-bodied long-headed birds? . . .

The force of Life seemed to be part of the answer. The questing, restless, mediating energy that brings the spirit into action; that is, to life. But what light did it throw on Hell?

I could look at this picture my whole life long, he thought, and still not find myself at the flower-stalked, bird-beaked bottom of it.

What a tribulation had been set up for him! Why did he not have done with it, and leave this place behind as one would leave a dream (as it sometimes seemed to be)? Why was he caught in this web of a picture? Why did it have to be him?

All his life, it seemed, he had been dogged by an inexplicable retribution for something he had not done.

Not for the first time, he wished he had a father and mother who could throw some light on his predicament.

Chapter 24

Elisabeth had no need to worry for the moment about her husband's reaction to the small rotundity that was beginning to plump out her stomach, and which could only be concealed with a great deal of fluffing of the kirtle. Mosman, Fierens, her father and the preachers were busying themselves with quite a different project – one that had occupied the Anabaptists' dreams for many months but could only now be put into effect.

It concerned the common ownership of wealth.

Hass, who was a sincere man in his self-engrossed way, fully believed that worldly riches were an impediment to entry into the Kingdom, and to a proper social harmony here on earth. He spelt it out in church one Sunday after a day-long meeting, with prayers, between the Leaders.

'God's will is that we should restore community of possession, my Brothers and Sisters, as it was in the beginning and as befits the Saints of God. We must put all our belongings into a common pool under the care of deacons and live from it according to our needs, for only thus can we truly help one another with a holy kind of service. Accordingly, my Brethren, everything that has served the purposes of self-seeking and private property, such as buying or selling, working for money, talking interest or practising usury – even at the expense of unbelievers – or eating and drinking the sweat of the poor . . . that is, making one's own people and fellow-creatures work so that one can grow fat . . . and indeed everything that offends against love . . . all such things are abolished amongst us by the power of love and community . . .'

There was a gasp from the body of the church as the full import of what he was saying sank in among the townspeople. Oh, they had had things requisitioned, they had gone along with the new ideas, even been baptized. It had seemed easier to, really. They didn't want any trouble. Keep your head down, that was their motto. But the notion of being asked to give up their gold, their possessions, everything they had worked for . . . well, it was asking a bit much.

'Ah, you murmur,' thundered Hass, 'you shift uneasily, you wriggle on your backsides, but you are no more than traitors, yes, traitors to God and to your fellows if you think otherwise. Personal wealth is an abomination to God. No Christian or Saint can satisfy Him if he does not live in such a community of ownership, or at least desire with all his heart to do so . . . So, Brethren, God wills that you hand over all your money, and all gold and silver ornaments, at Elim after the service today. If, for some reason, that is impractical, it must be within twenty-four hours.'

Fierens was in the church with the Provost, noting the names of those who seemed most uncomfortable with the preacher's recommendations.

Elim was the new name for the town square, and it was there that he repaired with the Provost to view the response of the command.

'There'll be evasions,' said the Provost as they walked. 'You see if there aren't. There were cries of real pain in that church.'

'It was the Devil's din,' said Fierens, 'depend upon it.'

It was as if his mind had spawned and there were now hundreds of little golden spider-minds – all his – each with its area of golden care. He could talk with the Provost, supervise the fortifications, know the heart and parts of Mosman at his prayers, entwine Konrad, prowl among the tents of the invaders, know the barrels of flour in the warehouse, walk with God, all without stirring his steps from Broad Street as he went.

The turn-out at Elim was disappointing. Some of the more passionate believers brought their all. A prosperous joiner named Hugwald came with a barrow-load and a wife who was in tears. He had always been inclined to enthusiastic gestures. There were one or two other large-scale donations. The rest were mere apologies.

'I told you,' said Mrs Hugwald to her husband, 'but you would not listen. No one takes this sort of thing seriously. You could have made a gesture but you had to go the whole hog. Now we're ruined.'

'Now you are saved,' said Fierens, suddenly descending, and addressing the joiner. 'You are saved. But she,' he continued, pointing a quivering finger at the woman, 'she is under arrest.'

The Provost bundled the protesting wife away while the joiner completed the hand-over. He had not liked his wife for many years.

'This is an outrage,' said Mosman, when he was summoned to the scene and shown the inadequate proceeds. 'It is an offence unto God.'

A crowd of townsfolk – as opposed to immigrants – had begun to collect, and it was clear that they had not brought their wealth with them. No one made any kind of overt resistance, for the lesson of the blacksmith was still fresh in their minds. Questions, however, were asked.

'Surely,' said one Karlstadt, a silversmith, stepping forward at last, 'surely you do not mean all our money? How can we trade? I can do nothing without my silver. If we cannot work and trade, the town will come to a halt. We will starve.'

Mosman approached him with a smile.

'Poor man,' he said. 'Your ears are stopped. All of you, oh my poor people, what? Has the Devil closed your understanding? Is Antichrist yet so rife?'

The people were silent. They feared him even more when he smiled.

'Go now to your homes,' continued Mosman, 'and do as the Lord commands. I want to see you all back here in one hour, bearing your money and your golden objects – yes, and your silver and your gems – ready and more than ready to hand them over to the community. Do you understand? Are your ears open?'

They nodded miserably, though there were still signs of mute resistance.

'Very well,' said Mosman. 'Go.'

One or two started to move off; the rest stood around sheepishly.

'Go,' shouted Mosman at the top of his voice.

The gathering broke up as he started to fumble for his sword.

Blommardine now came forward and laid a small pile of money and Julius's golden signet ring – the gift of Ammanati – at the prophet's feet, which she kissed.

'See,' said Mosman to the departing throng, 'you are shown up by a Magdalen. Rise, woman. Your sins are forgiven.'

Chapter 25

When the townsfolk returned, the response was better – wheelbarrows, even cartfuls of valuables appeared – but Mosman was still not satisfied.

Two of the Provost's men turned up saying they had caught a burgher burying treasure in his garden. Mosman fell down on his knees and prayed God to forgive the town.

'For,' he cried, 'you know, God, that where there is one caught in crime, there are many who practise it. Oh, miserable city that would cheat God of his portion!'

The people stood uncomfortably while he prayed, aware that they too had secreted money and objects in all manner of crafty places, and further depressed on hearing Fierens instruct the Provost to go and search the houses of all who had looked shifty in church.

The shadows lengthened. A chill wind sprang up and blew bitterly across the cobbles of Elim. The Provost returned with evidence of concealment and several eminent Rensburgers under arrest.

Finally Mosman stirred. His knees stiff with three hours of praying, he could hardly rise, but Blommardine, who had watched beside him, helped him up. The townspeople waited breathlessly for his verdict. He must surely let them go home now; night was falling; there were children who needed feeding.

Mosman slowly looked around.

'You are breaking God's heart,' he told them softly. 'You are like lost sheep who, being shown the true way, prefer the precipice. Yes, you may go to your houses now. I can bear no more of you tonight. Why should we waste our valiant soldiers' time looking for money that should readily be accorded? I am seriously debating whether I should leave Rensburg . . .'

At these words, the hearts of many citizens beat with a wild hope that he would indeed depart, for they had had enough and more; but there was a roar of protest from the crowd of several hundred new Rensburgers who had gathered to watch the events.

'Do not leave us . . . You are the prophet . . . Lead us to everlasting life . . .' and more ominously for the townsfolk . . . 'Don't bother with them . . . This is not their town. This is Jerusalem.'

Mosman lifted up his hand.

'Very well, I shall stay. There are still some righteous men in the city.

Go home now. It is nearly curfew time . . . Occupy yourselves in prayer and fasting. Pray for the unworthy that, through tribulation, they may come to the mercy-seat.'

The crowd dispersed, some to hymns and Bible study, others to closed shutters and a cold supper in the dark. It was not a good idea to be seen flouting the prophet's injunction even in your house. There were eyes – envious, malicious, monitory – which made it their business to spy out yours.

The town took to its bed gratefully. It was the one place you could be sure you wouldn't be preached at or reported. Even God seemed to turn a blind eye when you were asleep. You couldn't be blamed for your dreams . . .

At around five o'clock, in the middle of a rainstorm, suddenly all the townsfolk, both men and women, who had been baptized late – at the time of the expulsion of their contemporaries – received a terrible awakening.

Again, Fierens knew when to strike; the time of the lowest ebb, the hour of least resistance; he had breathed it into Mosman's inward ear, and Mosman had given orders to the Provost, and it was done.

Julius could hear everything from his eyrie above the shop where he often slept these days.

'Out, out, out.'

Bangings at doors, splinterings of wood, crashings of glass. He could imagine the frightened faces peering at each other in the dark.

'What is it?'

'Out, out, out.'

'I'd better go and see.'

'You'll get yourself killed.'

'We know you're in there. Everybody up. Five minutes you've got to get dressed.'

'This is an outrage.'

'It will be if you don't get a move on . . .'

Julius watched as his landlord and his wife joined the assembled company of unfortunates, and followed as they were marched into the square in the early light of dawn; young, old, sick, lame; all the reluctant baptizees who were more reluctant than ever as they saw the guard lined up with drawn swords in front of them.

The rain had stopped but a bitter, damp gale blew across Elim, sending its own little lances of cold through woollen hose and hastily wrapped shawl.

'What is the meaning of this? I must protest,' said an old schoolmaster called Hecker.

'Silence, you,' cried the Provost, striking him with the palm of his hand and making him fall in a sickening, crunching cartwheel across the slippery cobbles, where he lay silent, bleeding from the head.

'Don't move,' warned the Provost, 'or you'll get more of the same.'

'Blood,' said Mosman.

There was a pause. Mosman liked pauses. It gave him time to read the messages inside his head.

'Blood,' he repeated.

The people shivered. The single word coupled with the drawn swords made them feel colder than any north-westerly would make them.

'Yes, you may shiver,' Mosman continued. 'For God has spoken. Unless He decides to forgive you, you are to be put to the sword. You are to perish by the swords of the righteous. You are to be cut like stubble.'

Many of the townsfolk now fell to their knees.

'Mercy, oh God,' they cried. 'Mercy, mercy.'

'It is not as easy as that,' said Mosman. 'Anyone can fall down and cry mercy.'

'Mercy, oh mercy. We repent.'

'Guards,' shouted Mosman. 'Advance three paces.'

The armed men moved smartly forward and halted.

'Reach out,' said Mosman. 'Touch. Feel the sharpness of death. That is your death. Touch. Feel the pangs.'

The guards held out the blades towards them, while the townsfolk reached timorously out to stroke the shining metal. One or two of the more brutal soldiery jerked or twitched their arms so that the sharp edges actually cut into outstretched palms and fingers. Sounds of mingled pain and lamentation filled the square.

'Mercy, oh mercy.'

It was so cold.

'March them to the church of St Barnabas,' ordered Mosman, 'and lock them in. They must wait for God's decision. Let them pray to God as they have never prayed before – as perhaps they will never pray again. Take them away. The stench of their sinfulness is an affront to decent citizens. Elim is sullied by their presence.'

'Right, you lot, quick march,' said the Provost.

'Mercy. I have little children,' cried a distraught mother.

On an impulse, Julius stepped forward. His childhood had made him open to such appeals.

'I'll look after them. Tell me where they are.'

The Provost turned slowly round and looked.

'Oh yes? You'll look after them? And who might you be?'

'Love. That is Love. Love in a beard. Arrest him,' shouted a voice Julius recognized.

'Love? We'll look after you, Love,' said the Provost. 'We'll send you to the church with all the rest.'

Chapter 26

The doors banged shut and the great keys turned in the lock. The three hundred or so people inside the ravaged shell of the church – all paintings and effigies had been destroyed, the stained glass shattered – heard barriers being drawn up and knocked into position. There was no question of escape.

Every kind of emotion was manifested on the faces of the people around Julius – fear, horror, panic, a tendency still to plead, to compromise; all these were to be expected – but he was also comforted to notice occasionally fortitude, resolution and, yes, that expression which his master had painted so carefully in the middle section of the picture, loving carefulness, accompanied by that holding of the arm, the feeling of the life in the pulse with which the woman with the fruit had been comforting the dying man. A man he had never seen before, he looked like a minor merchant of some kind, was being held by his wife in this way. Her other hand was pointed upward with the three middle fingers pointing to the roof, the little finger and thumb stretching away to the side.

Julius made his way towards them, instinctively making the same sign with his hand. They saw him coming and smiled.

'How can you smile at a time like this?' asked a coarse-faced elderly woman. 'You think they don't mean it? Of course they mean it. We sinned, didn't we? You think that's funny? We're all for the chop, sinner.'

A young woman beside her fell in a swoon into the arms of her husband.

'Now see what you done. Here,' the old girl called aloud, 'there's someone not repenting here. We all got to repent or we'll never get out alive. Repent, you buggers.'

Julius and the couple moved away. The people were still too confused for mass repentance, mass anything. Each little group was locked in its own private misery.

'Welcome, Brother,' the woman said to Julius. 'You have the sign but I think you are not yet one of us.'

'Not yet,' he replied. 'I know the door. I am looking for the key.'

'The key you have already,' said the woman. 'It is only a matter of recognizing it.'

'You are not afraid?'

'Nothing we can do will alter anything here. If we live we will rejoice. If we die we will change from body to soul, from soul to spirit. Here, everything will go on. It is the lesson of the pool and the circle.'

'But don't you fear pain?'

'There is no pain greater than regret. The backward-lookingness of knowing what might have been. We live joyously while we can, and we die when we have to. What is that word you are looking for? You know it, don't you?'

Julius smiled at the couple and they once more smiled back. He closed his eyes for a minute as he concentrated on the word that he wanted. He knew it perfectly well, but it kept dancing like a wood-spirit between light and shade. When he opened his eyes the couple had gone.

'There's no water,' someone was shouting. 'How long they going to leave us here without water? We'll die of thirst.'

'There's water in the font,' someone yelled.

There was a rush to the font.

'I got to relieve myself,' said a fat chap with a red face and little pouting lips.

'You can't do it in church,' shouted another voice in panic. 'They'll kill us all if we desecrate the church.'

'But I got to,' moaned the fat man. 'I'll do it in the font now it's empty. They won't notice that.'

'You dare do it in the font. They're watching us, don't you see that? We don't know where they are but they're watching us. The old girl's right. We got to repent.'

'I have repented,' cried another voice. 'I can't repent any harder.'

An excitable little man who had made a name for himself in pageants – as official of the Notaries' Guild – climbed the pulpit and addressed the milling throng.

'Fellow-townsmen,' he cried, 'we are in a state of sin. If we were not in a state of sin, we would not be here. The sword of righteousness is hanging over us sinners. We must not just repent, we must be seen to repent. I want you all to join with me now and shout "we repent" so that those outside the church – those who are judging us, and God above all – may hear us. After me now . . . We repent.'

'WE REPENT,' shouted the people.

'I want to see the dust come down from the rafters.'

'WE REPENT.'

'You are still indistinct.'

'WE REPENT.'

'Let us now sing the hymn "Miserable Sinners here, we cry to thee below", and let us make the weathercock on our steeple skip in its frame.'

So it went on, with mingled prayers, lamentations, hymns, protestations and prostrations of every kind, sufficient you would think to turn iron into milk, but there was still no response either from above, or from outside the church. The doors remained resolutely locked.

Julius sat in a corner of the church looking fixedly at a rainbow pool of colours, like a tiny fractured piece of God's promise, thrown by the pale sun through a splintered corner of a window.

Morning passed into afternoon. None of the people gathered had had sufficient time to snatch so much as a crust that day, and hunger as well as thirst started to take its toll. The fat man, in spite of exhortations, had not been able to contain himself and had performed as far away as possible from the altar and main body of the church, in the room the bell-ringers used under the tower. Others followed him, and soon an unpleasant aroma started to seep into the nave.

Afternoon merged with evening, and it began to seem as though there would be no visitation that night. A questionable relief, however, for the more the uncertainty was prolonged, the more unbearable it became. Besides, a cold night in an increasingly vile-smelling church, on an empty stomach waiting for a death sentence, could not be considered a recipe for ease.

Suddenly there was a cry from those near the door.

'They're coming!'

People shrank away from the portal as it swung open with a doleful creaking of hinges. Every face turned to see whether life or death was to ensue. Julius, who had hitherto thought of himself as a spectator, a recorder of the scene (he had even tried to do a little charcoal sketching until he was warned off for not showing enough repentance), now felt more than a twinge of apprehension in his gut. Those swords were razor-sharp. How had the woman been so composed about death? He'd rather be regretful any day. Life was not, after all, an illustration. It was serious.

Mosman appeared with drawn sword, flanked by soldiers.

He made no move, but simply gazed down into the church while the soldiers wrinkled their noses at the effluvium. Mosman's sword-arm shot out, pointing straight forward, moving from one face to another until it stopped in front of the red-faced man.

'That one,' he said.

Two soldiers rushed forward and seized him.

'No, no,' shrieked the unfortunate fellow. 'I repent, I repent. I couldn't help the piss. I wasn't the only one.'

His fat wife joined in the appeal.

'Don't take him. He's all I have. His bladder's weak. We both repent. We'll do anything . . .'

'Take him away,' said Mosman.

The doors began to shut again as the fat man – who had buckled at the knees – was dragged ignominiously along the flagstones and out into the porch.

'We are all going to be killed. Oh, save him, save him,' sobbed the wife.

But the people huddled together and did nothing. They were too tired, too cold, too demoralized. If they were all going to be killed, at least tonight they were still alive. Perhaps after all it was better to be cold and hungry and smelly than dead. If anyone was to go, it was fair that it should be the fat man. Had he not been the first to defile God's building?

For all his search for the truth, Julius noticed with disgust that his own emotions echoed the general mood. Where was the equanimity with which the young couple had regarded the matter? And where were they anyway? He scanned the crowded aisles but could not see them. They made him think of Elisabeth. Why would she not let him see her again? He had felt that she had forgiven him. Life was full of mysteries, he thought, but perhaps that indeed was what it was about. Death was the only certainty.

Pulling his cloak lightly around him, he settled down in a corner beside the pulpit and fell into a fitful slumber.

Chapter 27

He awoke to a brilliant dawn and the sound of marching.

The doors cracked open and suddenly the church was full of soldiers. The townsfolk gathered themselves up as best they could and cowered back towards the bell tower, rubbing the sleep from their eyes and the ache from their bones.

Mosman, looking more than ever like some avenging Old Testament angel, surveyed them grimly from the altar steps.

'What? Not at your prayers?' he enquired. 'This does not argue repentance.'

'The spirit is willing but the flesh is weak,' cried the little man who had been good at pageants. 'We repent.'

'WE REPENT,' echoed the townsfolk with what strength they could muster.

'The stench of your sin riseth up,' announced Mosman.

It most certainly did. Fear had loosened their bowels, and the night had substantially increased the emanations from the bell-pullers' chamber.

'Draw your swords,' Mosman ordered his men.

Fifty bright blades appeared with a sickening susurration of metal. The townsfolk began to fall over each other as they backed away into the bell-pullers' room, slipping on the ordure that was seeping over the stones, besmirching themselves, utterly abased.

Julius suddenly saw a glimmer of hope. It was impossible to tell what Mosman's intentions were. To kill, to spare? Quite possibly Mosman did not know himself. (Indeed, it was true, he was waiting for the writing.) The only certain thing was flattery. If flattery didn't work, it would be out of fashion.

So, as the rest of the townspeople backed away, Julius sank to his knees and crawled a little in an attitude of penitence towards the Saint.

'Indeed, we are guilty,' he said. 'We deserve to die.'

'What?' cried Mosman.

The townsfolk turned appalled and angry eyes towards Julius. What was he saying? Deserve to die? This was an invitation to a massacre.

'No, no,' they called. 'Please. He is not one of us. Take him, not us.'

'Here at least we have an honest sinner,' said Mosman. 'Cut off his head and free his soul.'

The soldiers moved towards him but Julius did not move.

'Only you,' he cried suddenly.

Mosman raised his hand.

'Hold your swords,' said the Saint. 'Only I? What is your meaning?'

'You alone can intercede. Of all people, you alone have the favour in God's eyes that can save us. Only your prayers can prevail. We are feeble. We are weak. We have strayed, and the way is darkened . . .'

As he spoke, he began to edge forward on his knees again. The wiser of the townsfolk now saw the opportunity. They too knelt and started to crawl forward.

'Only you,' they cried, 'favourite of the Father.'

Gratification was not an emotion that registered easily on Mosman's stern features, but there was no doubt that he was inclined to accept the idea. More and more people sank to their knees. Soon the whole company – wretched, white-faced, shivering, spattered with their own ordure – were crawling towards the altar steps where the vengeful Leader stood rapt in his own greatness, basking in God's favour.

'Mercy,' they cried, 'pray for us, intercede, only you can do it, blessed Leader . . .'

This time it was Mosman who sank to his knees and started praying. Sometimes he prayed aloud, sometimes he prayed inwardly, mumbling and wrestling with unseen powers, crying out sometimes in strange tongues, sagging with the great effort he was making, and then again rising up as if he would drag mercy down from the skies. There came a time when he seemed to be losing the battle. He hung his head dejectedly and mumbled, 'If it is Your will, so be it, the blood of the unrighteous must be shed', but with a supreme effort he climbed once again up to the mercy-seat – you could almost see him scaling those unassailable heights; he would not be shaken off . . .

And these people whom he had so debased and humiliated began to love him. Who else would fight for them so? Who else gave a fig whether they lived or died? If he were successful, they would follow him forever.

Even some of the soldiers were impressed, though others wished he'd get on with it. But, as the Provost had told them, you can't rush a Saint. Four hours later, Mosman was still at it; and it was only around noon that he suddenly stopped, rose to his feet and confronted his congregation.

The swords came out again. The shivering started. Several of the penitents had pitched forward unconscious during the course of the intercession; but these, now roused, joined the others in a tremulous group to gaze at the Leader. There was no indication at the end which way the decision had gone.

Mosman now walked past them, gazing fixedly at each one of them, and finally ended his tour of inspection near the door.

'Fall in here,' he ordered the soldiers.

As they clattered into position on either side of him, the townsfolk turned fearful eyes upon one another. Was this to be the moment? Cut off from the door, they could only run round the church like chickens waiting for the axe. What did cold steel feel like as it sliced through your belly, ham-strings, gizzard?

'The Father is pleased to receive you into the community of the righteous,' Mosman informed them. 'Let me see the money tomorrow.'

He turned abruptly on his heel and left, followed by his guard.

The church erupted in general rejoicing. It was as though, instead of an ordeal of terror and abasement, the town had won a great victory.

One or two people congratulated Julius, clapping him on the shoulder and calling him a good fellow. The woman whose children he had offered to care for came up and thanked him.

He walked home alone. The cloud that had been slowly creeping up on the town out of the west had now covered the whole sky with its cloak. A few drops of rain began to fall. The ground seemed to be shaking. Was this the beginning of the End? He decided in the end that it was his own extremities not the earth's which trembled.

Chapter 28

The third stage of the Garden of Love, its hinterland, was the most intractable of them all. Whereas the first two at least had a preponderance of recognizably human figures, this one – the territory (if his notion was correct) of the spirit or the 'nous' as the Platonists had it – was peopled predominantly by strange half-humans, or even in-humans, though there was still a clump of dedicated men worshipping what appeared to be a giant strawberry, and one or two other people decorating and hand-standing upon a huge, veined reflective globe, crowned with strange, succulent turrets and fruited embellishments.

There was something about reflections he had read – that, when you looked in a mirror, into your own pupil, you could see your primal form, your own spirit. Was that what the woman upside down was doing? But what could one make of the dolphin-knights, some of whom were sporting in the tranquil waters with mermaids, while others in great procession came swimming up behind a great pink rock-building pierced with crystals? And the people – yes, there were more people – crawling into a huge split egg – or was it *out* of? – so pink they almost looked like roe?

It was a blissful bathing-pool. A black man was tenderly engaged with a blonde girl on a tiny horned skiff, while another swam towards them. Behind and to the right, other edifices, half-vegetable, crystalline, pierced with strange screws and vials and surmounted with veined fruit, upreared their peculiar summits – crowned in one instance by a rapturous youth looking at his reflection in a golden ball.

What was one to make of this? Julius had the strangest feeling that the intended recipient of the triptych was not the Brotherhood back in 'sHertogenbosch or anywhere else. It was himself – a last message from a magus, a conundrum from a Mercury.

That egg by the water's edge; the people as he looked, were returning to it, of course, not backing away. They were returning to oneness, to union. Even the bodies of the people higher up, the 'boy' with the golden globe, were sexless. This was the sphere of the spirit which was, after the washing out of sin, no more nor less than a very splinter of God. There was adoration in the boy's face, a contemplation not of his reflected self but of the Creator.

Something stirred at this point in his mind, a connection he could make; but it slid away, fish-like, before he could seize it. It would come back. Once these fishes of the mind started swimming, they returned. Fish, indeed, were very much part of this upper realm. Fish, after the fusion of man and fish that were the dolphin-knights, now surely became symbols of procreation and fecundity, carried on the right by an angel and on the left by a dolphin-knight with a great red fruit held on a spear.

And yet there was more to the symbol than that. Did they not stand for Christ himself, the *icthus*? And wasn't that why, in the top right-hand corner, floating like a promise of eternal order and redemption – for it was as close as could be to the division of the central panel with Hell – swam the Fish itself, alone, the One, towards whom a spirit was flying up, bearing the Fruit of Creation?

There were so many signs and symbols in this picture. Some so esoteric that Julius, who was fortunate in having received a southern as well as a northern tutoring, could still only guess at them; others religious, alchemical, classical that, by study and good fortune, he was able at least to have reasonable ideas about.

The whole of the first two panels were a perfect picture of classical religion and Platonic philosophy – just such a combination as the Florentine philosopher Ficino, friend of Cosimo and sometime mentor of Lorenzo de Medici, had extolled in his Academy, and whose teaching he himself had heard from Ammanati at the Villa Rosata.

The wheel had come full-circle, then. If he were right, he was not looking simply at an extraordinary and beautiful picture, or even at a complicated and dreamlike allegory . . .

All the clues and the questions, answered and unanswered, pursued their finny course through his mind as he sat, after a day's puzzling, before the picture in a peculiar kind of keyed-up trance. Finally, the answers at last began to take shape.

It was the man and woman that did it, they whose sign he had recognized last week in the church, the ones he could not find when he looked for them. It was now not only their sign he recognized, it was their faces – the same that peered out with that demonstrative, bright-eyed look from the lower right-hand corner of the painting. It was, of course, the magus, the Grand Master, and his bride.

A number of awkward pieces began to fit, and Julius knew he was being permitted a glimpse of the secret heart of the Mystery; it was as though the window which his master Bosch had shown him in the chapel were at last being inched wider.

This whole picture – at least, these first two sides of it – was a bible whose doctrine was, whose doctrine must be, Love.

And this was not a love of the somewhat abstruse, spiritual, milk and watery kind, which was sometimes offered as Christian love: love thy neighbour, love God, love them that despitefully use you. This was indeed love as a sacrament as Bosch had hinted, actual physical love, experienced in terms of the utmost tenderness and delight to the one – and no other – to whom your soul's destiny had allotted you, and to whom you were equally appointed. But, more than this, Julius saw, it was a symbol of the natural bounty, fruitfulness and earthly joy of the circle of life itself – which in turn was a symbol of a higher harmony and union, through which two became one, and with which all the myriad of other 'ones' could come at last, cleansed and refined, to join with that sublime and unimaginable One of Creation.

Was this after all what St John the Divine, the humanist's favourite, had meant? 'Beloved, let us love one another: for love is of God; and everyone that loveth is born of God, and knoweth God. He that loveth not, knoweth not God; for God is Love.'

No wonder the Grand Master would be so anxious to have it finished. And yet . . . how could he be there in the church and then not there . . . and anyway look no older than he did when the picture was painted eighteen years ago? There was magic in this picture. More even than a bible, it was a point of entry. Tired though he was, he set himself now to concentrate upon it, to open himself to it entirely, as the Gnostics did with their hermetic drawings; or, as he had heard in Florence, as Pythagoras had meditated upon certain diagrams . . .

'Love,' said the Grand Master, speaking to him from the painting. 'You are two-thirds of the way home now.'

'What? . . .' Julius could not tell where the voice came from. 'What?'

'It's no matter, Julius. Don't be astonished. It is plain to see you're not a Pythagorean. I go everywhere. White and black, light and dark. It is I. I was present at Eve's birth. That's why your master painted it to my instruction. I have been a Pharaoh and a gnat in my time. I have soared and cawed and swam and stung. I have been a woman and a panther. Now how much longer are you going to sit around?'

'I don't believe you,' said Julius. 'I'm dreaming.'

'What's the difference?' said the Grand Master. 'Now, to business. You know now the meaning of Paradise and the Earthly Garden. What are you going to do about Hell?'

'I . . . I don't know. I don't know what Hell is, except it looks very disagreeable. Someone's sliding down a knife-point, someone's getting skewered, a whore's being ridden by a goblin, another poor sinner's being strung-up on a harp-thing,' he listed feverishly.

'Do not make light of Hell, Julius. It is a very terrible state. You see the agitation, even here in the Garden, of those who border the panel to their right.'

Julius looked up and saw two lovers struggling in a tendrilly net of briars.

'They will get free. But Hell's influence disturbs even our Garden. I hope, Julius, you are not going to let it spread. It could, you know. It could seep out onto our green places. It could corrupt and darken and turn sour and negate everything that God wishes for us, just as it has happened in this town of yours in the very name of God . . .'

'It is not a town of mine.'

'It is until you leave it, one way or the other.'

His words struck a chill in Julius's heart.

'What do you mean?'

'I mean that I can promise nothing. Only your efforts will prevail. There is a gap in Hell which your master has left for you. Also some landscape at the top he could not finish. You know what you have to do.'

'And if I don't?'

'Oh, but you will, Julius. Is there anything now that I can do for you?'

'I want to see Elisabeth and take her into the Garden.'

'It may be done. But remember, Julius. Even in the Garden, until you are adept, you must be prudent. Things are still not yet quite what they seem. Last time you entered, it turned against you . . . and against your love . . . your love . . .'

The magus's features ceased moving and started to become mere line and colour again.

'Wait,' cried Julius.

What *had* happened in the Garden? For some reason, he could not exactly tell.

The bright eyes flicked towards him, the mouth set in a half-smile . . .

Julius stirred on his chair and awoke, shivering. Advancing on the picture he looked hard at the man in the lower right-hand corner, willing him to make a sign. But there was no movement in the face, not even so much as a crack in the pigment.

He stood, flapping his arms and thinking of Love. Well, he would see if Elisabeth did indeed come back to him. As for Hell . . . what was Hell? A punishment for sinners, a torment for the unrepentant? An absence from God? None of these seemed to fit the situation. There was that strange gap his master had left under a circular tray with a bagpipe on it, next to a huge desiccated carcase of – what? – a duck, with a diabolical tavern inside it, whose head and leg seemed to turn into a withered tree. What could conceivably be put there? Some hideous engine?

It was growing dark now as well as cold. A bleak wind blew through every crevice of the garret, every hole in his head. Time to go home. Of one thing he was certain; if he were looking for notions about Hell, he would surely find them on his doorstep.

Chapter 29

Blommardine had possessed the secret of the pomatum for many years. She had given it in mischief to her father and to Julius. He did not know that she had put it in the biscuits she had given him on that fateful day with Elisabeth. Nor did Mosman realize now that she was giving it to him. Along with various other properties, it served as a sauce of love. But it didn't sauce Mosman's love; or if it did, it was sublimed into an ever more intense relationship with the Almighty. This was a rare but not unknown effect of the strange preparation.

The pomatum was a witch's recipe, and the story of its finding was a typical Blommardine mixture of truth and evasion. She told the few she trusted that a Beguine had introduced her to it when she was fourteen in return for favours. You never knew with Beguines, those itinerant beggar-nuns, whether they were deeply religious or totally amoral. This one, she said, had been totally amoral. She had thought nothing, Blommardine declared, of seducing a young girl or indeed of delivering into her hand a dangerous secret; but then, of course, she did not know Blommardine's side of the bargain, for she was by no means an ordinary young girl. Indeed people who knew her well (there were not many; even her mother had died when she was young), people like her own old nurse, for instance, thought she was a child of the Devil. There was something immediately mischievous about her – a mischief that was not simply fun, a mischief that danced and twinkled, but something altogether more dangerous. You didn't get on the wrong side of Blommardine if you knew what was good for you. It was said she had turned a schoolfriend into a pig one afternoon 'just for fun', though no one else had seen it and the ex-pig was an unreliable witness. But certainly she had a strange way with her, and the incident of the nun was not the first of her sexual adventures. She was precocious in everything. Indeed, she had been on the look-out for the pomatum for some months. It was said to increase the carnal appetites enormously, as well as having other remarkable properties. The Beguine, though at first reluctant to part with any, finally yielded when Blommardine allowed her to put her hand up her skirts.

Once procured, Blommardine had wasted no time administering the stuff. She had fallen into a deep sleep upon taking it the following Sunday evening, at home – and soon began the strangest progression of dreams so vivid that they seemed more than dreams, and yet no reality could be so remarkable. She was flying. Oh, she had heard about witches doing that, but she had not expected the actual sensation of flight. Floating had been more her anticipation. But here she actually experienced the wind in her ears, the swoop and soar of a swan. At first she flew over places she recognized, the streets of 'sHertogenbosch – she could recognize her own house, the town hall, the church – then her flight took her east towards the German border. Soon after, she was skimming over the tops of the trees in a forest, then into a cave in a hill where she flew down and down through a narrow tunnel into a strange country she had never seen before.

Here she was given food and drink by strange creatures who did not speak, bird-heads and lizard-faces with human bodies who showed her many wonders – lamps that lit of their own accord, chariots that rolled at will, pictures whose images moved and spoke, guns that fired – pouf! – and destroyed whole cities.

As she watched, she became aware of the most wonderful sensation in her loins, a warmth, a craving, a benign sort of aching that could only be healed by contact. Other people, of angelic form but of both sexes (angels were not supposed to have gender), seemed to have gathered. They were stroking and caressing each other fulsomely, completely without any inference of love, doing the most obscene things (they were partly dressed) – handling breasts, putting hands into loins, licking behinds, all knowing that she was looking. Soon, lying on a cross-shaped bed, she could not stop rubbing herself, feeling her own nipples, thrusting her own hands into herself in an ecstasy of self-engrossment. They gathered around her and she showed herself to them. They watched judiciously as she reached climax after climax, and then, to show her pleasure could still be heightened, they started to couple and triple and quadruple with her themselves – their faces sometimes turning to snouts and muzzles, irresistibly bestial, while their members, whether male or female, remained accentuated, sublimed versions of the human. Her own seemed to have grown and blossomed and (yet) refined, so that it seemed the most beautiful in the world.

The smell of their sex was sweet and rank as ambergris. She remembered that later, for she had been told that the sense of smell was absent from dreams. Indeed, the whole experience was so vivid that she refused to believe it was phantasy.

And when she woke, warm and wet, her loins felt as though they had indeed played hostess to a company of angels, and she knew that what she had experienced was in some mysterious way more real than life itself. The over-riding impression, however, was not of sex but of power – the power of negation, desecration and darkness.

She did not meet the beguine again, but afterwards she never ceased to look for more of the pomatum. Without it life was pale and dull – though she did her best to devise amusements which emulated, however palely, her experiences in the underland. What witches she met produced sad stuff – it was mere beer after the finest Rhenish wine. She read books, she tried old recipes; nothing really worked and one or two made her ill.

And then one day Aleid Bosch – who was a friend of her father's, she said, and well disposed towards her – invited her to help sort some of the old man's papers. It was only after looking through certain drawings and sketches – she had never examined the paintings themselves, deliberately classing all religious pictures as not worthy of contemplation – that she realized the old boy had been to the same place that she had visited. Some of his monsters were identical to the ones whom she had clasped to her bosom and other places, she told her friends.

At this her heart quickened. If he had been there, perhaps he too had the secret. She busied herself to go through the four or five chests of work, documents and notes which Aleid had no stomach for; and finally, opening an old folio full of descriptions of places visited, a small piece of vellum fluttered out. She almost threw it away but something stopped her. She glanced at the inscription on it. 'A pomatum to open the eyes. Not to be taken lightly.' Underneath was a list of ingredients – some of them she recognized, some were completely unknown – and instructions both for the making and the taking of the mixture.

It took her many months to assemble all the items on the list. Camphor was easy, extract of blister beetle by no means so prevalent. In the end, however, she had them all assembled, prepared her mixture one long summer day when she knew Julius would be away working on a commission, and took a judicious quantity after sundown.

The results, though not identical in detail, were essentially the same: flying, entry into the garden of the underland, a banquet, urgent sensations in the loins, the coupling of strange, perversely beautiful monsters, inspection by those creatures, and finally delectable, intricate, flagrant, fragrant sex with those bittersweet sensations – a thousand times stronger than those of a naughty child – of power over the forbidden.

She awoke feeling like Prometheus. She had brought the fire – if not from Heaven, from somewhere much more delicious. She decided not to tell Julius about it, not to feed him any pomatum yet. It was her secret, her property. Julius was her contact with the pale waking world. She needed that, for she sensed without it she would lack something dull yet necessary, like salad. Without it, in fact, she could not last. And last she intended to. The experience was far too good to burn up in a year or so. She wanted to go on like this until she was seventy, eighty, perhaps for ever. As it happened, the thing had taken hold of her. There were drugs in it which, in the end, commanded addiction.

Meanwhile, important and erratic by day, she burned for the night. If she made love in her waking hours, with Julius, it was with a neurotic wildness that tried to catch (but never succeeded in catching) the ecstasy of the other place.

It was not mere luck for her that her husband was an artist – a man not perfectly in tune with the world, who did not care about her eccentricity. It was not mere luck because even at first she had chosen him partly for that reason. They were both detached; few questions were asked and even fewer answered. Recently she had left some pomatum cakes in his studio, but nothing seemed to come of it. It was a mistake anyway. She needed him as he was while she needed him at all.

There was, however, a different need in her waking life which curiously had grown with her nocturnal excursions. It was as though she felt she was slipping too far downward, that one day she would not return from that hall of lipping, lapping kisses, that too much of a good thing was not a good thing at all, that pleasure could spill over into pain once temptation had become a cage.

For this reason she felt she needed something stauncher to hold onto. There had always been that attraction towards strong men, those feelings about her father which in the end she had had to escape – not so much for moral reasons as for practical (though she knew the two could coincide). Her feelings now, firstly for the preacher Elijah and now for Mosman, marked an accentuation in these sentiments; they were not merely strong. They were Good. She could float in an equilibrium between two opposing forces. Perhaps it was her imagination, but the pleasures of the underland seemed to have become more intense (if that were possible) since she had taken up the role of Magdalen.

The trouble was, she was becoming obsessed with the need to sleep with the Saint. And, although she knew that the outcome could not be good, she felt a compulsion which grew to be irresistible to feed him more of the pomatum. The first time had not been enough. She disguised it, of course.

It wasn't easy, for the Saint ate sparingly and the brew had a peculiar if not unpleasant piscine tang to it. She tried it once in his gruel, but there wasn't enough flavour in it to mask the strangeness. He was by no means a fussy eater – regarding food as a painful duty – but he pushed it away.

'There is taint in the skilly,' he said.

'You must eat, Leader,' she urged, but he shook his head and fell into prayer.

She tried again with some rancid stew and this was much more successful. He ate quickly and retired to his chamber. Later she crept in and found him blissfully asleep. She wanted to slide beneath the cover with him, but she heard the step of someone outside.

Fierens entered and found her tidying the room.

'He is asleep,' she said.

She still did not like Fierens. There was something insidious about him. How different from the simple strength of her Good Man.

'Sin never sleeps,' he replied, looking at her strangely.

He knew what she was up to, but it was all part of God's purpose. When Mosman awoke he called for her.

'Are you rested, Master?'

'I communed with angels,' he said. 'I talked with seraphim.'

'What sort of angels, Master?'

'There is only one sort of angel.'

She let the matter drop for the moment. Angels? What sort of stirring was going on under that long, dark robe? He gave no indication. Later she increased the dose still further, but it seemed to find no sin in him.

Perhaps it had a different effect on men? Or on different people? Or on none but her?

Only his visions of righteousness and the wrath to come became more emphatic, more insistent.

She comforted herself with her own delinquent visions in which she took the snout-heads, the preposterous erections, to be the Leader's, and her power to be greater even than his.

Chapter 30

Konrad, once the defensive dispositions had been made and his lieutenants had been appointed, started to drill his soldiers in attack.

One or two more successful sorties were made, and it soon became clear that with one sudden offensive action they stood an excellent chance of routing the besiegers. He not only had a considerable body of experienced mercenaries in his force – the Anabaptists had picked up many converts from the drifting populace of ex-soldiers on the lookout for a cushy billet between wars – but he himself was on the way to becoming a good general.

He had imagination (he had a streak of cruelty), he was brave – perhaps a little headstrong – and he put the fear of God into the troops while leading from the front. Action was his balm.

He reported his readiness to Mosman, Fierens, the Deputy Burgomaster and other Leaders of the Town Council, and was expecting an enthusiastic endorsement of his plans, but he saw Fierens whispering to Mosman who thereupon shook his head.

'We are not ready,' he pronounced.

'But,' Konrad expostulated, 'we have the men and guns to do it. Surprise is on our side. One blow and poof! They will fly. You can see they are terribly stretched and poorly led. They never try anything. They just sit there. There is no discipline, no training. I promise you a victory.'

'Brother Konrad is a most valiant soldier,' said Fierens, politically, 'but, do you not see, this feeble threat from outside is exactly what we need to concentrate our minds within. Our New Jerusalem is only half won. There is still much to be done here. Half the town has still not pooled its money. How can it be called a truly godly community? We now have the opportunity provided by our unpaid guards outside to see that no corruption enters! Meanwhile we can establish more than equality of money. It is our belief that foodstuffs and all commodities should be shared. That is what community is about.'

He paused and looked deferentially towards Mosman.

'Everything should belong to everybody,' announced the Leader. 'Mine and thine should disappear.'

The Deputy Burgomaster, puppet though he was, did not much like this talk, nor did some of the other councillors.

'I thought we were handing our money in for the war,' he observed.

'You are handing your money in for the peace,' Mosman told him fiercely. 'The peace of God. That is, if you *have* handed all your money in, Mr Deputy Burgomaster.'

The Deputy Burgomaster blushed and shifted uncomfortably. The fact was, he did have a little stashed away in a garden pot.

'The Leader has expressed to me,' Fierens continued, after a pause to let the Deputy Burgomaster's discomfiture sink in, 'has vouchsafed his wish that we use this weak threat of a siege to perfect our City of God. For when we are perfect in God, who shall be against us?'

'Indeed, yes,' came the noises of assent from the various sources.

'For you, Brother Konrad, our trusted Captain, the Leader has a special honour,' said Fierens, turning to him, for it was by no means part of God's plan to have Konrad's nose put out of joint. 'Please tell him, Leader, what God has conveyed to you.'

'You are to be given the Sword of Righteousness,' announced Mosman. 'You shall be the scourge of the sinner and the protector of the Elect.'

He reached under the table and presented the weapon. It was indeed a fine blade and had belonged to a Teutonic knight. Konrad took it, experiencing proper gratitude. The position of town bully was now his. It would have been better for him, and for the town, if he had stuck to soldiering.

It was now his responsibility to see that all money and treasure were handed in on pain of death. Of course, the events in the church of St Bartholomew had left their mark, and most of those who had endured them wasted no time in bringing their wealth forward. But there were others in the town who were still not convinced that they should yield their hard-earned gold to a bunch of religious extremists. Oh, they had gone along with them. But not everybody believed they'd last; so resistance took the form of concealment.

Konrad now, with his darker side given free rein, began to pursue the hoarders in earnest, while promises of unending bliss and unequalled prosperity in God's city were lavished on the virtuous from every pulpit – alternating with the direct threats of divine wrath and earthly punishment to any that withheld.

Citizens came to dread the tramp of feet and the knock on the door when Konrad and his men came round. For, innocent or guilty, the place was turned upside down. Mattresses were ripped, floorboards yanked up, gardens dug, and wainscots torn from the wall. If cash, or anything of gold or silver were found, Konrad's demeanour would soften, become almost amorous.

'Well, now,' he would say, 'what have we here? A little trinket. An heirloom, is it? Belonged to your grandmother? Sentimental value? Oh,

I understand. I wish I had a groat for everything of sentimental value I've uncovered. People get so sentimental about things, don't they? I've even known people get sentimental about money. Like this bag of coins we found up your chimney. What do you say to that?'

'It's . . . oh, dear, I forgot. Not sentimental. My wife put it by for a rainy day. I'd no idea it was still up there,' the unfortunate householder would reply.

'Easily done.' Konrad could seem so sweetly reasonable. 'Memory's a funny thing. You probably also forgot that those who hoard money have been declared fit for execution.'

'Well, I . . . no, but . . .'

'But you didn't think it was serious, is that it?'

That was exactly what many householders had thought. After all, it was their money.

'Well, I . . . you know how it is . . .'

Konrad would now become venomous.

'I know exactly how it is. You felt you could cheat the community and get away with it.'

'No, no. I simply . . .'

'Simply! There is nothing simple about deceit. You will simply be executed.'

'No, no. You can't mean that. Look, take the money. I don't want it. Keep it yourself. I won't tell anyone.'

'You are a disgusting creature. Do you think you can bribe the Sword of Righteousness? Take him away. Yes, and his forgetful wife. They shall be examples.'

The householder would now realize what a mistake he had made in mentioning his wife at all. Both would sink to their knees. It had happened a number of times. Really, people were such sheep. Konrad sometimes wished someone would stand up and make a fight of it. Not that the outcome wouldn't be the same, but it would at least provide exercise.

Mr and Mrs Householder would be carried off and clapped in gaol. Sometimes they would be arbitrarily pardoned. Sometimes, if the Leader felt it fit, they would indeed be put to the sword, his Sword. The whole population would be made to come to Elim and watch. Konrad enjoyed the moment of killing. It wasn't just the fear in the face, the struggling, the shitting themselves. It was the moment the life in the eyes turned to glaze. It was the hiss the soul made as it left the body. It was the sound of the crowd as they realized they too were no more than soft engines.

At other times, the wretches would be brought out, blindfolded, caused to kneel, lectured, prayed over, made to wait an hour or two . . . before finally being tapped hard on the back of the neck with the broad of the sword – at this point they usually fainted – after which they were allowed to crawl home. At other times again, it would merely be a harangue for the malefactor in church. Nobody could be sure of anything.

Chapter 31

By methods such as this, within three weeks there was virtually no private money or treasure or object of gold or silver or gem or precious trinket, brooch or bauble in the town. It was frankly more fearful to have it than to hand it in – which was of course the object of the exercise.

New Jerusalem thus came to have considerable funds, but the money was never used inside the town. Instead it was employed in outside matters. Mercenaries were hired, supplies both military and domestic were bought; and propaganda in the shape of proselytes as well as pamphlets began to issue from the town in a steady stream (largely uninterrupted by the besiegers).

Those who worked in the town – for trade of a kind still carried on; food and clothing were needed, shoes had to be mended, barrels repaired, buildings patched – were paid not in money but in kind, and not by private employers but by the community.

Fierens thought on these matters with one of his minds – there were others on faraway matters and another still rapt in the ineffable – as he paced the walls on a May morning.

Fierens had been wise (but was he not all-wise?) to allow the siege to remain in force, for it meant the next move could be carried out under the pretext of necessity. Not that it was necessity, of course; the Saints believed in community of ownership but, as they had seen, there was some resistance to the notion among the newcomers to the Truth. And if there had been resistance to the pooling of money, how much more would there be to the sharing of the basics of life; of commodities like food, clothing, timber, soap, hardware, even medicine?

It was more expedient to call it necessity. Fierens knew (and he could put his thoughts into Mosman's head so Mosman knew also) that they needed to put the town on a proper footing with some despatch. The siege would probably in the end grow stronger; besides, the City of God must not be delayed a second longer than was needful.

Fierens paused in his tour. A smell of cooking rose from near the eastern gate where a mess-hall had been set up for the guards. Descending, he peered inside, where he found twenty men eating stew and listening to one of his deacons, a short-sighted Fleming reading from the Book of Isaiah.

'Where did you get that meat?' he asked.

He knew but he wanted to make a point.

The Fleming stopped reading and adjusted his spectacles.

'Brother Fierens?' he questioned.

'It is I.'

'We indented for it from Community Supply,' said one of the soldiers who acted as cook. 'Like what we always do.'

'It is wrong,' said Fierens.

'Wrong? Bbbbut . . .' the deacon stammered in perplexity.

'The fault is not yours. It is in our orders. Food must be foraged for, as if we were soldiering at large. We cannot be a drain on the central Commissariat. Go out next time and knock on the citizens' doors. Present them with a list of your needs. It is their city we are defending. Requisition what you want and – if there is any problem – send for the Sword of Righteousness.'

'Certainly we will,' said the deacon. 'And does that apply to boots?'

'Boots?'

'One of the men needs new boots.'

'There is no more mine or thine. Boots, clothing, sausage . . . the town is your wardrobe and your larder.'

'And Brother Joris here, just arrived from Antwerp, he doesn't have any lodgings. He's lodged in a real shit-house, if you'll pardon the expression,' said one of the men. 'Can he requisition himself a bed?'

'To be sure he can. Have I not said? Has the Lord not provided? There is no property that is not God's property. Knock and it shall be opened unto you; and if it is not, kick the door down. It is an offence to lock any door in the New Jerusalem.'

'I haven't seen that order,' said the deacon. 'I thought I was abreast of things.'

'It has just been made by our Leader. All doors must be left open day and night. See to it.'

'Very good.'

'And if they are not, you know who to summon. The Sword of Righteousness is hot as pepper on closed doors.'

Part Four

Behold, the King of Glory now is come
To reduce God and Devil to their Doom,
For *both* of them are servants unto Me
That lives and rules in perfect Majesty . . .

A Single Eye, No Darkness; or
Light and Darkness One
LAWRENCE CLARKSON

Chapter 1

The woods had exchanged their chaste displays of primrose for lavish invitations of cowslip, celandine and violet, and the shopkeeper-trees were busy putting out their awnings overhead. Blackbird and thrush warbled as if they were rehearsing for the Meistersinger contest.

Even the messenger of the Saints stopped to savour the relief that seemed to bubble from the earth. It had been a hard winter.

'What a beautiful day,' he said to the trees above him, and then, because it had come to be an essential sequel to any remark in the city, 'praise the Lord.'

Indeed, he really felt like praising the Lord today, for he was so glad to get out. Normally no one was allowed past the gates. But because he was young and fit and a good runner, he had been given the task of delivering Hass's pamphlets to the Duchy of Cleves where there was considerable support for the Rensburg revolution.

But he could not run just yet. The air was too sweet. There were anemones at his feet; and cherry blossom above him. It reminded him of his boyhood, when his father would take him for walks to pick flowers and boughs for his mother. They were both dead now, dead of the plague, six years ago.

A shadow fell across his thoughts which he tried to drive away by thinking of his sweetheart. It was May. How he wished he could take her to the woods and bring her home garlanded, with blossom in her hair! All he wanted was the simple, uncomplicated life his parents and his grandparents and their parents before them had known. Why did people have to go to such trouble to change things that nobody should change? Some people, it seemed, had an itch – they just couldn't bear to leave other people alone.

As if to echo the shadow on his mind, another more manifest shadow fell across his path. He looked up to see two men with drawn swords springing down the earthen bank towards him. He dropped his pamphlets and ran like the Devil. The men tried to follow him but soon gave up.

'You can't run far with a sword,' the first man panted to the other.

He was a thick-set fellow, and looked as if the only way he'd run far would be with a sword up his backside.

'We'd have had him soon enough without our swords,' agreed his companion, a taller figure with a beer-belly. 'Mind you, he did have a remarkable turn of speed.'

'Shit-scared, he was.'

'I'd have been shit-scared if I'd seen us running down a bank at me.'

'But then you wouldn't, would you?'

'What?'

'You wouldn't have seen us because you would have *been* us – or one of us at any rate.'

'I don't follow.'

'Hallo, what's this? He's dropped his bundle.'

'Let's see.'

Beer-belly crowded round while the other undid the hessian.

'Pamphlets, is it?'

'Too right it is. Filthy stuff.'

'Give us a read.'

'I shouldn't, really. You know what the Bishop says.'

'He says it's corrupting. But you couldn't corrupt me.'

'Why not?'

''cos I am corrupt.'

They both had a good laugh.

'All right, then. Here goes. "The poorest among us, who used to be despised as beggars, now go about as finely as the highest and most distinguished. By God's grace we have become as rich as the burgo-masters and the richest in the town."'

'That's terrible.'

'It's disgusting.'

'You know what?'

'What?'

'I'm not as corrupt as I thought.'

'You mean?'

'Exactly. If it's like that in the town, what the Hell are we doing here?'

The Bishop lost a number of men in this manner. It made his brother-in-law incoherent with rage.

Meanwhile, so persuasive were the pamphlets that got through that Anabaptism was made a capital offence, not only around Rensburg but in the Duchy of Cleves, the Archbishopric of Cologne, and even as far away as Antwerp.

Cavalry patrolled the roads, suspects were arrested, and great numbers of men and women in the towns – many of them quite innocent – were beheaded, drowned, burnt or broken at the wheel.

Chapter 2

Julius sat by the water-gate sketching and looking down through the reeds to the mud. What a beautiful thing mud was, he thought. The April rains had been late this year and turned into May ones, and, only recently subsiding, had created a wet mud-flat around the curve of the river. No cattle could get down there thanks to the siege, so the surface was untrampled. It would not last, of course. It would dry up and crack and flake. But while it remained it seemed the most marvellous wet manifestation, reminding him a little of the pool at which the three-headed ibis preened in Paradise, the slimy origins from which – so the Brethren held – all life first emerged, drawn by the Creator.

While he sketched, trying to catch the colours of the evening sky upon its surface, verses formed in his mind. He had always had a facility with rhymes and, in Italy, he had read Petrarch with great joy. This was poor stuff, of course, but he dared think it was the first verse in Praise of Mud which (roughly translated) is as follows:

> The common mud, it seems to me,
> Is much misunderstood.
> (I don't mean wetted earth that sticks
> To boots in field or wood.)
>
> But mud that by the water's edge
> Is neither stream nor land,
> Compote of elements it lies
> Sleeked out on either hand.
>
> The colours of the evening sky
> It catches and translates,
> To pink it adds its umber tones,
> To duck-egg blue its slates.
>
> It holds old boats in soft caress
> When they no longer swim,
> And gives them humped-up graves at last
> Along the water's rim.
>
> Mad whorls, stigmata, curlicues,
> Confuse, delight – and shock!
> What hippogriffs or nymphs made these?
> What arrow-footed roc?

315

Glitt'ring it lies, yet not so smooth.
Strange objects that appear,
Are made, with mud, a mystery.
(Resolved when you draw near.)

Old boots, and mangles, colanders,
Deposit of the flood,
Achieve new grace –
Religions too look better under mud.

Oh primal mud with whom we climbed
And, certain, will descend,
Mud unto shining mud – to Light
Translate us at the end!

Pleased with himself, as one is always pleased with any small talent at an alternative art, he wrote it down with a piece of charcoal on his sketching-paper.

It seemed in some way a fitting rejoinder to the inflated absurdities that were going on around him.

His heart sank, however, when he heard a cough behind him. Almost anything you did in public in Rensburg could be construed as Satan's work unless it were praying, soldiering or labouring to the common weal. Sitting by the water-gate writing foolish verse could well be a gaolable offence or worse. However, when he turned round, he was pleased to see his old acquaintance of the Cathedral crypt, the little Catholic priest.

Smaller than ever now, his face lined and his chest racked every now and then with a persistent cough, the man smiled at Julius and held out his hand.

'I came down to look at God's work, I mean Nature, for up there,' he gestured at the town, 'they would dis-nature Nature if they could. It is good to see a face that has no madness in it. How are things with you, my friend?'

'It is not as bad as with some. I know that I am involved since I am in this town, but somehow I don't feel part of it. I am an artist; I observe. Also I am in love, and trying to solve a puzzle.'

'It is often one and the same thing, I have heard,' said the little man, with a smile.

'You are probably right. I have two puzzles in that case.'

'Let me see your verse,' said the priest.

'By all means. It is extremely light.'

The little man read it intently, coughing now and then. At last he looked up.

'Very amusing,' he said, 'and well turned in places. Though I'm not sure about "Resolved when you draw near". Could try harder. As for the levity at the end, I suppose in these terrible times it is excusable. Anything that makes us smile must be clung to. Smiling is good for us, you know. I've always thought that.'

He coughed again.

'I think you are not smiling enough, Father.'

'It is nothing,' said the little priest, 'a mere cold, that is all.'

'How goes it with you?'

'Ah. They found the crypt. But not, I am glad to say, the passage or my Lutheran friend. We have our little network, but people are so frightened. I'm afraid we have to keep our heads down very low and bide our time. I only wish I thought more of the Bishop and his friends. The Bishop's all right in his way but . . . I don't know . . . Soldiers are soldiers. They sack, you know. Destroy. Rape. Pillage . . . I can't see a good end to this, though God knows I pray.'

'And pray you should, Brother,' said a hard voice behind them.

It was Fierens with a squad of soldiers.

'Seize them both,' he ordered.

Both knew enough about these people to try to escape.

'My friend and I were looking at the sunset,' said Julius. 'Is that a crime in this town?'

'Silence,' said Fierens. 'I know what you were doing. You were writing something, weren't you?'

'A little verse. In praise of God, really.'

'I don't like writers any more than I like painters. We don't need writers and painters in the New Jerusalem. Writers and painters make trouble. God is the only Author. Let me see the verse.'

He took the thing and scanned it.

'This is not verse. It is idolatrous.'

'I think you are misunderstanding it.'

'Misunderstanding?'

Fierens' pale, handsome face was so livid it was almost green.

'I misunderstand? Do you know what you are saying? You are saying God misunderstands!'

'But . . . you are not God . . .'

'I am with God.'

'He is mad,' said the little priest.

Fierens took a sword from one of the soldiers and was about to run him through; at the last instant, however, he thought better of it. A slow, ghastly smile spread across his face.

'Subtle,' he said, 'like the Devil your master. But not so subtle because God led me to you here. You want to make me kill you before I've questioned you.'

'Question?' repeated the little priest, his turn now to blanch.

He knew what it meant.

317

'You know what I mean,' said Fierens, unnecessarily. 'We have a spy in our midst,' he observed to the soldiers. 'One who would let the Bishop back, betray us to the Antichrist, and feed your bowels to his dogs.'

'I certainly would never do that,' said the priest, bravely. 'What a disgusting idea.'

Fierens stepped forward and struck him hard across the face with the back of his hand. The priest sagged, coughed blood and spat out a tooth. Then he walked back up to Fierens and turned the other cheek.

It was the bravest thing Julius had ever seen anyone do. Even Fierens was discomforted. He hadn't written that in his script.

'Time enough for that, and more,' he said at last. 'Come, soldiers. God's work will not wait.'

Julius stole a look of mutual commiseration at the priest but his companion's expression was blank, his mind turned inward, for he knew that, apart from pain and humiliation, he was already dead.

Chapter 3

Mosman was becoming more extreme, more vehement, almost mani-acally active, but whether it was the pomatum or the imminence of the Day of Righteousness, Blommardine could not tell. Her own dreams were changing too. The angelic forms were becoming still more diaboli-cal, obscene, grotesque; but no less enjoyable. It was as if she too was becoming one of them; so that what had seemed beautiful before was now gloriously foul. It was a banquet of disgusting delights from which she did not and could not draw back. Her sense of power – over the world if not the flesh – had correspondingly increased.

In her mind, and indeed in her body, she had left her marriage behind for good. She did not need Julius now. The fervour of the time, the magic of the Leader, made him quite unnecessary. She had removed what things she wanted from their lodging and slept now in an anteroom near the Leader's chamber, only returning when she needed to take the pomatum and to sleep undisturbed.

The latest phase of the revolution, one which gave Mosman the most active opportunities both as preacher and enforcer, was the suppression of learning in the town.

'The unlearned are the innocent,' thundered Mosman to a group of schoolteachers. 'They are the ones whom God has chosen to redeem the world.'

'What then shall we teach the children?' enquired the most learned of the headmasters.

'Cleanliness and the Old Testament,' replied Mosman. 'Teach them to fight the fight of righteousness. Teach them to fast and pray.'

'It is hardly a curriculum I am used to.'

'Then you had better retire and let some of the younger men take the job. You are obviously past it.'

'But . . .'

'Enough. It is decided.'

'I think it's a brilliant opportunity,' said one of the headmaster's younger colleagues, a greasy fellow who was generally disliked by the children. 'Just think! A whole young generation of junior Saints. We can have marches, prayer-meetings, a special Holy Innocents club for the under-fives, badges, Soldiers of Christ war-games . . . Oh, there's no end of things we can do. How brilliant of you to think of it, Leader.

I only hope you appoint someone big enough to pull it all together.'

'You are appointed, Brother.'

'Oh, I . . . well . . . I wasn't expecting such an honour, but . . . well, of course. I should be delighted, I'll start right away.'

'Your first task then is to see that all school books are gathered up and brought to Elim.'

'Gathered up?' asked the deposed head, dubiously.

'Gathered up and brought to Elim to be burnt. There are to be no books in the New Jerusalem.'

'No books in schools?'

'No books in all the city. Anyone I find who has a book that is not the Bible will be sorely afflicted. Great will be the tribulations.'

Sorely afflicted, as everyone knew, could mean anything from death to a lecture, but on the whole people didn't like to chance it any more.

Books began to appear, making an ever-growing pile in the square – illustrated manuscripts of priceless antiquity; and then all the spawn of that invention in Heidelberg: folios, octavos, chapbooks, pamphlets; treatises on religious subjects; treatises upon treatises on religious subjects – so no one could even begin to point to any scriptural authority other than that of the Saints themselves – books of recipes (cooking became very much simpler); ledgers; alchemical tractates; pagan authors (particularly pagan authors) like Cicero and Seneca and Virgil; romances; poetry; drama; histories; medical textbooks; logic; Euclid; Books of Hours; chivalry manuals; Castiglione's *Courtier*; even the great *Hammer of Witches*, the *Malleus Maleficarum* itself; all grist to the Saints' mill.

Of course, the ancient library of the Cathedral – one of the most important collections of manuscripts, texts and theological works in Germany – had been burned in a gleeful orgy of destruction on the night of the sacking of the Cathedral. But this time there was something even more disturbingly baleful about it. This time it wasn't merely religious knowledge; it was all knowledge. And the mood of the Saints had become, with the success of their excess, wilder and less restrained. There was, at the same time, a terrifying reasonableness about what they were doing – for if you truly believed the Millennium was coming, what need was there of further learning? Of belief there was plenty in the town.

Julius, squatting in his cell – there was nowhere to sit but the floor – reflected on belief. It had always seemed a strange thing to put so much emphasis on faith. He had found a little hole in the wall where the mortar had been picked out and through which he could whisper to the priest whose coughing he could hear next door. They had been left alone for a night and a day while the Sword of Righteousness attended to the book-gathering.

'I'm not sure I believe in belief, Father,' he said. 'It seems to get people into such mischief.'

'It all depends what you believe, my son.'

'But wouldn't proof be better?'

'If it were easy, everyone would do it. There is no virtue in taking your hand from a fire if you see that it is burning.'

'All the same, these people – some of them, many of them poor, homeless, ignorant, desperate – they have found a belief. They are told that faith is all-important. Wouldn't it be better to teach them to trust their senses?'

'If they trusted their senses alone, they would despair.'

Julius acknowledged that he had a point.

'But how are they to know which faith is good and which is mad?'

'Ah. There common sense comes in, and there again the inner sense – if one listens – the soul's sense must direct. These people are not listening to the soul. They are listening to themselves; even when they think they are at their highest reach and becoming one with God. They do not want to merge with God. They wish God to merge with them . . .'

Julius would have liked to have talked further on the subject. There was something here, even among their fear and filth and misery, that was very near the picture; near the riddle. But heavy feet sounded outside, and the door was thrown open.

Konrad loomed in the door, Sword of Righteousness at the ready, the inevitable squad of soldiers behind him.

'You are to come out, Painter, with your fellow-sinner, and see what happens to the works of idolatry, deception and error – the fire, Painter, that is waiting for you too, ever burning in the pit of Hell – but now waiting to consume the idle word and the vain image.'

They were led out under escort and forced to parade beside other prisoners in the square – a company that now included the ex-headmaster of the school.

Julius saw with dismay that indeed it was not just books that were being constantly piled on the mountain, but pictures too, torn from priory and private house and subject now to jeers and hissing as they were tossed in their gilded frames onto the pyre.

Mosman it was who bore the torch aloft.

'Behold the sacred flame,' he exclaimed rapturously. 'Let it light a fire and kindle a blaze on the altar of our hearts. Flare at your vain idols and false images. There is no truth but the Scriptures. There is no image but God.'

'No truth but the Scriptures, no image but God,' chanted the multitude, pelting the pile with rubbish and throwing themselves onto the books, tearing and defiling them in a delirium of vandalism, putting their feet through canvases, spitting on portraits, smashing carvings and cupidons. They hated learning as much as Art.

'It is worse than the Dark Ages,' whispered the priest. 'I never thought to see this in a Christian country.'

Julius desperately wanted the old man to keep his faith.

'You must believe in the soul's sense,' he said.

'Silence,' shouted a guard.

The old man pressed Julius's hand as the torch was thrust into the pyre. Soon the fire took, and smoke filled the evening air, as the spring breeze eddied in the square and bounced back from the buildings. Julius saw a beautiful woman in a portrait, certainly Italian, probably by Pontormo, burst exuberantly into flame, blister and blacken in scarcely more than a moment; a fine engraving by Dürer of St Hubert worshipping the stag turn to ashes; a landscape by van der Weyden; an interior by van Eyck . . .

'I can't watch this,' he said.

'Watch, Painter,' called Konrad. 'Your turn will come.'

'Do they mean to burn us?' Julius whispered to the priest.

'If you're lucky,' the little man whispered back. 'I fancy they have something more elaborate for me.'

There was nothing to say, nothing to do but watch. The heat, for which otherwise he might have felt grateful as the evening turned to night, seemed to have the quality of fever, of pestilence. A man was roasting sausages and offal a few yards away and distributing them to the crowd. There was a carnival feeling all around him. Some people were singing hymns, others urinating into the fire, some were even doing both at once.

Julius felt ashamed at being human. He was almost willing to walk into the fire to be consumed, and took a step forward – but was roughly jerked back by one of the guards.

'Not so fast, Painter. Your turn will come.'

It was the second time he had been told that. It did not bode well. At last they were marched back to the jail. Julius was thrown into his cell, but the priest was told to wait; he was to be taken somewhere else.

'Goodbye, Painter,' said the little man. 'We shall meet perhaps in the Garden.'

'You're not going to no garden. You're going to Hell,' said a guard.

'That is the puzzle,' said the priest, as they took him away.

It was the last Julius saw of his friend. He heard later that he had had his legs broken, his fingernails torn out, his testicles mashed to a skilly, a recorder stuck up his rectum – a favourite trick of the torturers; they jumped on your stomach and made it play – but he had still given nothing away.

Later, Mosman came to see Julius. It was his practice to visit prisoners at any time of the day or night, and harangue them. Blommardine accompanied him, carrying his Bible. Her eyes widened like a cat's when she saw Julius, but she said nothing. After praying and haranguing for an hour, Mosman rose, assuring Julius that there was no place for vainglorious idolaters in the New Jerusalem, and that he should look to his soul on this his last day on earth, for the city was certainly not going to feed sinners at a time of siege.

'May I pray with the sinner, Leader?' asked Blommardine.

'He is not worth the saving.'

'It would be practice for me. You pray so well, I feel . . . well, I should like to see if I can put what I have learned from you . . . into effect.'

'Very well. But do not be deceived by him.'

'Not any more I won't.'

'What did you say, Magdalen?'

'I won't be deceived any more by the tongue of sin. I was gullible once but being with you . . . you have opened my eyes, Leader.'

She meant it, thought Julius, even though it was the Saint – even herself – she was deceiving.

'There will be a guard outside the door,' said Mosman as he left. 'You only have to call.'

'You could rape me now,' Blommardine said to Julius. 'I wouldn't shout.'

'I don't think so, thank you,' said Julius.

He wasn't feeling like that sort of thing, not with the prospect of the rope over his head.

'I could rape you then,' she said. 'Would you call the guard?'

'Yes, I damn well would. What is it? Come here to gloat?'

'I have come here to save your hide, stupid. Just because you're a rotten lover doesn't mean . . .' Her voice trailed off. 'I have better lovers now than you could imagine,' she concluded.

'Saints?' asked Julius, incredulously.

Say what you would – and he did – about the Anabaptists, as far as carnality was concerned they were pillars of rectitude. Indeed, there had been executions for adultery.

'Devils.'

'Dear God.'

She told him about the pomatum (though not where she had found it).

He wasn't grateful to Blommardine for the trouble she had caused him – but at the same time there was something about her you couldn't totally dislike. She was reprehensible, irresponsible, wild, malicious; and yet you felt, in the end, it was she who was going to be burnt, whether or not she knew it. He was appalled at what she told him.

'You must stop taking that stuff immediately,' he said. 'It was wrong of you to take it in the first place. If anyone were to have it, it should have been me ... After all, I have to finish the picture.'

'It wouldn't work on you. You're too ... southernized. I bet old Bosch did it though. He took the stuff. You only have to look at his drawings.'

He looked at her strangely. She rarely offered any comment on art.

'What are they like, these lovers of yours?'

She described them, and he recognized the pig-nun, the tree-dog, the swollen beetle-abbot, and all the others that his master must have visited, embraced or observed.

'You can't observe much down there,' she said. 'You can't keep your hands off yourself.'

'Does Mosman know?'

'Of course not. I wouldn't tell him a thing like that. He's in another world.'

'Hell, I should think,' said Julius. 'He's even more of a devil than a tree-dog.'

'I'll go if you're going to talk like that. Guard,' she called softly.

'Wait,' said Julius.

'You called?' said the guard, opening the door.

'I wanted to know the time.'

'Just past two by the church clock. Leader said you was to be let out now.'

'Thank you. I shall leave shortly.'

'Very good.'

The guard withdrew and the door was bolted again.

'Have you given anyone else this pomatum?'

'Only Mosman.'

'Mosman?' Julius was aghast. 'But he's running the whole town. It will make him madder than ever.'

'He's saving my mind,' said Blommardine, soulfully. 'If it wasn't for him, tree-dog and company would have had me by now. They can't touch *him*. It doesn't affect him. If I stay with him, I'll be all right.'

'The trouble with you, Blommardine, is you can't see a patch of thin ice without feeling an irresistible urge to skate on it.'

'That's just one of the troubles with me,' she said, gathering up her Bible. 'I must go now. I may not be able to get you out of prison immediately, but I can probably have you excused death and torture. Will that be all right?'

'Yes,' he said, 'thank you, Blommardine. That would be a step in the right direction.'

'By the way,' she remarked as she went out, 'there was something else. Did you know I was your half-sister?'

'What?' he shouted, utterly aghast.

But the door had closed and he was alone. He fell to the ground and wept with frustration, beating the floor. He could not believe that she could have done this to him.

'You have ruined my life,' he cried.

Mocking laughter from the next cell told him the little priest had been replaced.

Chapter 4

The growing life inside her, while on the one hand it dismayed, even terrified Elisabeth – for who knew what her husband might not do; adultery was punishable by death – filled her at the same time with a joy she had known only in Julius's arms in the Garden. She felt she would not mind now, for herself, if she died, so long as the baby could live. Unfortunately or fortunately, whichever way she looked at it, the two issues were closely connected at the moment.

She still did not stir much from the house and garden, for the milder weather meant lighter clothes and, by the end of May, the baby was beginning to be undisguisable. Happily, her father was now too busy to pay more than sporadic visits to the house. He had found himself temporary sleeping-quarters nearer the 'barracks' so that he could be on hand in any emergency.

Frieda and her network of crones, although much depleted, still seemed to be able to keep abreast of his movements and, when he approached, a grey cloak was hung out to dry as a sign, from a window on the corner of the street. A black cloak was the sign for Fierens' appearance, and this occurred even more rarely, for Fierens had authority (as well as authorship) on his hands.

Even so, she knew that one day soon she was going to have to break the news to him. How she wished it was Julius she could tell! The weeks had lessened her sense of shock at his duplicity – she had read and re-read his letter of distraught regret; anger and pain had turned to compassion – and love, untroubled by hope, had slowly grown again with his child. She had such an instinct of his overwhelming joy at hearing of it. But why had he not written again? Had he perhaps tried to get in touch with her? Should she now risk putting him in danger by writing to him? Where was he now? Frieda, who normally knew everything, seemed unusually vague on the subject, beyond assuring her that he was still alive and doubtless loved her.

'What's this, Daughter?' said her father one day, returning unannounced and beating the grey cloak by a comfortable margin, 'growing fat in sloth? You should stir yourself more.'

'She has not been well,' said Frieda reproachfully.

'When I want your advice I shall ask for it,' said Konrad, curtly.

Being Sword of Righteousness had not improved his manners.

'It is true, Father. I have been weak. And Frieda here has been trying to feed me up.'

'Did no one tell you there's a siege on, woman. I cannot in my position be seen to be plumping up my family.'

'No, Father.'

'Eat less. Take more exercise. You should get out more. Help in the community.'

Elisabeth gave a little cough to indicate that her lungs were still not quite clear.

'And if you're still sick, I'll send for the doctor again.'

'Oh, no,' she said quickly. 'It's really much better.'

She didn't want a doctor poking about.

'Well, then. Look to yourself. You have a position in this town, you know. To be married to Fierens is a great honour. If anything should happen to our Leader, he will be the next.'

'I will take exercise,' she said.

'Help in the hospital. There is a war, you know.'

He kept reminding her of that.

'There's . . . nothing else, is there?'

His eyes, always critical, narrowed as he looked at her.

'Nothing else?'

Her heart beat faster.

'Nothing else you want to tell me? No . . . good news?'

There was no doubt what he was driving at. She pulled her baby in as far as she could.

'No other good news, Father.'

'Humph,' he said.

There was a call from the street. The Sword of Righteousness was needed at the arsenal.

'Coming,' he shouted.

He turned to go, and then turned back.

'I will tell Fierens you are better. He might give us cause for good news yet.'

They watched the door close.

'What did he mean, Nurse? Do you think he noticed?'

'I don't know, my duck. You can never tell with your father. He's no fool with his eyes. It's his brain that's a-squint.'

'What shall I do?'

'I don't know rightly, love. Truth's best when invention fails.'

'I'll have to tell him when he comes.'

'Pray to the good Lord, love. The eternal God is thy refuge and underneath are the everlasting arms. Pity about your young man being in prison,' said the old woman, as casually as she could.

It was time for the truth.

'Prison?'

Elisabeth's heart sank. She felt suddenly sick and clutched at a table for support.

'Why did you not tell me before?' she asked. 'You've been keeping it from me, haven't you? Oh, Nurse . . .'

'I didn't want you getting het up, did I, darling? He was found writing verses and talking to old Father Berthold. They've tortured and killed the poor old man, said he was hiding people, but he never talked. Your fellow won't be out just yet. But he's all right.'

'Thank God.'

She thought for a moment, and then smiled, feeling a ridiculous glow of relief and happiness.

'That's why he hasn't written again,' she said.

'Maybe,' said the old woman. 'Yes, I expect that's it.'

Chapter 5

Fierens in the city, about the city, at the walls, in the magazines, checking the stores, prowling the prison, flapping his ears at street corners, interrogating dissenters, harassing transgressors. Fierens on the Cathedral tower alone in the darkness, looking out beyond the town to the fires of the besiegers, twinkling like fallen stars in the water meadows below . . .

'It is very near,' said God. 'It will come to pass on Ascension Day. I will breathe in my servant Mosman's ear and he will be filled with a sublime exultation. Did he not promise the town that the Day of Judgement should be at Easter? He erred, for I did not speak thus to him, nor was the town sufficiently penitent. Howsoever, it is fitting that he should receive guidance and inspiration for some act that will be to the glory of the Saints and of Myself. If the town looks for a sign, it will not be disappointed. And you, my chosen Fierens, you shall at the last come unto my throne. And the last words of the Book of Life shall be written and the last act accomplished, and you shall sit with me as One in everlasting glory . . .'

God usually spoke in a biblical manner as was only fitting. He used Fierens' own voice, expressing his message in a hoarse little whisper. He didn't really have to speak at all, because one of Fierens' minds was God. God went off on His own independently, of course, doing things that Fierens did not have time to concentrate on, like making a storm come up or a child die; but when Fierens could locate his God-mind and make it stop running the world for a while, he found he could really get a great deal of Godness out of it, and so it was now.

He remained, locked in contemplation on the Cathedral tower, pondering the magnitude of the tidings that he and his mind were passing between them, until suddenly It was gone. Into the night, over the hills, beyond the stars It flew, the golden wire blown like gossamer in the winds of eternity, leaving him momentarily exhausted . . . He rested his head upon his hands as he gripped the parapet wall.

It was, in truth, extraordinary how much Fierens seemed to draw from these conversations – like a mystic, a medium, a madman, he appeared to be able to take ideas and truths which you would think he could not possibly know, straight out of the air. But then you would need to have extraordinary powers to think you or even part of you were God anyway. You would need to be touched by God one way or another.

Fierens stirred and lifted his head, feeling the strength return through the stone of the parapet. So far, of course, he had concealed his extraordinary powers. Mosman was still the Leader, the unwitting John the Baptist to his Saviour. So far he, Fierens, had been the arranger, the producer, the behind-the-scenes man, the orchestrator, the drummer, one of the leads, perhaps, but not yet the director, not yet centre-stage.

His extraordinary powers blazed beneath the cloak. It seemed incredible to him now that his arrival upon earth had been so ordinary. Born the illegitimate son of a village mayor – who would have thought he would rise up to meet God! Bastard was what he was told, of course. Now it seemed to him that his peasant mother might have concealed the truth from him. In fact, the more he thought about it now, the more certain he became. The village mayor was simply an excuse – a notorious philanderer whom his mother (a most unlikely conquest, being exceptionally quick on her feet) had been instructed by an archangel to name as parent. All the signs were there. He had been despised and rejected all right, shabbily treated, misunderstood, laughed at for being a bastard, railed at for a sluggard by the schoolmaster, mocked by the pastry cooks, cheated by Jews when he set up his own little business . . .

Yes, he was without question conceived immaculately. And the way he had come through all his tribulations – learning to watch and understand the play, to write and act his part, to see the way the other players and the groundlings reacted, to gratify the nobs – this was his Father's hand, guiding and urging him on, to take his place on the greatest stage of all – the stage not of history but of the End of History.

He was ready. But first Mosman must have his scene.

Chapter 6

It was, strangely, at this juncture that Mosman's grip on the town seemed stronger than ever. He enjoyed – if that was the word, since Mosman never really seemed to enjoy anything – an absolute dictatorship.

There was no private ownership any more. Property, possessions, food, drink, medicine, fuel, clothes, horses, wagons, everything came under the control of the community. And the community came under the control of Mosman.

Sin had been in many respects eradicated. Drunkenness was practically abolished, for there was no drink; gluttony was almost equally impossible. Sloth was met with a whip. 'Luxuria' or lust (if you felt like it after a supper of thin broth with dry bread and no beer) could only be practised in the connubial bed; otherwise you faced prison or worse. Even in the connubial, you could be reported by your spouse for excessive luxury.

Of anger there was plenty, but it was righteous anger meted out by the Saints; brawling of any kind was cured by the whip and the sword. Avarice was out of the question. Envy had little to feed on since all were equal. The only sin that really seemed to grow, like a tropical plant that has found at last the ambient home that it needs, was the last sin, the first sin, the worst sin of all: the sin of Pride.

Pride stalked the ranks of the Saints as ambition used to tickle the souls of the citizens. Since there could be no ambition here – for worldly things were at an end – all you could hope for was to be, not richer, cleverer, braver, more beautiful, but better than anyone else. And people went to enormous lengths to show how much better they were. They would pray for hours on cold cobbles. They would wear their hair-shirts and mortifying corsets. One man had proclaimed he would not touch food until the Day of Judgement came. (Pride unfortunately got the better of him and he expired.)

Some people would not sleep, resting on beds of shards. Others sang continually like cherubim and seraphim, though in not such tuneful quires. Others still scourged themselves and tramped the city, flagellating ostentatiously.

At the top of this heap of Pride was the Leader. He did not recognize it as Pride, of course. None of them did. But it coiled and writhed and seethed inside him – aided and abetted perhaps by Blommardine's pomatum which, though not showing him the devils of lust, was stoking him with even worse ones.

Easter had come and gone. And it rankled with him that the Day of Judgement had not occurred as he had initially promised. Oh, he had told the town that the fault lay with them. There had been insufficient repentance – that was abundantly clear. But even so mutterings had been heard that so far there had been a signal lack of divine under-pinning. People had seen crosses in the sky, of course. A dog had whelped a two-headed puppy. But this was tame stuff; a week in any town could show the same.

Mosman prayed for three days. The Saints' anniversary in Rensburg was a fitting moment for some great mark of divine approbation. He prayed for a fiery chariot but none was forthcoming. He fainted with lack of food but was revived by Blommardine, who brought him rough cakes and water. He prayed again, and this time it seemed his prayers were answered. He looked at his sword and it seemed, as it were, aflame.

Rising hastily, he called for eleven men with the strongest faith in town. Pride brought a hundred to his side.

'Just eleven,' he cried, 'the number of the Apostles. Come with me, you and you . . .'

He chose his eleven and told them what he intended.

'God has spoken,' he proclaimed. 'The enemy are given up into our hand. With these eleven and the Sword of Michael the Archangel which I hold, we will overcome the hosts of Midian and drive them with great slaughter from the field.'

Too late Blommardine saw what she had done.

'No, Leader,' she cried. 'They are too many. You are not well.'

But the Saints pressed around her angrily.

'Do not question the Leader. He has the Sword of Michael. He will deliver the enemy into our hand . . .'

Others said: 'She loves the siege. She would like us to be humbled.'

'Harlot,' some cried, especially the women who resented her influence on the Leader.

'Stay me not,' shouted Mosman, wildly, shaking his white hair in a flurry about his face. 'Sound the trumpets, open the town gate.'

'No, no, please no . . .'

She threw herself upon him but was roughly shaken off. The little band passed through the gates and charged across the meadow, calling on the name of Jehovah.

332

The Bishop's army, though not in the best of spirits, discipline or training, had no difficulty in cutting them to pieces, to a man.

It was the end of the silver-haired Leader and the start of the reign of gold.

Chapter 7

Julius heard the footsteps approaching with sinking heart. You never knew in this place whether someone had decided it was time, as they put it, to let your soul out. The door of his cell was flung open and the gaoler stuck his nose in. Julius decided not to jump to his feet. Reclining, you could stop your knees from shaking. The gaoler's first words, however, shook him another way.

'Hop it,' he said.

'What?'

'You're free to go.'

'But why?' he enquired. 'What have I not done?'

'Are you mad?' said the gaoler. 'Get up and get out. No one asks why and wherefore in this town. Do you question God's mercy?'

'I question man's,' said Julius. 'And I should like to know why I've been kept locked up for a fortnight or more without a trial.'

'There I can't help you,' said the gaoler. 'I'm just here to put 'em in and keep 'em in. But as for why you're out, the Leader's dead.'

'Mosman?'

'No less. Chopped to mincemeat. The Lord deserted him.'

Julius almost laughed out loud. This was wonderful news. The man was, had been a monster. But there was something about the gaoler's face which didn't encourage rejoicing.

'The new Leader,' continued the gaoler, 'the new Leader says it's because there's still wickedness among us.'

'I suppose there is,' said Julius. 'There's too much wickedness whichever way you look at it.'

'You're a fine one to talk,' said the gaoler. 'A gaol-bird like you.'

'Who is the new Leader?' asked Julius, changing the subject.

'It's not official yet but us guards say Brother Fierens. A lovely preacher. Ever heard him? To be honest, I think he's better than that late departed. One of us, know what I mean? A people's man, or Saint as I should say. Not so one-track-minded as poor late-departed, God rest his soul. He'll be with us again shortly on Resurrection day.'

Julius's heart had sunk anew on hearing the name of the new Leader, though indeed he had been half-expecting it. Poor town . . . it was out of the frying-pan into the fiery furnace.

'But why am I let out? Who ordered it?' he asked.

'Look, sonny . . .'

The gaoler changed his tone. He didn't like questions. They complicated things. He stepped inside the cell and showed Julius a fist that looked like a side of beef and smelt like one too.

'Know what this is?'

'It's a fist.'

'See it all right, do you?'

'It's a big fist.'

'Well you won't see it very soon because it'll be sticking out of the back of your head. Don't ask so many questions. I told you, didn't I?'

Julius, propelled by a kick, moved rapidly out of the prison, paused briefly outside to remember his friend, the little priest, who had died there, and walked home at a stiff pace, fearing that there might still be some trickery afoot. He could be followed. He feared that when he reached his lodgings he would find soldiers there who would confront him with some evidence of treason or unbelief – one and the same thing in the New Jerusalem – and would re-arrest him and take him back to the gaol. Such cat-and-mousery was becoming quite common under the rule of the Saints.

All he found on return, however, was Blommardine in a fearful state. (The lodgings, neglected for some time, were in a bad way too, but made less fuss about it.) Blommardine was sobbing uncontrollably. She had been sobbing all day. From the look of her, she would be sobbing all year.

He could almost have felt sorry for her if she had not been the cause of such a disaster in his life. Marrying him when she knew it was unlawful. Could she really be his half-sister? Or was it just another of her games? Indeed, he wondered as he looked at her whether games was the right word. Was she perhaps not a little mad?

Normally he would have felt happy about discovering a half-sister – his only living relative. The world was a bleak and dangerous place and it was good to have a family.

But to be married to your sister? This was taking proximity too far. And then there was the disturbing thought that, if she were mad, perhaps the seeds of that madness might lie in him as well.

'Hush,' he said at last, trying to calm her in a husbandly-brotherly sort of way.

'He is gone, he is dead,' she kept moaning. 'Would to God I had gone too.'

'They would have stopped you,' said Julius. 'Don't reproach yourself. Women aren't allowed on the battlefields.'

'What about Joan of Arc?' she sobbed. 'She wouldn't have stayed behind when the Saints went to war.'

'Joan of Arc was different. She had visions.'

'I have visions too.'

She did not specify the nature of her vision this time. Julius tried again.

'We must talk,' he said.

'Talk? Talk, talk, talk. Talk won't bring him back to life. I am lost without him. Damned.'

'Oh, come now.'

'Oh, come now?' she repeated savagely. 'How can you possibly know? You . . . worm. You half a man.'

'Half a brother,' he said, seizing his chance.

It seemed to do the trick, for she stopped howling and began to look more alert. Malice always perked her up.

'Oh, that.'

'Yes, that.'

'You might as well know. What does it matter now? You know who your father was?'

'No.'

'Your mother?'

'No, I've told you . . . no.'

She laughed bitterly through her tears.

'You poor idiot. Who do you think you are?'

What was she saying? Suddenly he felt that not just his paternity but his whole self was in question.

'I am who I think I am,' he replied nervously.

'No you're not,' she said.

He could feel his identity wobbling and slopping like junket. She sensed it and, even in her misery, it made her feel better.

'Who am I, then? Not . . . not your father's son?' It would be terrible to be the offspring of that monster.

She threw back her head and gave that terrible mirthless laugh again.

'Tell me,' he shouted.

'You are my mother's son. My elder brother . . .'

'You mean . . .'

'You are her bastard.'

Bastard? It was unthinkable that a well-brought-up young woman would have had a child out of wedlock, presumably even before wedlock.

'Did your father know?' he asked.

'Funnily enough, he didn't.'

'It must have been a well-kept secret.'

'Oh, it was.'

'But didn't he mind that she wasn't, you know, a virgin?'

'She had a good story. An awkward fall when she was young. He wanted to believe her so he did. He was in lust with her . . .'

'And my father?'

'You want to know, don't you?'

'Of course I want to know. Who am I? Tell me. I thought I would never find out. Now you tell me you've known all along. Who am I? Why do you torment me? I must know the other half. I'm only half a person.'

He was trembling with uncertainty and vexation.

'You are . . .'

'Yes? My father was . . .'

'I don't know. Really. Sorry.'

He stepped back, feeling momentarily faint. A well-born mother? Now at last it was becoming clear. The loveless childhood, the gruff apprenticeship, the unexplained sponsorship of his visit to Italy . . . It had to be the Grand Master, d'Almagaes. But why had he not married the unhappy girl? Surely Love would have dictated it?

'Why? Why?' he asked.

'Why anything? Why did Mosman have to die?'

She was beginning to huddle down into her chair again, but Julius caught her by the shoulders and shook her hard.

'Why?' he cried. 'Tell me, bitch.'

'I don't know why,' she shouted.

'Who told you anyway?'

'I found some papers among my mother's things. Secrets . . .'

'Show them to me. Give them. They are mine.'

'I've . . . forgotten where they are.'

'I don't believe you,' he howled. 'You've made the whole thing up.'

But in his heart he knew that wasn't true. There was a terrible likelihood about her story. He went onto another tack.

'And what about your mother?' he asked.

'Your mother,' she corrected. 'What about her?'

'Didn't she . . . miss her only son?'

'How should I know? You wouldn't expect her to speak of it, would you? Not with a man like Father around? He'd have killed her.'

Julius remembered the lawyer's chilly face, and shuddered. Poor Mother . . . He suddenly felt a great sadness that he had not known her, smelt her fragrance and taken her kisses.

'Anyway,' continued Blommardine, 'she never seemed very happy if that's any comfort to you. And she died when I was small. Unhappiness isn't good for you. That's why I shall probably die tomorrow.'

Tomorrow, as far as Julius was concerned, the way he felt about her at the moment, was a great deal too late.

'So why did you marry me?' he asked.

'I didn't know, then, did I? That was just coincidence. They say likes are attracted. It was just bad luck.'

'So when did you find out?'

337

'A couple of years later, when my father died. I was going through some boxes in the attic.'

'Why did you never tell me?'

'There didn't seem any point. One husband's much like another. And anyway you interested me then. Afterwards I thought . . . why rock the boat?'

One husband's much like another, Julius thought; it's the lovers that are so different. She could have been married to a clothes-horse for all she cared. Well, all that was going to change now. At least now he could be free of her. If only he had known before. He could have escaped with Elisabeth and they would be living in perfect love a hundred miles from this accursed town.

'We shall have to get an annulment,' he said firmly. 'The Church will have no problem with such an error made in good faith.'

'Annulment?' she enquired, eyes wide. 'What annulment? On what grounds?'

'On the grounds you've just told me. If it's true.'

'It's true all right. But where's the proof?'

'You have the proof.'

'Yes, I do. But I've lost it for the moment.'

'You bitch.'

She started to weep again – not at his words but at the condition of her life. Mosman had been strong enough to save her, but he was gone.

'Wrong letter,' she said.

'What?'

'It begins with W,' she told him. 'Witch is the word. Didn't you know?'

'I believe I did.'

Everything about his life was becoming clearer. He even felt sorry for Blommardine. There was a worm of evil devouring her; but it would not be doing so unless there was still some good in her. He glanced out of the window. Darkness was gathering like the works of sin.

'I must go now,' she said.

'Go?'

'They are calling me.'

She made no sign of going. Her tears were dry now, however. A change had come over her. Her cat's eyes shone and her hands moved about, stroking her dress.

'Will you not let our marriage be annulled?'

'Everything is null in this town.'

'This town is not going to last.'

'When it is over, we shall be over too. Do you want to make love to me now?'

'No! It is incest.'

'So much the better,' she said. 'Come, we are all in Hell.'

He could feel his loins stirring. There was an insidious appeal in her voice. Unlacing her bodice, she held out her right hand. He could see her thigh where her skirt had hitched up, and now she put her left hand between her legs.

It was one of those terrible moments when to do the wrong thing is infinitely attractive and totally irrevocable – you open a pretty little door and you drop into an abyss. The right thing, on the other hand, seems to have no immediate advantage in the short term. It seems tame, a little boring, really not at all the sort of thing an artist was supposed to do or be. And yet you know exactly what you should do; the abyss is there, clearly marked ABYSS; no one but a fool would follow that route; and yet . . .

Julius clutched the crucifix the little priest had given him, thought of his poor mother, and at last filled his mind with the picture of his love, the love that had seemed so impossibly remote and now – through Blommardine's news – might seem at long last to be nearer. His shame and his guilt no longer hung about his vision in clouds but purged themselves in tears which sprang to his eyes and rolled upon his cheeks. How could he consider incest with a sister-wife when the Garden of Love itself was in view? He looked at Blommardine and saw, instead of her pale, boyish face, a snout superimposed across the features. She moved scaled legs, feeling herself with talons.

'No!' he shouted. 'Never again. I have done with you.'

The vision faded. It was Blommardine still.

'Suit yourself,' she said, 'and pass me that jar over there.'

She motioned at a shelf beside the fireplace. He reached the pot down for her and lifted the lid as he passed it. A heady, deep, troubling, piscine vapour came up from it.

'Ugh,' he said. 'What is it?'

'Pomatum. Hell-brew. Leave me now. I shall sleep until tomorrow night. Go to your studio. You will find that Fierens wants to see you.'

Chapter 8

There was some agitation in the town after Mosman's death. It was said that God had let them down. It was even suggested that the Anabaptists weren't all they were cracked up to be.

Fierens called the townsfolk to the market-square, and spoke to them from a rostrum he had had knocked up by one of the chippies. It was more of a stage, really, since it had, behind it, a backdrop which concealed soldiers, spies, or special-effects men according to the nature of the gathering. He could have a host of angels flying out of it if he wanted to, seraphim and cherubim playing their harps, trumpets, psalteries and timbrels – he had only to say the word – but Jesus Christ his predecessor had not gone in for ostentation of that kind. Water into wine was more his line of country. And what was good enough for Jesus was good enough for him. Mind you, Jesus had been soft. Too soft on sinners; too soft on those who did not fully believe; and far too soft on those who were wishy-washy about the Last Judgement. Jesus had been the velvet hand in the velvet glove. Now it was time for iron. As brother of Jesus, he felt he could say these things without offence. Sorry, Jesus, time to move over.

'Our Leader, the Saint, has been taken up to Heaven,' he told the crowd.

'Where were you?' asked a voice with a Rensburg accent. 'Where were you when they were laying down their lives? Hiding behind the Sword of Justice?'

Fierens made a motion and three of the red-faced men moved directly into the crowd. The fellow who shouted, a brewer's drayman, was pinpointed. A word in his ear, a scuffle on the edge of the crowd, a dagger under the ribs, a discreet dragging away, and the argument was settled.

Fierens held up his hand.

'Oh, Brethren. My dear loves. Could you but hear yourselves . . . could you but see yourselves . . . could you but feel the filthiness of yourselves and dig inside and know your breathing . . . Why, then you would kneel and roar your apologies unto God. Your colleague – sadly taken ill – asks where was *I*? I was praying. Had you been praying . . . each and every one of you . . . why, the very clouds that we see overhead would have parted, and a beam of celestial overwhelmingness would have surrounded our brave Leader and his band, and nothing would have stopped them till they had slain the whole host of Midian that opposed them. Kneel now, all of you – oh dear, is it wet? Are you going to soil your nice gowns and your hose? I shall strew shards for you and you shall kneel on that.

'Shards,' he called.

Soldiers from behind the backdrop now appeared and emptied bags of pottery chippings on the ground.

'Down, get down,' ordered Fierens.

The assembled company, with some reluctance and considerable pain, proceeded to kneel.

'Now,' ordered Fierens, 'my sweet loves. Pray as you've never prayed before. Forget the pain. If you feel the pain, it means you are not praying hard enough. And I want you to pray hard. Pray for forgiveness for not having saved your Leader. Pray for triumph over iniquity. Pray for the New Jerusalem. And pray, oh good people, pray for your new Leader, whoever he may be, on whose shoulders must fall the burden of bringing us all to Jordan's farthest side. Are you praying?'

'Yes,' shouted the people.

'Are you praying hard?'

'Yes,' shouted the people.

'Do you feel the pain?'

'No,' shouted the people.

'Now, let me hear you praying. Shout it out. Don't be afraid. Let's get this thing lifting. I want to see those clouds break.'

A babel of noise burst over the square, so much so that the soldiers in the enemy camp across the river feared an imminent break-out.

'They're cross because we killed those lunatics,' said the Bishop, unhappily. 'I told you there'd be trouble.'

'Stand-to the guard,' ordered his brother-in-law.

But no trouble came from the town.

The people in the market-place prayed until they'd prayed themselves hoarse and then – it was regarded as a miracle – just at the moment when they thought they could pray no more, a great shaft of light pierced a narrow gap in the clouds, illuminating the whole square, and bathing Fierens' pale face in radiance.

'Up, up off your knees. Oh, my beloved, you have done it,' shouted Fierens.

They loved him for making their prayer work, for bloodying their knees. Was it good timing? Was Fierens a shrewd observer of the weather? Or was he chosen by God? To the townsfolk there was only one answer.

'Hurrah for Fierens our new Leader,' they shouted. 'Let the thousand-year rule begin.'

If there had been any doubt of the succession after Mosman's demise, Fierens had now effectively stamped his authority on the town.

It was a different rule, more political, more plausible, more subtle, more dangerous – and madder than anyone could guess.

Chapter 9

The soldiers broke into his studio without knocking and took him straight to Fierens' office in the Town Hall. It was cold out in the street, and raining in those fat, slow, portentous drops that presage a cloudburst. He would probably catch his death, but it hardly mattered. Readiness for death was part of the way of living these days.

He had been half-expecting arrest, and thought they meant to kill him without further ado. Painting had been forbidden as being tantamount to making graven images. Indeed, that was what Fierens began by telling him.

'Painting has been forbidden. It is tantamount to making graven images. I have imprisoned you for this before.'

'I am sorry,' said Julius, and he was.

The very rain, leaping off the flagstones of the square outside in little liquid explosions, seemed to underline the danger of the situation.

'However,' Fierens continued, 'we now require a celebration and record of these great days and the City of God has need of your services in this respect, so you shall be allowed to pursue your low craft.'

Fierens had worked with artists in the production of pageant and plays, and understood their presentational talents. Great effects could be achieved with a little artifice. Besides, was it not fitting that the image of the Leader should be on view at every possible vantage-point throughout this town, as an inspiration to the Just and a caution to the miserable sinner? Copies and copies of copies should be made.

So Julius was put to making a portrait of the new Leader, which offered him an opportunity of studying the man and his character over frequent sittings.

Fierens was not an easy subject. He had a fixed idea of the image that he wished to present and, over much of the month, he made Julius sketch at least a score of different poses. Finally, he hit upon the one that found favour – Fierens seated in a posture at once authoritative and judicious, one hand slightly upraised as if to indicate mercy to the faithful, his handsome features majestically severe but with a hint, just a hint, of clemency around the eyes; about his head not exactly a halo but a gathering of light as if to indicate immanence.

Once this was agreed upon, the work proceeded apace, although Fierens tended to go into a trance, neglecting the desired expression.

At other times, however, he would expand upon the End of Things, the nature of Antichrist and the glories of the General Resurrection. At others still, he would speak of his days in the theatre as though it was still his passion and his destiny.

Julius reflected that he might quite easily kill the man and liberate the city, but somehow he could not bring himself to do it. Although death had been in the Eden his master had painted – and it could be said to be a necessary part of the Brethren's Creed of Love – in the Earthly Garden itself there was no killing, only a little dying, and in Hell there was only violence without Death. Besides, Creed apart, he felt a natural revulsion to the act – a revulsion justified by the knowledge that he would be most vilely tortured by the guards if he perpetrated such a deed.

So Fierens lived, and it was the worse for everyone. By the time the portrait was finished (Fierens had insisted that it should be larger than life-size) it was late-June. Fierens spent a day looking at the picture, sometimes gazing upon it steadfastly, sometimes locked in prayer. At length he arose and pronounced himself satisfied.

'You have done fittingly, Painter,' he said. 'Now make me ten copies.'

'Ten copies?'

Julius was flabbergasted. It would take him months. What on earth did the man want ten identical portraits of himself for?

'That is what I command,' said Fierens.

There was no room for debate in his tone.

'I shall need help,' Julius told him.

'Get it.'

'I will have to set up a workshop, find an assistant . . .'

'Do so. There are other painters in the town.'

'Very well,' said Julius. 'I'll do my best.'

'I shall require all ten to be delivered by the end of July.'

It was an impossible commission but there was no arguing with the man. Julius had a further thought. Some good might come out of this tall order after all.

'What about your wife, Leader?'

'My wife?'

The man turned a puzzled look on Julius.

'Would it not be fitting to have a portrait of her too?'

'Fitting?'

'Seated, as your consort . . .'

'It would not be fitting.'

'Ah.'

The man seemed to resent the suggestion deeply. For a moment Julius thought that Fierens was going to say he had no consort, that he was not married. Could it be that Fierens was proposing to annul the

344

marriage, that Elisabeth might yet be free? He had not heard of her for days now. Perhaps she had been smuggled out of the town. Julius felt delight at the possibility of her safety and despair at such an absence.

And then Fierens said something which defied Julius's capacity to adjust expression.

'My wife,' he announced with some pride, 'is a Virgin.'

Chapter 10

It had been no longer possible to hide the truth behind apron or stomacher.

'You will have to tell him,' old Frieda had said. 'I swear you grow bigger by the minute. I've put the fear of God into that girl Billa, but soon she won't need to keep quiet. The whole world's going to see you're with child.'

'But I have not lain with him, Nurse. What is he going to say?'

'The good Lord will look after you, my darling. It is better that you speak to your husband in your good time rather than be found out in his.'

And so, fearful of the outcome and of the wrath both of husband and father, she had sent word to the Town Hall that she would be grateful for a visit from the Leader.

In due course, later that afternoon, after an agonizing three hours for her, he appeared. There was a peremptory knock at the door, and Frieda, who had been keeping watch at the window, hurried in with the announcement.

'He's here.'

'Oh, dear God.'

'You must be brave, child.'

'I must see him alone. I do not want my father to come too.'

'I will prevent him. It is fitting that you should see your husband alone after so much neglect.'

Frieda scurried off downstairs and Elisabeth was left by herself. Out of the window the house-martins flickered among the rooftops, teasing the eaves and flirting with the open casements.

The chestnut trees, whose tops showed behind the chimneys of the house across the way, thrust their last candlesticks (everything was late this year) at the sky so arrogantly you'd think they were flunkeys to a Hapsburg. A dog in the street padded urgently forward on some doggy matter that had nothing to do with repentance or the forgiveness of sins.

The whole of Nature – even the fly which busybodied at the window – seemed perfectly content with the way things were. Only man, Elisabeth thought, only man has this capacity to look at happiness and see misery.

She experienced a sudden, swallow-dipping lurch of longing for the father of her baby. Where was he? Why did he not come?

Presently steps could be discerned mounting the stairs – one set of steps, Fierens alone. It afforded some relief – not enough to change her opinion that this was the worst day of her life – but the respite was gratefully received.

The door opened and her husband entered.

'Well, spouse,' he said, and folded his arms, raising his eyes heavenward and averting his handsome head. It was clear he had other things on his mind.

Frightened though she was, the sheer impoliteness of the man enraged her. He had not noticed, she was sure, that she was pregnant. She began to feel that if she were delivered of a child upon the instant, he would still stand there in that disdainful and preoccupied attitude.

'Well,' she said. 'Are you not going to greet your wife and ask her how she does?'

'The Church is my bride,' he answered. 'The holy city is my spouse.'

She was tempted to ask why, in that case, had he married her, but she knew the answer to that. It was to bind the city – and her father – to the Anabaptists more closely. She had worked that out for herself and old Frieda had said as much.

Taking a deep breath she told him why she had asked for this interview.

'I am going to have a child,' she said.

Fierens had been walking with God again. There was something very big about to happen. It was time for another manifestation in the town. The creation of this pageant of life and death was now absorbing his whole being. Such things as food and drink, bodily matters, passed unnoticed. Lower angels attended to these for him while he created. He was here, in this room, because his lower angels had led him here. He spoke with the words the lower angel brought to his mouth. His higher consciousness, his power of creation, was enwrapped in the contemplation of Himself and with the destiny of his creature, man – a destiny that the affairs of this city of Rensburg would perfect or dash apart like a potter's vessel.

What was this woman saying, angel?

'A baby?'

'Yes.'

'But I have not known her.'

'No.'

'What does this mean?'

'I have known no man on this earth,' she said, for the union in the Garden had surely been in a world apart.

'But you are certain you are with child?'

347

'Look,' she said, and stood up revealing her fullness.

There was a pause while the lower angels muttered together, finally coming forward to him as he planned and contrived.

'It is a mystery,' they said. 'She has known no men. Her father would never allow it. She speaks truth.'

'What are you saying?' Fierens asked them.

They told him.

'It is the work of the Most High.'

'Of course it is,' he said. 'Have I not known it all along? Did I not tell the painter she was no crass consort?'

Fierens left his plans for the eternal city's establishment and came down to earth through the seven circles. Elisabeth was astonished to see his expression change to one of condescension.

'Blessed art thou among women,' he said to her.

'Blessed?'

'You were right to put yourself away privily,' he said. 'I should have instructed you to do so but I knew your wisdom in the matter.'

'I do not understand.'

'I have impregnated you from afar,' he told her. 'Behold, a virgin shall conceive and bear a son.'

'But . . .'

'It is a Sign. Wait now and watch. Great things are afoot in Heaven and earth. You have been chosen among women to be my vessel. Go in peace and attend my messengers.'

He departed without further word, leaving Elisabeth with the sensation that she had fallen off a cliff and landed on pillows.

Chapter 11

It was not going to be easy in a town as confused as Rensburg to find another artist of the necessary skill.

Julius finally decided there was only one recourse open to him. He would have to go to the police to see if they had a record of such a person; and this meant a visit to the Saint Provost. But might this not first furnish an opportunity to call on Konrad – a courtesy call to inform the Sword of Justice of his quest?

Memories of his last visit to the house made Julius shudder, but at least there was the chance that he might see Elisabeth again; and it could scarcely be that the Sword of Justice would belabour the servant of the Leader in his righteous pursuit of assistance.

That same evening, with wildly beating heart, he knocked at the door from which he had been so painfully ejected. A shadow at the upstairs window told him that the old nurse had spied him and would doubtless pass on news of his arrival to her mistress.

The door was answered at length by the serving-maid, who showed no little surprise at his appearance.

'The master?' she asked. 'Are you sure that's who you was wanting?'

'Of course I am sure,' he said loudly, hoping Elisabeth might be listening. 'It is a courtesy call.'

'Courtesy, is it?' the maid replied pertly. 'I hope you get more courtesy than you did last time.'

She showed him into the study and after a few moments Konrad appeared. His face betrayed astonishment and anger tinged with a kind of curiosity. Julius thought he looked thinner; the fire that had burnt in him was not extinguished, but it had changed its constituent in some way.

'You? What is the meaning of this? You have an impertinence coming back to this house. You want another beating?'

'You would surely not beat one who comes on a mission from the Leader?'

'The Leader? What can he want from you?'

'You heard perhaps I was making a portrait of him?'

'There has been talk of it.'

'He has commissioned me to make copies. I need to find at least one other artist in the town – perhaps two or three. I thought before I asked

349

the Provost if he knew of any, it would be civil to ask the Sword of Justice.'

'Humph.'

The change in situation was not lost on Konrad. His expression modulated into a tone of tolerance. One had to learn to modulate in Rensburg if one wished to stay on top. It was a town of altering situations. Besides, modulation was easier today.

He was in a high good humour for his daughter had just told him her news – not all of it, of course – just the fact that she was with child. (She felt that Fierens himself could impart whatever gloss he chose to put on the situation.)

The approach of grandfatherhood delighted Konrad. For a start it strengthened his daughter's position with her husband and underlined his own authority in the town. It would put out of his daughter's head any lingering infatuation with the painter. And altogether it would make life in the big house more familial; the baby would love its grandfather. (Konrad, like most bullies, wanted to be loved and couldn't understand why he was not. It made him treat people all the more bullyingly.)

'So, Painter,' he said. 'You have learned wisdom, I see. Yes, you may ask the Provost for your painters. I rather fancy there is one in gaol awaiting death. If it is necessary, we will spare him and set you over him. I dare say it will make him work the harder if he knows he'll be returned if he botches. I will speak to the Provost myself of the matter.'

Julius was about to thank him when there was a knock at the door. It was the serving-maid again.

'You are needed, sir, at once by the Leader. There's a messenger outside. Will you go with him?'

'Ay, ay, no peace,' said Konrad, importantly. 'Tell him I shall be with him on the instant. No hard feelings, Painter. You understand a daughter's honour? Fetch the painter wine, Billa.'

'Yes, sir.'

The maid closed the door and Konrad gathered up some papers.

'You'll stay and have some wine, Painter? We do not have to fret about you now. I am to be a grandfather.'

'Congratulations, sir,' said Julius, faintly, as the earth seemed to open in front of him.

'Yes, it is come in good time,' said the Sword of Justice.

He paused by the door.

'Thank you for your help,' said Julius.

'I will speak to the Provost of the matter,' Konrad told him again. 'Do not be afraid to ask for any further help you may need.'

Konrad left as Billa came back with the wine. Julius raised the cup to his departing bulk and drank a secret toast to Love.

It was some time since he had tasted wine, and the stuff helped to light certain beacons of hope in his heart which had lain damp and disused for many months. He knew of course that such optimism was unreasonable, merely wine-induced. The fact that his beloved was with someone else's child made any kind of resumption of their union doubly impossible. But then, he reflected, love thrives on impossibility.

He pondered on; looked up at last; and she was there.

He sprang from his seat.

'What?' he cried. 'Oh . . .'

She made no movement but continued to gaze on him.

'Speak to me,' he implored. 'Tell me that you hate me. No . . . that you are happy.'

'I do not hate you,' she said at last. 'You wounded me terribly. But slowly I came to understand a little. Frieda found out things about you . . . and about . . .' She could hardly bring herself to say the word '. . . and about your wife.'

'My wife,' cried Julius. 'She is not my wife.'

'Not your wife?'

Elisabeth turned pale and clutched at a chair for support. Julius rushed over to her and helped her to sit down.

'You must calm yourself,' he told her. 'Please . . . it is not good for you.'

A sudden thought made him go to the door which lay just ajar. Billa almost fell into the room.

'Get out,' he shouted at her. 'Go where you belong. If I find you listening here or telling tales I shall kill you. Do you understand that?'

He looked so fierce that Billa too almost fainted. She half-stumbled as she scuttled away towards the kitchen.

Julius closed the door firmly and turned back to Elisabeth.

'Not your wife?' she said again, more composed but still deathly pale. 'But you told me . . .'

'I did not know then,' he said. 'We were married but she has revealed that she is my half-sister. We cannot be man and wife by the laws of State and Church.'

'Oh, dear God . . .'

'Dear God indeed.'

They looked at each other. Finally she held out her hand to him. He took it and pressed it to his lips.

'It still does not excuse my weakness,' he said at last. 'I thought I was married – even though I sensed perhaps that there was something wrong in it – but I should have told you.'

'You have suffered for it, I think,' she said.

'God knows we both have. I could have endured it for myself, but to make you suffer too when I adored you . . .' He corrected himself. '. . . adore you . . . that was unforgivable.'

She looked at him again, searchingly, scanning his face as though it were a text in which she might find an answer.

'And are you happy?' he asked at length. 'Now that you are with child, his child?'

'Yes,' she said. 'And no.'

There was something else; something she was not telling him.

'Have you ever seen a sheep caught in a thicket?' she asked. 'It winds itself about and about, and the more it struggles the tighter it is entwined, until it pulls too tight and strangles?'

'I have,' he said.

'That is the way it seems with us. At every turn, we seem to get more tangled.'

'Tell me what it is,' he begged her.

'The child is yours,' she said.

Chapter 12

After his interview with Elisabeth, Julius had walked down to the water-gate again and watched the river, swollen now with the recent unseasonably heavy rains (the Saints said they were a portent), jostling the banks and bringing its tribute of boughs, casks, cartwheels and carcases to its distant rendezvous with the Rhine. The water eddied and chafed, covering the muddy reaches that had previously inspired him, and filling him now with images of the flow and counterflow of life and the relentless and unpredictable wheeling of fortune.

Just such confusion and turbulence fretted his own emotions. Elation, yes, that was the principal sensation – nothing could change that – but hatched about with fears. To be by some magic the father of her child and yet separated by obstacles so perilous for her (his own danger seemed insignificant) – these had to be the exquisite and deliberate machinations of a specifically malignant fortune.

Elisabeth and he had agreed that, for the moment, they should not meet unless the course of his duties necessarily took him to the house, which it had to be admitted was unlikely. He could not very well suggest to Konrad – even in his more accommodating mood – that he paint his daughter. There would be too many unfortunate precedents.

So, once they had embraced and declared undying love and wept a little, they had sworn patience and vowed to bide their time.

'I see only disaster in this town,' Julius told her. 'There will be at last a moment to escape, and we shall go together. But it will be after the child is born. Meanwhile you must rest and eat and live at peace, as much for the baby as yourself. The time will come when we will all of us need strength.'

'You are right,' she said, 'but we will miss you. This nightmare city is no place for a baby, even inside such a fat mother as me.'

'Big, not fat,' Julius corrected her gently, putting his hand on the lump.

'Thank you for that,' she laughed.

And then she had cried a little again, and he had embraced her once more, until there was a knock at the door, and old Frieda entered.

'It is time for you to go, Master,' she said. 'I cannot keep that Billa locked up for ever.'

'What will I do without you?' said Elisabeth. 'Now that I have found you again, I cannot just let you go.'

'It is better, darling,' said Frieda. 'If it is thought you have deceived the Leader, you will lose your head and your baby. Whatever he says now – blasphemously – about the work of the Most High. There'll be the Devil to pay.'

'She is right,' said Julius.

'Take care,' cried Elisabeth. 'The lump will want his father.'

She had determined that it was going to be a boy. It had to be.

'I should know,' said Julius. 'I wanted mine but never found him.'

He was not going to worry her now about what would happen if the child should be a girl. It would be tantamount to an admission of wantonness if not high treason.

'How are we going to hear from one another?' she asked.

'There will be ways. Frieda will help? The cronies . . .'

'Nearly all gone, Master. Just myself and one other whom you know. The rest are gone – exile, sickness, age and . . .'

She made a cutting motion.

'But two will be enough,' she continued staunchly.

'You must take care as well, Frieda,' he said. 'We need you to look after these two. Only contact me in extreme emergency. Not at the studio. It will be watched. There is a stone grave of a burgomaster behind St Michael's Church. One of its uprights has tilted a little sideways. A message can be left there. I take a walk in the graveyard every day.'

'And now you must go, Master,' said Frieda again. 'It would be a pity to have won so much and to lose it by being greedy.'

'She will be a nanny to the end,' said Julius, smiling.

'One more kiss.'

They clung together, and he was gone.

Chapter 13

The urgent summons that Konrad had received from the Leader concerned a sad slackening Fierens had noted in the city's progress toward salvation.

Konrad arrived to find the other six members of the inner circle – the Provost and five of the most senior deacons – already assembled and listening to a lucid appraisal of the situation.

It was strange, Konrad thought, how this man could on the one hand be transported to the heights, locked – as he himself declared – in communion with the Highest, and then be so meticulously attentive to the nuts and bolts of armaments, Commissariat or, as now, to the sensitive pulse of a whole city. How he loved and feared the man . . .

'Something will be done. I assure you, Brethren. The town is locked in the winter of sin! These fair flowers that we see deceive us. But I feel stirrings within me, Brethren, that are shoots of God. I shall go to prayer now. Tomorrow you must see how things fall out. Watch . . . listen . . . trust in the Lord.'

'Amen,' cried the inner circle.

Next day Fierens ran naked through the town in a frenzy.

The nakedness was symbolic of the stripping away of earthly trammels, but it did much to commend the handsome Saint to the ladies of the city. He was well-appointed for such a holy person.

Soon he was followed by a motley crew of enthusiasts who flung off their garments and joined the chase. Wobble-breasted matrons, strapping louts of the town, scrawny starveling Saints, who had but recently entered town after God knew what privations on the way . . . a bobbing, exalted throng who did their best to follow the Leader as he foamed and cried in strange tongues, letting the lower angels take the reins as he contemplated a Deity who, more and more, presented to his enraptured gaze a mirror-image of himself.

The lower angels at length brought him back to the town square, where he fell into a silent ecstasy for three days.

The motley crew of followers mostly did the same, though some sneaked off after a while, finding silent ecstasy not half such fun as frenzy.

The inner circle led by Konrad and the Provost with his guard kept watch and waited as the Leader had ordained.

On the fourth day, Fierens arose and – in the most matter-of-fact of tones – as if he had been no more than napping – called for the entire population of the town to gather in the market-square.

When they were assembled, he climbed upon his podium and addressed them as follows:

'Good news, Saints and Brethren. We are to hasten forward. There is little time. The Lord has made it plain, however, that if our town is to be saved – and we do want to be saved . . .'

'Yes, we do,' shouted Konrad, the Provost and the guard.

'I cannot hear you,' said Fierens.

'YES WE DO,' shouted the town.

'But we cannot be saved with a city constitution that has been created by man. We must have one created by God . . .'

'BY GOD,' thundered the town.

'And God has said no burgomasters or town council. Where do we read in holy writ of burgomasters and town council?'

'Nowhere,' yelled the town, for burgomaster and council had never been popular. 'NO BURGOMASTER OR TOWN COUNCIL!'

'What God has ordained instead is a leader of the people . . . that is, myself.'

'LEADER, LEADER . . .'

The crowd took up the chant, repeating the word like a mantra, till the sound bounced off the bricks and rolled back in waves across the water meadows, making the dozing mercenaries stand-to with widened eyes.

'And, on the model of Ancient Israel, twelve Elders. A list of those Elders will appear tomorrow at the Town Hall. I can tell you now it will include Acting Burgomaster Konrad Harting and several other members of the guilds, as well as some former councillors, for these are men known to you, and God does not want to raise only strangers over your heads. But there will be Saints as well, for you have grown to love and respect those whom God hath put among you. Rejoice, therefore. You are rid of your old imperfect systems and now have God to thank for such freedom as you now possess.'

'THANKS BE TO GOD.'

'But it is no light matter, Brethren. We are at war. Not just with the sin in ourselves but with those servants of Antichrist outside who wish us ill and would drag us back into the stench of mortality. Our rule, God's rule, must be obeyed. The new government has absolute authority over us – yes, I include myself as subject as well as Leader. All matters, public and private, spiritual and material, shall come under its jurisdiction. It will have the power of life and death over all. Naturally the just will have nothing to fear. Only the transgressors need tremble. The rest of us can rejoice in the knowledge that the Great Day is now closer than ever. And to mark that inestimable blessing, I proclaim this day a holiday. Open the stores, Provost. Bring out the bread . . .'

'Hurray for the Leader,' someone shouted, 'three cheers for the Leader!'

'HURRAY, HURRAY, HURRAY,' yelled the populace. 'FREE-DOM . . . LEADER . . . BREAD . . .'

'What the Devil's all that noise in the town?' asked the Bishop. 'I don't like it. They should be shaking in their shoes. I thought we'd killed their Leader chap. It should've been bad for morale.'

'Don't ask me,' said his brother-in-law. 'They're all mad in that town of yours. I wouldn't want it back if you gave it me on a plate. For two pins, I'd pack up and go home.'

'Oh, come on,' said the Bishop. 'We can't give up now. The whole of Germany would laugh at us.'

'The whole of Germany *is* laughing at us,' said his brother-in law. 'And it isn't just Germany.'

Chapter 14

Next day, as the new Council met for the first time, Julius called on the Provost with his request for whatever artists might be in the town.

'Artists are shit,' said the Provost. 'Do you want me to spell it out for you?'

'That is not what the Leader thinks,' replied Julius, brave in his new privilege.

'Watch yourself, Painter. You may strut now but the Leader has a way of changing his mind . . .'

'Look . . . I don't want to cause trouble. I just need more hands . . .'

'Cut you some if you like.'

The Provost smiled grimly at his little joke – or was it a joke? Julius tried a new tack.

'Mr Harting said there might be one in prison.'

'Artist? I think we strung him up yesterday.'

'Please. Could I go and ask? It's urgent. The Leader wants ten copies of his portrait by the end of the month.'

'Oh, very well. Take this note to the gaol. If he's there, you can have him. Nasty little piece of work. Drawing funny pictures of the Saints, he was. That's unlawful. He'd be laughing at God next. You tell him I'm watching him.'

'Any more?'

'Any more what?'

'Any more artists you know of?'

'Not if I can help it. Reckon we hanged them all. That's good, though, isn't it? We don't hang pictures here. We hang artists. Ho ho ho.'

And ho very ho to you, thought Julius, hurrying over to the gaol, because he might, or might not, just be in time to save the sinful dauber.

As luck would have it, the artist still survived, though only just. He was due to be executed next day.

'It doesn't seem right to release him with the Leader just out of an ecstasy and all,' said the gaoler. 'Still, you can have him if you want. The executioner'll be pleased. All this executing is giving him executioner's elbow.'

A small, tousle-haired young man was brought out of a cell and presented himself to Julius as Hans-Peter Schedel, painter, of Cologne.

'Am I glad to see you,' he said.

'You are well met,' replied Julius. 'I hope you can paint.'

'I learned under a man who had worked for Dürer,' he said.

It was a promising start.

'And what are you doing in Rensburg?'

'I had been commissioned to paint a mural in the Abbey. It was a long job. The town was taken over before I was fully paid. I had no money so I had to stay. I wish I'd never seen the place.'

'Come over to my studio, and let's see what you can do.'

As they walked through the town, a fellow detached himself from a wall where he was lounging and followed them unnoticed, while Julius told his companion something of his own history in the town.

'I was sent here, I don't know why, to do something, I don't know what, and in so doing I met the greatest joy and the hardest misfortune,' he said.

He had taken a liking to the fellow. It was good to have the company of a painter again.

'It sounds like a riddle.'

'Indeed. That is just what it is.'

'Like life itself, as you might say.'

Julius smiled cautiously. It was not exactly forbidden to smile in public but it was not encouraged.

'Yes, perhaps that is the nature of the riddle. Tell me, what brought you to the gaol,' he said.

'Simply some sketches I was doing in my room, looking out on the square. The Saints present wonderful subjects. There is no need for caricature. My landlady reported me and I was accused of mockery.'

'Mockery is unlawful,' said Julius in the Provost's tones. They both laughed.

They had now arrived at Julius's studio, and he took him up the rickety stairs over the shop. Throwing open the door, he ushered his companion into the room, and removed the drapes from the wall.

Hans-Peter stopped short with a whistle.

'What on earth is that? It is astonishing . . . wonderful . . .'

'It is the puzzle, or part of it,' Julius told him. 'I put it on the wall so I could study it the better.'

'But that is not your work?'

'No. That is Hieronymus Bosch.'

'I have heard and even seen something of his.'

'I was born in his town.'

The little painter advanced to the wall and studied it more closely.

'A man could spend a lifetime on that puzzle,' he said at last. 'Do you know what any of it means?'

'Some of it, not all. But the hardest part is, I have to finish it and I

359

shall not find happiness until I do. How do you finish something whose meaning you don't know?'

'It will be shown to you perhaps,' said the little man. 'This town has not finished with us yet.'

They stood awhile in front of the Garden whose secret remained within.

'Come,' said Julius, 'let me show you the portrait that we have to copy.'

He lifted the drapes off Fierens' picture, and the little painter whistled again.

'Not bad,' he said, 'for a portrait of a madman. You have caught those eyes which see God and through which God looks out. We believe that Thou wilt come to be our Judge, eh? Perhaps Fierens really is God. Have you thought of that?'

'I have. And sometimes the idea seems quite credible. For who but someone as mad as Fierens could have created such a place as this?'

The two men laughed bitterly.

'Come,' said Julius. 'Let us to work.'

Outside, the listener shifted his position the better to put his ear to the door.

Chapter 15

The first thing the Council of the Elders did was to abolish money (having previously collected all they could).

Anyone not on military service who worked for a living became an employee of the city. The good of the community was considered to be reward enough.

The guilds, whose job it had been in the past to monitor and regulate reward, now had little more to do, and died with their function.

As for crime, murder and stealing were already punishable by death, but to the list were added lying, slander, avarice and quarrelling. Nor was this all. Death was now to be meted out as a punishment for all manner of insubordinations. A son who reviled his father; a wife who challenged her husband; anyone who disobeyed God's commands and those of his instruments on earth, the Elders of Rensburg; all were, at least in theory, candidates for the high jump.

Some of these offences might not, of course, always be reported – although there were now instances of children exposing their mothers for domestic disobedience and even vice versa – but whatever happened in practice, the new measure served as a stick with which to beat the populace. You never knew who might report you, or for what. You never knew when the Sword of Justice and his bodyguard might not come a-knocking at your door . . .

As for man's oldest pastime, the Elders came down on that like a ton of pricks, as Blommardine so elegantly put it. The only sexual coupling allowed was in marriage between two Anabaptists – and that was only in the interest of procreation (a difficult one to prove, but nevertheless in the statute book, and at least one Saint paid the penalty for lusting unprocreatively). Anything else, including marriage with a 'Godless one', was viewed as adultery and/or fornication, which were of course capital offences and to be shunned like the plague. Masturbation was another black mark, and people went to great lengths to avoid being caught at it.

'Fuck me,' said Blommardine when Julius told her of the latest fusillade of edicts, as she came swimming up drowsily from an orgy of incubi.

'I fear that would be a capital offence,' said Julius.

He returned home but rarely now, preferring to sleep in his studio away from the reek of pomatum.

'We are married. We are both re-baptized,' replied Blommardine.

'You are my half-sister,' insisted Julius. 'Even the Saints would give that the thumbs down.'

'You will go on about it, won't you?' she said, crossly. 'I wish I'd never told you now. It was just a joke.'

'You're lying,' he said.

'Prove it.'

'Give me the papers.'

'No.'

'That's insubordination.'

'Go and fuck yourself.'

'Please, Blommardine.'

'Well, lie with me, then.'

'No.'

'No song, no supper.'

'Look,' he pleaded. 'I've done you no harm. Why've you got it in for me? I've helped you. I don't know why but I even quite like you.'

'Thanks very much.'

'But we cannot be married.'

'Look,' she said. 'All right. I'll let you off the hook. Sometime. In a little while. Not now. This town is so boring. Why should you be happy if I can't? Why did Mosman have to die?'

'It wasn't my fault,' he said. 'Why don't you get your claws into Fierens? Bet you can't.'

She could never resist a challenge like that.

'What d'you bet?'

'Anything you like.'

'I'll hold you to that,' she said.

It crossed his mind that, if she did succeed, Fierens might be hoist with his own petard and be arraigned by his own Elders – which would be no bad thing – and then of course Blommardine would be too, and that would be hard commons for the little cow. He didn't want to cause her death.

'Perhaps you'd better not,' he said.

'What? Afraid you'll lose?'

'Afraid that if you win you might be strung up for fornication. You are after all my sister.'

'Oh, that,' she sniffed scornfully. 'D'you really think Fierens would let them? Still, nice of you to think of it. You're not such a bad old fart.'

'Give me the papers, then.'

'Down, boy. Later.'

362

Chapter 16

The sexual winter, coming as it did in the buoyant time of year, caused a number of long faces in the town. Even the Sword of Justice drooped a little, though Konrad had put that side of his life resolutely behind him – violence was anyway a better substitute for lust, and legal with it. Still, you couldn't help feeling a sweet ache sometimes in the loins, or waking up with egg-white on your nightshirt. Meanwhile all who were reported to the Provost were arrested, and Konrad himself took over from the arm-sick executioner.

Julius and Hans-Peter worked away resolutely on their copies, though Hans-Peter did sometimes turn and look longingly at the girls in the Earthly Garden.

Outside, flagellation made quite a revival as people sought for diversions from their more natural inclinations. Even people who were never before much interested in carnality became quite fidgety.

And then suddenly everything changed.

How Blommardine effected the alteration Julius never asked and never knew. That it was a result of some intervention of hers he did not doubt for a moment. One day she just appeared and said:

'You lost.'

'Congratulations,' he replied.

He did not question the truth of her claim. She did not lie about such things.

'He is going to establish polygamy,' she said.

'He is what?'

'Polygamy,' she repeated, as naturally as if it were peppercorns.

'I don't believe it.'

'Go out and listen in a day or two. After he's told the Elders.'

He went to the window and gazed out at the town. Smoke drifted from a hundred chimneys. Washing wagged in the breeze. Children played. It didn't look like Gomorrah.

'I thought they were supposed to be Saints,' he said.

'They make their own rules. God is in them. They are free spirits.'

'How did you do it?'

She smiled slyly.

'You have started mischief,' he told her.

'He is God, you know,' she said. 'I am Magdalen. The devils have gone. It was better than anything I have known.'

'It would be, wouldn't it?' said Julius.

'The notion came to him as we lay together. "I have a wife already," he said. That's your fancy one, Julius, he was talking about. "But I cannot sin," he went on. "Therefore it must be that it is lawful to have many wives even as Father Abraham. The Lord has spoken it." My God, he gave me a humping. He'd been holding onto that since I don't know when. Doesn't seem to care for your Elisabeth, though. Heaven knows how she got pregnant.'

She looked at him with her green eyes.

'You wouldn't know anything about that, I suppose?'

'Certainly not,' he snapped.

'Keep your hair on, brother-lover. Just teasing.'

'One day you'll go too far,' he said.

'And then what will you do, brother-lover? Hm? Anyway, now I'm his second wife . . . third wife . . . sorry . . . did you know he had a wife in Leyden?'

Julius's heart leaped. His early instinct was confirmed. Elisabeth was not married to the man after all! He was a bigamist, even if he was tin-pot god of this town. Once this madness was over, as surely it must be one day, they could be legally married. He made a mental note to leave the news for Elisabeth by the burgomaster's tomb. At least it would comfort her in the weeks ahead.

'What are you thinking, brother-lover?'

'I'm thinking that you cannot be married both to me and him. Abraham's wives didn't have husbands,' he told her.

'Quick, aren't you?' she said. 'All right, yes. You have your severance. No papers yet, though. Let's see how you behave. You owe me, remember. Not the other way round.'

'For God's sake, Blommardine.'

'For Fierens' sake. He makes puppets of the rest of you – yes, even Mosman.'

'Some of the town aren't going to like it,' Julius observed.

'Some of the town aren't here to have it. They left their women behind when they skedaddled. There's three times as many marriageable women as men in this town. Polygamy makes sense. We must breed for the future.'

She was already beginning to talk like a politician's wife.

Chapter 17

Fierens had drawn a new strength and exaltation from his encounter with Blommardine. He had known of her, of course, in the town, had felt her presence, experienced with her the dives into the pit and the wriggling of the loins with the myriad satyrs that enflamed, gratified her body and gnawed away at her soul. But even she who was low, engulfed in sin, even she had become the servant of the most high, the Magdalen now to his own Godhead. Besides, the lower angels who were housed in his gender related that they had never seen such pure and sinless delight since the very days of Eden itself.

He had always been a highly sexed man, and now he was a highly sexed God.

He explained the change in the marriage laws to an attentive meeting of preachers and Elders.

'God has revealed to me,' said he (it was not yet quite time to tell them that God and he were one), 'God has revealed that we shall not be strong enough to come to His eternal throne or to be ranked as City of God when we are but a village.'

'A village,' cried Hass, who was faithful as ever but a Rensburger all the same, 'but Rensburg is a city. We have a Cathedral, we had a . . .'

He was going to say bishop but bit his tongue just in time.

'Such trappings as these are insignificant in God's eyes. God wants souls, Brother Hass. We are short of souls. Or we shall be . . .'

'There are more in the town than there ever were, Leader.'

'But they are women, Brother Hass. Three women to one man. What does that mean?'

'It means we shall dwindle,' said the Sword of Justice, as Hass floundered. 'Unless . . .'

'Unless what, Sword of Justice?' said Fierens coaxingly.

'Unless husbands can be found for them.'

'Ah. Husbands,' said Fierens, peering round. 'Husbands . . . But where shall we find husbands for them when the hosts of Midian are encamped around?'

'We shall not find them,' said Hass at last, looking glum. 'We shall dwindle as the Sword of Justice has said.'

There did indeed seem to be an impasse.

'Fear not,' said Fierens, 'for the Lord has spoken.'

The Elders looked at him wonderingly. Was he going to produce husbands out of a hat? With Fierens it seemed anything was possible.

'Your seed shall be as the flowers of the field, as the sand that is upon the sea-shore,' Fierens continued. 'And how may this be, my Elders? Why, the Lord commands that we follow the precept of "increase and multiply", *crescere* and *multiplicamini*, Brethren.'

'That's all very well, Leader,' said one of the Elders who had previously been a minor aristocrat, selected by Fierens as having some influence in the Old Town. 'But how do we do it? No husbands, no *multiplicamini*.'

'We adopt for the New Jerusalem the sacred practice of the Patriarchs of Israel.'

There was no need to explain to the Elders what that meant. A gasp arose from a dozen throats, and the argument started.

Fierens did not want to order them. His position was not yet so strong that such a radical if natural progression would be accomplished without the agreement of these lieutenants. Of course he knew – because He knew all – that by breaking down the tradition of marriage, the most stabilizing force in society, the rest of his plan could follow the more easily. But this was the vital step. He allowed the debate to last for several days.

On his side initially were the Provost (who was *always* loyal to the Leader), the Sword of Justice (who saw a way at least of combining severity with lubricity), and the prophets Mordecai and Habakkuk (who believed in the Old Testament way of doing things).

In the middle were waverers such as Hass, who truly wanted to believe but took some persuading. And in the other camp were the aristocrat Elder (who said he'd never heard of anything so disgusting in his life), the ex-leader of the Ropemakers' Guild, and two ex-councillors, all men who represented the interests of the former Rensburg.

'That is what you are,' said Fierens, his patience finally running out on the fifth day. 'You are more involved in the past than the future. You seek the old Rensburg, not the New Jerusalem. Go, then. Find it. Walk the streets. Ask for it where it may be. Where is the old Rensburg? It is smoke, Brethren. A dream. Dirty water that has been flushed down the sewer. If that is where you are, you are nowhere.'

'But some of the past is good,' cried the ropemaker. 'It is not all bad. You yourself invoke the Patriarchs of Israel.'

'Do not dare,' said Fierens in a terrifying, quiet voice, 'do not dare to compare your miserable town with those of the Fathers of our Religion. Was Antichrist abroad then? Was the Day of Judgement looming, pendulous as that cloud you see out of the window? This was a wicked town and it is to be cleansed. It is to be scrubbed and fubbed and washed and brushed until it is fit to house the Community of Saints.

He that is not with me is against me, and the wrath of God – I swear it – shall pursue him to the bubbling gates of Hell. Is that not so, Sword of Justice? Shall we take a vote, then, Brethren?'

The motion was carried unanimously, and the preachers went forth to propagate the new doctrine in market-place and pulpit.

Chapter 18

Hans-Peter and Julius were collecting new materials from the chandler's beside the square a week later when they were aware of a commotion beside the Town Hall.

A body of citizens, old Rensburgers – Julius recognized many of them – ran along with drawn swords calling on all who loved God and their wives to join them in a rising against the new government and its order of polygamy. The edict, it seemed, was the last straw to those who had already borne almost every other humiliation in the name of a rectitude that seemed now to be arbitrarily cast aside.

'We should watch this, Hans-Peter,' said Julius. 'Have you your charcoal and paper?'

Catching the Provost and the guard by surprise, the Rensburgers surrounded them and threw them into prison. They then proceeded to the Burgomaster's chamber and arrested Fierens, who was in consultation with the Sword of Justice.

Fierens walked out with an air of absolute composure.

'Oh, my poor sinners,' he cried, halting the little procession when it emerged.

'Silence, Dutchman,' shouted a saddler whom Julius knew slightly.

'I have no country,' replied Fierens. 'I am of the kingdom of God. But you, Rensburger, enjoy this day, for I have it on the highest authority that it shall be your last.'

The saddler turned pale at the words. There was something prophetically convincing about Fierens' utterances.

'Move him along,' he shouted roughly. 'We are the masters now.'

But Fierens had more to say and, though surrounded by armed men, there were none that dared stop him.

'Blow ye the trumpet of Zion,' he cried, and it was as if his voice came from a great height, reverberating like thunder across the square, 'and sound an alarm in my holy mountain.'

Even the guards on the wall, who could not possibly hear, turned towards the scene as though the words were carried to their inward ear.

'Let all the inhabitants of the land tremble, for the day of the Lord cometh, for it is nigh at hand . . .'

'Are you getting this, Hans-Peter?' whispered Julius.

'Yes, yes. He is magnificent.'

368

'You don't turn a city upside down with a croak and an apologetic cough,' said Julius.

'Shhh,' people near them cautioned – some of them townspeople, Julius noted.

'A day of darkness and of gloominess,' continued Fierens, warming to his text, 'a day of clouds and of thick darkness, as the fog spread upon the mountains. A great people and a strong there hath not been ever the like, neither shall there be any more after it, even to the years of many generations . . .' He paused momentarily, then began again with a voice like a trumpet. 'Are ye that people? Do ye embrace that glorious hope of joy everlasting? Or are ye just . . . Rensburgers?'

He spat the word as if it were a toad on his lips.

'Rensburgers,' he repeated, 'married to the gross filth of worldliness, wedded to vices and possessions and beastly transitoriness which will all be swept away and you along with it – a tumbling of arms and legs and carts and candlesticks and ribbons and blood – when the Day of Justice comes? Take me to prison, Saddler. Yes, I know who you are. I do not wish to be here. I would rather be in prison when vanity walks free. Take me, I say.'

The saddler barked an order and the little procession moved on. Already there were calls from the crowd to set the Leader free. There were little sallies forward, but they were beaten back by swords and the procession continued.

'Should we not join the townspeople?' asked Hans-Peter, quietly. 'They want to end this madness. Surely they need all the help they can get?'

Julius reflected. The painter was right, and yet instinct told him there was something wrong with this uprising. There were thousands of Saints in the town who would not give up their Leader lightly. This little venture had all the appearance of being badly planned and hurriedly organized. A proper revolt would have seen to it that the armoury was barred, that the Saints were surprised in their beds, that the Leader was killed as soon as arrested. It was no good taking him to gaol. What were they planning? Some kind of trial?

'I don't mind dying,' he told Hans-Peter. 'But there are things I have been charged to do and one – no two – whom I must protect. I'm afraid these Rensburgers are too muddled and too few to do anything but be taken and executed.'

'That is my opinion,' said Hans-Peter, 'but it hurts me to watch and do nothing.'

'It is sometimes the hardest part,' said Julius.

But when he watched next day as the Saints surrounded the company of Rensburgers, overpowered them, and began to execute them under the ordinance of Fierens and the Sword of Justice (both unwisely left

369

alive), he knew it was much harder to be taken out and decapitated in the presence of your wife and children.

Some met their death bravely, seemingly proud and unmoved, disdaining the madness of the Saints. Others uttered dreadful oaths and imprecations. Others still – this was the most disturbing – wept and grovelled and begged for mercy and had to be dragged, shitting themselves, to the block, where half a dozen blows would finally separate them from their seats of reason. Only when thirty headless bodies lay on the carts drawn up in the town square – with another cart for the heads – did the Sword of Justice pause.

There was one man left: the saddler who, it seemed, was ringleader.

'What will you do with me, Masters?' demanded the wretched man.

'Spare him,' sobbed his wife, a pretty woman with golden hair.

Her beauty was one of the reasons the saddler had been up in arms.

'Daddy,' shouted his little girl, fair as an angel.

She wrenched herself away from her mother and ran to where he stood. He bent and gave her a kiss, though his arms were bound. She hugged him close and sobbed. Julius had never seen such misery in a man's face.

'Take her away,' shouted Konrad, 'or by God she will share her father's punishment. Away, brat.'

Rough guards jerked her arms away and threw her back at her mother.

'Look to her, wench,' shouted the Provost.

'Take her away. Go,' cried the wretched saddler to his wife.

'No,' ordered Fierens. 'Make them watch. We have no wives, or children, no husbands here. We are the family of God. And we must see what punishment falls on those who lay hands upon the Lord's anointed.'

The saddler was first stripped to his shirt, then made to mount a box under the gibbet.

'You'll hang me, then?' he asked the Sword of Justice.

'Hanging's too good for you,' Konrad replied.

A terrible realization started to dawn on the poor man, but he was determined not to whimper in front of his child.

'String him up,' ordered the Sword of Justice.

The box was knocked away and the saddler dangled, kicking. His bowels loosened.

'Let him down,' ordered the Sword of Justice.

The saddler, half dead, fell heavily into his own shit and lay there, stunned, a terrible red wheal, like a choker, around his neck.

A ghastly cry was torn from his wife, who held her hands tight over her daughter's eyes.

'Let her see, Mistress,' observed Fierens.

Her arms were held back by strong hands, and the little girl was thus able to witness the next part of the proceedings.

As her father swam back to consciousness, his shirt and cod-piece were taken off, and a sharp sword slit all the way up his belly from his penis to his breastbone. A great mass of bowel and blood tumbled out and lay on his lap, pulsating like a dog. The man, who had behaved with the greatest bravery until now, emitted a noise that should never come from a human.

The little girl fainted. The man turned appalled eyes at his wife, who hung motionless in the arms of the thugs behind her.

Julius suddenly heard himself shouting:

'Stop, stop, stop.'

It was, of course, far too late, and made not the slightest bit of difference. Hans-Peter looked at him aghast.

Fierens, however, was quite pleased by the interruption.

'By all means, wait, Sword of Justice. Our painter wants to make a record.'

And so the whole repulsive procedure had to wait while charcoal and paper were found.

'You'd better do it,' said Hans-Peter. 'Remember what you said.'

'See all right, Painter?' asked Fierens. 'Good. I shall want to see your findings. Proceed, Sword of Justice.'

The saddler, not dead by any means, in fact still horribly alive, but in a terrible limbo where death was certain and infinitely preferable, started to make bubbling noises. Agonized and shocked though he was, he did not want the next part.

The Sword of Justice lifted the axe of Justice and started cutting off the saddler's arms and legs.

The crowd was riveted. Oh, there had been executions before, but never so many. And hanging, drawing and quartering, well ... you didn't get one of those in a month of Sundays.

'Funny, really, seeing a man like that. Makes you realize we're all just meat,' said a red-face to his neighbour.

Piercing liquid noises which had never been heard in an abattoir, which shouldn't be heard in a nightmare, accompanied the dismembering of the man.

At the end, he lay there, just a trunk with a head, bleeding from every extremity, eyes fluttering and rolling, a travesty of a thing you could never believe had once been a mother's baby.

'Daddy,' screamed the little girl, who had recovered from her swoon.

The eyes fluttered.

'You couldn't call a thing like that Daddy, could you, now,' said the

371

Sword of Justice. 'That thing's been prepared for the Devil's kitchen. That thing's going to roast on the Devil's spit. Leave him . . .'

He raised his hand as one or two, friends of the wife, came forward.

'Let him be like that as a caution. He won't last long. The dogs will finish him off.'

Chapter 19

After such a display, it was perhaps not surprising that polygamy caught on fast in Rensburg.

The preachers gave the lead, and it was quickly clear that you could not be taken seriously as a preacher unless you had at least half a dozen wives sitting attentively, pew-deep, at your every sermon. Soon all the men, with varying degrees of willingness, adopted the idea and the hunt was on for wives.

The women themselves had mixed views on the notion. There were those who were more carnally inclined who liked the concept and who made it their business to get bagged by the most attractive husbands – men whom previously perhaps, they had merely eyed in church and whose images had presented themselves only in the sticky fingertips of darkness. There were others who found the idea of great imposition. A statute was passed requiring all women under the age of fifty to be married to one of the godly. It was the misfortune, for instance, of a certain pious and chaste spinster of Carver's Lane to find herself now fourth wife to a 'faithful' syphilitic from Nijmegen. Another gentle virgin, sweet but somewhat retarded, became the property of a sadist. Such cases were not uncommon, since there were few single men, and such as there were got snapped up by the more attractive or pushier young ladies.

Hans-Peter was momentarily gratified to find himself the centre of many attentions, finally selecting a bubbly red-head from Cleves with all the characteristics a painter most enjoys. It was true he had to take on another sickly-faced matron from Arnhem as second wife, but since she spent most of her time in church it did not seriously inconvenience their exercises.

Julius was nearly required to marry again, but – whether because of Blommardine's influence with Fierens, or because he pleaded his work for the Leader was his 'wife' – he was allowed to remain undisturbed.

Disturbed he would almost certainly have been. Several women in a household all married to the same man was a recipe for trouble, and all manner of domestic disturbances began to break out, even though quarrelling incurred the death penalty.

A dozen women were, in fact, executed for domestic strife. Others who wished to remain faithful to their absent husbands (prudently departed from the town to seek work and opportunities for their families elsewhere), and refused to accept the new marriage laws, were publicly stripped and whipped, and the more intractable were also put to death.

However, like the grass under the roadway which finally pushes through the cobbles, the wonderful capacity for domestic dissonance that two women in a household can evoke won the day, and soon divorce came to be permitted; and not long after that the marriage service in church was abolished, and a single civic ceremony could close as well as open the nuptial tie – sometimes in as short a span as a single day.

Free love had come to Rensburg. But though some spoke of the return of the Free Spirits – and there were those in the town, as Konrad knew, who professed to be their representatives – the practice of love in Rensburg was as far from the Religion of Love as Hell is from the heights of the Empyrean.

Julius, reflecting on the extraordinary perversion of human institutions that had come to pass, and harking back to his days in Italy where the human spirit, though inevitably sullied in some areas, had soared so gloriously in others, could not see the condition of the town as an example of God punishing man but of man punishing himself. It was as if man, peering into a mirror, had seen only his imperfections, and become enraged, heaping up the imperfections a hundredfold.

As he toiled away in his studio on the sixth copy, alone – his colleague being engaged upon the red-head – his mind turned once more upon his predicament here in the town. For two pins, for less than two pins, for half a pin, he would leave today, go down to the water-gate, swim across the river. Oh, he might be shot, or drowned, or taken prisoner the other side and hanged. Worst of all, he might be captured and publicly tortured in the town square – for the Sword of Justice was very hot on deserters. But he would do it – for reiterated nightmares tend to infect their occupants just as a prison pales the skin and rots the spirit of its inmates. He could feel himself changing for the worse. Surfeited with horrors, he was becoming hardened. He had wished the saddler would stop bubbling, not out of sympathy but almost from irritation.

Why had he been sent here? You will do it, the Grand Master had said. He did not have to obey. The money had not been enormous. He could have obtained commissions elsewhere. He had gone along with it because – as so often in his life – he had had no clear idea of what he wanted to do, where he wanted to go, who he wanted to be.

'You will do it.'

Almost as if it had been some kind of Grail, the hunt for something superb, amidst horrible dangers and monstrous adversaries, that would finally make all whole; the magisterium; the Elixir.

And what had he found? Love.

He looked at his master's picture again. Yes, love was the word one kept coming back to. Love was the Academicians' theme, love was the Grand Master's creed, love was Christ's teaching even in this hellish town.

'Beloved, let us love.' Love, not as lust, but sometimes severe, sometimes adamantine, totally demanding, strong as death. In fact, as he gazed, his mind sucked into that beckoning foreground in front of the whirl of the riders on their strange and various mounts, following the bride and bridegroom, he saw that Love was death as much as life, an act of giving as much as receiving. The comforting women offering refreshment, the bird offering fruit, hovering above the mouths of the dying, were almost like bees upon a flower. It was food, it was fertilizing. The wheel was everything and the wheel was Love.

He closed his eyes. He could hear the murmuring of rivers, the flutter of soft wings, and flowers that rang like bells, and bird-song, music that the breezes play upon strings, and the distant lolloping upon turf of gentle, terrible paws.

'Julius. Julius.'

It was the voice of the man in the corner, with the woman's beautiful face beside him; the clothed man, the knowing man, the man he had known all his life.

'What is it?' he heard himself say, though he did not open his lips.

'You must endure, Julius. No turning now. You are more than halfway there.'

'I could take her now and go.'

'That is not the way. You are the one, Julius. The world is near to death – no, not to death, for death is life – it is near to nothing, to the End. Only Love can save it.'

'But . . . Why me?'

'You were appointed. Do you not want to save the world? Your love, your child?'

'Yes, yes,' he groaned. 'But I am weak.'

'You will find strength.'

'And when may we go from here?'

'When you have finished Hell.'

The voice faded. Other voices took over, a cheerful distant babble as at a happy gathering, snatches of song, drowsy-making as for one who listens with eyes half-closed, too weary to take part, at the corner of a party.

Julius did not know how long he slept. At one point in his dreams, or out of them, he was aware of thunder but, when he awoke, the sky was clear and Hans-Peter was shaking him excitedly. There was the sound of cheering from the street.

'What . . . what is it?' he asked, cross with himself for sleeping when the deadline for the pictures was so close.

'They have fired pamphlets into the besiegers' camp, offering the mercenaries money to join us. The Bishop cannot pay them. And now two hundred of them are coming in, while others have simply packed up and gone home.'

'You seem pleased, Hans-Peter.'

'Well . . .'

The little artist's enthusiasm subsided as he thought about it.

'I suppose not,' he said. 'Though I must say domestic life with Carlotta is turning out to be rather jolly. I don't want that to end.'

'I don't want anything to end until Elisabeth has had her child.'

He had told Hans-Peter something of their story. It was probably a mistake. It was a mistake to trust anyone in Rensburg. But he had after all saved the man's life.

'It is typical of this town,' said Hans-Peter. 'You can't even take sides. Heads you lose and tails you lose.'

'At least if the Bishop wins things can get back to some kind of normality – even though I suspect he'll have his revenge on the town. On the other hand, if Fierens wins, the curtains come down. Madness becomes the rule of law. And not just cities but whole nations go into the dark,' said Julius.

'You have a strange turn of phrase, Julius. Where did you pick up such things?'

Julius laughed.

'Oh, in Italy, I dare say. You know what dramatists they are.'

Hans-Peter nodded, though he had never been out of North Germany.

'I say,' he remarked, indicating the pile of copies. 'We are doing well.'

'Yes, we are,' said Julius. 'And we would do even better if you gave your paint-brush as much exercise as you give your pencil.'

Hans-Peter giggled.

'Speak for yourself,' he said. 'A pencil may be what they call it in Brabant but in Cologne we have a stouter term.'

Julius threw a brush at him.

'It's a bit rich, though, isn't it?' said Hans-Peter after a while, picking up a fresh board – they were painting the copies on wood – and placing it on his easel.

'What is?'

'Offering them money when we don't even pay our own men. How does Fierens square that with his conscience?'

'Fierens doesn't have a conscience,' Julius told him, 'it's one of the reasons he thinks he's God.'

Chapter 20

Blommardine was not the only one of Fierens' wives acquired during that hot high summer. Indeed, he came to have fifteen in all, for he had discovered prodigious powers in his loins and liked to unleash them as often as the lower angels thought it necessary, which was often. Blommardine, however, was the chief wife, and had a hand in selecting most of the others. Some were quite young girls of fifteen or sixteen – the lower angels liked them young – and she took great pains and some pleasure in instructing them in the matter of their bodies and the best way to please the Leader. She gave them baths and washed their breasts for them; and then lay with them afterwards in friendliness, putting her hand between their legs, testing them ingratiatingly for virginity. She had decided that, apart from herself, only virgins could marry the Leader, the French sickness having several times been reported in the town and spreading like wildfire in the provinces.

So Blommardine patted and stroked and tweaked, and gave the young virgins more pleasure, it was said, than the lower angels themselves but the lower angels didn't seem to mind, and sometimes came and supervised the proceedings.

At the same time as this increase in uxoriousness, however, Fierens did not – as some commanders do – show any sign of diminution or loss of interest in the war. He was in no means a sapped Mark Antony. Indeed, tireless energy was one of the outstanding qualities of his leadership – a leadership which by any reckoning had to be rated as impressive. Admittedly, he would have said he had the advantages of an all-seeing eye, but he did indeed seem to possess (as Konrad had noted) a remarkable grip of detail.

He laid in stores, he organized a proper commissariat, he first imported gunpowder and later even made it, he saw that arquebuses and pistolets were regularly cleaned (he specified lint and wire brushes), his armourer turned out a regular supply of halberds, good-quality cannonballs and light-duty cuirasses. He held regular exercises on the walls, practising repulsion of invaders with stones, boiling water, flaring pitch and night-soil. In the town, discipline was mustard-hot. All knew their task and station, whether it were to fight, support, recruit, train, refresh, replenish or repair.

Guard duties were strictly defined and rosters properly organized.

Guards were visited by a deacon two or three times a night, and woe betide any that were caught sleeping. Sleep eternal was threatened and occasionally executed – though on the whole the soldiers were a privileged body.

Some of the mercenaries, however, who had been lured in with gifts of money, spending it illegally in an illicit tavern and causing a near-riot when they should have been on duty, were rounded up and shot, thus ridding the town of poor soldiers and unseemly expense.

In three separate sorties on the besiegers – how different from the Mosman debacle – enemy guns were spiked and important prisoners taken. And when the Bishop tried to take a leaf from Fierens' book and shot pamphlets over the walls proclaiming a general pardon if the town gave in, Fierens responded with a typical mixture of practicality and rigour.

Anyone reading them would be executed.

There were many pamphlets lying around Rensburg that week, only eventually collected by special contingents of long-sighted Saints, who picked the paper with averted gaze . . .

Perhaps infuriated by the lack of response to this latest ruse, or enflamed by the heat of the summer – there was a near-drought in the camp – or fearful that his limited supply of allies, vassals and mercenaries would dwindle away toward harvest-time – it was always a tendency – the Bishop, listening to his generals, decided on a make-or-break attack upon the city wall.

Siege-ladders were prepared, summer-sleepy halberdiers were rounded up, cannon wheeled forward . . . The trumpet sounded and the Bishop and his brother-in-law advanced with their motley soldiery.

Before they were even near the walls, a murderous fire started from the town's cannon. Fierens – in a stroke of typical genius – had applied the naval use of chain-shot to siege defence, and the guns now mowed down the massed attackers on the open space as easily – in almost as leisurely a manner – as the scythes that would soon be sweeping the blond corn in the fields behind.

Those who reached the walls with their ladders were greeted not simply with flaming pitch but a new ingredient which Fierens had caused to be added to the brew – something that made it stickier, and nastier, burning even when it was on the skin and burrowing into the flesh. Hell-fire, the defenders called it.

The attackers – what was left of them – soon drew back and the Bishop (feeling as usual ridiculous in his armour) and his brother-in-law retired with them, lucky to have escaped with their lives.

'Blow this for a game of soldiers,' said his brother-in-law, when they returned. 'You haven't got a hope in Hell of taking that town the way you're going on. I'm off.'

Actually, the attack had been his brother-in-law's idea.

'No, don't do that,' said the Bishop. 'Something'll turn up.'

But one by one the local landlords and petty nobles who owed allegiance to the Prince Bishop formed up and said what amounted to the same thing.

'It'll be harvest-time,' they said. 'Must get back. Crops to get in. Sorry and all that. Knew you'd understand.'

And the mercenary captain said it too.

'Sorry, sir. But we're mercenaries, like. And the thing about mercenaries is ... well, we're mercenary. And when there isn't, as there hasn't been for some time, mercenary incentives, as you might say, the mercenary gets restless and suddenly decides to bugger off, saving your holiness, and follow his trade elsewhere. Which is what we're doing. Got a little job in Strasburg, cash up front. Let us know when you've got the dibs and we'll be back. Farewell, sire.'

He ended formally because you never knew when you might not be grateful for a job or recommendation.

'Farewell,' said the Bishop, feeling helpless, which indeed he was.

In fact, if Fierens had chosen that moment to follow up his victory, he would have captured the Bishop, destroyed his camp and perhaps consolidated his hold on Rensburg for ever.

But he did not. Something else had come up.

Chapter 21

The garden was past its best, and the earth in the beds was cracked and dry.

The stock, having turned in a delectable performance, with wafts of heart-breaking fragrance all summer, now looked as though it had been too long in the chorus-line.

Even the musk-roses were beginning to grow blowzy, and the snap-dragons and gillyflowers nodded listlessly like maiden aunts at a party. The lavender, it was true, still flickered with bee and butterfly, but it was a desiccated harvest, and there seemed just a touch of desperation in the flapping of the peacocks, holly blues and red admirals as they rushed greedily at the flowers, which – if they sucked enough – might give them, just a few of them, strength to last until the spring – if there was going to be a spring. In this town on the edge of time, nothing could be taken for granted.

For all that, it was a pleasant place to be on a September day, sheltered from a light east wind with the first touch of chill upon it, sitting in a corner of her father's walled garden and feeling the stir of the child inside her.

Overhead, emphasizing fecundity, as if for a masque, the trees teemed with fruit. Apple and plum, apricot and peach, medlar and quince, sagged under the weight of harvest all around, and behind her, at the south wall, the vine was so shrouded in purple clusters you'd think the brick had been blest by St Vincent himself.

Sitting there almost in a trance, in that pleasant state of motherhood-to-be when nothing can be hurried, and blanking and dreaming are the order of the day, Elisabeth did not notice the figure that appeared over a wall and crept stealthily along the pleached lime-walk to the corner where she was sitting, and it was only when a shadow fell across her face and two hands were gently put over her eyes and a kiss was placed on her forehead that she realized that the man who filled her dreams – and, yes, her body – was standing beside her.

'You,' she murmured drowsily, 'you should not be here, dearest. And yet I'm so glad you are.'

She turned and kissed him on the mouth, a red-admiral kiss seeking strength for whatever was to come. They embraced in this manner with a passionate tenderness, while the grapes and the figs and the medlars swelled around them in the sun.

At length they paused.

'What news?' he asked.

'No news, I'm glad to say. I grow bigger, as you see. We try to keep the world out. It is easier here. But we hear of terrible things . . .'

She shuddered.

'You must not think of them,' he said. 'Be calm and rest. You must grow like a grape. There is nothing else you can do.'

'And what of you?' she asked. 'How did you get in?'

'My painter helped me over. The rest of the town has gone off to the square. There is some revelation or other. We are excused because we must finish still more pictures of the Leader, your husband. They are almost ready now, but we delay as much as we dare. What he wants so many for I cannot think. Perhaps he will give you one.'

'I hope not,' she shuddered. 'He only visits occasionally and then he looks at me as if I were a holy mare.'

'It is good at least that he has married Blommardine. It lets me out. Even she confesses we are not married now.'

'It is horrible in a way. Has the whole world gone mad? Fifteen wives! You'd think he would not need me. I think he . . . doesn't want to touch me. It is almost as though I burn him.'

'There is a virtue in you that affects him. That is why he wants the child – to take the virtue from you and proclaim him as a god, the Son of God.'

'It is worse than blasphemy,' she said. 'And yet . . . what if the baby is a girl? He would kill us.'

So she had been worrying about it, he thought. Why should she not? It was an appalling predicament whichever way you looked at it.

'It will be a boy,' he said, stoutly.

'We must escape.'

'We shall. Just let the child be born. Grow strong a little. Then we'll find a way, I promise you.'

'I wish we could step into that Garden of yours, and never ever come out of it.'

'I wish it too. But I don't yet have the key. It doesn't open to order. The answer lies in Hell, and that is where I have to look.'

'Not Hell?' she asked and crossed herself (a forbidden gesture in Rensburg).

'Not Hell itself, I hope. Though if Hell could open and engulf a town, I think we do have Hell in Rensburg. No, Hell in my master's picture which I have to finish. There is a meaning in those images which I cannot . . .'

He broke off.

'Go on,' she told him.

'You do not need to hear of Hell,' he said. 'You must think of fruit and flowers, good thoughts. The Garden...'

'Tell me,' she said. 'If it helps you it will be flower and fruit enough.'

'Let me describe it, then, for you only glimpsed it when you came to me. Here, I have a plan of it which I always carry with me. Consider that the whole is lit not by a sun or single source but – this is my master's genius – by irregular fits and starts of light as if from intervals of hell-fire.'

He spread out the folded sketch for her inspection. He had made it half in the hope of enlisting her advice.

'That is a rare effect,' she said. 'There is nothing like it I have seen.'

'Here are various torments in the foreground. The pig-nun embracing some unfortunate ... the hare nibbling a girl's toes like carrots ... the harlot-queen, see, crowned by a dice ... the bandogs devouring the dying man...'

'What do they mean?' she asked. 'There seems sense in it, almost as though it were this town itself... and yet it is sense mixed with nonsense and the sum is nightmare ... Nature disnaturing itself ... healing turned to poison ... monsters half-man, half-beast ... half-tree and half-engine...'

She did not know exactly where the words came from.

'You are right,' said Julius excitedly. 'It is like this town. I have been seeing it as somewhere but it is here. See, the Leader, with bird-head, on his throne swallowing men and voiding lost souls. The soldiers ... torturers ... preachers ... Yes, and that gave me, gives me, something of the background that is missing. The city walls, the mill, the bridge over the river ... flood and fire ... I put them in so...'

'There is no flood and fire, my dearest.'

'Not yet,' said Julius, with a sudden vision of things that he would have wished unseen.

'And the Leader does not have a throne...'

'Elisabeth. Elisabeth...'

It was her father's voice calling from the house.

'Quick,' she said. 'My dearest, you must go. If he finds you here, he will...'

She did not need to complete the sentence. He knew what Konrad would do. He kissed her, told her he would be back at the next opportunity, bade her keep happy, ran down the hidden tunnel of the limes and sprang over the wall where Hans-Peter waited, drowsing in the sun.

'Elisabeth, where are you?'

Her father came down the path, red-faced from hurrying in the heat. 'Why did you not call, child?'

Normally he would have been angry, but he had latterly adopted a more respectful manner. Today he seemed almost obsequious.

'I must have been asleep. It is so peaceful here.'

Her heart belied her words. What could her father want in such a hurry?

'Great news, Daughter. You are to be a queen.'

Chapter 22

A fellow called Bahlmann – quite a prosperous chap he must have been, for he was a goldsmith by trade until, forsaking all, he had come to Rensburg from Paderborn – had set up as a new prophet late in August. Nathan, he called himself.

Nobody took much notice of that, for new prophets set up almost every day, speaking strange tongues, many of them, and witnessing like nobody's business. Indeed, there were already five other Nathans in the town.

Bahlmann, however, prophesied very lucidly, and had come to the attention of Blommardine, who had many conversations with him and told him something of the divine purpose and the world's imminent destruction – details of which she had received from the Leader.

On this day in September, then, without any warning, and unprompted by Fierens who had spent the morning inspecting the defences, punctu-ated by a brief spell of Christerie with a pretty dark-haired girl from Bruges, this goldsmith ran like a whirlwind to the town square and mounted the preacher's podium which had been erected near the Leader's for any who felt like delivering themselves of a revelation.

It so happened that Konrad was in the Town Hall when he started, and was able to catch something of his drift in good time to fetch Fierens fresh from his 'path to the heights' (a path, Fierens was finding, much more direct and commodious than the golden wire which had served him in the past).

'Hearken unto me, oh ye nations,' cried Bahlmann-Nathan, 'and tremble all you lords of the earth, for it has been revealed to me this day that there is one mightier than thou.'

It did not matter to the passers-by, putting down their various errands and burdens to listen (a 'witnessing' was always better than work, since there was no money to be earned), that there were no lords of the earth present. Prophets were always like that. Playwrights and prophets used high-flown lingo. It gave the thing style; you could respect it. You didn't want a prophet talking like a tapster, although a ripeness of phrase was nice too if they could throw it in from time to time, for effect.

'He is matchless in might with incontestable dominion,' continued Bahlmann, warming to his theme. 'And where is this paragon, this prince, this potentate whose authority shall exceed all the powers that are upon the earth?'

'Where?' asked the crowd, caught up in a strange excitement.

'He is coming. I feel his imminence. Can you not feel the very buildings moving back?'

'Who? Who?' shouted the crowd. 'Is it the End?'

'It is the Beginning,' cried Bahlmann. 'Oh lucky Rensburg that art but little among the cities of the world. For out of you shall come a Monarch that shall be called Magnificent, Omnipotent . . . Princeps Orbis . . . Gem of Justice . . . He shall inherit the sceptre and throne of his forefather David and shall possess the kingdom until God himself reclaims it . . .'

'Who? Who?' shrieked the populace in a frenzy.

'I see him . . . Yes . . .' The prophet shaded his eyes. 'Yes, I see him, my people. Your Leader, now the world's. Down, down on your knees. Let none stand in his presence.'

There was some grumbling at the back, but you never knew who was watching, so they all knelt.

Fierens and Konrad, accompanied by the guard, advanced towards the podium from the direction of Fierens' quarters.

'What is your text, Prophet?' asked Fierens sternly.

The prophet himself, off his perch and kneeling now, raised his head just sufficiently to kiss Fierens' shoe. Fierens received the attention gravely and lifted the man to his feet.

' "Zadok the priest and Nathan the prophet anointed Solomon King",' said Bahlmann. 'Pray kneel, sire, for I must anoint you Princeps Orbis.'

He thereupon reached into his robe, pulled out a small vial, and sprinkled its contents on the kneeling Fierens (who seemed to be taking the whole thing in good part); he thereupon grabbed the Sword of Justice from Konrad (who released it none too keenly) and presented it to Fierens, declaring him in a great voice 'King of the New Jerusalem'.

There was a stunned silence while Fierens prostrated himself upon the ground, crying out to God for direction on this new road.

'I am unworthy, I am unworthy,' he called.

'No, sire, you are worthy,' cried Konrad, making the best of his loss of sword.

'I am unworthy,' Fierens repeated.

But later he got up and mounted the podium himself.

'Thus,' he said, looking around him with those eyes that could catch a flicker of sedition at a hundred paces, 'thus was David, Solomon's father, a lowly shepherd boy, anointed by the prophet at God's command as King of Israel. God has often done such works; and whoso resists His will invokes God's wrath upon himself.'

385

There was an uneasy shuffling at this point. The townsfolk had hoped perhaps that there might be rejoicing. A feast wouldn't come amiss. All this talk of God's wrath seemed bleak under the circumstances. But there was more.

'Now it is given me to have power over all princes and all lands. And now, my subjects, I have the right – given me with this sword – to wield it to the confusion of the evil-doer and to the defence of the righteous. So let none of you . . .' Here he let his eyes once more wander round the steadily filling square, seeing into each soul. '. . . let none of you besmirch yourselves with sin or crime, or resist God's will, or by Heaven this righteous sword will fall on you swiftly with the sharpness of death in its blade.'

There was a little ripple of noise in the crowd at this point, more perhaps of surprise than remonstrance. Had they not just beaten off a major attack? Had they not shown their zeal? But, on the other hand, had they asked for a king to be set over them – especially a king who as Leader had chastised them with whips and now seemed ready to bring on the scorpions? They had, they knew, requested no such thing, but they understood that the matter was now out of their hands.

The murmuring appeared to sting Fierens. His sense of unworthiness had quickly evaporated.

'Fie upon you,' he cried, 'that you mutter against God's command. Come at me, what?, with knives and stones. Run at me with halberds . . . Shoot at me . . .'

The soldiers around him stiffened their guard. Konrad, who at a judicious moment had taken back the Sword of Righteousness, raised it threateningly.

'Do what you will, I shall still be your king and rule not just over this murmuring town of yours . . . but the whole world shall be my foot-stool and all who inhabit it; for that is God's will, and of my kingdom there shall be no end until time itself is rolled up and put away!'

He turned, disgusted, from the podium and walked away in close consultation with the prophet, attended by the Sword of Justice who shot grim glances at the crowd.

He need not have bothered. Even among the former Rensburgers, there was no will to resist any more. They had seen too much. They knew what Fierens could do. And those who had arrived, the newcomers who outnumbered them, the desperate and dispossessed as well as the Company of Saints; why, they had roofs over their heads, water to drink and bread to eat; they knew which side it was buttered. There would be no help from them. So, one way and another, it seemed better to bite the bullet once more and adjust to their new role as subjects. After all, they had been subjects of the Prince Bishop. They had been here before.

And it was interesting to learn from the preachers over the following day or two just how exactly Fierens fitted the picture of the Messiah as portrayed by the prophets of the Old Testament.

Chapter 23

In due course, Julius received a summons to attend the King at the Bishop's Palace (which was now the Royal Palace), which he had taken over along with all the other large houses around the Cathedral.

Fierens sat in state in a large hall attended by various courtiers who only a few days ago had been Elders. The change seemed to suit them. They appeared much more relaxed, though no less self-important.

'Bow,' hissed the Provost, who was hovering around as Julius approached.

Julius did so.

Fierens lifted a gracious hand a few inches from the horizontal.

'We have waited long enough,' he said, 'for our portraits. We could call on any Italian to do it, summon him here, it would be an honour. We might condescend to Holbein. But since you are here, we give you the opportunity to finish what you have started.'

Julius and Hans-Peter had now completed two orders of five portraits each and were in the process of finishing three more. The first batches were already in place at salient points around the town, reminding the virtuous and the sinful that the Leader was ever-watchful.

'Thank you,' said Julius, he hoped not ironically.

'Thank you, sire, painter-shit,' said the Provost.

'Thank you, sire,' said Julius, and bowed extravagantly.

The King nodded.

'Our emblem,' he said, 'is the orb of earth, a crystal globe transfixed with swords topped with a cross and with a crown over all. It indicates our absolute supremacy. I wish to see the emblem printed in gold, around my neck, supported by a golden chain, and I will have it repeated at the top left-hand corner of the picture. Is that clear? You will paint it on the original and all the copies you have made. Further, I will have the portraits ready in two weeks' time. Let there be no delay.'

'No, sire.'

'So, Painter. What do you think of our palace?'

'It is very fine, sire.'

'It is not as fine as it will be. The best craftsmen in the town are already at work, and when we have finished even the so-called Emperor himself, the impostor Charles, who will kneel here, will feel but a petty baron.'

388

Julius glanced around. Already rich brocades were in evidence; silks, and gilded furniture; God knows where they had come from. Fierens himself, forsaking the drab black cloak and hat which had been the badge of the Anabaptist from high to low, was clad in purple velvet trimmed with ermine, and glittered with rings and chains studded with precious stones.

The courtiers too wore clothes of the finest quality, as befitted their position as lieutenants and functionaries of the King of Kings. There seemed already to be dozens of them.

A flurry at one of the great side doors announced the arrival of the queens. Music sounded from a small consort of viols and rebecks somewhere behind the throne. Headed by Blommardine, the queens proceeded in line towards the King, and spread out in two rows before him, curtseying. Julius had never in his life – even in Florence – seen such finery on so many beautiful women.

There was a hush from the buzzing courtiers as the girls made their entry. You could tell what the men were thinking, even though they had their own wives who were all of them doubtless plums of their kind. But these were something different.

Blommardine, for a start, had never looked lovelier. She seemed to have filled out a little. Her dress was low-cut so that her breasts came within a hair's breadth of bursting their banks as she gracefully sank to the floor before her Lord. Her hair shone with a witch's gloss. Her skin was as white as a Paderborn goose. And her huge green eyes gazed at Fierens with an almost narcotic devotion. She appeared not to see Julius. Indeed, she seemed to see no one else when Fierens was present. He would have it no other way.

'Rise, my queens,' commanded Fierens.

There was, you had to admit it, something extraordinarily imposing about the man. He had taken to regality as if he had been born to it – although those born to it seem sometimes to be extraordinarily lacking in those attributes – no, it was as if he had been rehearsing the part all his life and now had it perfect.

The girls glided upward from their curtseys with a delicious rustle of long legs and delectable rumps in skirts of silk and taffeta sarsenet.

You could not help desiring them; they were so beautiful to begin with; and Blommardine had spent many hours with them, teaching them the arts of beauty and the precepts of arousal; so that their beauty had more than natural powers of attraction about it. They radiated allure like houris in a harem.

In the queens' mansion, Blommardine reigned supreme, and any wife who objected to her methods was quickly evicted. Her technique of preparation was now to make love to the queens – one by one, and sometimes in larger numbers – herself. Indeed, she encouraged them to make love to each other. She knew it would create a riper, more hot-house atmosphere of pleasure and guilt (some of the girls did feel guilty, although guilt about this kind of thing was now officially a crime in the Royal Household). Such arts, performed in the languorous hours of the autumn afternoons when the King was at business, brought the harem to an almost perpetual state of interest, intrigue and arousal.

Julius gazed and gazed at them, and would have fallen in love with at least three of them had he not loved Elisabeth, and wondered not for the first time just what sort of man could convert from morality of the severest rectitude to capering polygamy in a matter of days, and still hold his head up to the world, his God and himself.

Did he really think of himself as being beyond sin? Did he think of himself as being mortal at all? Did he not sometimes have headache or pain in the gut, feel nausea or nurse a boil? Without such touches of Nature, he must be a rare man indeed. With them, how could he say to himself, 'I am nearer God than man?'

A trumpet sounded, and Fierens arose.

'Come,' he said. 'It is the hour for dinner. You will eat with us, Painter.'

It was not an invitation.

Julius followed the procession of queens and courtiers into the great hall of the palace. Tables were laid out in a great double-L shape, joined by the high table at the top, at which Fierens now seated himself beside two of the most beautiful queens, who were in turn flanked on one side by Konrad, who was now Chief Minister, on the other by Hass, who had been appointed Royal Orator. Julius seated himself near the bottom of the table as was customary for painters – below the knights (newly created) and doctors, but above the armourers.

The meal was long and miraculously elaborate. Cooks who you would think would have fled months ago had cropped up in the most unlikely places and sprouted in the new dispensation, like seedlings under glass.

There was carp and lark, shrewdly stuffed; capon; duckling; a boar's head; venison; beef; pikelets; sallets of various kinds; syllabubs; marzipans and tarts; all accompanied by the finest Franconian wines and hippocras which did not – as so often happened – disguise with its spices and Grains of Paradise what was tantamount to vinegar, for it was made from the best burgundy.

While the banquet progressed, music – played by the consort of rebecks and viols, now joined by serpents and crumhorns – occupied the feast, and a jester gambolled about making insinuating remarks that had the ladies in stitches.

What Julius found particularly eerie about the occasion was the fact that his neighbours, on both sides, seemed totally unaware of the

390

incongruity of the proceedings when weighed against the town's recent history and the privations of the townsfolk at large.

'We've come a long way in a short time,' he ventured to the man on his left, a former grain merchant who had been made a Holy Knight.

'A long way, fellow?' the knight remarked insolently. 'Not as far as we shall go.'

It didn't seem too promising, so Julius tried his right-hand neighbour, an immigrant carpenter, now Palace Joiner.

'I must say,' he said, 'I feel a little awkward sitting here in such state while those outside have little to eat but gruel.'

'They eat it rejoicing,' the man replied seriously. 'It tastes to them like the pomegranates of Paradise, for it has been blest by the Messiah of the Last Days.'

There was something profoundly disturbing about sitting here in the presence of such beauty, in a state of such wantonness, supping on so lavish an excess of meats, and surrounded by such glassy conversationalists. It was like going to an orgy in a madhouse.

The other even odder thing about the whole performance was the behaviour of Fierens himself. Julius suddenly knew what it was that made him so disconcerting a companion. You had the strangest feeling in his presence that what you had always felt were your independent powers had never existed, or were at any rate replaced by something else; that your part in life was not a thing of infinite choice and possibility, but was so entirely circumscribed that it could have been written for you – or that you could have been written for it.

Indeed, he could see it now. Fierens, sitting at the high table, aloof yet by no means inattentive, had the look of preoccupation that Julius had seen writers and, yes, painters wear.

They were all – this room, these gentlemen-at-arms, the queens, the Public Orator, the very dogs beneath the table – mere figments of his imagination.

Nonsense, of course, thought Julius; but the uncomfortable notion persisted. How else could one account for such violent swings in the moral and emotional climate of the town, accepted by all save a token few, whose resistance might be no more than a judicious tremor written into the script to make the whole charade more credible?

His thoughts were interrupted by the Public Orator, who stood up, over the fruit and canary wine, to make a speech.

'In honour of our great Lord, spiritual and temporal, with whom we have had the honour of breaking bread,' cried Hass, 'it has been decided to rename all the streets and squares of the town. Henceforth, the High Street shall be called Fierens Street. The market-square shall be called Lord's Square. The Westgate, Jerusalem Gate. And so forth. Notices will be erected through the town which will provide the details.

391

'Further, the very days of the week shall be changed, for they have at the moment lewd names which reflect the names of devils. Saturday was Saturn's Day. Sunday, the Sun's. Monday, the Moon's ... How we have laboured under these evil names. Sunday will now be known as Abraham Day. The rest will follow alphabetically. Monday will be Benjamin's Day. Tuesday will be Canaan. Wednesday, David. Thursday, Ezekiel, Friday (yes) will be Fierens Day and Saturday will be Salem.'

He went on to describe how all the main streets of the town and even new-born children would be named after a special system of the King's, and how gold and silver commemorative coins would be struck (there was no need for money, of course) bearing Fierens' head with the words 'One King over all' and 'The Word has become Flesh and dwells in us'. The motif the coins would bear would feature a device (already familiar to Julius) that illustrated the King's absolute spiritual and earthly authority – a globe, representing the earth, pierced by two swords (one for the Pope, the other for the Emperor) over which would rest a crown bearing the legend 'One King of Righteousness over all'.

While this was going on, Julius stole a look at Fierens, who was sitting – with an expression that reminded him now of an old puppet-master he had known as a youth in Bois le Duc – rapt and yet totally involved with the proceedings.

Julius shifted his gaze to two of the queens, sitting together, whom he sensed were looking at him. One of them winked. He did not wink back. It would have cost him his head. He rather thought she had her hand up her neighbour's placket.

The meal lasted, with entertainments, well over four hours. Some of the participants fell asleep over the tables, dazed with hippocras. Some of the older courtiers made their excuses and left. Others now began to dance. One or two of the queens and some of the other women started to embrace their companions.

The musicians began to play louder, more insistently. Julius, although he had drunk sparingly, felt his head begin to throb.

A troupe of girls with horned coifs now entered the room dressed in the Turkish manner, in scarves and gauze, and performed voluptuous ballet. Fierens – still with a detached air – and some of the other courtiers got up from the table and mingled with the whirling dancers, while servants cleared the tables and threw rugs and furs upon the dais.

The wine must have been drugged, for it seemed to Julius that the candlelight was turning darker, redder. A smell of enticing, disgusting sweetness filled the air. Bodies began to mingle; nipples appeared, shockingly red against white breasts that hung like lanterns in the gloom; thighs curved and glistened; grape-red homunculi sprang from cod-pieces . . . Julius could not tell whether he saw these things or whether they were shadows.

'Come on,' said Blommardine at his shoulder. 'He won't mind. He is the King of Love.'

She was up to her old tricks.

He looked across to where Fierens was lying with arms outstretched in a travesty of crucifixion. The forefingers of each hand rested lightly between the legs of two dancers who lay rigid, one on either side of him, trembling as if his very touch had powers beyond Nature. A third dancer, kicking ecstatically like a votary of Cybele, squatted on his man-godhood.

His face was completely void of emotion.

An urge to be part of this obscenity, this feast of foul delight, swept over Julius. Perhaps Lust really was the father of all sins, as the Church said. Or were lust and love different sides of the same coin, as the Free Spirits had it? Another minute and he would be lost. I am grass, he thought, hay, bent by any wind . . .

The image saved him. He recalled a day, long ago, when Bosch had taken him into his inner workshop – the day after Julius had stolen in for a secret viewing (it was almost as if Bosch had known of it) – and shown him the commission he was working on. It was the interior of the locked triptych whose outside had so haunted him; the Pilgrim of Love on the dangerous road of life. Revealed inside was a painting, in the most beautiful pinks and blues and yellows imaginable, of a haywain – flanked on the left by a scene of Original Sin, with angels falling from Heaven like mosquitoes, and on the right by Hell.

The great cartful of hay topped by a pair of lovers, flanked by an angel and a devil playing music out of his nosepipe, was surrounded and scrabbled at by a whole squabbling flock of people – labourers, notaries, nuns, merchants, mountebanks, young, old – followed by a pope and an emperor, and led by masked devils. Christ, in the clouds of glory above, looked down in sorrow and resignation.

'What does it mean?' he had asked after he had praised it, for he had never seen anything so weirdly, so astonishingly beautiful.

'Hay,' his master had told him. 'The stuff of the world. Everyone grabs at it but it is vain. Hay . . . It means "nothing". All is vanity, saith the preacher.'

'Come,' said Blommardine, clutching at his arm, stroking him familiarly. 'You know what I mean, brother-lover.'

Julius shook himself. He thought of Elisabeth patiently waiting for him. He had the strangest sensation that by his action now he could make her baby an angel or a devil.

'Come on, slow-balls. What you waiting for?'

He tore himself away from her.

'No,' he muttered. 'Hay . . .'

'Hay? What are you talking about? Hay? You want a tumble?'

'Hey,' he said, waving his arms and hoping an excuse would come. 'Hay . . . that's it. Got no sleep. Must hit hay.'

She stared at him as if he were deranged. Then her eyes narrowed; green witch's eyes that weren't deceived by floundering.

'You're in love,' she told him. 'You're still in love. You're in love with the Queen.'

He could not deny it.

'You'll be sorry for this,' she said, and turned, tripping lightly away to a group around the Sword of Justice.

When she said he'd be sorry he usually was, he thought.

'He's in love with the Queen,' he thought he heard her say.

They turned to look at him. He realized she had never intended him to make love to her. It was a ruse. She never liked to let go.

Julius stumbled from the hall, through the heavy doors, and out into the night. The cobbles fizzed with early frost and the moonless sky was throbbing with pinpoints of light.

He went to the usual place.

As he watched, a shooting-star like a homing angel seemed to drop straight into the house where his true love lay.

394

Chapter 24

The people of the town did not know exactly of all the excesses of the Court. Not that there was anything enacted there that could possibly give rise to guilt in the participant for, if it was sanctioned by the Lord of All the Earth, it was sanctified indeed. If God was in the Leader and if the Leader – as in some cases indeed he was – in them, there could be no question of evil-doing. It was in fact evil to think that there could be.

But the town had a fair idea of what was going on, and there was some muttering on the subject of such pomp and magnificence as everyone could see with his own eyes. It was all very well for the King, his wives and friends to dwell in splendour, but everyone else was living like church-mice – and low church-mice at that.

Muttering was forbidden in Rensburg, so the situation must have been bad. Now the prophet Bahlmann-Nathan made it worse. He got up one day in the market-place and announced that God hated all excess of costume. He spoke on the subject for three hours, but that was the gist of it. And it was enough for Fierens.

An announcement went out that all clothing and bedding were to be strictly rationed; all that was superfluous was to be handed in on pain of execution. Every house was searched and eighty-three wagon-loads were collected; and though much of it went to warm and encourage the zealous newcomers who still streamed in from Holland and Frisia, and the deserting mercenaries from the Bishop's army, the very best found its way to the palace by the Cathedral.

There was now, of course, more muttering in the town. The weather – it was late autumn now – was beginning to turn cold again. A chill and poisonous east wind had set in, bringing with it rheums and fevers. The gap between the surfeits of the Royal Court and the hardships of the ordinary citizen was becoming intolerable, even for those who had previously acquiesced.

Fierens, however, who foresaw all (had he not created these people?) understood their littleness and limitations; so he prepared a pomp for them. He knew they loved a spectacle.

A huge throne was raised on the dais in the market-place. Covered with cloth of gold, it dominated the entire square, towering over the pews for the royal councillors and prophets. Around the square at judicious intervals were now placed such further copies of the King's picture as Julius and his studio had been able to finish.

Trumpets sounded, the population was convened, and to a stirring fanfare a procession of Officers of the Court, preceded by the Sword of Justice and including Hass, the Royal Orator, marched solemnly into Mount Sion. The Royal Bodyguard, composed of immigrants and mercenaries, took up its station, forming a great circle around the throne. When at last they were posted, yet one more blast of the trumpets announced the arrival of the King of the World himself, riding on a white palfrey, holding an orb and wearing a golden crown.

Dismounting, he climbed the steps of the throne while the Provost and his men went about the populace coercing cheers and generating enthusiasm.

His face a mask, his eyes burning through to your very soul if his gaze should rest on you, he waited impassively for a time while the crowd took in the majesty of the spectacle. On either side of him stood a beautiful blond boy – the one on the left held a copy of the Old Testament, demonstrating that the King was of David's line, giving him the necessary authority to re-interpret God's Word; the one on the right held a naked blade.

Suddenly the King's right hand shot up in a salute. There was a gasp of awe from some of the more suggestible ex-nuns, and all sound ceased. Even the east wind, which had been chasing leaves around the cobbles, seemed to lower itself in deference.

'Pomp,' said the King, and stopped, looking around for effect, searching each soul with his glittering eyes. 'What is pomp? What is the purpose of pomp?'

'It's to cover your carcase with finery while honest men go bare,' shouted a voice from the crowd.

The Provost moved hissing through the throng like a red-hot poker through a toddy.

'Oh, my dear people,' Fierens continued. 'What evil still lurks among us. That was the Devil's voice you just heard. But I am thankful that you heard it, for it means that our Adversary is desperate. He knows that the End is very near and that here in this town, our New Jerusalem, he knows he has scant chance of overcoming. Do not think that I do not understand your fears, your privations. And do not imagine that it does not grieve me to live in pomp – yes, pomp – that word which caused the Devil to cry out – to live in pomp while you struggle in privation. Ah, my people, if I could exchange my pomp with you I would, for the fact is that wearing fine clothes and eating delicately mean nothing to me. I am dead to the world and the flesh. I merely do these things because, while we are *of* the world, the King and his Court must be seen *by* the world. We must live in due majesty and, yes, pomp –

for the greater splendour of God and his State on earth. We cannot be seen to be inglorious. But I assure you, my sweet people, if you do bear with me, yet but a little while, then I shall bring you to such joys, such splendours, such pomps of your own as you yourselves may taste and delight in. You shall sit on silver chairs, and feast at silver tables heaped with flesh and fowl and fruits more succulent than any that I know. And I shall, if it please you, wait on you. For the Third Age is come at last. Tell the people, Royal Orator.'

Hass duly stood up and in ringing tones declared how the First Age was the age of sin and endured until the Flood; the Second Age was the age of persecution and the Cross, which had lasted until now; and the Third Age was the age of vengeance and triumph of the Saints. He told them how Christ had striven to restore Truth to the sinful world; how the Church had taken His teaching and corrupted it; how Christianity lay bound in a captivity worse than Babylon; and now Christ was about to come again.

'He has already established His Kingdom in Rensburg and set over it His new David. Already all the prophecies of the Old Testament have come to pass,' declared the Royal Orator, wagging his big head emphatically.

Some, though not all, of the crowd, seemed inclined to confirm his vision.

'Now you, the Saints, must go forth, the Sword of Justice before you, to enlarge God's Kingdom until the whole world is encompassed,' Hass continued. 'Now, before long, Christ will come in might as King and ruler, and with your help, my children, with you the people of Rensburg, select and elect, He will vanquish the Devil and those who do his work and will utterly cast out the abomination of desolation. Say it with me, my children. The glory of all Saints . . .'

The crowd was well drilled in the litany, and roared it as though they were actually advancing on the enemy.

'The glory of all Saints . . .' they yelled.

'Is to wreak vengeance . . .' shouted Hass.

'Is to wreak vengeance . . .' they replied.

'Revenge without mercy must be taken . . .'

'Revenge without mercy must be taken . . .'

And they hollered with him in unison the concluding apostrophe.

'On all who are not marked with the Sign.'

'What is the Sign?' he asked them.

'IT IS THE SIGN OF THE SAINTS.'

'Then, indeed,' Hass told them, 'there will appear a new heaven and a new earth, in which you, my children, freed from your long serfdom to the ungodly, will live without hunger or pain or fear or weeping. For the former things will have passed away. There will no longer be princes

397

or powers, all will be held in common, and gold and silver will no longer serve the lust of the great but only the Children of God, for they will have inherited the earth. And God knows, even more than I do . . .'

'God knows,' repeated Fierens suddenly from his towering throne, and you could sense that he knew too, 'God knows. For who knows better than He the tribulations, sorrows, pains, hardships, privations, sickness, humiliations, trials, obstacles, jibes, galls, chafes, inclemencies, thumb-nosings, insolences, rigours, hungers, purges, mockeries and perturbations under which you have laboured. But the greater the suffering, the greater the glory. And in the days to come, when it shall be asked of me, who shall sit at my right hand, I shall speak out for you and you and you . . .'

His hand shot out again, pointing hither and thither in the crowd so that people jostled and fought to be caught in his line of sponsorship.

'And me . . . and me, Lord.'

'And you and you . . . For . . .' he told them at last, 'you are dearer to me than my own life, and I shall speak for you righteous ones and shepherd you in, even though, at the end, Jerusalem's Gate shuts in my own face.'

'No, never,' they cried, 'you first. The King shall come into his own.'

The nuns' eyes were streaming tears. Strong mercenaries dabbed their faces. There were no mutterings now. Julius, who had been working his way around the crowd to get a better view of the proceedings, felt his foot slip as he walked. He looked down and saw that he was treading in a pool of warm blood.

Chapter 25

The more he looked at this painting, the more it seemed to exercise power and drawing-in-ness upon the meditator.

It was after all the intention of most religious painting to bring understanding and faith to the beholder. It was not perhaps surprising that this Garden, so supremely and intricately planned, so consummately executed, should have its own more powerful effect.

Some great mind was at work upon his own – charming, inspiring, soothing, enchanting, compelling – so that, increasingly, all he had to do was yield to it and it would talk to him or, as it had done on that fateful occasion months ago, it would one day, oh yes, open once again to absorb him and his Love utterly; or, it would speak to him as it had done before.

However, recently the Garden of Delight itself – and Eden too – had stayed resolutely shut to him, admitting only his wonder and conjecture. It was Hell which more and more seemed to be closer. As he wandered in the town, there were faces that seemed familiar, and he would trace them again in the picture when he came in – that soldier, that fiend, that girl with the dice upon her head. Not that there were any girls with dice on their heads in the town – they would have had them cut off, the dice and their heads with it. But that expression of vapid curiosity. Oh yes, indeed, there she was, next to the hare nibbling the toes, he had seen her that very day on Mount Sion.

He had come in now, once again, here now, to escape the crowds and the Court, and his endless pictures of the King which stared from every corner, to pit himself once more against the problem. He was thankful for the studio. It was difficult to be alone in this town these days – so many people, so many voices and witnesses, strange tongues, preachings, punishments, guards, deacons, arrests, announcements, flagellations, and death.

He had taken a workshop in the palace. The Royal Orator had suggested he should do a portrait of him, and Julius had asked for a room where he could paint undisturbed.

'Nothing simpler,' said the Royal Orator, using his first short phrase of the week.

It had been a splendid opportunity to work somewhere warmer – there was no shortage of wood in the palace – and to establish

399

Hans-Peter who, though a cheerful enough fellow, seemed to jar in the studio. The studio was a place where he needed to be alone.

And here he was, once more, alone here with that wretched, pestilential east wind blowing outside; leaves falling and twirling like lost souls, and the rags he had stuffed in the lattice to keep out the draught straining to join them.

He was not looking forward to winter. Nobody in the town was. The general feeling seemed to be that if Christ was coming again, he'd probably wait till the spring.

He addressed himself once more to his wall, checking out the detail on the panel that he had made ready to convey to the chapel upon completion. He had already begun to sketch in certain scenes drawn from the town in the upper third of the board . . .

The herded victims of eviction, for instance, escorted by friends, made a suitably infernal procession. And, higher still, there were already the possibilities of fire. The town had already seen a number of abnormal conflagrations, some caused by carelessness on the part of the newcomers, others by lucky pitches of the enemy.

He had been impressed by the besiegers' firing of a windmill, which had stood on a small hill by a bridge not far from the town. It had glowed like a lantern, with its blazing sweeps looking like fiery rays in the darkness.

There had been another fire in which the flames had flowed like a torrent of light surging through a gateway. A fine effect: this too had been sketched in. He could feel optimistic about the possibility of all that, but he was still no nearer the central problem – that gap under the tray which held the bagpipe with, beneath it, the sinners escorted by the beetle-nun, the bird-man and the horned lady.

He had been looking again at the scene to its right, hoping that it might throw light on the problem. It showed a sinner sliding backward, down a razor-sharp knife, while on a plate overhead hounds devoured a knight in armour. The knife's handle rested on a curious double-breasted jug, while the reverse end of its blade was balanced on a smooth-pointed pitcher. Below it a gaunt-faced bearded ghoul with impatient gesture rode a big bridled mare of a woman, who shamelessly crawled along showing her heavy breasts and buttocks, while a sponge on a lance advanced both to mop her quarters and goad her on to further lubricities.

'What does it mean?' he groaned.

He was beginning to be oppressed by the notion that there was not much time, that he would not leave the town with Elisabeth and their child unless the timing could be completed. Hell glowed with a cold, unwarming warmth like sunstroke. He shivered. Perhaps he was catching a fever.

It was then that the voice spoke again.

'Carnality, sexuality, that is the knife-edge. If it is mastered, the building of life remains intact. If it is misused, it falls apart.'

'Who are you? Speak to me again,' he called.

Had it really spoken, or was it another of these chimaeras that seemed so to afflict him these days?

There was no answer. The wall confronted him with its limpid hues and its hellish flushes. Out of the bottom right-hand corner of the Garden, the Grand Master fixed him with glittery eyes.

'Father,' he said hopelessly. 'Why me?'

There was nothing for it but try to work it out again. If the lesson of the jugs and the knife meant that life broke down when love was misused, then surely that monstrous creation in the centre, part burst carcase, part egg, part ruined tree with its dead roots in boats locked in ice . . . surely that must also be life broken down?

The tree was withered, the egg was rotted and broken, the ocean was frozen, the boat was going nowhere . . . Life was broken down all right. And so it should be. This after all was Hell. The picture was like this town. It was why he had been sent here.

There must be some other clues. There was indeed a key – you might have thought it represented enquiry – it was to the left of the ruined egg-carcase, but it was an instrument of torture. There was a lantern to throw light – but it was a prison for the damned who burned like moths caught in a candle. There was even that huge pair of testicle ears – but they were not for understanding – separated by the penis-like blade; they represented, he supposed, the attentive auxiliaries of lust. Perhaps these clues contained the answer, but he could not read them. He returned to the centre.

What did that desolate and devastated monster, half animal, half vegetable, require? What horror could be added to it?

He thought of hideous talons and ghastly orifices, of red-hot droppings and molten vomits, leprous breasts and animated pudenda; he considered slimed half-reptiles and crocodilian-vegetable chimaeras; he even toyed with the idea of a monstrous birth, part alchemical-homunculus, part insect.

But in the end – as it was growing dark and bitterly cold (there was a shortage of candles as well as firewood) – he had to confess himself once more defeated.

He wept in his frustration and railed on his father, on the Brethren who had brought him to this pass, on life and even love, which had made him so miserable.

As he left, to return to his cold and cheerless lodging – at least Blommardine had kept the place warm – he turned to look at his reflection in the glass.

401

He was shocked by the gaunt features and haunted eyes that stared out at him. How could Elisabeth love such a scarecrow? He hadn't eaten for some time. Perhaps he should try to find something for supper . . .

And then the voice spoke to him again. Or was it his father's voice? Or his old master's? And did it come from the Garden? Or his head? At any rate he found himself repeating words that he had heard many years ago in Bois le Duc.

'When you look at a figure, any figure, what do you look at first?'

'Why,' he spoke up now to his mirror-image, 'the head, to be sure.'

That was what the monster needed: a head. And not just any head, mark you. The space was only suitable for one particular head. A head which this town and all history had proved more monstrous than any hellish cacodaemon you could imagine: the human head, of course. Was it not the human head, thirsting for the fruit of the tree of knowledge, which had provoked all the trouble in the first place?

The only question now was whose.

The head was half the answer to the puzzle.

Chapter 26

Taraaa. Tarantarantaraaa.

Julius had come to dread the sound of trumpets. They had once been martial. Before the declaration of the Kingdom, they had served warlike purposes, depressing perhaps but necessary. But these, though just as alarming to those who disobeyed, were not necessary trumpets.

By no means the sinew-stiffening clarions of the battlefield, they were, Julius realized, the old trumpets of Bois le Duc, stage trumpets to alert the people to a procession, a flourish for a show. Fierens was up to his old tricks. Sound the trumpets, we're going to have a stunt.

Taraaa. Tarantarantaraaa.

You could sense the beginning of involvement in the town, the unbolting of doors, the tying of tunics, the straightening of hose, the fidgeting of feet.

Taraaa. Tarantarantaraaa.

The trumpets sounded for the third time – it was one of those golden mornings of Indian summer, with the promise of a glorious day ahead – and the people poured onto the square of Mount Sion, as they had been bidden a week before by the prophet Bahlmann.

'The men shall come armed. But the women and children, yea the newly born, shall accompany them. For together you, the Children of God, will march out of the town. Your strength will be as the strength of twenty. Enflamed with the Lord's might, you shall appear like angels. At your approach the enemy will bow down and flee. Thus you shall march to the Promised Land and you will feel neither hunger nor thirst nor fatigue upon the way. The zeal of the Lord of Hosts will perform this.'

So they all formed up. Many of the mothers, timorous for their children, pleaded with the prophet, but he was adamant.

'The new-born shall speak with the wise tongues of serpents,' he cried. 'They will confound all who oppose them.'

'Where are we going, Mother?' asked a child.

'To glory everlasting,' answered the prophet.

'Will it be warm there?' asked the child.

'As warm as Abraham's bosom,' came the reply.

'But it is cold now,' the mother cried. 'My younger one is yet suckling.'

'He shall suckle this day on the milk of truth,' vouched the prophet, 'pressed from the paps of righteousness.'

'Truth?' cried the mother. 'Truth is a hard skilly.'

'Enough of gossip,' exclaimed the prophet, sternly. 'See! The King rides forth to war.'

And indeed, Fierens with all his Court was even now riding into Mount Sion, gorgeously apparelled and caparisoned.

He inspected his troops solemnly – the men with their swords and pikes, the ex-nuns with their staffs of faith, the mothers with their children – and appointed officers to lead each company. The inspection took a great deal of time because the King insisted on praying over all the children, especially those with the prettier mothers; but at last it was finished, and the King took his place at the head of the procession.

He raised his arm in a Roman salute, cried in a great voice, 'Revenge without mercy', and then, 'One sheepfold, one flock, one King', spurred his white palfrey, and moved on down the road towards the massive oaken portals of the Westgate.

Before them he stopped and shouted imperiously to the watch:

'Unbar the gates and let the Lord's host pass.'

But even as the great bars of seasoned wood, thicker than the mast of a ship, grumbled back and the huge hinges began to groan open, the King's voice was heard again.

'Stop!'

The mighty doors snapped fast. Bars rolled across again, snug in their iron hoops. Soldiers, guards, ex-nuns, mothers and children looked at each other in amazement.

'It was but a test,' said the King. 'I am now perfectly assured of your loyalty and zeal. And now, back to Mount Sion where I have ordained a banquet to reward you.'

It was typical of the man, thought Julius. What an entertainer he would have made! Indeed, Julius corrected himself, indeed, what an artist he was proving to be. A whole town for cast, a world for audience. Surprises, illusions, histrionics, mystery, stunts, pathos, cruelties, spec-tacles – every trick of the dramaturge was being exercised in a headlong cornucopia of effect.

Back to the market-place they all rushed – and there, in their absence, huge tables had been set up and benches drawn, a place for everyone, young and old. And now cooks started to distribute loaves and cooked meats while butlers poured ale and wine. It was a feast the like of which many had never tasted – and for those who were still of the old town stock, such as they had not known for many months.

Fierens and Blommardine and many of the courtiers helped to serve it. By the time all had eaten and drunk their fill, it was late in the afternoon. Some were beginning to be drowsy, others, whose stomachs could not cope with the sudden ingestion of rich viands, were beginning to feel ill; but they all had to sit on as King, Queen and courtiers distributed small loaves and yet more wine. For the Royal Orator had a treat for them. They were privileged, he said, to be the first people in the world to take the New Communion of the Second Coming.

None, however sleepy or sick, was allowed to move until Hass had had his say. The New Communion service was a long and rambling one. Its gist was that the bread was the body of the returning Christ and the wine was his already pulsing blood, which – as they drank and ate – would become flesh and blood in them, making them his very Brothers and Sisters.

A few of the diners threw up discreetly during the course of this long dissertation, and it was with sensations of relief that the mothers finally hauled their children off to bed, though the ex-nuns and immigrants and converted mercenaries declared themselves profoundly affected.

Now it was time for the King and Court to dine, which they did on a specially prepared high table in full view of the people.

'No favours, see,' cried the Lord of all the earth. 'We eat what you eat. We drink what you drink. One sheepfold, one flock, one King.'

The people, held back by the guard, took up the cry.

After dinner, the King, acting on a sudden illumination, sent for a captured mercenary and had him beheaded right in front of the high table. Some of the queens exclaimed crossly when their gowns were splashed.

'And I heard a voice that cried "So shall all perish",' adjured the nasal-voiced Bahlmann the prophet, '"who sin against the Truth and will not turn from the error of their ways. They shall be brought before the King and sentenced and struck down with an hewing blade. Their memory shall be blotted out and they shall find no mercy at the Day of Judgement. Thus spake the Lord."'

The people were impressed, as ever, at a public execution, though God knew there had been enough of them. What did it mean, that 'sin against the Truth and will not turn'? It could mean anything, really.

Chapter 27

Fierens with his wives. A warmed chamber filled with soft hangings, whose whole floor seemed to be pillow. The queens either naked or in shifts caressed themselves or each other in a day-long exercise of lovemaking. The Queen-in-Chief, Blommardine, supervised their pastime, distributing sweetmeats cooked with pomatum and occasionally calling to the King to enjoy some particularly dainty exploit – not that he normally responded, for he was not of this earth, but she did it to encourage momentum.

It was like some hot spring of love whose welling occurred now here, now there, as this or that group or couple came to the bubble; and when at last one was gaspingly and deliciously exploded, another would start lazily inflating again in some other corner.

The room was never still. Nor was it silent. A little gale of sighs, a breeze of whispers, a showerlet of laughter one after another, would play about the chamber, making it seem now a spring garden, the gentle vagaries of whose climate served to emphasize the amorous nature of the season.

Blommardine had given Fierens the pomatum; of course she had. But whether it had any effect on him was impossible to say. He made love prodigiously on occasion. There had been one amazing day when he had pleasured each one of his wives in the course of an afternoon.

'My seed shall cover the earth,' he had remarked.

If he went on like this, it probably would, she had thought, reaching across and touching the face of the last of the wives after he had left. The girl was still moaning with pleasure. He had that effect on them. Blommardine liked the notion of the whole world – fields, lawns, walks, terraces, towers, deserts, mountains and the sands of the sea-shore as on some primal morning – glistening with the dew of the King's love upon them.

She liked it still today, as she lay in the lap of one of the younger queens. She would have liked to have told him about it now, but he was not in today. He lay there motionless upon his couch, eyes open, staring at the world from a pinnacle of Heaven. She knew that it would have been more than her life was worth, Chief Queen though she was, to try to bring him down before he was ready. He had told her so.

'I am holding the world together,' he had said.

She turned her head and addressed herself to her pretty companion. 'We are lost,' she mumbled. 'Lost.'

'I know,' said the girl. 'But I'd rather be lost than find I was a serving-maid again.'

Chapter 28

After so long, so very long, so many humiliations and set-backs, the Bishop was rather pleased with the way things were going.

Chastened by his previous set-backs, he had found new mercenaries, trained them in the light of his experience, and renewed the siege. Not only had his forays met with increasing success under the walls of the town, but he had even been able to make a breach with one of his cannon. The wall had been repaired, of course. But it showed it could be done.

The last time anything like that had happened, the Saints had sent a strong party out and exacted swift revenge, spiking the guns and killing a company of mercenaries, and indeed occasioning desertions.

This time there had been no such break-out. It was good for morale. And, as is the way when Fortune starts to turn, another benefit accrued hot on the heels of the first. The Prince Bishop of Paderborn, doubtless concerned for his own neck – pamphlets as well as prophets had streamed unstintingly out of Rensburg, urging all the cities and States of Germany to overthrow their rulers – the Prince Bishop had sent reinforcements. And, as if that wasn't enough – which it wasn't – the Imperial Stadtholder had promised some more, whereupon Count Mansdorf also agreed to chip in.

'Soon we shan't have to break down the walls,' the Bishop told his brother-in-law. 'We shall simply be able to sit here and starve them out.'

'Soon, maybe. Not yet, definitely,' said his brother-in-law.

His brother-in-law was somewhat piqued because he loved what he called a 'good dinging battle', but the Bishop managed to make him see the advantages. The Bishop was becoming, by dint of trial and error – a great deal of trial, he would say, and even more error – a not totally incompetent general. His sister, he liked to think, looked at him sometimes with a positive lack of scorn.

'It's strange,' he told her. 'They could have opened the gates, marched out and cut us down where we stood after that last attack of mine. Botched, I'm afraid.'

'You were not brought up to be a general. The thing was thrust upon you. You were learning.'

'I was learning, but at a cost. I was deserted by mercenaries and allies alike. They could have had us, but for some reason they didn't follow up.'

'Don't talk about reason,' his sister told him. 'Don't expect reason. Reason is not part of their currency.'

'I understand they don't have currency,' he said. 'They pay each other in kind.'

'And their King takes most of it. What does he give in return? Kind? Unkind and plenty of it.'

'He gives them hope. He gives them faith. I wish for their sakes he would give them charity.'

'You sound as if you feel sorry for them. I hope I am not going to have to revise my recent better opinions of you. You cannot be lenient with a disease. You cannot be milk-and-watery with a contagion like that. You have to lop it off, root and branch. You must hate it as you would a mad beast.'

'I know, my dear,' said the Bishop, sighing. 'That is what my allies have told me. But in all charity, I can't help feeling sorry for them, can I?'

Chapter 29

Elisabeth had her baby in early December, over a week late, and a message was smuggled by the old nurse to the effect that the birth had been (thank the Lord) uncomplicated. The boy was strong though small, the mother weak but well under the circumstances, and he might see her very quickly the following Friday if he came over the garden wall after Mr Harting had left for the Court.

He found Elisabeth in bed with her baby, looking pale but beautiful.

'You can only stay ten minutes,' said Frieda, and left them together.

'Say hullo to Richard,' she said.

He kissed her first and then bowed to the pink-headed pupa in her arms.

'Richard *Coeur de Lion*,' he said. 'I think the name suits you. Except you're a bit more like *Coeur de Papillon* at the moment.'

'Hold him,' she said, handing the caterpillar-shape over.

'He's rather small. Will he break?'

'Not unless you drop him. He's probably tougher than you are.'

'He has his grandfather's grip,' he said ruefully, as the little hand grabbed his finger.

'How are you? You look thin,' she said.

'I'm all right. Food's getting scarce out there. They've stepped up the siege, I'm afraid.'

'We need you strong,' she said. 'I'll tell Frieda to bring you food.'

'No, no. Keep what you've got. I know your father's important but things could change. You can't depend on anything in this town. The sooner we leave the better.'

'I can't leave quite yet, dearest. In a month or so.'

He looked at her, handing the baby back into her arms. Mother and baby were both so frail. They would never survive the journey in this cold. She took his hand and squeezed it.

'Have you told Fierens?' he asked. 'He'll have to think it's premature.'

'Father says don't tell him just yet ... He has much on his mind. Wait till Christmas.'

'What? Why should he do that?'

'Father says it'll make a nice present for him.'

Julius knew better.

'He wants to make him Jesus. He wants a Second Coming.'

'No.'

Elisabeth held the baby tightly.

'Don't you want our baby to be the second Christ?'

She looked at him wide-eyed.

'Do you?' she asked.

'I want him to be the King of Love. Richard the Big Heart.'

She relaxed.

'That he will be,' she said. 'Like his father. What are we going to do?'

But old Frieda came in at that point.

'Come along,' she said. 'Time's up. I can't have her exhausted. It'll stop the milk. And there's a fellow skulking outside in the street I don't like the look of. So be off quick round the back while I open the front door.'

'Goodbye, my dearest heart,' said Elisabeth. 'Come and see us soon.'

'Only when I say so,' said Frieda. 'We're playing with fire in a pitch-yard if you ask me.'

Julius kissed the baby and drew Elisabeth to his heart. A terrible feeling swept over him that he might never see her again.

'What is it?' she asked him.

'Nothing. Everything . . .'

'I know. But it'll be over soon. We'll go away and be the happiest people in the world.'

He kissed her once more and left. Frieda stopped him at the bottom of the stairs.

'I've seen bad times,' she said. 'But this . . . it's as though Hell has opened. I'll look after her, depend on it. And you, look after yourself. I do believe you're her only chance.'

He kissed the old woman which, to his amusement, made her blush.

'All this kissing. Now go you on,' she said. 'Keep your ears wide, your nose long and your eyes at the back of your head.'

Chapter 30

Konrad could hardly believe the way fortune – or, rather, Fierens – had so coincided his two great delights. On the one hand he held the Sword of Justice; on the other he could now legitimately indulge the Wand of Priapus.

He now had the wives that were the proper allocation for a senior official of the Court. Not one of them was over nineteen. He did not bring them home to the house in Broad Street. It had too many associations he would rather leave behind. Besides, there was a little secret he wanted to keep for a while. Instead he had them installed, as was proper, in his quarters in the palace itself. He prevailed upon Blommardine to see that they were instructed and entertained while he was about his more disciplinary business – though, of course, he brought back a touch of the iron fist to enliven the softer disciplines of Venus. In fact, one of his wives had her arm broken and another a fractured cheekbone, but it was wonderful to see how they all clustered around him when he returned from a foray.

Today, he was sitting in his office in the palace after a busy night and a hearty breakfast, reflecting on the Kindness of Fate – or, rather, Fierens – which had raised him from a mere tradesman to one of the princes of the world – and wondering whether he should not go down to his distillery to see to the consignment of aqua vitae which he had promised the Royal Butler – when there was a knock at his door.

The man who entered did not walk straight in. He came sidelong. You could recognize Schwenk from half a mile by his distinctive manner of sidling. Such creatures were busy in Rensburg these days – spying, reporting, being called as witness, lying, conniving, poisoning reputations, falsifying evidence. There had been a time when Konrad had feared he knew too much, might denounce him (unless suitably sweetened) to the Saints for those visits to the hypocaust under the Town Hall. But now all that was past. Things went on these days that made the hypocaust seem like a nursery playground.

Now Schwenk was his man, and he rewarded him with trifles. Nothing too much, mind, or he would grow overweening. But a raw-boned country girl here, a square meal there; such things worked wonders with the little sneak; and up he came with all manner of morsels of his own.

'Ah, Schwenk,' said Konrad. 'Something afoot?'

'I've been following the painter as you suggested.'

'The Royal Painter?'

That was now Julius's title – conferred upon him for his portraits of King and Court and his record, in a multitude of skilful drawings, of the history of the New Jerusalem.

'That's right,' said Schwenk. 'There's something going on.'

Konrad had never trusted that fellow. There was something about him – something behind those watchful eyes – that smacked of heresy and worse. He had to move carefully, for the man seemed to be in favour with the Court, although that of course could change overnight; but he had decided weeks ago that the man must be monitored, both for the good of the city and himself, the two being naturally indivisible.

If, for instance, as he guessed, the painter was still harbouring an affection for his daughter and the King found out, would not that reflect badly on the Sword of Justice? Might he not himself be a victim of the royal volatility? He could not bear to lose those wives – especially lovely Kirsten of the perfect buttocks who yelped so prettily when he whipped her. There would be many, if he fell, who would be after his blood.

'The painter,' he repeated slowly to Schwenk.

A horrible thought struck him. Suppose, just suppose, that the painter and his daughter had got together, made the beast with two backs, before the King married her. It was impossible, of course, but just suppose even a rumour of it got out . . . Well, it wouldn't, of course. But if it did, if so much as a whisper reached the King's ear, both Konrad and painter – and whoever it was who had whispered – would be cut off out of the land of the living and floated down the river for fishmeat.

No one likes being a cuckold at the best of times, thought Konrad, but bearing in mind the proposed paternity of the child, God's Own . . . could God be cuckolded? . . . the implications did not bear thinking of.

He fingered his collar uneasily and spoke again to Schwenk.

'The painter? What of the painter?'

'He's got something going on in that place of his. Paintings . . .'

Konrad knew he had a studio over a shop.

'What of it? He's a painter.'

'I couldn't get in, but what I could squint . . . he's painting on the wall.'

'I understand painters do sometimes. It's called a mural, Schwenk.'

'Yes, but . . . he stares and stares at it. He talks to it. I can't hear most of what he says. "Master", he says sometimes. And then "Elisabeth" . . .'

Schwenk stopped and looked craftily up at the Sword of Justice. He could see he had made a hit.

I'm going to have to kill you, Schwenk, thought Konrad. You have just signed your warrant. But first I must use you a little more.

He leant forward and grasped Schwenk high up by his doublet so that he almost choked.

'You report only to me, don't you, Schwenk? You wouldn't blab to anyone else?'

'Who? Me? Gracious heavens, no. We are old fffriends . . .'

The little man was suitably scared, but Konrad turned the knife.

'If I hear that you've told so much as a word, a syllable, a letter, Schwenk, of what you've seen to any but me, you are not merely dead. You are flayed alive by the Royal Tanner, your guts are spilled by the Royal Butcher, and your eyes are put out by the Royal Glassblower. What else does the painter do?'

'I . . . I don't know for certain. I lost him. But . . . you won't be angry?'

'I am angry, but not with you, Schwenk. I shall only be angry with you if you do not tell me everything. If you do not tell me everything, I shall be very angry with you indeed.'

He grasped a small dagger, serving as a paper-knife, which lay on his desk. Schwenk blanched and swallowed.

'I think he has visited your daughter,' he said.

Chapter 31

Fierens' control of the town was now absolute. Anyone who disobeyed the increasingly arbitrary ordinances of the King was stamped on. Not that there was no disagreement with this state of affairs. The Saints, of course, said he could do no wrong. But some of the townsfolk who had stayed on for whatever reason – fear, self-interest or misguided acquiescence; especially the women – now began to say very quietly that he could do no right. It came to the same thing in the end, however. There was nothing anyone could do about anything anyway.

What you could say about Fierens – with Konrad at his side – was that he had built an exceedingly efficient and brutal means of keeping order. It was called the King's Bodyguard. Composed entirely of immigrants and ex-mercenaries, men who had nothing when they came to Rensburg but who now were the King's men – privileged, richly clad, generously fed, and supplied with all the women they could service – they were the embodiment of the King's power and law. They alone in the town were allowed to ride horses (apart of course from the Court), and they drilled and clattered urgently about the town on their terrible errands. When you heard that noise you hid as fast as you could.

It was evident to all that their function was a civil not a military one. The man who was known as the Provost – the implacable, iron-souled, beetlingly suspicious ex-gaoler from Leyden, where he had been sacked for brutality – commanded the bodyguard and was known to take orders only from the King and the Sword of Justice.

On the second day after the banquet, it came to the Provost's notice that some of the women had been heard to be grumbling. He reported it to Konrad who reported it to the King.

Fierens was a thousand miles up in the empyrean, but he already knew about it, of course. He had planned it. Women were always the troublemakers, the serpent tongues, the deceivers. Had the Fall not been perpetrated by a woman? That fair, soft flesh, those long shanks, those savoury loins – those eyes, those lips – all this was but a shadow. Within they were ripe for corruption. But yet they too had souls, and they too must be saved. If they could not be saved by faith and love such as he had shown these people in the great work that he had prepared for them, why, then, they must be taught a lesson. They must learn by fear.

The script at once began to take shape.

(Scene change to Mount Sion. A large crowd has gathered. The clattering of hooves is heard and three young women are led in escorted by foot-soldiers and the mounted PROVOST with bodyguard. They are thrust roughly towards the throne.)

THE KING: Who are these prisoners?

PROVOST: They are women, sire, who persist in the error of their ways.

THE KING: What are these ways?

PROVOST: This woman, sire *(indicating a handsome dark-haired girl)*, will not allow her husband to have congress with her.

THE KING: Is this true?

DARK GIRL: Yes.

PROVOST: *(yanking her hair)* Yes, sire.

DARK GIRL: Yes, sire.

THE KING: Why?

DARK GIRL: He has four wives already and I love my betrothed who is away from the town.

THE KING: How can you have a betrothed if you are married?

DARK GIRL: I do not think . . . *(desperately)* . . . I do not think myself married to this man.

THE KING: Take her clothes off. Let us see why she is ashamed to lie with her husband.

(The PROVOST and another soldier tear her garments from her. She is a well-built woman and tries to hide her shame from the crowd.)

THE KING: I see nothing to be ashamed of. Let us give her something worthy of her shame. Cut off her breasts.

(The PROVOST draws his blade. The struggling woman is held fast. He holds each nipple in turn and the breasts are severed. The woman falls down in a faint, bleeding among her breasts.)

THE KING: Next.

SECOND WOMAN: No, no.

(The SECOND WOMAN is a comely girl of some twenty-three years. She is golden-haired, plump, and would have a lazy forwardness about her if she

were not so frightened. She keeps looking at where the DARK GIRL *lies moaning now, holding her bloody hands to her chest.)*

THE KING: What is she charged with?

PROVOST: Bigamy, sire.

THE KING: Bigamy? But this is an outrage.
Speak, woman.

SECOND WOMAN: Well, first this man Thomas come along and said I could be his third wife, but he didn't take no notice of me, so I walked out and met this geezer called Fred. Fred says I could be his second wife and he was very attentive and all was well till we met Thomas in the street and he says 'Oi, that's my number three.' Please, sir, I didn't know it was wrong. Honest, I thought what was sauce for the gander was sauce for the goose, like.

THE KING: Take her clothes off. She is a whore.

SECOND WOMAN: No ... no ... no ...

(She is stripped although she struggles violently.)

THE KING: Tie her so that she shows her shame like the whore that she is.

(The woman is tied to a wooden 'horse' which pulls her head down and thrusts her rump up for public view.)

THE KING: Now, since you have acted like a beast, you will be treated like one. Provost ...

(The PROVOST *leads on a jack-ass which is made to mount the woman and have congress. He is too large for the woman and tears her as he penetrates. The crowd gasps and watches, shocked and fascinated. The woman's screams echo across the square. Even the* DARK GIRL *raises her head to watch.)*

THE KING: And now the third prisoner.

(The THIRD PRISONER *is a proud, quick-witted young woman with a sharp-intelligent face. She is the oldest of the three. She is afraid but she is also defiant.)*

THE PROVOST: The prisoner's charged with insulting a preacher, mocking his doctrine, and murmuring against your leadership, sire.

THE KING: That is the worst of the offences that I have heard this morning. Is it true?

THIRD WOMAN: Do you want it to be true ... sire?

THE KING: Do not chop logic with me. I want the truth.

417

THIRD WOMAN: 'What is the truth,' said Pilate, jesting.

THE KING: Her evasion proclaims her guilt. Strip her naked.

THIRD WOMAN: You won't find the truth there.

(While they are stripping her, the SWORD OF JUSTICE grabs her head and cuts out her tongue. She chokes and splutters on her own blood. The SWORD OF JUSTICE holds the tongue up for all to behold as she sinks to the ground with a beard of blood.)

THE KING: See what happens to those who speak against the Lord. Execute them, Sword of Justice.

(The DARK GIRL and THIRD WOMAN are too shocked to struggle, and their heads are taken off with a single blow. The SECOND WOMAN, though badly hurt, writhes like a devil, and the axe cuts half her face off. She is still struggling when the final blow falls.)

THE KING: So perish all who do not follow the Way.

(The PROVOST gathers up the heads and the crowd disperses, chastened and instructed.)

Chapter 32

Mid-December now. The watchmen's fires on the rampart hissing in the flurries of snow. Lips beginning to chap, blains beginning to form, the cold seeping under doors, through chinks, putting fingers down your back just when you thought you'd drawn up to a nice blaze. Not that there were many nice blazes in Rensburg – apart from those the enemy started. Wood was scarce, coal non-existent. Wet leaves smoked in slow bonfires around which children gathered, coughing, holding out raw hands.

Not so easy now to break out in the dark and bring fuel in from the woods. The enemy's lines were widening, trenches spreading. And, worse than lack of fuel, food was becoming harder to bring in. It was still arriving. The enemy were not yet that secure but, among those deacons who were still more of this world than the next, there was cause for concern.

'Do you know what worries me, Brother?' said one such grizzled veteran to a mercenary-turned-Saint as they huddled over a brazier. 'There isn't going to be no Last Things. It's going to be the same old things all over again.'

Chapter 33

Christ-tide had come round again. There seemed to those townsfolk who had retained any hold on reality not simply little to celebrate but even less to celebrate with.

After the Feast at Mount Sion, it had been ordained that Apostles should go forth armed with the tongues of angels and Hass's latest pamphlet, *Restitution*.

This mighty river would spread its fertilizing tributaries all across north-west Europe; to Paderborn and Magdeburg, to Groningen and Westphalia. And indeed, insurrections were springing up in many cities; monasteries were being seized, town halls taken over. But, in nearly every case, the authorities – alarmed by the events in Rensburg – were bestirring themselves with unaccustomed vigour.

Other Hass pamphlets, printed in their thousands, were being read hungrily by the poor and disaffected right across Holland and Frisia. But the more the poor rose up, the livelier was the response of the powerful.

Representatives of the States of the Upper and Lower Rhine, meeting in mid-December in Koblenz, passed a motion agreeing to supply the money, troops and equipment that would make the Bishop's already improving siege properly effective.

The great proselytizing flood had turned into a stream and lately a trickle. Prophets were finding it harder to get through. (If caught, they were tortured as a matter of course and summarily executed.)

Equally, supplies of every kind were becoming harder and still harder to secure. People were starting to hoard, though it was forbidden on pain of death.

It was a particularly cold Christ-tide Eve, with a north wind bringing a little fine snow and then dropping to stillness, making way for a bitter frost. Even among the more resolute of the Saints, optimism had sunk and shrivelled like the very sap of the world.

On Christ-tide Day, however, the sun came out and jumped off a myriad of icicles; slid shimmering down a thousand snowy roofs, hurting the eye as it dazzled across the broad expanse of square; and danced now here, now there as you looked, spinning away at last across the river to bathe the enemy in brilliance. It was hard to feel dejected on such a morning. Children appeared out of nowhere and slid down slopes on trays. Even in the Court, after a night of particular surfeit, the queens emerged and threw snowballs.

It was at this juncture that the trumpets sounded. People had become wary of trumpets.

'Not today,' breathed a young mother, calling her children to her.

And yet today the trumpets did not seem to have that peremptory, authoritarian, military sound. They seemed altogether more joyful, more seraphic. What could it mean?

The people all gathered themselves up, wrapped themselves in what warmth they could, and trudged out onto the cracklingly flat white slopes of Mount Sion.

They did not have long to wait. Soon the bodyguard marched onto the square. They were not mounted this time. It was most unusual, and excited comment.

'It's on account of the frost,' explained a father to his son.

'It's on account of a joyful occasion,' said the Provost, grudgingly.

He did not approve of joyful occasions, but it was the King's prerogative to have one if he wished. Mind you, if you were to have a joyful occasion, this one offered a better pretext than most.

The soldiers took up their position round the square, and then the Court appeared. They had ridden in closed carts down the straw-strewn road from the palace, and filed onto their benches with looks of satisfaction at each other, while the populace gasped at their finery and furs.

At last the King appeared, drawn in a small closed cart by a milk-white pony. The Sword of Justice preceded it. The Royal Orator attended it. The Keeper of the King's House led it. The two boys, one with the Bible, the other with the naked blade, advanced on its either side.

The King emerged and raised his hand to the crowd.

The crowd replied with their customary spontaneous enthusiasm, conducted by the Provost.

Fierens turned and climbed the steps of the throne, then turned again and addressed the multitude.

'"Then shall the eyes of the blind be opened,"' he said, '"and the ears of the deaf unstopped. Then shall the lame man leap as an hart. And the tongue of the dumb shall speak."'

He paused. They recognized the quotation. It concerned the coming of the Messiah. But since they had been told about the coming of the Messiah every day for the last year, it did not really seem worth getting them out on Christ-tide Day for.

'"Rejoice,"' he continued, '"rejoice greatly, O daughter of Jerusalem . . . get thee up into a high mountain. Arise, shine, for thy hour is come."'

They were still none the wiser. Even the ex-nuns couldn't get up into a higher mountain than horizontal Mount Sion. There was none to be had.

Fierens changed quote again.

'"For unto us a child is born, unto us a son is given. And his name shall be called Wonderful, Councillor, the Mighty God, the Prince of Peace."'

The crowd looked at each other in astonishment, in slowly dawning comprehension. Did he mean . . . ? Could it be . . . ?

'Yes,' Fierens shouted, 'we have been a people in darkness. We have dwelt in the land of the shadow of death. We have known terror by night and pestilence by day. We have been abused, persecuted bloodily, put to the sword, but . . . but, my people, we have been sustained, we have been nourished, we have been fortified by the knowledge that one day our dear Lord . . .'

'Dear Lord, dear Lord,' said the ex-nuns, becoming agitated.

'Our dear Lord will come again to us as once he did so long ago. Today, oh my people, it is my joyous duty to tell you that after so many signs and portents, that we have ourselves witnessed, unto us is born, in the city of David . . . a Saviour which is Christ the Lord . . .'

Out of the cart now stepped a nurse – not old Frieda but a denizen of the Court – carrying a small bundle closely wrapped in fur. She was handed down by the Sword of Justice and carefully ascended the stairs of the throne with her charge, which she extended to the King. He took the bundle and held it up to the crowd.

'And here, oh good people be joyful, here he is,' he announced. 'Born this very day to my Queen who – the Royal Surgeons can vouch for it as can her father, the Sword of Justice; take it up with him if you will – has never known man. She has lived at home chastely ever since our marriage, and has been put away privily on account of this great joy and privilege . . .'

A few of the people, it is true, looked sceptical at the news, but for most of the crowd the King's words had the authority of Gospel. A very small number, who had known Elisabeth, could not believe that she would lend herself to anything so blasphemously fraudulent, and went along with the general rejoicing.

Only Julius, who watched the whole scene with growing horror, felt sick and turned away. He had anticipated, of course, that Fierens would make capital out of the child, but he had not foreseen the impact of the actual event.

To see his child held high and named as the returned Saviour filled him with mingled disgust and terror. Disgust for humanity and its false prophets, terror for the boy who would never be let out of these people's sight. What of old Frieda? More important still, what of Elisabeth? They must be beside themselves with worry. Elisabeth would surely be moved to Court to be with the baby?

And what would happen when the end came? The first to be slaughtered by the Herods out there would be the tiny child.

His heart went out to it and he wept.

The town had never had a Christmas like it.

Chapter 34

By mid-January, the blockade was really beginning to bite. Rensburg was surrounded by trenches and blockhouses, and a double line of infantry and horse. It was for the first time completely cut off.

The besiegers made no effort to take the town, however, preferring to wait, as the Bishop had suggested. They were, if cold, at least well supplied. There was no shortage of wood to burn and wine to give cheer.

Inside the town things were different. The first item to run short was, of all things, soap. The Saints had always prided themselves on cleanliness and this deficiency cut hard; but they were reassured by the Royal Orator, who told them cleanliness was in the heart and mind.

There was no doubt, however, that the lack of soap had a lowering effect on morale. The next thing to be rationed was flour, which caused not just discomfort but alarm.

The Royal Orator had no immediate answer to that; but the Sword of Justice had firm views. He ordered the deacons to search every house and requisition every crumb of food that they found. Evidence of hoarding was punished with the utmost rigour of the law.

It was becoming a difficult choice now, whether it was preferable to die as a result of imminent starvation, the axe of the Royal Executioner, or the pikes of the besiegers. At this juncture, the Royal Executioner was still the least-preferred option, but it was beginning to be a close-run thing.

All the horses in the town were now killed, apart from some of those of the Royal Bodyguard, which were held back for emergencies. Their flesh was salted and barrelled and sent – like most of the extra food gathered – up to the Royal Palace to be stored.

The snows of January and February turned into the floods of March and – though there was no shortage of water – the general populace had seen no proper food for days. Famine, first of the Horsemen, stalked the town. Every creature that could be eaten – cat, rat, dog, mouse, hedgehog, snail, bat – had been killed. People began to eat lichen and grass, old shoes, scraps of leather from the tanneries, slugs, distemper from the walls, bodies of the newly dead.

A watch was set up to discourage this last vile aberration, but it was discontinued when the watch itself gave way to it.

People ate what and where they could; and sometimes they did not wait for the dying to expire. Mothers fought off the clutching hands that reached out for their sick babies; warned their small children not to play down by the warehouses where the immigrants lived, telling them tales – all too true – of children who had disappeared. But soon there was no shortage of bodies as the Second Horseman, Pestilence, moved in; nothing dramatic as yet, an epidemic of fever, a mysterious and recurring stomach ailment, jaundice, whooping-cough; but enough to weaken an already weakened populace.

A child playing football with a skull . . . A girl collecting human bones for soup . . . There was plenty of material for his old master Bosch, Julius reflected, as he went about the town. Sometimes the very paper he drew on was stolen to fill some wretch's belly.

Even the birds seemed to have disappeared – either in fear or disgusted with the thin peckings to be had in the town. Only huge verminous crows, too vile to tempt even the starving, still remained (though surely bigger than before?), hopping monstrously about among the dying.

'The child thrives. He is growing in strength and wisdom,' Fierens announced one day on Mount Sion. 'He shall testify to you at Easter and we shall be delivered. Thus saith the Lord.'

Not even the Provost could rouse the crowd to more than a feeble cheer at this piece of news. It was even doubtful which end of the announcement they were cheering for.

Fierens was full of notions at this time. He was obsessed with the Christ-child and devoted a great deal of his time – much to Blommardine's annoyance – to listening to its cooings, which he would interpret as if they were the utterings of the Godhead. Elisabeth, who was now lodged in the palace, hated his attention but could do nothing to prevent it.

'He shall preach at Easter on Mount Sion,' he kept telling her.

It made her dreadfully afraid. What would a starving populace make of a plump, gurgling baby? They would rise up and rend him when no Salvation came.

Another of the King's ideas elicited a happier reception. He came down from one of his raptures, summoned Julius, and instructed him to paint the Virgin and Child.

'Blessed art thou among painters,' he told him, 'for whereas every other of your kind has had to make do with mere imitations of the Virgin and the Christ, you have the ineffable honour of depicting the real thing. Down on your knees, Painter, before the child, and beg his grace in your endeavours.'

Julius did as he was told, silently asking his baby's forgiveness for bringing him into this blasphemy. He was careful not to look at

Elisabeth, feeling that his blaze of love received would give them all away. Fierens began praying as Julius knelt.

The great question, he thought, shutting out the King's voice, is why the innocent seem to be punished in this world as much as the guilty – more so, because a punishment for the innocent is double punishment. Why would God do that? Is it because we are all guilty? Or is it because we are all innocent – even Fierens, even the Sword of Justice and the Provost? They cannot help what they are, they know not what they do. You'd think I was reasonably innocent; I like to think I'm a reasonably good man – but I know what I do, I am aware of what is right and wrong, and I still do wrong. Oh, it may be only a lesser wrong. It wouldn't be killing people or cutting out tongues or luring ten thousand people to starvation and death with wild promises. But perhaps my lesser wrong is as big in its way as Fierens' monster wrong. He would still be a pastry cook if all my little wrongs – and those of people like me – were little rights. Our lesser wrongs simply open the way for the thumping big ones. Perhaps the notion of Original Sin, which the Grand Master dismissed, is after all the right one. We deserve Fierens because we are guilty and have not yet been proved innocent. Or perhaps it is not Sin which leads us astray, it is self. Or perhaps . . . his heart beat faster . . . self is sin. He felt he was on the brink here of something tremendously important if he could but catch it. If sin is self, that must be why Love – the opposite of self – is so important . . .

He was so pleased with the idea that he looked up as Fierens concluded his invocation, and smiled at Elisabeth. She stared back at him, unblinking.

'Do not smile at the Madonna, Painter. She is holding Eternity in her lap,' the King admonished him.

Julius apologized.

'I require the picture to be painted with the Virgin, seated, holding the Child in the foreground with myself as Father, standing behind them – not too far behind.'

'I understand,' said Julius.

'I will come and go,' said the Lord of all the earth. 'You must do the best you can.'

The rising of the moon and the setting of the sun were in his care.

Julius was not able to speak to Elisabeth on this occasion but, at the first sitting, Fierens had to leave after half an hour.

'Carry on as you may, Painter.'

'I will, sire.'

'I will return in due course.'

'Very well, sire. Would you like me to complete your part of the portrait first? I could concentrate on you next time.'

But Fierens was away, his thoughts soaring across the ether, uncatch-
able, unknowable.

'Ummmm,' he said as he left, 'ummmm.'

'You can fetch me some more sienna from the store,' Julius
said to Hans-Peter, who was busying himself in the workroom.

'We have some here . . .' Hans-Peter began.

'More sienna.'

'Ah.'

'We cannot talk,' whispered Elisabeth when he had gone. 'I am
watched all the time. It is some idea of my father's.'

'What about the boy?'

'He is looked after by some nurse of theirs but I am allowed to
feed him. The King will have no one feed him but his Virgin
Mother.'

'Are you a virgin mother?'

She blushed.

'I cannot explain,' she said.

'I cannot explain either,' he whispered. 'Are you ready to leave
the . . .'

'Shhh.'

She knew he meant escape.

'Just two weeks more. At the first warm weather,' she murmured.
'There are listeners everywhere.'

'Where is Frieda?'

'She is here. I insisted she came. The King will not have the child's
mother upset! He says it is bad for the milk. She hates it here but she
wanted to be with me.'

She paused, and then she said in an adamantine tone he had not
heard before:

'And I will not have that woman near me.'

'Woman?'

'Your . . .' She wanted to say wife but could not.

'She is not my . . .'

'Shhh . . .'

'She is my sister.'

There was a scuffling sound at the door. Julius strode over and
wrenched it open. Hans-Peter stood there with an armful of supplies,
trying to get in.

'I brought some more,' he said, dropping pigment, 'in case we needed
them.'

Could Hans-Peter be a spy? Julius would not have thought so a month
ago, but now anything seemed possible. Everyone was afraid for their
skins.

427

Elisabeth made a little face at him and whispered voicelessly when Hans-Peter's back was turned. I love you, it said, Frieda will tell you when we are ready.

Chapter 35

It was the sense of absolute mastery of himself – through God, and later as God – that had given Fierens absolute mastery of the town.

It was a remarkable achievement and owed much to Nature: his fine voice, tall figure, handsome bearing and piercing brown-black eyes all contributed to his charm. But it was his total enrapture in his own rightness that shone through all his dealings, both public and private. Strong men's, hard nuts', tough veterans' characters all seemed to go into a sort of recess when he was present. Even Konrad would find he had to leave meetings after a few hours in order to regain his energies. Being in the man's magnetic presence left him exhausted and void.

The Provost went to the palace as little as possible for the same reason.

'I cannot do my job without my own initiative. I must have my own initiative. The King, all glory to him, makes me knackered and that's a fact.'

Neither of them would dispute, however, that the King had total power. Nobody, not even Julius, would dispute that in Rensburg. The question was, how far that power went outside the town.

Fierens, buoyed by his absolute sway at home, was convinced that it extended across the earth.

People like the Sword of Justice and the Provost were too committed to the New Jerusalem to consider that there was any alternative. Neither of them could survive failure. They truly believed that angels with flaming swords would rout the forces of darkness gathered at their gates.

Others, like Julius, saw no hope for a town where food was exhausted, whose munitions were running low, and whose leaders showed increasing signs of an abdication of – not simply reason – but instinct. It was not a matter of if, but of when the town should fall.

Fierens, however, was still coming up with ideas. On one occasion in March he produced the Holy Child to the assembled populace and told them that – rather than allow them to starve – the Babe would change the cobbles into loaves. The Child gave a pretty little gurgling shriek, and Fierens indicated to the faithful that they should eat.

Such was the power of his presence that down they went and scrabbled up the stones, gnawing at them desperately in their need.

'They're stones,' lamented the credulous Saints, 'alas for us.'

'You have not sufficient belief,' Fierens told them. 'O ye of little faith.'

Light in the head with hunger, the people wept.

'Go and fast and pray,' they were admonished. 'For ye know not when the time comes.'

Easter came and went, and some remembered that the King had said he would be burnt on Mount Sion if deliverance had not arrived. The crowd assembled in the square. The bodyguard had built a fire.

'I bet he doesn't come,' said a disenchanted mercenary. 'Guzzling up at the palace most like.'

'Name?' said a bodyguard, advancing. 'What was that you said?'

'The King . . .' stammered the mercenary. 'He'll be puzzling up at the palace.'

'Puzzling? The King doesn't puzzle.'

'He puzzles how to save mankind from its wickedness . . .' said the mercenary in a rare show of invention.

Further argument was curtailed by the arrival of the Holy Babe with the King himself – on foot, wearing only hose and shirt. He advanced upon the pile of firewood, stepped across, and stood against the central pole.

'Tie me, guards, then put the torch to it.'

Many of the people rushed forward.

'No, no. Do not leave us.'

'I have heard muttering that you have not been delivered.'

'Well. We have not,' said one sturdy burgher, emboldened by the King's imminent fricasseeing.

He looked, to some of the crowd, as if he had been hoarding – too plump by half he was.

'So,' said the King, turning upon him. 'You are not saved?'

The burgher spotted the trap but too late.

'Well,' he said. 'No . . . Not by arms . . .'

The King raised his hands to the crowd.

'Are you saved?' he shouted.

'Yes,' they roared back.

'What do we do with those who are not marked with the Sign?'

'REVENGE WITHOUT MERCY MUST BE TAKEN.'

The fat burgher was torn limb from limb. Some of the limbs indeed disappeared, and went to the stewpots down by the old warehouses.

The King stepped nimbly out of the firewood with the Holy Child and returned home in triumph where, after a good dinner, he spent the evening in group activity.

That was by no means the end of his inventiveness, however. Whether it was Blommardine's judicious administering of pomatum which stimulated his appetite for dramatic interlude, or simply his realization of the need for ever more fantastic diversions to keep the people's minds off their predicament, he reported that his next move was the production in the Cathedral of an obscene masque – or Massque as he called it – parodying the Catholic Mass. It ran for several days to great applause, and was then replaced by an even more popular satire (again written by himself) lampooning the rich and powerful with a wonderfully comic Lazarus who kept popping up out of his coffin with jokes and digs that made you 'corpse' with laughter, just when you least expected it. Some people actually hurt themselves they laughed so much.

Then there was the Sports Day.

The whole population of the town – no excuses – was bidden to form up for three whole days of dancing, racing and athletics. It was a strange choice of diversion for a people that was now too weakened by hunger and sickness to do much more than put one foot in front of the other. But faith – and the King's presence – worked their usual magic. One fellow, a lanky Saint from Malines, actually ran all the way round Mount Sion.

True, he collapsed at the end and had to be taken off to the kitchens, but it was a wondrous achievement and showed that the Spirit was moving strongly in the town.

In dancing, the slower measures were preferred, the Pavane proving most popular, though some of the court ladies showed a pretty leg in the Galliard. It was a shame about the casualties in the country section. The Sword Dance, particularly, claimed a number of victims.

As for athletics, the tug of war was the most popular event, although in several cases it was adjudged that the rope won. And in the long jump, one emaciated fellow literally jumped out of his skin.

'Well done, good and faithful servants,' said Fierens in his concluding speech. 'You have run the great race and the Lord, our great Spectator, is not indifferent. To all shall be given the prize . . .'

Everyone in the crowd inched forward at this news. Perhaps there might after all be a banquet.

'The prize is life eternal,' concluded the King. 'Refreshment will now be served at the tables behind you. Do not abscond with the beakers.'

There was a rush for the tables, but all they found was water.

'If we pray hard enough it will be wine,' cried a zealot, undiminished by previous disappointment.

It was strange, indeed, how disappointment seemed to inflame faith rather than diminish it; though there were exceptions.

'I've prayed till I've ruptured myself,' a tinker muttered to a disillusioned hosier. 'But all I've ever turned water into is piss.'

Chapter 36

It is very easy for those who are not in love – but have at some point been so – to forget the pain of it. Those whose self is too large to have been in love are the less for it; and if they think themselves lucky that they have escaped the leaden stomach, the terrible longing, the loss of appetite, the anxiety, the obsession, the depression, the anatomizing of tiny gestures, phrases, inflections – they are wrong. Love – not to be confused with jealousy – love, however painful, is a state of grace, even when it is not returned. Love reciprocated is to the state of lovelessness as colour is to grisaille.

Julius had for so many months existed with this benign distress that he did not think anything could make it more extreme. But the arrival of his son had that effect. It added to his burden of anguished concern – and yet it was not quite the same. It was not one and one making One. It was one and one making three.

He sat in his studio – tired, for he had not slept – with aching heart and aching brain. Lack of food, lack of sleep, tension, and frustration at his failure to find the missing Face, overwhelmed him. He had tried Fierens, the Sword of Justice, the Provost, Blommardine even. He had invented countenances of terrifying malignancy. But none of them seemed to fit. Now at last he lifted his gaze from Hell and looked once again, with that sense of refreshment, at the Garden. Why were there no children in the Garden? What was the meaning of the childless throng? Not one baby among them.

Of course! There were no children in Eden. They only came after Adam and Eve were thrown out.

It meant, then, that what he was looking at was the state of things that would have been if Adam and Eve had never sinned. No, that could not be right, for how would the other inhabitants of the Garden have arrived? Rather, what the painting must be showing was the true Millennium: a condition that would come about if – after Sin and Death had been laid low by Love – humanity were allowed to go back to the Garden and live there in peaceful bliss embracing all Creation.

Where did that leave his son? Not as a rival for his mother's love. That would make no sense. Not as an impediment to Love's union; but surely, yes, as an eventual candidate for union of his own. These people in the painting had no age. They were beyond Time . . . Generation to generation, they were Love's children and Love's children's children . . .

His head fell forward and he dozed.

'A child is the outward and visible outcome of union. He must be protected and nurtured and raised up. But is there not another outcome – a fruit of the Spirit? Look, there it is, floating heavenward to join its origin, borne by a winged Genius through the firmament. Love's sublimation . . .'

Julius started. Had he himself spoken? He had taken to mumbling. The great thing about talking to yourself, he used to say to Blommardine when she mocked him, is you can be sure of a sympathetic ear.

But this voice again . . . was it his? . . . was it his sympathetic tongue? . . . were there spirits here? . . . fruits of spirits . . . geniuses? He focussed his attention on the picture again; on Hell; on the two far from sympathetic ears pierced by the penis-knife, poised like a siege-engine over the gap that he had to fill.

His thoughts were interrupted by a noise that sounded as if Hell had belched or Armageddon had been joined – coming, it seemed, not far from the market-place itself. Something had exploded with an enormous, dull kerbooomff, causing the sky to light up as if Mount Sion had suddenly sprouted a volcano.

Hastily making notes of the sky's lurid gradations of colouring, he huddled on his cloak and went out to investigate.

He found the source of the conflagration to be none other than Konrad's distillery, which for some reason, whether arson or malfunction – certainly not enemy missile, for no activity had been reported – had suddenly taken upon itself to blow up. The raw spirit made a combustion the like of which Rensburg had never seen. Fire simply spurted out of the distillery as if it were auditioning for a part in Judgement Day.

The whole town, it seemed, had turned out to see it, though it was well past curfew-time. Firelight flickered on sweaty faces toasting in the enormous heat.

It occurred to Julius that Fierens might just have organized its firing himself. He would certainly have enjoyed the effect. And there he was, perhaps a shade early on the scene, standing with the Sword of Justice, who was looking rather green at seeing his alembic go up in smoke. The Sword of Justice was blaming the alchemist for the disaster.

'I'll kill him when I find him,' he kept repeating.

In fact the poor man was in a thousand morsels scattered over half the city.

'It is a Sign,' said the King. 'It is the hand of the Most High. Only a miracle can save the town. I shall pray to the Infant for rain.'

'Pray. Pray all of you,' shouted the Provost.

433

The cloud that had been threatening all day obliged with a downpour, and the fire was contained.

'The Lord shall come. He shall not be slow,' said Fierens. 'The Infant today gripped my dagger and cried "Awawahwahwoe to my enemies".'

Fatherhood (albeit surrogate) had made a difference to Fierens. He was proud of the child. But being the Son of God, he considered him also his brother. So he had a close family interest.

When the excitement was over, Julius walked back to his studio, lit a precious candle and finished his notes. The background was taking shape nicely now. He would place the distillery centre-left. He had an idea for a huge and menacing shape, half beast, half burning mill, looming over it. All that was needed was something else before it – straight lines to throw the hellish disorder into effect. What was this picture saying? Disorder, yes – disorder in the heart, the head, the soul, the spirit; disorder in the town, the land, the world. Nature itself in revolt . . .

He looked out of the window again, across the city walls to where the besiegers' fires twinkled in the darkness, reflected in the flooded water meadows below.

Flood, that was it. Hard edges and a flaming sky reflected cold upon the surface.

He blew out his candle and lay cold on hard edges of his own. Hell was coming nearer now.

Chapter 37

The worsening situation in the city appeared to have absolutely no effect upon the King. He almost seemed to delight in adversity, for it exercised his powers more, indulged his interest in obstacles. There was no drama in a play that had no challenges, no spectacle, no surprise. A breach in the wall, a fire, a rumour of treachery, all helped to build the tension in the town.

Meanwhile Blommardine plied him with pomatum in the most extravagant manner. Strange and wonderful that the drug which had so cast her downward among the devils should now have quite the opposite effect upon him. He was permanently elevated. Only a small part of him moved sentiently on earth. The rest was all glory, and he could completely cast that earthbound portion off when he chose.

For the moment, however, he did not choose. It was quite clear to him that these people among whom he moved must be taught a lesson. Those who were serious about salvation must be sifted from the gross and lumpen worldlings. He had not created all these characters for them simply to mill about the stage.

Accordingly, he summoned the population to Mount Sion once more on yet another rainy April morning. The crowd was noticeably thinner now. Famine had ridden among them, cutting them down, tumbling them into huge communal graves beside which emaciated relatives sobbed tearlessly; some rocked in utter desolation to and fro, and raved, sometimes tipping over and dying in the pit, too exhausted to crawl out.

'God is not pleased with you,' announced Fierens from his throne to the bedraggled multitude. 'He has commanded me to let you go. Open the gates, Provost.'

'No, no,' begged many of the people. 'We will stay.'

They had come too far, believed too much to turn back. They would go on, faithful unto death. But others were not of their persuasion. They had gone along with things this far because that had seemed the only option. Any chance to get out with their wives and children must now be seized with both hands. Old men and women, the sick and the disabled – all sensed that now was the time to go.

'Those who wish to go may leave,' said Fierens. 'But I sob for your souls. Yea, you shall be accursed of the Lord and your portion shall be everlasting damnation.'

Water gurgled from the Town Hall gargoyles and muttered in the gutters.

'Fall out all those for the road to everlasting damnation,' commanded the Provost.

They made a sorry sight – several hundred of them, many barely able to walk; some on crutches, others carried by their family on litters. Only a handful of able-bodied men went with them – more or less the last of the true Rensburgers, people who could finally take no more, who had lost everything, even their pride.

The gates groaned open, and hoppity-limp, away they straggled down the road beside the marsh and the water meadows.

It looked to some of the faithful, of course, as if the King had weakened. It was the first time in more than a year that anyone had been allowed to escape the iron bands of salvation. But the King was ahead of them as ever. Not only was the town rid of a great number of useless mouths to feed, but the weight of their sickness and disaffection was removed as well.

That would have been enough in itself, but the King had more of a lesson for the defenders than this. He knew that the general appointed by the States of the Upper and Lower Rhine would not be prepared to allow the Bishop to let these people pass. He knew that he would put the able-bodied men immediately to the sword and – fearing that the rest would spread heresy, and whatever other foulness they carried, behind the lines to his rear – would order that they should be stopped at the first line of trenches and instructed to wait his pleasure in the marsh until he had decided what to do with them. The Bishop's instinct was for leniency. The general's was for blood. And so they debated for a while . . .

Meanwhile, the King's expectation was justified in every particular, and when it came to pass he showed no mercy.

Some of the exiles now returned to the city and pleaded to be let in, beating and tearing at the gates with their bare hands; but they stayed shut fast. Others attempted to erect shelters, pitifully inadequate, beside the marshes.

Many lay down and died.

All the while it continued to rain.

Chapter 38

The town was now divided into twelve dukedoms, each of which was commanded by a desperado totally loyal to the King – men who had everything to gain and nothing to lose by the continued condition of the town.

If any within the walls was heard to speak of leaving the city or, worse, of surrender, he or she was hauled to Mount Sion, stripped, beaten and beheaded – that is, if they were lucky. Others were drawn while the life was yet in them and left to rot in their own ordure. Every available spike on gate and rampart carried a bloody head.

If you wore an air of resentment, or bravado, or insolence, that was enough to have you arrested and despatched. The only face to wear was a cowed, subservient, trusting one – unless you were a soldier, and then you had to look resolute. Laughter was tantamount to treason; not of course, that there was much to laugh about.

The atmosphere – and smell – in the town was little better than that which pertained outside.

While these horrors were being perpetrated, Julius worked on at the portrait with Elisabeth and her baby, filling in with Fierens as and when he appeared. Whenever she came to him these days, he noticed that Hans-Peter would be resolutely in attendance, his ear attentively flapping. Sometimes too he would be aware of other ears at the door, footfalls in the passage as he opened the door, noises in the rain outside the window.

The baby was now over four months old. The time to leave had arrived. Elisabeth had signalled as much to him and they had exchanged a scrap of paper. 'We could go now,' he read, 'but I am watched.' There had to be an opportunity for them to talk.

It came a few days later, when Hans-Peter had forgotten to bring over the madder from the studio. Julius had told him the day before it would be needed for the Madonna's dress.

The little painter was enormously apologetic.

'Stupid me,' he cried, beating his forehead. 'Call this a brain. It is a bat's nest. I won't keep you long.'

'Don't hurry,' they said.

When he had gone, Julius looked carefully out of the window – it was a particularly unpleasant rain that morning; even a Tom would have

437

had second thoughts about peeping in that chilly downpour. Then he walked softly towards the door, pounced upon it, and thrust it open wide to catch any who might be skulking in the passage. Still nobody.

He shut the door quietly again, then turned and took Elisabeth in his arms. They kissed each other hungrily, as if they would exchange their souls. Then he picked the child up and embraced it too, for, he told her, he knew how it was as a child to be unembraced.

'We must not be long,' she said. 'He will be back. We have to leave very soon. I do not think the town can hold much longer.'

'Nor I,' he said. 'But it will be difficult. The dukes are ranging far and wide. The gates are watched and, just in case we should fail to take the point, they are topped by heads and quarterings of others that have tried. Even if we should succeed, the only thing you can say about the picture outside is that it has helped me very much in my view of Hell.'

'Poor people,' she said. 'Poor town. It was a good town really, you know. Ordinary. At least I thought it was. I suppose it was like our old apple-tree. Covered in reds and gold from a distance, until you got up close and saw the . . . What is it, dearest?'

Julius had started.

'I thought I heard a . . .'

He ran to the door again and quickly opened it.

'Nothing,' he said, returning.

'There is a way,' she said.

'How?'

'I won't tell you now. I do not trust this place.'

'You trust me?'

'Completely.'

'I love you. If anything . . . should happen . . . remember that.'

'We have one heart,' she said. 'It happened when we made love. In spite of everything – I felt it.'

This time there was a discernible noise outside.

'Hans-Peter,' he told her.

'I will send for you in a week's time. Be ready at eight o'clock in the evening, a week from today. I love you.'

The door opened. It was the little painter.

'Here we are,' he said, holding out the little parcel. 'Madder.'

Chapter 39

It was a desperate pass. A week later and he still had not finished.

It was such a little thing. Just one small section of a complex picture, but it was the key to it: the centre. Everything would fall into place when he had found it. Until it was finished he knew they could not leave. Whoever was leading him on this strange course would not allow it. Panic was setting in.

He had tried more faces; faces he had seen in crowds of unspeakable brutality, that he had earmarked for a Carrying of the Cross; faces that recalled other faces: the Bishop's, Savonarola's, the Medici Pope's, he with the fistula that stank like the miasma coming up from the marshes. He even tried the face of his old master Bosch, but that too – though, yes, there was something to it – still failed to provide the answer. He knew he would know it when he saw it. It would be blindingly obvious. It would stare him in the face.

Wait a minute, now.

He got up and walked to the looking-glass that stood upon the table near the window. He sank his face into it, pushing it down as if it were in a pool, shimmering thought over it, rippling the surface with anxiety.

It was a common enough face, a little on the long side, blue eyes with rather heavy lids, wide-set, a straight nose, high cheekbones and a mouth that for the most part seemed to express a sort of self-deprecating resignation, brown hair with tinges of red and gold.

It might as well do, he thought. I've tried everything else.

He started to draw. As the work progressed, he became aware of a very light creaking, scratchy sort of sound, which he thought must be an intermittent drip from the roof falling on paper – there was enough of it about – although the noise he heard sounded almost more like metal upon metal. It did not disconcert him. For some reason, he was beginning to feel sure that he was on the right track.

And indeed, why should it not be him? Bosch had first instructed him to do it. It was his commission. He had been sent here to this hellish place, trapped in a bad marriage to fall in love in impossible circumstances. He had been tormented by fate – or by someone or something else – in order to solve someone else's problem.

He tried various expressions on his face, but none of them seemed right. They all seemed to be looking out at him with a sulky, petulant, hard-done-by air. It was like a child having a tantrum at a tidal wave.

And then he thought: it is true that I believe I have been a victim of some malevolent design, but I have, after all, turned the tables on it, since I have met on the way the greatest good fortune that life offers. I love and am loved. Whoever planned my evil pilgrimage did not think of that.

So how should I be looking, if I were in Hell, but back with regret and resignation and without a shadow of hope to the Garden of Love that I have lost?

And then he thought: perhaps that pilgrimage is not the work of a devil. Perhaps it is I with my little I that have been too selfish to see. That face of mine that I am putting in the picture must be the face of my self. Hell is my self, the Garden is Love which is my selflessness.

Since even in Hell I am capable of remembering Love, there is still hope for my redemption, so I shall take out the hopelessness and put in a shadow of possibility. There. It is done. How does it look?

Even as he put his brush down, he was aware of a curious sensation of permission; the noises that he had heard ended with an almost inaudible but distinct iron percussion that sounded like a click upon his inner ear. He had made the grade. Something had opened.

With inexpressible relief, hurriedly, expertly, he copied the face that he had painted onto the panel that must be despatched to the appointed place.

He completed the final touches in the late afternoon and sat, as the paint dried, still dazed with relief. He had finished the strange task that had been set him. There would be no more money – it had continued to arrive throughout his time in Rensburg (though latterly, of course, he had handed it in). There would be no more obligation. He was free.

He must have dozed again because he started and looked up, and it was nearly dark. Clouds the colour of a boiled pudding admitted no departing light from the sun. He wrapped his painting as best he could to protect it on whatever course Elisabeth had decided upon. He had no affairs to settle if the worst befell them. Elisabeth and their son were all the affairs he had. He had no regrets that he had not expressed. He was leaving Rensburg – if indeed they managed to find a way to do so – as gladly as he had ever left anywhere in his life. Hell and Rensburg . . . he would be overjoyed to put both behind him.

At last there came the longed-for tap at the door.

Even at this stage he felt that something might have gone wrong, that she would not have been able to get away. But there she was at his door, heavily cloaked and hooded, with the baby snugly wrapped.

They kissed.

'You got away all right?'

'They are at a feast. Afterwards there will be the usual revels. I shall

440

not be missed. I placed a bolster in my bed and gave the child's nurse some poppy which Pastor Joachim found for me.'

'Pastor Joachim?'

'You have met him once before. Do you remember the two priests you met when I was being married?'

'I certainly do. I thought they were both dead. One of them most certainly is. I spoke to him before he died.'

'Pastor Joachim is still with us by a miracle – a number of miracles. He will help us to escape.'

'Will he come here?'

'There would be too much risk. We will meet him at ten o'clock.'

'It is only eight now.'

'I know.'

She smiled at him and put the baby down.

'He will sleep,' she said. 'He's very good. I fed him before I came.'

They held hands and stepped into the Garden.

Soft wings, gentle breezes, scents of flowers, perfumes of fruit and fresh grass, running water, sweet laughter, flower-bells and the sound of bees folded about them as they walked.

There was all the time in Creation.

Hands helped them, pointing the way; smiles attended them; they were greeted without surprise as though everyone had known they were coming.

Fruits profuse and marvellous were there to eat; pitchers full of exquisite, reviving juices and liquors refreshed their senses.

At last, in the fragrant recesses of a rose, they lay and took the Sacrament.

Chapter 40

'I tell you I followed them here,' said Schwenk to the Sword of Justice.

In league with Hans-Peter, he had actually been lying in a clothes-chest in the palace workroom when Elisabeth had outlined her plan.

He had come up the stairs behind mother and baby to make certain where they were going, and then hurried back to call the guard.

'No sign of them,' said Konrad. 'But what the . . .'

There was a little gurgle and a coo from the bundle on the artist's bed.

'It is the Child. Take him to the palace,' cried Konrad. 'They cannot be far away. Keep watch by the door downstairs. They'll be back shortly, if I know my daughter. She will not leave the Child long.'

The baby started to cry.

'Strange painting,' said Hans-Peter, 'but well done.'

He pointed at the painted wall whose hanging lay gathered on the bed.

'What?' said the Sword of Justice, turning. 'Foh! It is an idol. We'll send someone to remove it later. Look to the door.'

They clattered out and there was silence in the room . . . And then there came the sound of purling water and bird-song and the murmur of bees and distant voices and rippled leaves again . . . and a translucent mist came from the wall like the rainbow misting of a waterfall . . .

And there was suddenly Elisabeth's voice.

'I thought I heard him call. I'm sorry. We could have stayed for ever. But we had to come back.'

'I know,' said Julius. 'We had to come back. But it doesn't matter now. Nothing matters because we are one. Nothing can stop that.'

She hurried to the bed; stopped; turned a face towards him that was deathly-white.

'Oh sweet Jesus,' she cried. 'Our baby. He is gone. They've taken him.'

Fear held his heart.

Oh, God, he thought, was it always to be like this; give with one hand, take away with the other? Haven't I done enough? Must there always be one more monster in the maze?

'What shall we do?' she said. 'We can't leave him.'

She didn't blame him or Love, nor would she. It wasn't Love's fault;

442

rather that Antichrist's of Love, Uitwaarden-Fierens, tin God of self, King of the Castle, pulling heaven and earth down after him.

He drew a deep breath. There was no fear any more. He gathered up the completed panel and gave it to her.

'There's nothing for it. We had better go downstairs. Take the painting for me. They will not hurt you. And kiss me a last time. I may not see you again on this earth.'

Chapter 41

Konrad decided that, for cosmetic purposes, it would not do to have the Mother of the Returned Christ arraigned for misdemeanour. He swore Schwenk and Hans-Peter to silence, and issued the direst of threats to anyone of those involved in the arrest who should doubt that his daughter had been abducted.

The public line was that the painter was to be charged with the attempted rape of the Queen.

Later, half-mad with anxiety and the ravages of excess, Konrad visited his daughter in her apartment. She sat white-faced, looking at the floor as he shouted.

'You do this to me, Daughter? How dare you? By God I'll . . .'

He made as if to strike her. Suddenly she turned and faced him with blazing eyes.

'I am still the Queen, Father. Remember that. You touch me and you die. I want my child.'

Konrad was disconcerted at such talk from one who had always seemed subservient.

'Your child?' he blustered. 'A fine mother, leaving him alone for any intruder to pick up.'

'He was not alone. I was in the room.'

'The room?'

He still puzzled over how they could have come down the stairs when he had so searched the place.

'We were both there.'

'You lie.'

Doubtless there was some secret avenue.

'My baby?' she said again.

'He is with the nurse. You are to be confined for the moment to your quarters. It seems you are not to be trusted, madam.'

'And Julius?'

'The painter? He is to be charged with high treason.'

'But that's ridiculous! What treasonable thing has he done?'

'The attempted rape of the Queen is reason enough.'

'He did not attempt.'

For a moment Konrad did not take in the import of her statement. Hans-Peter had not yet thought it safe to tell him all he knew.

'You would, of course, defend . . .'

And then he stopped, swinging his ponderous head like a bull about to charge.

'You mean?'

'I mean I lay with him.'

Suddenly all the fight went out of Konrad. He sat down on a bench and passed a hand over his face.

'Don't say that,' he told her. 'Don't ever say that.'

If this got out it would be the end of everything.

'I will say it if there's a trial. I'll say . . . he's the father of my child.'

'No trial,' said Konrad, wearily.

It was some time since there had been trials.

And then her words sank in. He looked at her aghast.

'What did you say?'

'I'll say he's the father of my child.'

'Shhhhh. Impossible,' whispered Konrad. 'Don't speak so loud.'

'Not impossible. I came up to his room once before. I love him completely. He is mine and I am his.'

'Oh, my God,' Konrad moaned. 'This is the end of me.'

He looked completely broken. The months of surfeit had left their mark. The rodents of vice had been at his stuffing. The man who had struck terror into the hearts and brains and bowels of the town was now a ragbag of nerves.

'Where is he?' asked Elisabeth, pressing home her advantage.

He did not reply for a moment but sat hunched, thinking of Fierens' extraordinary facility for knowing what went on. Did he know of this? Surely he could not or he would have punished them both to the limits of his genius. Or was he playing a game, winding them in? He had watched him do this with a number of the Royal Household. One moment you'd be supping with them, the next you'd be scraping their skin off a cell wall.

'Where is he?' asked Elisabeth again. 'You haven't . . . he's not . . .'

She could not bring herself to say the word. He must be alive. If he were dead, she would pull the sky down.

Konrad roused himself.

'Oh, he's alive all right. Fierens has a job for him to do.'

445

Chapter 42

Fierens had come to him in the dungeon where he had been thrown.

'So,' he said, 'Martens. You thought I did not recognize you? Have you forgotten my name?'

He was wearing a golden cloak with a crown of gold upon his head. In his left hand he carried a golden sceptre, in his right a crystal globe surmounted by a golden cross. His very beard and moustache seemed made of the stuff. Gold twinkled and nodded at his mouth and chin in the gleam of the soldiers' torches. He looked like an archangel.

Julius said nothing. One of the soldiers kicked him.

'Answer His Majesty, painter-pig.'

'Uitwaarden,' said Julius.

The sceptre came crashing down across his thigh.

'Wrong. It is Lord of All the Earth.'

'Ahh,' said Julius.

'Do you know me?'

'Yes,' said Julius.

'Yes, Majesty,' said the soldier.

'Wrong.'

The golden rod came flashing down on Julius again.

'I am Unknowable.'

'Ohhh,' groaned Julius.

'What am I going to do with you?'

'Spare me?' suggested Julius.

'Wrong once more. You are a man of such sin that our city can hardly breathe, our river out there can hardly flow while you remain in our midst. But yet I will stay your punishment. Your devil's gift shall be used to God's purpose at the last. It is our pleasure that you finish our picture of Mother and Child, Martens. We shall stand over you while you work so you will not even dare to think beastliness at our Queen.'

Chapter 43

Next morning, at daybreak, after a shivering night spent lying on rancid straw, Julius was shaken awake by a gaoler and given a crust and a bowl of dirty water.

Soon after, the guard arrived and escorted him, shackled, back to the Queen's apartment where he found Fierens waiting with Elisabeth and the baby.

The easel was set up. The paints and brushes were ready to hand. Nothing was said. Fierens made one movement with his hand. The inference was clear.

So Julius set himself to complete his masterpiece – for masterpiece it was going to be. All the constraints he had felt when he wrestled with old Bosch's Hell were gone. He was free. His brush flowed smooth as a stream. It was going to be a work – he could see it as though it had a being quite separate from his own – of great tenderness and grace.

Fierens, as he had promised, stood beside him attended by two soldiers with drawn swords. There was no chance to speak to Elisabeth or even to delay a little in the painting. All he could do was look now and then from the canvas he worked on to his Love and their little son, with a hopeless adoration that dared not, for her sake, ask for return. Meanwhile, she gazed ahead with huge, sad eyes as the baby was placed and replaced upon her lap by the nurse. He had never seen Elisabeth look more beautiful.

'You are taking too much time,' said Fierens after a while. 'Bustle, Painter. I have the world to manage.'

'Will the Queen turn her head a little to the left?' said Julius.

On the fifth day, it was all but complete.

Weak from lack of food – he was still given only crusts and water – Julius was beginning to feel light-headed. But the picture glowed and breathed under his touch. It was a marvellous thing and fitting for the Mother of God or the Bride of Love, whichever way you looked at it. All the time his heart ached as if there were a knife in it, as if it were being eaten by eagles.

On the sixth day, Julius fainted, but was revived with water and dragged back to his easel.

'It is finished,' he said at last. 'All it needs is the varnish. The other painter can do that.'

'Do you like it, Queen?' asked Fierens.

She rose from her seat and came round to examine it. Fierens pushed Julius roughly away. There was a profound silence while she gazed. Even the little child was quiet, though awake, looking adoringly up at his mother.

'It is the most beautiful picture I have ever seen,' she said at last, speaking neither to her husband nor to Julius, but to the world. 'It is a masterpiece.'

'Excellent,' said Fierens.

And he took a sword from one of the soldiers and ran the picture through, slashing and tearing at it until it was completely destroyed.

'What . . .' shouted Julius, struggling. 'No . . .'

'Why?' cried Elisabeth.

'It is faeces,' said the Lord of All the World. 'Take them to the dungeons.'

Chapter 44

Julius was cast into darkness alone. He had no idea where they had put Elisabeth and her baby. There was no sound save the cold drip-drip of water on stone and the distant scuffle of a rat.

And so he lay nursing his bruises for a long while, consumed by the most horrible anxiety and remorse – had he not led Elisabeth into this danger? Would it not have been better after all never to have known Love than to have exposed her and his innocent child to such horrors?

He could have endured it for himself, but to know that they were prisoners too caused him bitter grief. There was nothing he could do but wait. At least, he thought, in the Hell that I have been studying so intently, full of vileness though it was, there was light. You could not even paint this scene. It is blind-black as our predicament.

At last, however, hours (as it seemed) later, he became aware of a ghost of a flicker from the direction of what he supposed to be the door. A line of reddish glimmer showed. There, he thought, that is more like Hell. It grew in intensity as its source advanced towards him.

Thoughts began to assail him that made him wish again for blackness, for nothing but evil would be bringing light down here. And when the door burst open, revealing Fierens, with the Sword of Justice, and six soldiers with torches, he knew that his fears were realized. They had not come to let him out.

Julius prepared himself to die. He had no fear of death now, however dreadful the throes of dying might be. He would be united again with his Love and together they would rise, as one, to be united with the one Beginning and End of all things.

Fierens, as ever, knowing or seeming to know what was in all minds and conditions, smiled.

'Ah, Painter,' he said, 'but you're not going to die yet.'

'Not die,' cried Julius. 'Then let us out. If you play God, you can play merciful God.'

'Play?'

There was a terrible chill in the voice.

'You remember the play, do you, Martens?'

'I remember the play. It wasn't my fault you didn't get the part. And anyway, it was nearly twenty years ago. Is all this because of *that*?'

'God is God not just in great matters, Painter, but in minute particulars. You are a bad liar. And you are to be finished. You have seen too much and understood too little. It is time to put the lights out.'

He motioned to two of the soldiers, who brought forth a brazier in which two irons rested.

'Hold him.'

The other four soldiers seized Julius by his arms and legs. Julius could see Konrad's face, deathly pale in the firelight.

'What do you mean to do?' shouted Julius, struggling.

'Your eyes have made mischief for you, Painter. There is only one cure. It is time, as I say, to put the lights out.'

Seizing an iron, he thrust it without stopping straight into Julius's eye.

Blackness turned to red, pain beyond any torment in Creation.

Somewhere a voice started screaming – a thin, high noise, like a sound heard at night in a wood.

The body bounced and writhed but the soldiers held it fast.

'And now the other one.'

The pain of the first by no means prepared him for the agony of the second. But now another, kinder blackness closed over the red, the high noise stopped, and the body fell back insensible.

Chapter 45

Her cell was more comfortable than a dungeon; there was at least the reflection of sunlight off a stone wall; and a window-sill with moss and bird droppings; but it barely served for a mother and child. As well, thought Elisabeth, that Fierens had insisted she feed the child herself (Mary had fed the infant Jesus, he said). Otherwise, it seemed, there would have been nothing for the baby to eat, as indeed there was nothing for herself. She waited in anguish for whatever decision might come, worried more for her child and Julius than her own fate, and frightened for all of them. She had heard things in a night of fitful sleep that should not be heard.

Finally, the door opened and her father appeared. He seemed to sag more every time she saw him.

'Father,' she exclaimed, relieved that at least it was he and not the iron-bound Provost.

'I am not your father,' he said loudly, looking round with the door still open. 'You have forfeited that right.'

He closed the door and sat down heavily.

'Well, Daughter,' he said. 'It seems I am to kill you.'

'Kill me?' she exclaimed.

The baby gave a little gurgling cry of pleasure.

'Hear that, little one? Your grandfather wants to kill your mummy,' she said.

'Gerrga,' said the baby.

'Yes, it is, gerrga. It's very gerrga indeed,' she said.

She was on the verge of tears, but she would not cry in front of him.

'It's either I kill you or I kill myself. That's the way Fierens looks at it. And I don't have the heart to kill myself.'

He could not kill himself and he could not kill her. If he didn't do it, somebody else would. What was to become of him?

Funny, he thought. I never did discover the secret way of the Adamites.

'My God,' she cried, suddenly enraged. 'You are a fool. Look what you've done to us all.'

He nodded, dully.

'It's either you or me,' he said. 'He doesn't trust me otherwise.'

'And what about the baby?' she asked, clasping the child to her breast.

'The baby will be spared. No, more. He will be Prince of Peace.'

That at least was one dread removed. She had been fearful that they would cast him from the battlements.

'And Julius?' she asked. 'What is to happen to him?'

He looked uncomfortable. That high rabbit-scream still rang in his ears. Funny, really, when he had heard so many screams, that this one should linger. It seemed to have wound its way right into his head and wouldn't come out.

'What is it?' she shouted at him. 'What have you done?'

Terrible visions of her mangled love assailed her – Julius broken and bleeding from the bastinado or the rack; flayed, fingernailed, hamstrung, swollen with forced water; incarcerated in little-ease, where he could not stand or lie or stretch . . .

'What is it?' she cried again, attacking him with her fists.

He put up his hands, weakly fending her off.

'Fierens did it,' he said, 'not I. It was your husband.'

'My husband? Foh.' She spat on the floor. 'What did he do?'

And then he said the one thing that she hadn't thought of. The worst thing, the impossible thing for her painter with his speedwell eyes, so quick and kind.

'Blinded him,' her father said. 'Put out his eyes with a red-hot poker.'

And he covered his ears involuntarily as if the scream would come out of his head and volley round the walls.

Chapter 46

When Julius regained consciousness, in double darkness, the agony had scarcely abated. If he could have found some way of hastening his end, he would have embraced it. Pain like this was more than a mortal was meant to bear. Its only virtue – if it could be called that – was that it almost stopped him thinking of his loss. Almost, but not quite . . . As he hovered between consciousness and swoon, a pain as cold as the other was incandescent filled his heart.

He would never see the sweet fields, counterpoints of green in the forest, or the clouds, or the waters, or the buildings, or the graceful beasts, or the men and women little lower than the angels, or the children, or his own child, or the dear face of his beloved; never again; never, never. Oh, fair world, I have lost you.

There were no tears to weep, no eyes to wash, only a gaping, aching hole of torn flesh which he could feel wet in his hands.

The high scream had given way to bitter, deep, retching groans of hopeless pain and sadness without solace.

I am adrift on a dark ocean. Take me, currents, and let me drown . . . Take me . . .

But . . . here was a strange thing . . .

It could not be . . . but something . . . was growing brighter. Perhaps, after all, they had not truly done it, only feinted at a blinding. Yes, he could positively discern something now. It must have been another of Fierens' games, for he could quite plainly see greens and pinks, and the beginning of shapes, pale and tall, that were – of course they were – he could see now, men and women little lower than the angels, and flowers, huge and huddled, and a great silver haddock which lay on the grass for some reason, though it seemed perfectly natural for it to do so. Let the haddock lie.

He was overjoyed, of course, for he had thought sight gone for ever; and yet here he was in the Garden again, seeing as well as ever, if not better. For whereas before it had had a dreamlike quality, a sort of delicious mistiness, this time it was sharper and deeper. Indeed, as he looked up, he could see the plain beyond with the prancing animals and their riders circling the pool, and beyond them the lake with the globe and the wonderful vegetable-mineral castles.

He lay back. He was still feeling weak. A naked girl approached him, smiling.

'That's better,' she said. 'Would you like some more of the fruit?'

She showed him the great pointed blackberry she was carrying, upon whose end a drip of moisture was already forming. So that was what had eased his pain and given him his sight back.

'More fruit, please,' he said, and drank gratefully as she held the blackberry's point to his mouth.

He could feel the strength returning as he sucked the juice. And now he rose thankfully and wandered among the crowd. And whereas before he had been a visitor with Elisabeth, like strangers in a village, though welcome – now they all seemed to know him, and he them. There was Philipp and Bernt, and lovely Magda, naked as a sixpence. He too was naked. They all stopped what they were doing as he passed by, and greeted him.

A lovely black girl, Shuna, balancing a cherry on her head, standing beside Adela and watching her fly her tame swallow, turned and said:

'Hullo, Julius. You were a long time.'

'It's not easy,' he smiled back.

'Oh, it's not easy. If it were easy, there'd be no point.'

Round and round went the swallow; then came back, at a whistle, to settle on Adela's hand.

He strolled on, pausing beside a couple, Friedrich and Inge, languorously stroking one another in a transparent seed-pod. He smiled at them and watched their lovemaking without a shadow of shame. Below, in the bulb of the plant, Thomas looked out through a tube at his tame rat, which also answered his call.

'Play with my rat, Julius?'

Julius took the animal which before he had always regarded with horror. Now its little face looked up at him so wisely and trustingly he felt nothing but love for it. He returned it to Thomas who received it happily.

He was walking beside the lake now. A boy, doing cartwheels in the water, stood upside down with a huge raspberry held between his thighs. He was holding himself fulsomely – though the raspberry thorns and that hooded crow (again) said his carnality should be tempered by love for a partner. And there she was!

'It's lovely, in,' cried the boy.

'Wait for me!' came her cry from across the lawns.

Further on two lovers, bobbing on the water in a great pink oak-apple, looked out to pick a sweet berry which floated by, surrounded by nibbling swimmers.

How jolly it all was! How gorgeous that great tortoiseshell butterfly

454

which whirred like clockwork right past him and landed on a thistle flower.

He paddled in the water, looking back at it. Beyond, more people, more faces he knew, streamed forward joyously up the steps from a dim grotto.

'Look out! So sorry!' He had nearly bumped into another couple, who were themselves looking backward. It was Charles and Anneliese, moving out of the way of a procession of gorgeous birds.

'Apologies, Charles and Anneliese.'

'Don't mention it. Our fault entirely. I say, are you all right?'

'All right?'

To tell the truth, he was beginning to feel odd again . . . weak . . . The pain was coming back. Everything was going dark . . .

'Quick. He'll help you,' said Charles.

The great gold finch stopped, and the birds behind him halted too.

In its beak it held another blackberry whose juice welled out in a stream of pure refreshment.

'Aaah . . . Aghh . . .'

He writhed and struggled in the water like a sail half overboard, his limbs the livid-green of death.

'Arrrgh . . .'

'Peace . . . peace . . .' called the bird, and peace enfolded him as he drank.

When he awoke, he was lying in another part of the Garden, and Ammanati's voice was speaking in his ear.

'"Just as our mother's womb holds us for nine months, preparing us not for itself but for the place in which we seem to be released, fit already to take on a mind and to lead an existence in the open light of day . . ."'

Wait a minute. That was the Grand Master's voice. Of course, he was Ammanati too. He could see him now, looking gravely down at him and reading from a book.

'"So also during this time,"' continued the magus, '"which extends from childhood into age and in which we grow ripe for another birth, a new birth awaits us, a different state of things. Although you dread that day as your last, it is in fact the nativity of the eternal. Lay down the burden. Why do you hesitate? Did you not once already come forth from a body in which you lay hidden, a body that you abandoned? You clutch fast, you struggle and resist – just as it was through your mother's intense effort you came into the world. You sigh, you weep; this too is the lamentation of birth-pangs. But consider instead your good fortune in being granted grace – and reflect that it is nothing new for you to be separated from something of which you were formerly a part."'

The Grand Master folded the book and sat for a while looking down at Julius, who felt both moved and amazed by the words.

'Seneca,' said the Grand Master, turning his sharp brown eyes upon him and perceiving Julius to be ready for conversation, 'to his friend Lucilius.'

'Am I dead or alive?' asked Julius.

'You are in labour – preparing in due course to throw off your soul. You have learnt to dissolve your self in Love. Your next course is to do the same in Death. Life, Love and Death are three points of the wheel. Through Death, literally, comes Life, Julius. As you will find in due course. That is why there is no shame or sting in it. That is why Death was at the Creation. It could not exist without life, and vice versa.'

Julius raised his head and looked about him. Immediately to his right he saw, reclining in a crystal tube, his dearest love, Elisabeth. She seemed to be listening to something profound, for she inclined her head in her hand and turned her face attentively.

'Elisabeth, my love,' he called.

'She cannot see or hear you,' said the Grand Master.

In her hand she carried an apple; on her lips was a seal. Julius felt that he could lie here gazing at the mystery for ever, but the Grand Master gently broke in on him.

'It will shortly be time to go, Julius. More pain, I'm afraid. But it will not be for long.'

'Will I come back here?'

'This place that you see is only an image of what is to come, Julius. It uses earthly images because that is all that earthbound creatures can comprehend. I planned it and designed it myself over many, many years to teach and to encourage and to warn. We see here the spheres of Earth, Moon and Sun. The Sun, symbol of the Creator, sows Spirit into the cosmos. This is conceived by the Moon which gives birth to Soul. The Earth then clothes it with substance which is Body. In death, the reverse takes place and Love lifts the purified Soul from Body back to Spirit – and in due course back to the Sun. As it is written in the Adamites' hymn: "They who know the joys of Love, rise to join the God above".'

'But I thought my master Bosch . . .'

'He painted the picture to my instruction.'

Julius took in the news with some amazement.

'But what . . . why? . . .'

'He had transgressed against the Brethren. It was a way of atoning for some of the harm he had done.'

'What harm?'

'Well . . . you, Julius, for one thing.'

'I?'

This was extraordinary. And yet there had to have been some reason for so many of the rigours of his life.

There was another question he had to ask, which had been burning in him for almost as long as he could remember.

'Tell me,' he said. 'You are my father, aren't you?'

'Oh, Julius . . .'

The Grand Master smiled.

'What a life you have had. If I had been your father, I would not have . . .'

He stopped.

'Go on, please.'

'There are times when . . . even if you have been at the beginning of things and have, under God, such power and knowledge as might make you prodigious . . . There are times when even God himself has to watch. For to interfere would be to break Nature.'

'So you are not my father. Who is?'

'The man you call master. Master Bosch.'

'But he cannot be,' Julius said, astonished.

'I assure you.'

'Why did he not claim me? Make much of me? He never even hinted that he . . . He let me think that it was you.'

'He married in weakness a wealthy woman. He liked position, fine things, influence. It was not a sin, he thought. The money allowed him to choose the commissions he wanted. It was very reasonable.'

'Reasonable,' repeated Julius, nodding.

It was strange he did not feel anger.

'We know no thought of vengeance here,' said the Grand Master, reading his mind. 'But what I have to tell you will exercise your forbearance to the limit.'

'Please go on,' said Julius.

'Everything went well with him. He became famous and respected which was no surprise, for he was a painter of genius. We were strong in Bois le Duc in those days and your father joined the Brethren. It was my doing, for I had come there with the purpose of persuading him to paint our cryptograph, our secret, Julius. And then, disaster. Or was it disaster?'

He paused.

'Was it disaster?' asked Julius.

'You will see. He fell in love with a young woman, little more than a girl, of good family in the town, daughter of a noble. What was worse – or better – was that she fell in love with him. It was, you could see, the love of both their lives. What were they to do?'

'What did you suggest?'

'To the Brethren there was only one answer. There can be no impediment to such a sacrament.'

'But he was married.'

'The Brethren say – especially if there are no children – that such a marriage is meaningless. Bosch and his love should simply have left and found a home elsewhere. We could have helped them. She was willing, but Bosch for some reason – comfort, reputation, respectability – felt that they should wait a little while. This, in that perfect universe of Love, was when the imperfection entered. For when she became with child – which she did – she did not tell him at first for fear of losing him. Can you believe it?'

'I can,' said Julius, who had also known weakness in Love.

'And then, of course, when she did tell him, it was too late. Any day now, she would be discovered. Bosch panicked. He knew his wife would take it badly. He had just received a commission for the Cathedral. He was honoured in the town. Though he loved the girl, he loved his selfish life. He could not do it.'

'Selfish,' said Julius, thinking of his face in Hell.

'Yes,' smiled the Grand Master. 'You had that right at the last, Julius. To continue. The girl would surely have been in disgrace with her parents, and Bosch would have been pilloried – literally – but Fate took a hand. Plague visited the town and the whole family with the exception of the girl and a loyal old serving-maid died within a week. Thus she was able, on the pretext of a lowering sickness, to keep inside the house, and finally left, under cover of darkness, when the baby was due. The child was born in the stews down by the river. And Bosch, who had arranged for her lodging and her midwife, waited outside while the child was born. I have perhaps underplayed his love for the girl. I do not believe he ever recovered his happiness. Unable to blame himself, he blamed the child . . . you . . .'

Julius had understood where this was leading, but it was still a shock to hear it.

'I . . .' he murmured. 'It was not my fault.'

'No, but he became almost mad in his vindictiveness. He wanted you placed where he felt you would be least happy. We reasoned with him and obliged him finally to take you on. He could be very . . . veiled. You never even suspected what he thought of you. For a time, we did not fully appreciate it either.'

'What did he think of me?'

'He hated you. You had destroyed his happiness. Worse, he continued to blame you for what happened to your mother.'

'What did happen to her?'

'She never really recovered from the sorrow of losing you and the pain and anxiety of the situation. Her uncle from Aachen, who became the head of the family, moved to the town and obliged her to marry that lawyer, your wife Blommardine's father.'

'So she *was* my half-sister!'

'Yes, but only Bosch knew that. The tale is nearly over. The girl died shortly after giving birth to Blommardine, which turned Bosch against you still further. He was half-mad, I think. There was a kind of madness in his painting.'

'He did send me to Florence,' said Julius, trying to find kindness in his father.

'That was the Brethren, Julius. We thought it would be good to separate you. And indeed he did seem to moderate. But all the while he was hatching his last two stratagems. First, he was jealous of your skill, especially when you came back from Italy. You could do things he could never attempt.'

'Jealous of me?' said Julius. 'He was the master.'

'Even so, he hit on this ruse of making you finish this great picture of his – which was, of course, finished already. It was a trick of his. He believed it would intrigue and unsettle and even obsess you – which it did (he knew you well; it was perhaps a little like knowing himself). It was easy for him to arrange your payment. The rest he left to your sense of duty. He knew it would both tie you to his style, show his superiority and, most important, waste your time.'

'Do you mean to say . . . it was all for nothing?' asked Julius. 'Why did no one stop me?'

He did not feel aggrieved but astonished.

'For one thing, the Brethren did not know. I was away in another part of the world – in another body, Julius; yes, I will show you how to do that at last, since I perceive you are of the stuff that will make a master. At any rate, when we did know what was going on, through the picture itself, we found that the exercise was working its own magic. You were in fact becoming wise. It could only continue.'

'What was the other stratagem of my father's?'

'Ah. That was heinous. It should hardly be mentioned.'

'Please go on.'

'He gave Blommardine – when she was fourteen or so, and he had got to know what sort of person she was – he gave her the secret of his vile pomatum, a mixture he used to find his hellish images. He suborned her into promising eventually to marry you, her half-brother – a notion that immediately attracted her. And, just in case this wasn't enough, he bribed her father (who at the time was in financial trouble) into selecting you as son-in-law.'

'But why? Why?'

'He wanted you to repeat his own mistakes but more so.'

'I did,' said Julius, not angrily but reflectively. 'How very much I did.'

459

'He will be punished, I assure you,' said the Grand Master. 'It will be his head in Hell. Can you not imagine that face – wan, desolate, bleak-eyed, turned back with infinite regret to the memory of sweet Love and the joys of union? It will be like an eternal ulcer in his heart, that he could have had such bliss. Instead, he plunged from grace and would not be content until he brought others with him.'

'But he did not bring me there.'

'Very nearly, Julius. You nearly failed. You were given a second chance. That is why you are here today.'

'And is there no second chance for him?'

'No. There is none . . . unless . . .'

The Grand Master seemed to be fading. What was this? As he looked, the shadows gathered; streaming in like battle-smoke from over to the right where Hell lay.

'Grand Master,' he called, 'Elisabeth . . .'

All he could see was their dim expressions now – she, pensively rapt, he, gravely attentive.

'Unless . . . unless . . .'

The darkness covered him; all he could feel was pain; all he could hear was the rumble and thunder of Hell's destruction.

'Dear God, why can I not die? Leave me not in Hell.'

'Julius . . . Julius . . .'

He could hear the voice calling very faintly, somehow both near and far away, like an insect or a giant across a gulf.

'Julius . . .'

Go away. Leave me with my pain. He would know the voice anywhere. It was that of his master, his father.

'Son . . .'

He could see the face now – white, the eyes sidelong, looking to left of picture, the lips loosely compressed into an expression of rueful desolation and despair.

'Help me . . .'

Oh, God, that he should come to me who can help no one, he thought. He was about to open his mouth and shout his own pain and grief. But suddenly, in his fear and loneliness and agony, a single beam of that Sun beyond the sun, penetrating every darkness, shone in the deepest recesses of his heart, and he croaked out in a voice, hoarse from screaming, hardly recognizable as his own:

'I forgive you, Father.'

He did forgive him. There was no point in anything else. We know no thought of vengeance.

Like the exhalation of one of Hell's bagpipes translated suddenly to Paradise, the harsh voice became expressive of an ineffable relief.

'Ahhhhh . . .'

The sound withdrew, as it seemed across vast distances, and Julius was left once more in darkness and the rumble of battle. He stirred at last and propped himself up on one elbow. He supposed he must have been delirious before, but he now found himself as awake as eyelessness would permit. Those were not Hell's guns, surely? There was a battle going on up there if he wasn't mistaken.

The constant screaming pain of his eyes had now subsided into a thudding, raw, aching soreness. He crawled painfully to the wall, holding his hand in front of him, and at length found the stonework and stood up. There he remained for a while, feeling the texture of the stone with hands that must now be eyes.

Later, he heard the sound of bolts being drawn, and felt a damp draught stir the air. The heavy door creaked open. A familiar voice spoke.

Chapter 47

'What have they done to you, you poor bugger?'

Blommardine's question came from over to his right. He heard her now step towards him.

'Here,' she said. 'I've brought bandages and salve for your eyes.'

'Where's Elisabeth?' he asked, and then he screamed as Blommardine gently touched him.

'Sorry,' she said, 'but we'll have to do it. We can't let you walk around like that.'

It felt as if the hot irons were being plied all over again; but at last it was done and he began to feel the benevolence of the ointment.

He repeated his first question.

'Where's Elisabeth?'

'She's all right. She gave me this salve. She's down at the water-gate, waiting for you now with the baby. Pastor Joachim's looking after her. He has a little boat hidden down there.'

'How did you do it?'

He motioned with his hands, indicating their release.

'They breached the walls last night. A couple of townsfolk told them where they were weak. There's been a devil of a battle going on. Everyone who can fight is down there, even the Royal Orator. I made Konrad give me the keys and the rest was easy.'

An extra-large explosion shook the walls.

'Is this the end?' he asked.

'It's the end for you. I'll take you down to the water-gate and after that it's in the hands of the gods ... The Bishop has barred the river further down so it's a matter of crossing, not a ride downstream, I'm afraid.'

'What about you?'

'Oh, I'll stay with him. I love him, do you see?'

An unfortunate phrase, he thought. He could not see. He thought, I used to think I would rather be dead than blind. Soon enough I shall be both.

'Does he love you?' he asked.

'Not in the least.'

'Strange that one who would be God should be so cruel,' he told her.

462

'Or perhaps not,' she said, bitterly.
She gave him her hand and he pressed it.
'Come, my brother . . .'

Chapter 48

Smoke from the burning buildings drifted across the marshes at night, sometimes hiding the dark shapes clumped in the open, sometimes revealing them in the glare of the fire.

The sack of the town had been completed a week before, but the General had told his army again that no inhabitants must pass through the lines, for they might spread the contagion.

As a result, the old and the weak, children, pregnant women and young babies, men with dreadful wounds and burns to the bone, were left to grub for roots and grass in the already scavenged waste between the town walls and the line of the encampment.

Almost unbelievably, those who were already there, lurking half-starved in their make-shift shelters, seemed to resent the newcomers, offering no help and sometimes even attacking them.

Sometimes a sortie would ride out from the besiegers' camp (the General had won the argument with the Bishop), men in armour and peaked steel helmets, hacking at any group that showed signs of defending itself, and at many that did not. Babies were put to the sword, women were split open like squashes, men lived for days transfixed by arrows or with pikes protruding from their entrails.

One former defender of the town had a shaft transfixing his hat so that it was pinned to his skull. The pain was so appalling that no one dared try to remove it.

In that mild weather, between spring and summer, it seemed to take everyone a long time to die.

A terrible noise went up from the land – of wailing and howling; cries for mercy; shrieks of desolation and fear; and of children who could not be comforted. Disease now began to take its toll. Bloated corpses, rotting on the ground, sent forth a foul miasma; or floated like monstrous fish in the greasy waters of the mere.

It was the time of the springing of leaves, and here and there grass and fronds, even saplings, sprang up, turning the dead into vegetation.

A plague of toads, either drawn to the decay or as a matter of obscene coincidence, was reported by the marauding soldiery. Toads squatted on the pale bodies of the dead and the not quite dead; hopped carefully among the bloodstained rags and bandages; clambered into mouths gaping in terminal agony; even made their nests in the pudenda that lay exposed in the carelessness of death.

Flocks of birds – ravens, jackdaws, crows, owls – hopped and fluttered and feasted at their will.

In a corner of this swampy Golgotha, under a little stone conduit hidden from the soldiers, lay a man who had been recently blinded and terribly wounded. He was tended by a young woman. Beside them lay a baby.

'Is it dark?' asked the man.

'Yes.'

'You must go,' said the man. 'Leave me. You must save yourself. They won't be watching so closely now. You could get past in the dark.'

The girl shook her head.

'No,' she said.

There was a pause. They had had this conversation before. Suddenly the man gave an exclamation. She tried to restrain him but he sat bolt-upright.

'I see it now,' he said.

'Shhh. What do you see?'

She knew he could not see anything.

'See,' he said, 'what my father saw. The tunnel of light . . . And yet there is something more . . .'

He sank back exhausted. Tenderly, the girl opened her dress, leant over and squeezed a few drops of milk from her breast into his mouth. It was all she had to give him.

'Ah,' he murmured. '*Rorate coeli*. The heavens are opened. The end is as the beginning.'

'Hush,' she said again.

His head turned towards her once more.

'In the midst of Hell we are in Heaven,' he said.

He smiled at her and died.

Historical Note

My story of the disturbed city of Rensburg was inspired by the events that took place in Munster between 1533 and 1535.

Many of the incidents I describe did indeed happen (though, equally, many of them did not). Some of the characters, too, are drawn from the shadowy stage of history. Fierens, Mosman and Hass are loosely based upon what facts we know of Jan Bockelson, Jan Mathys and Bernt Rothmann, leading figures in the real drama.

Other characters are even more tenuously connected with recorded fact. Blommardine owes almost nothing, as far as I can see, to the Lord of All the Earth's principal queen, Divara. Julius and Elisabeth did not, as far as I know, exist. The Grand Master probably did and – who knows? – still does.

The sensualist-brutalist interpretation of Konrad's character may seriously malign Knipperdollinck, leading citizen of Munster and notable collaborator – and then again it may not do justice to the man's capacity for evil.

Fictitious or factual as the contents of the story may be, it will perhaps be of interest to give here the account of the actual fate – recorded in *The Pursuit of the Millennium* – of three of the principal participants in the Anabaptist takeover of the town.

'Bockelson . . . was for some time led around on a chain and exhibited like a performing bear. In January 1536, he was brought to Munster; and there he, Knipperdollinck and another leading Anabaptist were publicly tortured to death with red-hot irons.

'Throughout their agony, the ex-king uttered no sound and made no movement. After the execution, the three bodies were suspended from a church-tower in the middle of the town, in cages which are still to be seen there today.'